Nora Roberts

Loving the Enemy

Mills & Boon™

First Published 1988
Third Australian Paperback Edition 2012
ISBN 978 174306845 8

First Published 1984
Fourth Australian Paperback Edition 2012
ISBN 978 174306845 8

LOVING THE ENEMY © 2012 by Harlequin Books S.A.

REBELLION
© 1988 by Nora Roberts
Philippine Copyright 1988
Australian Copyright 1988
New Zealand Copyright 1988

STORM WARNING
© 1984 by Nora Roberts
Philippine Copyright 1984
Australian Copyright 1984
New Zealand Copyright 1984

Published by
Harlequin Mills & Boon®
Level 5
15 Help Street
CHATSWOOD NSW 2067
AUSTRALIA

® and ™ are trademarks owned by Harlequin Enterprises Limited or its corporate affiliates
and used by others under licence. Trademarks marked with an ® are registered in Australia
and in other countries. Contact admin_legal@Harlequin.ca for details.

Printed and bound in Australia by Griffin Press

MIX
Paper from
responsible sources
FSC
www.fsc.org
FSC® C009448

CONTENTS

Dear Reader,

One of Nora Roberts's most adored creations is a series of books about a powerful, passionate, love-resistant brood known as the MacGregors. Since the release of the first MacGREGORS book over twenty years ago, the irresistible clan has captured more than its share of hearts, and readers have enjoyed learning about everyone in this formidable and fiery family.

Earlier this year, Silhouette Books was delighted to offer fans of the MacGREGORS series the chance to discover the splendor of the first four MacGREGORS books with *The MacGregors: Serena~Caine* and *The MacGregors: Alan~Grant.* And in this very special edition, Silhouette Books is pleased to bring you a prequel—and to introduce you to an earlier, equally opinionated, Serena MacGregor....

This first historical romance by Nora Roberts tells the story of the fiery Highland beauty Serena MacGregor and how, despite her dedication to the Stuarts in the uprising of 1745—not to mention her hatred of all Englishmen—Serena found herself utterly captivated and tempted by one. And just like all the MacGregors to come after her, it was just a matter of time before her pride was ultimately conquered by passion and true love.

We hope you enjoy this enchanting story, and we hope that you continue to read all about the other MacGregors in the collections that will be published in the coming year.

Happy reading!

The Editors
Silhouette Books

Rebellion

This story is told for the MacGregors,
all who came before, all who come after.

Prologue

They came at dusk, when the villagers were at their evening meal, and the peat fires sent smoke curling from the chimneys into the chill November air. There had been snow the week before, and the sun had beaten down and then retreated until the frost had set hard as rock under the bare trees. The sound of approaching horses rang like thunder through the forest, sending small animals racing and scrambling for cover.

Serena MacGregor shifted her baby brother on her hip and went to the window. Her father and the men were returning early from their hunting trip, she thought, but there were no shouts of greeting from the outlying cottages, no bursts of laughter.

She waited, her nose all but pressed against the window glazing, straining for the first signs of their return and fighting back her resentment that she, a girl, was not permitted to join hunting parties.

Coll had gone, though he was barely fourteen and not as skilled with a bow as she herself. And Coll had been allowed to go since he was seven. Serena's mouth became a pout as she gazed out through the lowering light. Her older brother would talk of nothing but the hunt for days, while she would have to be content to sit and spin.

Little Malcolm began to fuss and she jiggled him automatically as she stared down the rough path between the crofts and cottages. "Hush now, Papa doesn't want to hear you squalling the minute he walks in the door." But something made her hold him closer and look nervously over her shoulder for her mother.

The lamps were lighted and there was the scent of good, rich stew simmering over the kitchen fire. The house was neat as a pin. She and her mother and her little sister Gwen had worked all day to make it so. The floors were scrubbed, the tables polished. There wasn't a cobweb to be found in any corner. Serena's arms ached just thinking of it. The wash had been done and the little lavender sachets her mother loved so much were tucked in the chests.

Because her father was laird, they had the best house for miles around, built of fine blue slate. Her mother wasn't one to let dust settle on it.

Everything looked normal, but something had set her heart to racing. Grabbing a shawl, Serena wrapped it around Malcolm and opened the door to look for her father.

There was no wind, no sound but the horses' hooves beating against the hard frost on the path. They would ride over the rise any moment, she thought, and for a reason she couldn't name, she shuddered. When she heard the first scream, she stumbled

backward. She had already righted herself and started forward
when her mother called out to her.

"Serena, come back in. Hurry."

Fiona MacGregor, her usually lovely face pinched and pale,
rushed down the stairs. Her hair, the same red-gold shade as
Serena's, was pinned back and caught in a snood. She didn't
pat it into place, as was her habit before welcoming her husband home.

"But, Mama—"

"Hurry, girl, for God's sake." Fiona grabbed her daughter's arm
and dragged her inside. "Take the bairn upstairs to your sister.
Stay there."

"But Papa—"

"It's not your father."

Serena saw then, as the horses crested the hill, not the hunting plaid of the MacGregor but the red coats of English dragoons. She was only eight, but she had heard the tales of pillage
and oppression. Eight was old enough to be outraged.

"What do they want? We've done nothing."

"It's not necessary to do, only to be." Fiona closed the door,
then bolted it, more out of defiance than of any hope it would
keep out intruders. "Serena—"

A small, slender woman, she gripped her daughter's shoulders.
She had been the favored daughter of an indulgent father, then
the adored wife of a loving husband, but Fiona was no weakling.
Perhaps that was why the men in her life had given her their
respect, as well as their affection.

"Go upstairs into the nursery. Keep Malcolm and Gwen with
you. Don't come out until I tell you."

The valley echoed with another scream, and with wild weeping. Through the window they saw the thatched roof of a cot-

tage rise in flames. Fiona could only thank God her husband and son hadn't returned.

"I want to stay with you." Serena's wide green eyes overwhelmed her face, damp now with the beginnings of tears. But her mouth, the one her father called stubborn, firmed. "Papa wouldn't want me to leave you alone."

"He would want you to do as you're told." Fiona heard the horses stop at the door. There was a jingle of spurs and the sound of men shouting. "Go now." She turned her daughter and pushed her toward the stairs. "Keep the babies safe."

As Malcolm began to wail, Serena fled up the steps. She was on the landing when she heard the door burst in. She stopped and turned to see her mother face a half-dozen dragoons. One stepped forward and bowed. Even from a distance, Serena could see that the gesture was an insult.

"Serena?" little Gwen called from the stairs above.

"Take the baby." Serena pushed Malcolm into Gwen's pudgy five-year-old arms. "Go into the nursery and shut the door." She lowered her voice to a whisper. "Hurry—keep him quiet if you can." From her apron pocket she dug a sugarplum she'd been saving. "Take this and go before they see us." Crouching at the top of the stairs, she watched.

"Fiona MacGregor?" said the dragoon with the fancy stripes.

"I am Lady MacGregor." Fiona kept her shoulders back and her eyes level. Her only thought now was to protect her children and her home. Since fighting was impossible, she used the only weapon at hand—her dignity. "By what right do you break into my home?"

"By the right of an officer of the king."

"And your name?"

"Captain Standish, at your service." He drew off his gloves, waiting, hoping, to see fear. "Where is your husband...Lady MacGregor?"

"The laird and his men are hunting."

Standish signaled, sending three of his men on a search of the house. One overturned a table as he passed. Though her mouth was dry as dust, Fiona held her ground. She knew he could order her home torched, as easily as he had her tenants' cottages. There was little hope that her rank, or her husband's, would protect them. Her only choice was to meet insult with insult, and calmly.

"As you've seen, we are mostly women and children here. Your...visit is ill-timed if you wish to have words with the Mac-Gregor or his men. Or perhaps that is why you and your soldiers come so bravely into Glenroe."

He slapped her then, sending her staggering backward from the force of the blow.

"My father will kill you for that." Serena flew down the stairs like a bullet and launched herself at the officer. He swore as she dug her teeth into his hand, then swept her aside.

"Damn devil's brat drew blood." He lifted his fist, but Fiona flung herself between him and her daughter.

"Do King George's men beat small children? Is that how the English rule?"

Standish was breathing fast. It was a matter of pride now. He could hardly let his men see him bested by a woman and child, especially when they were Scottish scum. His orders were only to search and question. It was a pity the sniveling Argyll had convinced the queen, in her role as regent, not to enforce the Bill of Pains and Penalties. Scotland would indeed have been a hunting ground if she had. Still, Queen Caroline was furious with her Scottish subjects, and in any case she was hardly likely to hear of an isolated incident in the Highlands.

He signaled to one of the dragoons. "Take that brat upstairs and lock her up."

Without a word the soldier scooped Serena up, doing his best to avoid her feet and teeth and pummeling fists. As she fought, she screamed for her mother and cursed the soldiers.

"You raise wildcats in the Highlands, milady." The officer wrapped a fresh handkerchief around his hand.

"She is unused to seeing her mother, or any woman, struck by a man."

His hand was throbbing. He would not regain his men's esteem by thrashing a puny child. But the mother... He smiled as he let his gaze wander over her. The mother was a different matter.

"Your husband is suspected of involvement with the murder of Captain Porteous."

"The Captain Porteous who was sentenced to death by the courts for firing into a crowd?"

"He was reprieved, madam." Standish laid a hand lightly on the hilt of his sword. Even among his own kind he was considered cruel. Fear and intimidation kept his men in line; the same would work with one Scottish whore. "Captain Porteous fired on a group of rioters at a public execution. Then he was taken from prison and hanged by persons unknown."

"I find it difficult to sympathize with his fate, but neither I nor anyone in my family know of such matters."

"If it's found differently, your husband would be a murderer and a traitor. And you, Lady MacGregor, would have no protection."

"I have nothing to tell you."

"A pity." He smiled and moved a step closer. "Shall I show you what happens to unprotected women?"

Upstairs, Serena beat on the door until her hands were raw. Behind her, Gwen huddled with Malcolm and wept. There was no light in the nursery but for the moon and the flames from the fired cottages. Outside she could hear people shouting, women wailing, but her thoughts were all for her mother—left below, alone and unprotected, with the English.

When the door opened, Serena stumbled back. She saw the red coat, heard the jangle of spurs. Then she saw her mother, naked, bruised, her beautiful hair a wild mass around her face and shoulders. Fiona fell to her knees at Serena's feet.

"Mama." Serena knelt beside her, touched a tentative hand to her shoulder. She'd seen her mother weep before, but not like this, not these silent, hopeless tears. Because Fiona's skin was cold to the touch, Serena dragged a blanket from the chest and wrapped it around her.

While she listened to the dragoons ride off, Serena held her mother with one arm and cuddled Gwen and Malcolm with the other. She had only the vaguest understanding of what had happened, but it was enough to make her hate, and to make her vow revenge.

Chapter One

Brigham Langston, the fourth earl of Ashburn, sat at breakfast in his elegant town house and frowned over the letter. It was certainly one he'd been expecting, one he'd been waiting and watching for. Now that it was here, he read each word carefully, his gray eyes serious and his full mouth firm. It wasn't often a man received a letter that could change his life.

"Damn it, Brig, how long are you going to keep me waiting?" Coll MacGregor, the quick-tempered, redheaded Scot who had been Brigham's companion on certain journeys through Italy and France, seemed unable to sit quietly while Brigham read.

In answer, Brigham merely lifted one narrow hand, white-skinned and foaming with lace at the wrist. He was accustomed to Coll's outbursts, and for the most part enjoyed them. But this time, this very important time, he would hold his friend off until he'd read the letter through again.

"It's from him, is it not? Damn you to hell and back, it is from him. From the Prince." Coll pushed away from the table to pace. Only the manners hammered into him by his mother kept him from tearing the letter from Brigham's hand. Although the knowledge that, despite the difference in size and girth, Brigham could hold his own in a fight might also have played a certain role in his decision. "I've as much right as you."

Brigham looked up at that, letting his gaze pass over the man who was now striding around the small salon with enough force to make the china rattle. Though his muscles were tense and his mind was shooting off in a dozen directions, Brigham's voice was mild.

"Of course you do, but the letter is, nonetheless, addressed to me."

"Only because it's easier to smuggle a letter to the high-and-mighty English earl of Ashburn than it is to a MacGregor. We're all under suspicion of being rebels in Scotland." Coll's sharp green eyes were alight with challenge. When Brigham merely returned to the letter, Coll swore again and dropped into his chair. "You're enough to try a man's soul."

"Thank you." Setting the letter beside his plate, Brigham poured more coffee. His hand was as steady as it was when he gripped the hilt of a sword or the butt of a pistol. And, indeed, this letter was a weapon of war. "You are quite right on all counts, my dear. The letter is from Prince Charles." Brigham sipped his coffee.

"Well, what does he say?"

When Brigham indicated the letter with a wave of his hand, Coll pounced on it. The missive was written in French, and though his command of the language was not as good as Brigham's, he struggled through it.

As he did, Brigham studied the room around him. The wall-
paper had been chosen by his grandmother, a woman he remembered as much for her soft Scottish burr as for her stubbornness.
It was a deep, glassy blue that she'd said reminded her of the
lochs of her homeland. The furnishings were elegant, almost
delicate, with their sweeping curves and gilt edges. The graceful Meissen porcelain figurines she had prized still stood on the
little round table by the window.

As a boy he'd been allowed to look but not to touch, and his
fingers had always itched to hold the statue of the shepherdess
with the long porcelain hair and the fragile face.

There was a portrait of Mary MacDonald, the strong-willed
woman who had become Lady Ashburn. It stood over the crackling fire and showed her at an age very close to what her grandson claimed now. She'd been tall for a woman and reed-slim, with
a glorious mane of ebony hair around a narrow, fine-boned face.
There was a look in the way she tilted her head that said she
could be persuaded but not forced, asked but not commanded.

The same features, the same coloring, had been passed down
to her grandson. They were no less elegant in their masculine
form—the high forehead, the hollowed cheeks and full mouth.
But Brigham had inherited more than his height and his gray
eyes from Mary. He'd also inherited her passions and her sense
of justice.

He thought of the letter, of the decisions to be made, and
toasted the portrait.

You'd have me go, he thought. All the stories you told me,
that belief in the rightness of the Stuart cause you planted in
my head during the years you raised and cared for me. If you
were still alive, you'd go yourself. So how can I not?

"So it's time." Coll folded the letter. In his voice, in his eyes, were both excitement and tension. He was twenty-four, only six months younger than Brigham, but this was a moment he had been awaiting for most of his life.

"You have to learn to read between the lines, Coll." This time Brigham rose. "Charles is still holding out hope of support from the French, though he's beginning to realize King Louis would rather talk than act." Frowning, he twitched back the curtain and looked out at his dormant gardens. They would explode with color and scent in the spring. But it was unlikely he would be there to see them in the spring.

"When we were at court, Louis was more than interested in our cause. He has no more liking for the Hanoverian puppet on the throne than we," Coll said.

"No, but that doesn't mean he'll open his coffers to the Bonnie Prince and the Stuart cause. Charles's notion of fitting out a frigate and sailing for Scotland seems more realistic. But these things take time."

"Which is where we come in."

Brigham let the drapes fall back into place. "You know the mood of Scotland better than I. How much support will he get?"

"Enough." With the confidence of pride and youth, Coll grinned. "The clans will rise for the true king and fight to the man behind him." He rose then, knowing what his friend was asking. Brigham would be risking more than his life in Scotland. His title, his home and his reputation could be lost. "Brig, I could take the letter, go to my family and from there spread word throughout the Highland clans. It isn't necessary for you to go, as well."

One black brow rose, and Brigham nearly smiled. "I'm of so little use?"

"To hell with that." Coll's voice was bluff, his gestures wide. Both were as much a part of him as the rumbling cadences of his homeland and his fierce pride in it. "A man like you, one who knows how to talk, how to fight, an English aristocrat willing to join the rebellion? No one knows better than I just what you can do. After all, you saved my life more than once in Italy and, aye, in France, as well."

"Don't be boring, Coll." Brigham flicked at the lace at his wrist. "It's unlike you."

Coll's wide face folded into a grin. "Aye, and there's something to be said for the way you can turn into the earl of Ashburn in the blink of an eye."

"My dear, I *am* the earl of Ashburn."

Humor kindled in Coll's eyes. When they stood together like this, the contrasts between the men were marked. Brigham with his trim build, Coll with his brawny one. Brigham with his elegant, even languid manners, Coll rough-and-ready. But no one knew better than the Scot just what lay beneath the well-cut coats and the lace.

"It wasn't the earl of Ashburn who fought back-to-back with me when our coach was attacked outside of Calais. It wasn't the earl of Ashburn who damned near drank me, a MacGregor, under the table in that grimy little gaming hell in Rome."

"I assure you it was, as I remember both incidents very well."

Coll knew better than to banter words with Brigham. "Brigham, be serious. As the earl of Ashburn you deserve to stay in England, go to your balls and card parties. You could still do the cause good here, with your ear to the ground."

"But?"

"If I'm going to fight, I'd like to have you beside me. Will you come?"

Brigham studied his friend, then shifted his gaze up and beyond, to the portrait of his grandmother. "Of course."

The weather in London was cold and dank. It remained so three days later, when the two men began their journey north. They would travel to the border in the relative comfort of Brigham's coach, then take the rest on horseback.

For anyone who remained in London during the miserable January weather and chose to inquire, Lord Ashburn was making a casual journey to Scotland to visit the family of his friend.

There were a few who knew better, a handful of staunch Tories and English Jacobites whom Brigham trusted. To them he left in trust his family home, Ashburn Manor, as well as his house in London and the disposition of his servants. What could be taken without undo notice, he took. What could not, he left behind with the full knowledge that it probably would be months, perhaps even years, before he could return to claim them. The portrait of his grandmother still stood above the mantel, but on a sentimental whim he'd had the statue of the shepherdess wrapped for the journey.

There was gold, a good deal more than was needed for a visit to the family of a friend, in a locked chest beneath the floor of the coach.

They were forced to move slowly, more slowly than Brigham cared for, but the roads were slick, and occasional flurries of snow had the driver walking the team. Brigham would have preferred a good horse beneath him and the freedom of a gallop.

A look out the window showed him that the weather to the north could only be worse. With what patience he'd learned to cultivate, Brigham sat back, rested his booted feet on the opposite seat, where Coll sat dozing, and let his thoughts drift back to Paris, where he had spent a few glittering months the year before. That was the France of Louis XV, opulent, glamorous, all light and music. There had been lovely women there, with their powdered hair and scandalous gowns. It had been easy to flirt, and more. A young English lord with a fat purse and a talent for raillery had little trouble making a place in society.

He had enjoyed it, the lushness and laziness of it. But it was also true that he'd begun to feel restless, fretting for action and purpose. The Langstons had always enjoyed the intrigue of politics as much as the sparkle of balls and routs. Just as, for three generations, they had silently sworn their loyalty to the Stuarts—the rightful kings of England.

So when Prince Charles Edward had come to France, a magnetic man of courage and energy, Brigham had offered his aid and his oath. Many would have called him traitor. No doubt the fusty Whigs who supported the German who now sat upon the English throne would have wished Brigham hanged as one if they had known. But Brigham's loyalty was to the Stuart cause, to which his family had always held true, not to the fat German usurper George. He'd not forgotten the stories his grandmother had told him of the disastrous rebellion of '15, and of the proscriptions and executions before and after it.

As the landscape grew wilder and the city of London seemed so far away he thought once again that the House of Hanover had done little—had not even tried—to endear itself to Scotland. There had always been the threat of war, from the north or from across the Channel. If England was to be made strong, it would need its rightful king.

It had been more than the Prince's clear eyes and fair looks that had decided Brigham to stand with him. It had been his drive and ambition, and perhaps his youthful confidence that he could, and would, claim what was his.

They stopped for the night at a small inn where the Lowland plains started to rise into the true Highlands. Brigham's gold, and his title, earned them dry sheets and a private parlor. Fed, warmed by the leaping fire, they diced and drank too much ale while the wind swept down from the mountains and hammered at the walls. For a few hours they were simply two well-to-do young men who shared a friendship and an adventure.

"Damn your bones, Brig, you're a lucky bastard tonight."

"So it would seem." Brigham scooped up the dice and the coins. His eyes, bright with humor, met Coll's. "Shall we find a new game?"

"Roll." Coll grinned and shoved more coins to the center of the table. "Your luck's bound to change." When the dice fell, he snickered. "If I can't beat that…" When his roll fell short, he shook his head. "Seems you can't lose. Like the night in Paris you played the duke for the affections of that sweet mademoiselle."

Brigham poured more ale. "With or without the dice, I'd already won the mademoiselle's affections."

Laughing thunderously, Coll slapped more coins on the table. "Your luck can't hang sunny all the time. Though I for one hope it holds for the months to come."

Brigham swept his gaze upward and assured himself that the

door to the parlor was closed. "It's more a matter of Charles's luck than mine."

"Aye, he's what we've needed. His father has always been lacking in ambition and too sure of his own defeat." He lifted his tankard of ale. "To the Bonnie Prince."

"He'll need more than his looks and a clever tongue."

Coll's red brows rose. "Do you doubt the MacGregors?"

"You're the only MacGregor I know." Before Coll could begin an oration on his clan, Brigham asked quickly, "What of your family, Coll? You'll be pleased to see them again."

"It's been a long year. Not that I haven't enjoyed the sights of Rome and Paris, but when a man's born in the Highlands, he prefers to die there." Coll drank deeply, thinking of purple moors and deep blue lochs. "I know the family is well from the last letter my mother sent me, but I'll feel better seeing for myself. Malcolm will be nigh on ten now, and a hellion, I'm told." He grinned, full of pride. "Then so are we all."

"You told me your sister was an angel."

"Gwen." The tenderness invaded his voice. "Little Gwen. So she is, sweet-tempered, patient, pretty as new cream."

"I'm looking forward to meeting her."

"And still in the schoolroom," Coll told him. "I'll be around to see you don't forget it."

A little hazy with ale, Brigham tilted back in his chair. "You've another sister."

"Serena." Coll jiggled the dice box in his palm. "God knows the lass was misnamed. A wildcat she is, and I've the scars to prove it. Serena MacGregor has the devil's own temper and a quick fist."

"But is she pretty?"

"She's not hard to look at," said her brother. "My mother tells me the boys have started courting this past year, and Serena sends them off with boxed ears, scrambling for cover."

"Perhaps they have yet to find the, ah, proper way to court her."

"Hah! I crossed her once, and she grabbed my grandfather's claymore from the wall and chased me into the forest." The pride came through, if not the tenderness. "I pity the man who sets his sights on her."

"An amazon." Brigham pictured a strapping, ruddy-cheeked girl with Coll's broad features and wild red hair. Healthy as a milkmaid, he imagined, and just as sassy. "I prefer the milder sort."

"Isn't a mild bone in her body, but she's true." The ale was swimming in Coll's head, but that didn't stop him from lifting the tankard again. "I told you about the night the dragoons came to Glenroe."

"Yes."

Coll's eyes darkened with the memory. "After they'd finished shaming my mother and firing roofs, Serena nursed her. She was hardly more than a bairn herself, but she got my mother into bed and tended her and the children until we returned. There was a bruise on her face where that black bastard had knocked her aside, but she didn't cry. She sat, dry-eyed, and told us the whole."

Brigham laid a hand over his friend's. "The time's past for revenge, Coll, but not for justice."

"I'll take both," Coll murmured, and tossed the dice again.

They started out early the next morning. Brigham's head ached, but the cold, blustery air soon cleared it. They went on horseback, allowing the coach to follow at a sedate pace.

Now they were truly in the land he'd been told of as a child. It was wild and rough, with crags rising high and moors spread out and desolate. Prominent peaks pierced the milky gray of the sky, sometimes cut through with tumbling waterfalls and icy rivers thick with fish. In other places rocks were tumbled as though they had been dice rolled by a careless hand. It seemed an ancient place, one for gods and fairies, yet he saw an occasional cottage, smoke belching from the central opening in the thatch.

The ground was heaped with snow, and the wind blew it in sheets across the road. At times they were nearly blinded by it as Coll led the way up the rising, rut-filled hills. Caves opened out of rock. Here and there were signs that shelter had been taken in them. Lakes, their waters a dark, dangerous blue, were crusted at the edges with ice. The effects of the ale were whisked away by a damp cold that stung the air and penetrated even the layers of a greatcoat.

They rode hard when the land permitted, then picked their way through snowdrifts as high as a man's waist. Cautious, they bypassed the forts the English had built and avoided the hospitality that would have been given unhesitatingly at any cottage. Hospitality, Coll had warned Brigham, would include questions about every aspect of their journey, their families and their destination. Strangers were rare in the Highlands, and prized for their news as much as their company.

Rather than risk the details of their journey being passed from village to village, they kept to the rougher roads and hills before stopping at a tavern to rest the horses and take their midday meal. The floors were dirt, the chimney no more than a hole in the roof that kept as much smoke in as it let out. The single cramped room smelled of its occupants and of yesterday's fish.

It was hardly a spot the fourth earl of Ashburn would be likely to frequent, but the fire was hot and the meat almost fresh.

Beneath the greatcoat, which now hung drying in front of the fire, Brigham wore dun-colored riding breeches and a shirt of fine lawn with his plainest riding coat. But though it might be plain, it fit without a wrinkle over his broad shoulders, and its buttons were silver. His boots had been dulled a bit by the weather but were unmistakably of good leather. His thick mane of hair was tied back with a riband, and on his narrow hands he wore his family seal and an emerald. He was hardly dressed in his best court attire, but nonetheless he drew stares and curious whispers.

"They don't see the likes of you in this hole," Coll said. Comfortable in his kilt and bonnet, with the pine sprig of his clan tucked into the band, he dug hungrily into his meat pie.

"Apparently." Brigham ate lazily, but his eyes, behind half-closed lids, remained alert. "Such admiration would delight my tailor."

"Oh, it's only partly the clothes." Coll raised his bicker of ale to drain it, and thought pleasantly of the whiskey he would share with his father that night. "You would look like an earl if you wore rags." Anxious to be off, he tossed coins on the table. "The horses should be rested; let's be off. We're skirting Campbell country." Coll's manners were too polished to allow him to spit, but he would have liked to. "I'd prefer not to dally."

Three men left the tavern before them, letting in a blast of cold and beautifully fresh air.

It had become difficult for Coll to contain his impatience. Now that he was back in the Highlands, he wanted nothing so

much as to see his own home, his own family. The road twisted
and climbed, occasionally winding by a huddle of cottages and
cattle grazing on the rough, uneven ground. Men living here
would have to keep an eye out for wildcat and badgers.

Though they had hours to ride, he could almost scent home—
the forest, with its red deer and tawny owls. There would be
a feast that night, and cups raised in toasts. London, with its
crowded streets and fussy manners, was behind him.

Trees were scarce, only the little junipers pushing through on
the lee side of boulders. In Scotland, even the brush had a difficult time surviving. Now and then they rode by a rumbling river
or stream, to be challenged by the eerie, consuming silence that
followed. The skies had cleared to a hard, brilliant blue. Above,
majestic and glorious, a golden eagle circled.

"Brig—"

Beside Coll, Brigham had suddenly gone rigid. Coll's horse
reared as Brigham pulled out his sword. "Guard your flank," he
shouted, then wheeled to face two riders who had burst out from
behind a tumble of rock.

They rode sturdy garrons, shaggy Scottish ponies, and though
their tartans were dulled with age and dirt, the blades of their
fighting swords shone in the midafternoon sun. Brigham had
only time enough to note that the men who charged had been
in the tavern before there was the crash of steel against steel.

Beside him, Coll wielded his sword against two more. The
high hills rang with the sounds of battle, the thunder of hooves
against hard-packed ground. Gliding overhead, the eagle circled
and waited.

The attackers had misjudged their quarry in Brigham. His
hands were narrow, his body slender as a dancer's, but his wrists

were both wiry and supple. Using his knees to guide his mount, he fought with a sword in one hand and a dagger in the other. There might have been jewels on the hilts, but the blades were fashioned to kill.

He heard Coll shout and swear. For himself, he fought in deadly silence. Steel scraped as he defended himself, crashed when he took the offensive, driving at one foe and outmaneuvering the other. His eyes, usually a calm, clear gray, had darkened and narrowed like those of a wolf that scents blood. He gave his opponent's sword one final, vicious parry and ran his own blade home.

The Scot screamed, but the sound lasted no more than a heartbeat. Blood splattered the snow as the man fell. His pony, frightened by the smell of death, ran clattering up the rocks. The other man, wild-eyed, renewed his attack with more ferocity and fear than finesse. The violence of the advance nearly cut through Brigham's guard, and he felt the sting of the sword on his shoulder and the warm flow of blood where the point had ripped layers of clothing and found flesh. Brigham countered with swift, steady strokes, driving his quarry back and back, toward the rocks. His eyes stayed on his opponent's face, never flickering, never wavering. With cool-headed precision, he parried and thrust and pierced the heart. Before the man had hit the ground, he was swinging back toward Coll.

It was one on one now, for another of the attackers lay dead behind Coll, and Brigham took time to draw a deep breath. Then he saw Coll's horse slip, nearly stumble. He saw the blade flash and was racing toward his friend. The last man of the band of attackers looked up to see the horse and rider bearing down on him. With his three comrades dead, he wheeled his pony and scrambled up the rocks.

"Coll! Are you hurt?"

"Aye, by God. Bloody Campbell." He struggled not to slump in the saddle. His side, where the sword had pierced it, was on fire.

Brigham sheathed his sword. "Let me see to it."

"No time. That jackal may come back with more." Coll took out a handkerchief and pressed it to the wound, then brought his gloved hand back. It was sticky but steady. "I'm not done yet." His eyes, still bright from battle, met Brigham's. "We'll be home by dusk." With that, he sent his horse into a gallop.

They rode hard, with Brigham keeping one eye out for another ambush and the other on Coll. The big Scot was pale, but his pace never faltered. Only once, at Brigham's insistence, did they stop so that the wound could be bound more satisfactorily.

Brigham didn't like what he saw. The wound was deep, and Coll had lost far too much blood. Still, his friend was in a fever to reach Glenroe and his family, and Brigham would not have known where else to find help. Coll accepted the flask Brigham put to his lips and drank deeply. When the color seeped back into his face, Brigham helped him into the saddle.

They dropped down out of the hills into the forest at dusk, when the shadows were long and wavering. It smelled of pine and snow, with a faint wisp of smoke from a cottage farther on. A hare dashed across the path, then crashed through the brush. Behind it, like a flash, came a merlin. Winter berries, as big as thumbs, clung to thorny limbs.

Brigham knew Coll's strength was flagging, and he paused long enough to make him drink again.

"I ran through this forest as a child," Coll rasped. His breathing came quickly, but the brandy eased the pain. He'd be damned if he would die before the true fighting began. "Hunted in it, stole my first kiss in it. For the life of me, I can't think why I ever left it."

"To come back a hero," Brigham said as he corked the flask.

Coll gave a laugh that turned into a cough. "Aye. There's been a MacGregor in the Highlands since God put us here, and here we stay." He turned to Brigham with a hint of the old arrogance. "You may be an earl, but my race is royal."

"And you're shedding your royal blood all over the forest. To home, Coll."

They rode at an easy canter. When they passed the first cottages, cries went out. Out of houses, some fashioned from wood and stone, others built out of no more than mud and grass, people came. Though the pain was streaking up his side, Coll saluted. They crested a hill, and both men saw MacGregor House.

There was smoke winding out of the chimneys. Behind the glazed windows lamps, just lighted, were glowing. The sky to the west was ablaze with the last lights of the sun, and the blue slate glowed and seemed to turn to silver. It rose four stories, graced with turrets and towers, a house fashioned as much for war as for comfort. The roofs were of varying height, strung together in a confused yet somehow charming style.

There was a barn in the clearing, along with other outbuildings and grazing cattle. From somewhere came the hollow barking of a dog.

Behind them more people had come out of their homes. Out of one ran a woman, her basket empty. Brigham heard her shout and turned. And stared.

She was wrapped in a plaid like a mantle. In one hand she

held a basket that swung wildly as she ran; the other hand held the hem of her skirt, and he could see the flash of petticoats and long legs. She was laughing as she ran, and her scarf fell down around her shoulders, leaving hair the color of the sunset flying behind her.

Her skin was like alabaster, though flushed now from delight and cold. Her features had been carved with a delicate hand, but the mouth was full and rich. Brigham could only stare and think of the shepherdess he had loved and admired as a child.

"Coll!" Her voice was low, filled with the music of laughter, rich with the burr of Scotland. Ignoring the horse's dancing impatience, she gripped the bridle and turned up a face that made Brigham's mouth turn dry. "I've had the fidgets all day and should have known you were the cause. We had no word you were coming. Did you forget how to write or were you too lazy?"

"A fine way to greet your brother." Coll would have bent down to kiss her, but her face was swimming in front of his eyes. "The least you can do is show some manners to my friend. Brigham Langston, Lord Ashburn, my sister, Serena."

Not hard to look at? For once, Brigham thought, Coll hadn't exaggerated. Far from it. "Miss MacGregor."

But Serena didn't spare him a glance. "Coll, what is it? You're hurt." Even as she reached for him, he slid from the saddle to her feet. "Oh, God, what's this?" She pushed aside his coat and found the hastily bound wound.

"It's opened again." Brigham knelt beside her. "We should get him inside."

Serena's head shot up as she raked Brigham with rapier-sharp green eyes. It wasn't fear in them, but fury. "Take your hands off him, English swine." She shoved him aside and cradled her brother against her breast. With her own plaid she pressed against the wound to slow the bleeding. "How is it my brother comes home near death and you ride in with your fine sword sheathed and nary a scratch?"

Coll might have underplayed her beauty, Brigham decided as his mouth set, but not her temperament. "I think that's best explained after Coll's seen to."

"Take your explanations back to London." When he gathered Coll up to carry him, she all but pounced on him. "Leave him be, damn you. I won't have you touching what's mine."

He let his gaze run up and down her until her cheeks glowed. "Believe me, madam," he said, stiffly polite, "I've no desire to. If you'll see to the horses, Miss MacGregor, I'll take your brother in."

She started to speak again, but one look at Coll's white face had her biting back the words. With his greatcoat flapping around him and Coll in his arms, Brigham started toward the house.

Serena remembered the last time an Englishman had walked into her home. Snatching the reins of both horses, she hurried after Brigham, cursing him.

Chapter Two

There was little time for introductions. Brigham was greeted at the door by a gangly black-haired serving girl who ran off wringing her hands and shouting for Lady MacGregor. Fiona came in, her cheeks flushed from the kitchen fire. At the sight of her son unconscious in the arms of a stranger, she went pale.

"Coll. Is he—"

"No, my lady, but the wound's severe."

With one very slender hand, she touched her son's face. "Please, if you'd bring him upstairs." She went ahead, calling out orders for water and bandages. "In here." After pushing open a door, she looked over Brigham's shoulder. "Gwen, thank God. Coll's been wounded."

Gwen, smaller and more delicately built than her mother and sister, hurried into the room. "Light the lamps, Molly," she told the serving girl. "I'll need plenty of light." She was already pressing a hand to her brother's brow. "He's feverish." His blood stained his plaid and ran red on the linen. "Can you help me off with his clothes?"

With a nod, Brigham began to work with her. She coolly sent for medicines and bowls of water, stacks of linen were rushed in. The young girl didn't swoon at the sword wound as Brigham had feared, but competently began to clean and treat it. Even under her gentle hands, Coll began to mutter and thrash.

"Hold this, if you please." Gwen gestured for Brigham to hold the pad she'd made against the wound while she poured syrup of poppies into a wooden cup. Fiona supported her son's head while Gwen eased the potion past his lips. She murmured to him as she sat again and stitched up the wound without flinching.

"He's lost a lot of blood," she told her mother as she worked. "We'll have to mind the fever." Already Fiona was bathing her son's head with a cool cloth.

"He's strong. We won't lose him now." Fiona straightened and brushed at the hair that had fallen around her face. "I'm grateful to you for bringing him," she told Brigham. "Will you tell me what happened?"

"We were attacked a few miles south of here. Coll believes it was Campbells."

"I see." Her lips tightened, but her voice remained calm. "I must apologize for not even offering you a chair or a hot drink. I'm Coll's mother, Fiona MacGregor."

"I'm Coll's friend, Brigham Langston."

Fiona managed a smile but kept her son's limp hand in hers. "The earl of Ashburn, of course. Coll wrote of you. Please, let me have Molly take your coat and fetch you some refreshment."

"He's English." Serena stood in the doorway. She'd taken off her plaid. All she wore now was a simple homespun dress of dark blue wool.

"I'm aware of that, Serena." Fiona turned her strained smile back to Brigham. "Your coat, Lord Ashburn. You've had a long journey. I'm sure you'll want a hot meal and some rest." When he drew off his coat, Fiona's gaze went to his shoulder. "Oh, you're wounded."

"Not badly."

"A scratch," Serena said as she flicked her gaze over it. She would have moved past him to her brother, but a look from Fiona stopped her.

"Take our guest down to the kitchen and tend to his hurts."

"I'd sooner bandage a rat."

"You'll do as I say, and you'll show the proper courtesy to a guest in our home." The steel came into her voice. "Once his wounds are tended, see that he has a proper meal."

"Lady MacGregor, it isn't necessary."

"Forgive me, my lord, it's quite necessary. You'll forgive me for not tending to you myself." She picked up the cloth for Coll's head again. "Serena?"

"Very well, Mother, for you." Serena turned, giving a very small and deliberately insulting curtsy. "If you please, Lord Ashburn."

He followed her down through a house far smaller than Ashburn Manor, and neat as a pin. They wound around a hallway and down two narrow flights because she chose to take him down the back stairs. Still, he paid little notice as he watched Serena's stiff back. There were rich smells in the kitchen, spices, meat, from the kettle hung by a chain over the fire, the aroma of pies just baked. Serena indicated a small, spindle-legged chair.

"Please be seated, my lord."

He did, and only by the slightest flicker of his eyes did he express his feelings when she ripped the sleeve from his shirt. "I hope you don't faint at the sight of blood, Miss MacGregor."

"It's more likely you will at the sight of your mutilated shirt, Lord Ashburn." She tossed the ruined sleeve aside and brought back a bowl of hot water and some clean cloths.

It was more than a scratch. English though he might be, she felt a bit ashamed of herself. He'd obviously opened the wound when he'd carried Coll inside. As she staunched the blood that had begun to run freely, she saw that the cut measured six inches or more along a well-muscled forearm.

His flesh was warm and smooth in her hands. He smelled not of perfumes and powders, as she imagined all Englishmen did, but of horses and sweat and blood. Oddly enough, it stirred something in her and made her fingers gentler than she'd intended.

She had the face of an angel, he thought as she bent over him. And the soul of a witch. An interesting combination, Brigham decided as he caught a whiff of lavender. The kind of mouth made for kissing, paired with hostile eyes designed to tear holes in a man. How would her hair feel, bunched in a man's hands? He had an urge to stroke it, just to see her reaction. But one wound, he told himself, was enough for one day.

She worked competently and in silence, cleaning the wound and dabbing on one of Gwen's herbal mixtures. The scent was pleasant, and made her think of the forest and flowers. Serena hardly noticed that his English blood was on her fingers.

She reached for the bandages. He shifted. All at once they were face-to-face, as close as a man and woman can come without embracing. She felt his breath feather across her lips and was surprised by the quick flutter of her heart. She noticed his eyes were gray, darker than they had been when he'd coolly assessed her on the road. His mouth was beautiful, curved now with the beginnings of a smile that changed his sharp-featured aristocratic face into something approachable.

She thought she felt his fingers on her hair but was certain she was mistaken. For a moment, perhaps two, her mind went blank and she could only look at him and wonder.

"Will I live?" he murmured.

There it was, that English voice, mocking, smug. She needed nothing else to drag her out of whatever spell his eyes had cast. She smiled at him and yanked the bandage tight enough to make him jerk.

"Oh, pardon, my lord," she said with a flutter of lashes. "Have I hurt you?"

He gave her a mild look and thought it would be satisfying to throttle her. "Pray don't regard it."

"I will not." She rose to remove the bowl of bloodstained water. "Odd, isn't it, that English blood runs so thin?"

"I hadn't noticed. The Scottish blood I shed today looked pale to me."

She whirled back. "If it was Campbell blood, you rid the world of another badger, but I won't be grateful to you for that, or anything."

"You cut me to the quick, my lady, when your gratitude is what I live for."

She snatched up a wooden bowl—though her mother would have meant for her to use the delft or the china—and scooped out stew and slapped it down so that more than a little slopped over the sides. She poured him ale and tossed a couple of oatcakes on a platter. A pity they weren't stale.

"Your supper, my lord. Have a care not to choke on it."

He rose then, and for the first time she noticed that he was nearly as tall as her brother, though he carried less muscle and brawn. "Your brother warned me you were ill-tempered."

She set her fist on her hip, eyeing him from under lashes shades darker than her tumbled hair. "That's fortunate for you, my lord, so you'll know better than to cross me."

He stepped toward her. It couldn't be helped, given his temper and his penchant for fighting face-to-face. She tilted her chin as if braced, even anxious, for the bout. "If you've a mind to chase me into the wood with your grandsire's claymore, think again."

Her lips twitched even as she fought back the smile. Humor made her eyes almost as appealing as anger. "Why? Are you fast on your feet, *Sassenach?*" she asked, using the Gaelic term for the hated English invader.

"Fast enough to knock you off yours if you were fortunate enough to catch me." He took her hand, effectively wiping the smile from her eyes. Though her hand curled into a fist, he brought it to his lips. "My thanks, Miss MacGregor, for your so gentle touch and hospitality."

While he stood where he was, she stormed out, furiously wiping her knuckles against her skirts.

It was full dark when Ian MacGregor returned with his youngest son. After his quick meal, Brigham kept to the room he'd been given, leaving the family to themselves and giving himself time to think. Coll had described the MacGregors well enough. Fiona was lovely, with enough strength in her face and bearing to add grit to beauty. Young Gwen was sweet and quiet with shy eyes—and a steady hand when she sewed rent flesh together.

As to Serena...Coll hadn't mentioned that his sister was a

she-wolf with a face to rival Helen's, but Brigham was content
to make his own judgments there. It might be true that she had
no cause to love the English, but for himself, Brigham preferred
to weigh a man as a man, not by his nationality.

He would do as well to judge a woman as a woman and not
by her looks, he thought. When she had come racing down the
road toward her brother, her face alive with pleasure, her hair
flying, he'd felt as though he had been struck by lightning. For-
tunately, he wasn't a man who tarried long under the spell of a
beautiful pair of eyes and a pretty ankle. He had come to Scotland to fight for a cause he believed in, not to worry because
some slip of a girl detested him.

Because of his birth, he thought as he paced to the window
and back. He'd never had any cause to be other than proud
of his lineage. His grandfather had been a man respected and
feared—as his father had been before death had taken him so
early. From the time he was old enough to understand, Brigham
had been taught that being a Langston was both a privilege and
a responsibility. He took neither lightly. If he had, he would have
stayed in Paris, enjoying the whims and caprices of elegant society rather than traveling to the mountains of Scotland to risk
all for the young Prince.

Damn the woman for looking at him as though he were scum
to be scrubbed from the bottom of a pot.

At a knock on the door he turned, scowling, from the window. "Yes?"

The serving girl opened the door with her heart already in
her throat. One peep at Brigham's black looks had her lowering
her eyes and bobbing nervous curtsies. "Begging your pardon,
Lord Ashburn." And that was all she could manage.

He waited, then sighed. "Might I know what you beg it for?"

She darted him a quick look, then stared at the floor again. "My lord, the MacGregor wishes to see you downstairs if it's convenient."

"Certainly, I'll come right away."

But the girl had already dashed off. She would have a story to tell her mother that night, about how Serena MacGregor had insulted the English lord to his face—a face, she'd add, that was handsome as the devil's.

Brigham fluffed out the lace at his wrists. He had traveled with only one change of clothes, and he hoped the coach with the rest of his belongings would find its ponderous way to Glenroe the next day.

He descended the stairs, slender and elegant in black and silver. Lace foamed subtly at his throat, and his rings gleamed in the lamplight. In Paris and London he'd followed fashion and powdered his hair. Here he was glad to dispense with the bother, so it was brushed, raven black, away from his high forehead.

The MacGregor waited in the dining hall, drinking port, a fire roaring at his back. His hair was a dark red and fell to his shoulders. A beard of the same color and luster covered his face. He had dressed as was proper when receiving company of rank. In truth, the great kilt suited him, for he was as tall and broad as his son. With it he wore a doublet of calfskin and a jeweled clasp at his shoulder on which was carved the head of a lion.

"Lord Ashburn. You are welcome to Glenroe and the house of Ian MacGregor."

"Thank you." Brigham accepted the offered port and chair. "I'd like to inquire about Coll."

"He's resting easier, though my daughter Gwen tells me it

will be a long night." Ian paused a moment, looking down at the pewter cup held in his wide, thick-fingered hand. "Coll has written of you as a friend. If he had not, you would now be one for bringing him back to us."

"He is my friend, and has been."

This was accepted with a nod. "Then I drink to your health, my lord." He did, with gusto. "I'm told your grandmother was a MacDonald."

"She was. From the Isle of Skye."

Ian's face, well lined and reddened by wind and weather, relaxed into a smile. "Then welcome twice." Ian lifted his cup and kept his eye keen on his guest. "To the true king?"

Brigham lifted his port in turn. "To the king across the water," he said, meeting Ian's fierce blue gaze. "And the rebellion to come."

"Aye, that I'll drink to." And he did, downing the port in one giant gulp. "Now tell me how it happened that my boy was hurt."

Brigham described the ambush, detailing the men who'd attacked them, and their dress. As he spoke, Ian listened, leaning forward on the big table as though afraid he might miss a word.

"Bloody murdering Campbells!" he exploded, pounding a fist on the table so that cups and crockery jumped.

"So Coll thought himself," Brigham said equably. "I know a bit about the clans and the feud between yours and the Campbells', Lord MacGregor. It could have been a simple matter of robbery, or it could be that word is out that the Jacobites are stirring."

"And so they are." Ian thought a moment, drumming his fingers. "Well, four on two, was it? Not such bad odds when it comes to Campbells. You were wounded, as well?"

"A trifle." Brigham shrugged. It was a gesture he'd acquired in France. "If Coll's mount hadn't slipped, he would never have dropped his guard. He's a devil of a swordsman."

"So he says of you." Ian's teeth flashed. There was nothing he admired so much as a good fighter. "Something about a skirmish on the road to Calais?"

Brigham grinned at that. "A diversion."

"I'd like to hear more about it, but first, tell me what you can about the Bonnie Prince and his plans."

They talked for hours, draining the bottle of port dry and cracking another while the candles guttered. Formalities faded and disappeared until they were only two men, one past his prime, the other only approaching it. They were both warriors by birth and by temperament. They might fight for different reasons, one in a desperate attempt to preserve a way of life and land, the other for simple justice. But they would fight. When they parted, Ian to look in on his son, Brigham to take the air and check the horses, they knew each other as well as they needed.

It was late when he returned. The house was quiet, fires were banked. Outside the wind whistled, bringing home to him the isolation, the distance from London and all he held familiar.

Near the door, a candle had been lighted to show him the way. He took it and started up the stairs, though he knew he was still far too restless for sleep. The MacGregors interested him— they had since the first time he and Coll had shared a bottle and their life stories. He knew they were bound together, not just through family obligation but through affection and a common love of their land. Tonight he had seen them pull together with unquestioning faith and loyalty. There had been no hysterics when he had carried Coll inside, no weeping and fainting women. Instead, each had done what had needed to be done.

It was that kind of strength and commitment Charles would need over the next months.

With the candlelight sending shadows leaping, Brigham walked past his room to push open the door to Coll's. The bed-curtains were pushed back, and he could see his friend sleeping yet, covered with blankets. And he saw Serena sitting in a chair beside the bed, reading a book by the light of another taper.

It was the first time he'd seen her look as her name described. Her face was calm and extraordinarily lovely in the soft light. Her hair glowed as it fell down her back. She had changed her dress for a night robe of deep green that rose high at the throat to frame her face. As Brigham watched, she looked up at her brother's murmur and placed a hand on the pulse at his wrist.

"How is he?"

She started at the sound of Brigham's voice but collected herself quickly. Her face expressionless, she sat back again to close the book she had in her lap. "His fever's still up. Gwen thinks it should break by morning."

Brigham moved to the foot of the bed. Behind him, the fire burned high. The scent of medicine, mixed with poppies, vied with the smoke. "Coll told me she could do magic with herbs. I've seen doctors with less of a sure hand sewing up a wound."

Torn between annoyance and pride in her sister, Serena smoothed down the skirts of her robe. "She has a gift, and a good heart. She would have stayed with him all night if I hadn't bullied her off to bed."

"So you bully everyone, not just strangers?" He smiled and held up a hand before she could speak. "You can hardly tear into me now, my dear, or you will wake up your brother and the rest of your family."

"I'm not your dear."

"For which I shall go to my grave thankful. Merely a form of address."

Coll stirred, and Brigham moved to the side of the bed to place a cool hand on his brow. "Has he waked at all?"

"A time or two, but not in his right head." Because her conscience demanded it, she relented. "He asked for you." She rose and wrung out a cloth to bathe her brother's face with. "You should retire, and see him in the morning."

"And what of you?"

Her hands were gentle on her brother, soothing, cooling. Despite himself, Brigham imagined how they might feel stroking his brow. "What of me?"

"Have you no one to bully you to bed?"

She glanced up, fully aware of his meaning. "I go when and where I choose." Taking her seat again, she folded her hands. "You're wasting your candle, Lord Ashburn."

Without a word, he snuffed it out. The light of the single taper by the bed plunged them into intimacy. "Quite right," he murmured. "One candle is sufficient."

"I hope you can find your way to your room in the dark."

"I have excellent night vision, as it happens. But I don't retire yet." Idly he plucked the book from her lap. "*Macbeth?*"

"Don't the fine ladies of your acquaintance read?"

His lips twitched. "A few." He opened the book and scanned the pages. "A grisly little tale."

"Murder and power?" She made a little gesture with her hands. "Life, my lord, can be grisly, as the English so often prove."

"Macbeth was a Scot," he reminded her. "'A tale told by an idiot, full of sound and fury, signifying nothing.' Is that how you see life?"

"I see it as what can be made of it."

Brigham leaned against a table, holding the book loosely. He believed she meant just what she said, and that interested him. Most of the women he knew could philosophize about no more than fashion.

"You don't see Macbeth as a villain?"

"Why?" She hadn't meant to speak to him, much less hold a conversation, but she couldn't resist. "He took what he felt was his."

"And his methods?"

"Ruthless. Perhaps kings need be. Charles won't claim his throne by asking for it."

"No." With a frown, Brigham closed the book. "But treachery differs from warfare."

"A sword is a sword, thrust in the back or in the heart." She looked at him, her green eyes glowing in the light. "If I were a man I would fight to win, and the devil take the method."

"And honor?"

"There is much honor in victory." She soaked the cloth and wrung it out again. For all her talk, she had a woman's way with illness, gentle, patient, thorough. "There was a time when the MacGregors were hunted like vermin, with the Campbells paid in good British gold for each death. If you are hunted like something wild, you learn to fight like something wild. Women were raped and murdered, bairns not yet weaned slaughtered. We don't forget, Lord Ashburn, nor forgive."

"This is a new time, Serena."

"Still, my brother's blood was shed today."

On impulse he placed a hand over hers. "In a few months more will be shed, but for justice, not revenge."

"You can afford justice, my lord, not I."

Coll moaned and began to thrash. Serena turned her full attention to him again. Automatically Brigham held him down. "He'll break open his wound again."

"Keep him still." Serena poured more medicine into a wooden cup and held it to Coll's lips. "Drink now, darling." She poured what she could down his throat, murmuring, threatening, coaxing all the while. He was shivering, though his skin was like fire to the touch.

She no longer questioned Brigham's presence, and she said nothing when he stripped off his coat and tucked back the lace at his wrists. Together they bathed Coll with cool water, forced more of Gwen's mixture past his dry lips and kept watch.

During Coll's delirium Serena spoke to him mainly in Gaelic, as calm and steady as a seasoned soldier. Brigham found it strange to see her so unruffled when from almost the first moment of their acquaintance she had been animated by excitement or fury. Now, in the deepest part of the night, her hands were gentle, her voice quiet, her movements competent. They worked together as though they'd spent their lives doing so.

She no longer resented his assistance. English or not, he obviously cared for her brother. Without his aid she would have been forced to summon her sister or her mother. For a few hours, Serena forced herself to forget that Lord Ashburn represented all she despised.

Now and then, over the cloth or the cup, their hands brushed. Both of them strove to ignore even this minor intimacy. He might have been concerned for Coll, but he was still an English nobleman. She might have had more spine than any other women he'd known, but she was still a Scots terror.

The truce lasted while Coll's fever raged. By the time the light turned gray with approaching dawn, the crisis had passed.

"He's cool." Serena blinked back tears as she stroked her brother's brow. Silly to weep now, she thought, when the worst was over. "I think he'll do, but Gwen will have a look at him."

"He should sleep well enough." Brigham pressed a hand to the small of his back, where a dull ache lodged. The fire they had taken turns feeding during the night still roared at his back, shooting light and heat. He had loosened his shirt for comfort and a smoothly muscled chest could be seen in the deep V. Serena wiped her own brow and tried not to notice.

"It's almost morning." She felt weak and weepy and tired to the bone.

"Yes." Brigham's mind had shifted suddenly, completely, from the man in the bed to the woman by the window. The first hints of dawn were behind her, and she stood in shadow and in light. Her night robe cloaked her as if she were royalty. Her face, pale with fatigue, was dominated by eyes that seemed only larger, darker, more mysterious, for the faint bruises beneath.

Her blood began to tingle below her skin as he continued to stare at her. She wished he would stop. It made her feel...powerless somehow. Suddenly afraid, she tore her gaze from his and looked at her brother.

"There's no need for you to stay now."

"No."

She turned her back. Brigham took it as a dismissal. He gave her an ironic bow she couldn't see, but stopped when he heard the sniffle. He paused at the door. Then, dragging a hand through his hair and swearing, he moved toward her.

"No need for tears now, Serena."

Hurriedly she wiped at her cheek with her knuckles. "I thought he would die. I didn't realize how afraid I was of it until it was past." She swiped a hand over her face again. "I've lost my handkerchief," she said miserably.

Brigham pressed his own into her hand.

"Thank you."

"You're welcome," he managed when she handed it back to him crumpled and damp. "Better now?"

"Aye." She let out a long, steadying breath. "I wish you would go."

"Where?" Though he knew it was unwise, he turned her to face him. He only wanted to see her eyes again. "To my bed or to the devil?"

Her lips curved, surprising them both. "As you choose, my lord."

He wanted those lips. The knowledge stunned him as much as her smile did. He wanted them warm and open and completely willing under his own. Light broke through the sky and tumbled like gold dust through the window. Before either of them were prepared, he reached out so that his fingers dug through her hair and cupped her neck.

"No," she managed, amazed that the denial was unsteady. When she lifted a hand in protest, he met it, palm to palm. So they stood as the new day began.

"You tremble," he murmured. Lightly he ran his fingers up her neck, kindling small fires. "I wondered if you would."

"I've not given you leave to touch me."

"I've not asked for leave." He drew her closer. "Nor will I." He brought their joined hands to his lips, dropping a soft kiss on her fingers. "Nor need I."

She felt the room tilt and her will drain as he lowered his head toward her. She saw only his face, then only his eyes. As if in a dream, she let her own eyes close and her lips part.

"Serena?"

She jerked back, color flaming into her face at the sound of her sister's voice. Shaken, Serena gripped her hands together as Gwen stepped into the room. "You should be resting yet. You've only slept a few hours."

"It was enough. Coll?" she asked, staring toward the bed.

"His fever's broken."

"Ah, thank God." Her hair more gold than red, curtained her face as she bent over him. In her pale blue night robe she looked very much like the angel Coll had described. "He sleeps well, and should for a few hours yet." She glanced up to smile at her sister and saw Brigham by the window. "Lord Ashburn! Have you not slept?"

"He was about to retire." Serena moved briskly to her sister's side.

"You need rest." Gwen's face puckered into a frown as she thought of his shoulder. "You'll do your wound no good else."

"He does well enough," Serena said impatiently.

"For your concern, I thank you." Brigham bowed pointedly to Gwen. "As it appears I can be of no further use, I will seek my bed." His gaze swept down Serena and up again. Beside her sister she, too, looked like an angel. An avenging one. "Your servant, madam."

Gwen smiled after him as he strode out, her young heart fluttering a bit at the sight of his bare chest and arms. "So handsome," she sighed.

With a sniff, Serena brushed at the bodice of her robe. "For an Englishman."

"It was kind of him to stay with Coll."

Serena could still feel the determined press of his fingers on the back of her neck. "He's not kind," she murmured. "I don't believe he's kind at all."

Chapter Three

Brigham slept until the sun was high. His shoulder was stiff, but there was no pain. He supposed he owed Serena for that. His lips curved into a grim smile as he dressed. He intended to pay her back.

After he had pulled on his breeches, he glanced at his torn riding coat. It would have to do, as he could hardly wear evening dress. Until his trunks arrived he would be roughing it. He ran a hand over his chin after shrugging into the coat. His stubble was rough and his lace far from fresh. How his valet would have cringed.

Dear, dour Parkins had been furious at being left in London while his lord traveled to the barbarous Scottish Highlands. Parkins knew, as few did, the true purpose of the trip, but that had only made him more insistent about accompanying his master.

Brigham tilted the shaving mirror. Parkins was loyal, he thought, but hardly competent to do battle. There was no finer—or more proper—gentleman's gentleman in London, but Brigham hardly needed, or wanted, a valet during his stay in Glenroe.

With a sigh, he began to strop his razor. He might not be able to do anything about the torn jacket or the drooping lace, but he could manage to shave himself.

Once he was presentable, he made his way downstairs. Fiona was there to greet him, an apron over her simple wool gown. "Lord Ashburn, I trust you rested well."

"Very well, Lady MacGregor."

"If you're a man such as I know, you'll be wanting to break your fast." With a smile, she laid a hand on his arm and began to walk. "Would you care to sit in the parlor? It's warmer than the dining hall, and when I have a solitary meal I find it less lonely."

"Thank you."

"Molly, tell the cook that Lord Ashburn is awake and hungry." She led him into a parlor where a table had already been set for him. "Shall I leave you now, or would you prefer company?"

"I always prefer the company of a beautiful woman, my lady."

With a smile, she accepted the chair he held out for her. "Coll said you were a charmer." Apron or not, she sat as gracefully as any drawing room miss Brigham had known. "I wasn't able to thank you properly last night. I'd like to make up for that now and give you all my gratitude for delivering Coll home."

"Would that I had delivered him under better circumstances."

"You brought him." She offered her hand. "I owe you a great deal."

"He's my friend."

"Aye." She squeezed his hand briefly. "So he's told me. That doesn't lessen the debt, but I won't embarrass you." Molly brought in coffee and Fiona poured, pleased by the opportunity to make use of her china. "Coll asked for you this morning. Perhaps after you've eaten you would go up and speak with him."

"Of course. How does he?"

"Well enough to complain." Fiona's smile was maternal. "He's like his father, impatient, impulsive and very, very dear."

They spoke idly while his breakfast was served. There was porridge and thick slabs of ham, portions of fresh fish with eggs and oatcakes and numerous jams and jellies. Though he chose coffee over the breakfast whiskey, it occurred to him that, while remote, this Highland table could easily rival one in London. The lady sipped her coffee and encouraged Brigham to eat his fill.

He found her burr charming and her conversation direct. While he ate, he waited for her to ask him what he and her husband had discussed the night before. But the questions didn't come.

"If you'll give me your jacket this evening, my lord, I would mend it for you."

He glanced at the ruined sleeve. "I fear it will never be the same."

Her eyes were sober when they met his. "We do what we can with what we have." She rose, bringing Brigham to his feet. Her skirts swished quietly into place. "If you'll excuse me, Lord Ashburn, I have much to see to before my husband returns."

"The MacGregor has gone?"

"He should be home by evening. We all have much to do before Prince Charles makes his move."

Brigham's brow lifted as she left. He'd never known a woman to take the threat of war quite so complacently.

When he returned upstairs, he found Coll a bit pale and shadowed around the eyes but sitting up and arguing.

"I won't touch that slop."

"You will eat every drop," Serena said threateningly. "Gwen made it especially for you."

"I don't care if the Blessed Virgin dipped her finger in it, I won't have it."

"Blaspheme again and you'll wear it."

"Good morning, children." Brigham strolled into the room.

"Brig, thank God," Coll said feelingly. "Send this wench on her way and get me some meat. Meat," he repeated. "And whiskey."

After crossing to the bed, Brigham raised a brow at the thin gruel Serena held in a bowl. "It certainly looks revolting."

"Aye, that's just what I said myself." Coll fell back against the pillows, relieved to have a man on his side. "No one but a thick-skulled woman would expect anyone to eat it."

"Had a rather nice slab of ham myself."

"Ham?"

"Done to a turn. My compliments to your cook, Miss Mac-Gregor."

"Gruel's what he needs," she said between her teeth, "and gruel's what he'll have."

After a shrug, Brigham sat on the edge of the bed. "I've done my bit, Coll. It's up to you."

"Toss her out."

Brigham fluffed his lace. "I hate to disoblige you, my dear, but the woman terrifies me."

"Hah!" Coll set his chin and eyed his sister. "Go to the devil, Serena, and take that slop with you."

"Fine, then, if you want to hurt little Gwen's feelings after she nursed you and took the time and trouble to make you something fit to eat. I'll just take it down and tell her you said it was slop and you'd rather have nothing than touch it."

She turned, bowl in hand. Before she'd taken two steps, Coll relented. "Hell and damnation, give it to me, then."

Brigham caught her smirk as she swept aside her skirts and sat. "Well done," he murmured.

Ignoring him, she dipped the spoon in the bowl. "Open your big mouth, Coll."

"I won't be fed," he said just before she shoved in the first bite of gruel. "Curse it, Serena, I said I'll feed myself."

"And spill gruel all over your clean nightshirt. I'll not be changing you again today, my lad, so open your mouth and be quiet."

He would have sworn at her again, but he was too busy swallowing gruel.

"I'll leave you to your breakfast, Coll."

"For mercy's sake." He grabbed Brigham's wrist. "Don't desert me now. She'll yap at me, nag and bluster and set me mad. I—" He glared as Serena pushed more gruel into his mouth. "She's the devil of a female, Brig. A man's not safe with her."

"Is that so?" Smiling, Brigham studied Serena's face and was rewarded by the faintest rising of color.

"I haven't thanked you for getting me home. I'm told you were wounded," Coll said.

"A scratch. Your sister tended it."

"Gwen's an angel."

"Young Gwen had her hands full with you. Serena bound me up."

Coll looked at his sister and grinned. "Ham-fisted."

"You'll be swallowing the spoon in a moment, Coll Mac-Gregor."

"It takes more than a hole in my side to devil me, lassie. I can still put you over my knee."

She wiped his mouth delicately with a napkin. "The last time you tried you walked with a limp for a week."

He grinned at the memory. "Aye, right you are. Brig, the lass is a Trojan. Kicked me square in the—" he caught Serena's furious look "—pride, so to speak."

"I'll remember that if I ever have occasion to wrestle with Miss MacGregor."

"Beaned me with a pot once, too," Coll said reminiscently. "Damn me if I didn't see stars." He was drowsy again, and his eyelids drooped. "Fire-eater," he muttered. "You'll never catch a husband that way."

"If it was a husband I wanted to catch, so I would."

"The prettiest girl in Glenroe." Coll's voice wavered as his eyes shut. "But the temper's foul, Brig. Not like that pretty Frenchie with the gold hair."

What pretty Frenchie? Serena wondered, sending Brigham a sidelong look. But he was only grinning and fiddling with the button of his jacket.

"I've had the pleasure of discovering that for myself," Brigham murmured. "Rest now. I'll be back."

"Forced that gruel on me. Nasty stuff."

"Aye, and there's more where that came from. Ungrateful oaf."

"I love you, Rena."

She brushed the hair from his brow. "I know. Hush now, and sleep." Serena tucked him up while Brigham stood back. "He'll be quiet for a few hours now. Mother will feed him next, and he won't argue with her."

"I'd say the arguing did him as much good as the gruel."

"That was the idea." She lifted the tray with the empty bowl and started past him. Brigham had only to shift to block her way.

"Did you rest?"

"Well enough. Pardon me, Lord Ashburn, I have things to do."

Instead of moving aside, he smiled at her. "When I spend the night with a woman, she usually calls me by my name."

The lights of war came into her eyes, just as he'd hoped. "I'm not some golden-haired Frenchie or one of your loose London women, so keep your name, *Lord* Ashburn. I've no use for it."

"I believe I have use for yours…Serena." She delighted him by snarling. "You have the most beautiful eyes I've ever seen."

That flustered her. She knew how to handle flattery, how to accept it, evade it, discount it. Somehow it wasn't as easy with him. "Let me pass," she muttered.

"Would you have kissed me?" He put two fingers under her chin as he asked. Serena held the tray like a shield. "Would you have, this morning, when the need for sleep was all over your face and the light just going gold?"

"Move aside." Because her voice was husky, she shoved the tray at him. Brigham caught it instinctively to keep it from falling. Unencum-bered, Serena headed for the door with him two steps behind. The sound of running feet stopped them both.

"Malcolm, must you sound like a great elephant? Coll's sleeping."

"Oh." A boy of about ten skidded to a halt. His hair was a deep red that would probably darken to mahogany with age. Unlike the other men in his family, he had fine, almost delicate features. He had, Brigham noticed immediately, the deep green eyes of his sister. "I wanted to see him."

"You can watch him, if you're quiet." With a sigh, Serena shook his shoulder. "Wash first. You look like a stableboy."

He grinned, showing a missing tooth. "I've been with the mare. She'll foal in a day or two."

"You smell like her." She noticed from the mud in the hall that he hadn't done a thorough job of cleaning his boots. She would sweep it up before their mother saw it. She started to speak to him about it, then noticed he was no longer attending.

Brigham found himself being studied and assessed, quite man-to-man. The boy was lean as a whippet and smudged with dirt, and there was sharp curiosity in his eyes.

"Are you the English pig?"

"Malcolm!"

Both ignored her as Brigham stepped forward. Calmly he handed the tray back to Serena. "I'm English, at any rate, though my grandmother was a MacDonald."

Mortified, Serena stared straight ahead. "I will apologize for my brother, my lord."

He shot her a look ripe with irony. Both of them knew where Malcolm had come by the description. "No need. You would perhaps introduce us."

Serena's fingers dug into the tray. "Lord Ashburn, my brother Malcolm."

"Your servant, Master MacGregor."

Malcolm grinned at that, and at Brigham's formal bow. "My father likes you," he confided. "So does my mother, and Gwen, I think, but she's too shy to say."

Brigham's lips twitched. "I'm honored."

"Coll wrote that you had the best stables in London, so I'll like you, too."

Because it was irresistible, Brigham ruffled the boy's hair—and grinned wickedly at Serena. "Another conquest."

She lifted her chin. "Go wash, Malcolm," she ordered before she flounced away.

"They always want you to wash," Malcolm said with a sigh. "I'm glad there'll be more men in the house."

Nearly two hours later, Brigham's coach arrived, causing no little stir in the village. Lord Ashburn believed in owning the best, and his traveling equipment was no exception. The coach was well sprung, a regal black picked out with silver. The driver wore black, as well. The groom, who rode on the box with him, was enjoying the fact that people were peeking out their doors and windows at the arrival. Though he'd complained for the last day and a half about the miserable weather, the miserable roads and the miserable pace, he felt better knowing that the journey was at an end and that he'd be left to tend to his horses.

"Here, boy." The driver pulled up the steaming horses and gestured to a boy who stood beside the road, ogling the coach and sucking his finger. "Where will I find MacGregor House?"

"Straight down this road and over the rise. You be looking for the English lord? That be his carriage?"

"You got that right."

Pleased with himself, the boy gestured. "He's there."

The driver sent the horses into a trot.

Brigham was there to meet them himself. Braced against the cold, he stepped out as the coach pulled up. "You took your sweet time."

"Beg pardon, my lord. Weather held us up."

Brigham waved a hand at the trunks. "Bring those in. The stables are around the back, Jem. Settle the horses. Have you eaten?"

Jem, whose family had been with the Langstons for three generations, jumped down nimbly. "Hardly a bite, milord. Wiggins here sets a mad pace."

Appreciating the truth of it, Brigham grinned up at the driver. "I'm sure there will be something hot in the kitchen. If you would—" He stopped as the coach door swung open and a personage more dignified than any duke stepped out.

"Parkins."

Parkins bowed. "My lord." Then he studied Brigham's attire, and his dour face changed. His voice, filled with mortification, quivered. "Oh, my lord."

Brigham cast a rueful glance at his torn sleeve. Undoubtedly Parkins would be more concerned with the material than with the wound beneath. "As you see, I have need of my trunks. Now, what in blazes are you doing here?"

"You have a need for me, as well, my lord." Parkins drew himself up. "I knew I was right to come, and there can be no doubt of it. See that the trunks are put in Lord Ashburn's room immediately."

Though the cold was seeping through his riding coat, Brigham planted himself. "How did you come?"

"I met the coach yesterday, sir, after you and Mr. MacGregor had taken to horse." A foot shorter than Brigham, and woefully thin, Parkins pushed his shoulders back. "I will not be sent back to London, my lord, when my duty is here."

"I don't need a valet, man. I'm not attending any balls."

"I served my lord's father for fifteen years, and my lord for five. I will not be sent back."

Brigham opened his mouth, then shut it. Loyalty was impossible to argue with. "Oh, come in, damn you. It's freezing."

Cloaked in dignity, Parkins ascended the stairs. "I will see to my lord's unpacking immediately." He gave a shudder as he studied his master's attire once more. "*Immediately*. If I could persuade my lord to accompany me, I could have you suitably clad in a trice."

"Later." Brigham swung on his greatcoat. "I want to check on the horses." He strode down the steps, checked, then turned. "Parkins, welcome to Scotland."

The faintest ghost of a smile touched the thin lips. "Thank you, my lord."

Jem the groom seemed well on the way to making himself and the horses at home. Brigham heard his cackling laughter as he pushed aside the wooden door.

"You're a right one, ain't you, Master MacGregor? Sure and Lord Ashburn has the best stable in London—England itself, for that matter—and it's me who's in charge of them."

"Then I'll have you look at my mare, Jem, who'll be foaling soon."

"Pleased to have a look at her I'll be—after I've seen to my loves here."

"Jem."

"Eh—" He turned and saw Brigham standing in a beam of thin winter light. "Yes, sir, Lord Ashburn. I'll have everything set to rights in a twinkle."

Brigham knew that Jem couldn't be faulted with horses, but

he also had a free hand with the bottle and language the Mac-Gregors might not deem proper for their youngest. So he lingered, supervising the settling of his team.

"Fine horses they are, Lord Ashburn." Malcolm had taken a hand in the grooming. "I can drive very well, you know."

"I wouldn't doubt it." Brigham had stripped off his greatcoat, and since his jacket was ruined in any case, he added his weight to the work. "Perhaps we'll find an afternoon so you can show me?"

"Truly?" There was no quicker way to the boy's heart. "I don't think I could handle your coach, but we have a curricle." He gave a manly sneer. "Though my mother won't let me drive anything but the pony cart by myself."

"You'll be with me, won't you?" Brigham swatted one of the horses' flanks. "They seem to be in good shape, Jem. Go have a look at Master MacGregor's mare."

"Please, sir, would you look in on her, too? She's a beauty."

Brigham laid a hand on Malcolm's shoulder. "I'd be delighted to meet her."

Satisfied he'd found a kindred spirit, Malcolm took Brigham's hand and led him through the stables. "She's Betsy." At the sound of her name, the mare poked her head over the stall door and waited to be rubbed.

"A lovely lady." She was a roan, not beautifully distinguished, but dignified and trim enough. As Brigham lifted a hand to stroke her head, she pricked up her ears and fixed him with a calm, questioning eye.

"She likes you." The fact pleased Malcolm, as if he often trusted the opinions of animals over those of people.

Inside the stall, Jem went about his business in a calm, capable way that impressed the young Malcolm. Betsy stood tolerantly, sighing occasionally so that her heavy belly shook, and switching her tail.

"She'll be foaling soon," Jem pronounced. "Another day or two by my guess."

"I want to sleep in the stables, but Serena always comes and drags me back."

"Don't fret about it, Jem's here now." With that, Jem stepped out of the stall.

"But you will send word when it's time?"

Jem looked at Brigham for affirmation, got it and grinned. "I'll send up a shout for you, never fear."

"Could I impose on you to show Jem to the kitchen?" Brigham asked. "He hasn't eaten."

"I beg your pardon." Abruptly proper, Malcolm straightened his shoulders. "I'll see that the cook fixes you something right away. Good afternoon, my lord."

"Brig."

Malcolm grinned at the man, and at the hand he was offered. He shook it formally, then skipped out, calling for Jem to follow.

"A taking little scamp. If I may say so, milord?"

"You may. Jem, try to remember he's young and impressionable." At Jem's blank expression, Brigham sighed. "If he begins to swear like my English groom, the ax will fall on me. He has a sister who would love to wield it."

"Yes, milord. I'll be the soul of propriety, I will." Breaking into a grin, Jem followed Malcolm out.

Brigham didn't know why he lingered. Perhaps it was because it was quiet, and the horses good company. It was true that he'd spent a good part of his youth in the same way as Malcolm, in the stables. He'd learned more than a few interesting phrases. He could, if necessary, have harnessed a team himself in only half again as much time as his groom. He could drive to an inch or doctor a strained tendon, and he had overseen his share of foalings.

Once it had been his dream to breed horses. That had changed when the responsibilities of his title had come to him at an early age.

But it wasn't horses or lost dreams he thought of now. It was Serena. Perhaps because his thoughts were on her, he wasn't surprised to see her enter the stables.

She'd been thinking of him, as well, though not entirely kindly. Throughout the day she hadn't been able to concentrate on ordinary things. Instead she concentrated, unwillingly, on that moment she had stood with him by her brother's window.

She'd been tired, Serena assured herself as she wrapped the plaid securely around her. Almost asleep on her feet, if it came to that. Why else would she have only stood there while he touched her in that way…looked at her in that way?

And how he'd looked. Even now, something stirred in her at the memory. His eyes had gotten so dark; they'd been so close. She knew what it was to have a man look at her with interest, even to have one try to steer her into the shadows to steal a kiss. With one or two, she'd permitted it. Just to see if she might care for it. In truth, she found kissing pleasant enough, if unexciting. But nothing before had come close to this.

Her legs had gone weak, as if someone had taken out the blood and replaced it with water. Her head had spun the way it had when she'd been twelve and sampled her father's port. And it had felt, Lord, as though her skin were on fire where his fingers had touched it. Like a sickness, she thought.

What else could it be? She shook the feeling off and straightened her shoulders. It had been fatigue, plain and simple. That, and concern for her brother, and a lack of food. She was feeling a great deal better now, and if she chanced to come across the high-and-mighty earl of Ashburn she would handle him well enough.

She shook off her thoughts and peered around the dim stable. "Malcolm, you little heathen," she called, "I'll have you out of those stables and into the house. It's your job to fill the woodbox, hang you, and I've done it myself for the last time."

"I regret you'll have to hang Malcolm later." Brigham stepped out of the shadows and was pleased to startle her. "He isn't here. I've just sent him along to the kitchen with my groom."

She tossed up her chin. "Sent him along? He's no servant of yours."

"My dear Miss MacGregor." Brigham stepped closer, deciding that the dull colors in the plaid were the perfect foil for the richness of her hair. "Malcolm has formed an attachment for Jem, who is, like your brother, a great horse lover."

Because her heart was softest when it came to Malcolm, she subsided. "He's forever in here. Twice this week I've had to bundle him up and drag him into the house past his bedtime." She caught herself and frowned again. "If he pesters you, I'd appreciate it if you'd let me know. I'll see that he doesn't intrude."

"No need. We deal together easily enough." She was frowning over that as he stepped closer. She smelled of the lavender that always seemed to waft around her. "You need more rest, Serena. Your eyes are shadowed."

She had nearly stepped back before she was able to resist the unusual urge to retreat. "I'm as strong as one of your horses, thank you. And you're very free with my name."

"I've taken a liking to it. What was it Coll called you before he fell asleep? Rena? It has a pretty sound."

It sounded different when he said it. She turned to study his horses. "You've impressed Malcolm with these, I'm sure."

"He's more easily impressed than his sister."

She glanced over her shoulder. "You have nothing that could impress me, my lord."

"Don't you find it wearing to despise all things English?"

"No, I find it fulfilling." Because she was feeling weak-kneed again, and needful, she turned on him, letting anger replace longings she did not yet understand. "What are you to me but one more English nobleman who wants things his way? Do you care for the land? For the people? For the name? You know nothing of what we are," she spat out. "Nothing of the persecutions, the miseries, the degradations."

"More than you think," he said softly, guarding his own temper.

"You sit in your fine house in London or your manor in the country and dream by the fire of values and great social change. We live the fight every day, just to hold on to our own. What do you know of the terror of waiting in the dark for your men to return, or the frustration of not being able to do more than wait?"

"Do you blame me, too, for your being born a female?" He caught her arm before she could spin away. Her shawl fell away from her hair and onto her shoulders so that the evening light struggling through the doorway and the chinks in the wood glowed over it. "I might curse myself for preferring you that way."

He resented bitterly his automatic response to her. "Tell me the truth, Serena, do you despise me?"

"Aye." She said it with passion, wanting it to be true.

"Because I'm English?"

"It's reason enough to hate."

"It's not, but I think I'll give you one."

To please himself, he thought as he dragged her against him. To undo the knots in his stomach, calm the thunder in his loins. She jerked back and might have landed a blow, but he was prepared for her, and very quick.

The moment his mouth came down on hers, she went still. He heard her breath suck in, then only the buzzing in his own head. She had a mouth like rose petals, soft, fragrant, crushable. With an oath, he wrapped an arm around her waist and locked her to him. He could feel her breasts yield and her body tremble. His own was rigid with the shock of the sensation that poured through him.

Behind them the horses blew and shifted weight. Dust motes danced in an errant sunbeam.

She couldn't move. She thought she might never move again, because all the bones in her body had dissolved. Behind her eyes was a rush of colors, so vivid, so brilliant, that they would certainly blind her. If this was a kiss, then she had never experienced one before, for this was all heat, all light, all movement, in one meeting of lips.

She heard a moan, such a soft, such a sweet moan, and never recognized it as her own. Her hand was on his arm, fingers tangled in the tear of his sleeve. She might have swayed, but he held her so close.

Was she breathing?

She had to be, for she lived still. She could smell him, and the scent was much the same as it had been on their first meeting. Sweat, horses, man. And he tasted... Her lips parted, she thirsted for more. He tasted like honey warmed in whiskey. Wasn't she already drunk from him?

Her heart began to thunder, drumming in pulses she hadn't known existed. If there was more, she wanted to find it. If this was all, it was enough for a lifetime. Slowly she slid her hands up his arms, over his shoulders and into his hair. Her kiss changed from one of shock and surrender to one of demand.

He felt her teeth nip at his lip and a fire centered in his loins. Suddenly desperate, he pressed her back against a post and savaged her mouth even as it opened and invited him in. In that instant he was more her prisoner than she his.

He surfaced like a man drowning, gulping in air and shaking his head to clear it. "Good God, where did you learn to do that?"

Right here, right now. But shame and confusion stained her cheeks. However it had happened, she had let him kiss her and, Lord help her, she had enjoyed it. "Let me go."

"I don't know if I can." He lifted a hand to her cheek, but she jerked her head away. Struggling for patience, Brigham stood where he was and tried to catch his breath. A moment ago she had kissed him in a manner to rival the finest French courtesans. But now, right now, it was painfully clear she was innocent.

He could kill himself—if Coll didn't beat him to it. Brigham set his jaw. Seducing the sister of his friend—the daughter of his host—in the stable, as though she were a tavern wench. He cleared his throat and stepped back. When he spoke, his voice was stiff.

"I offer my deepest apologies, Miss MacGregor. That was unforgivable."

Her lashes swept up. Beneath them her eyes were not sheened with tears but bright with anger. "If I were a man, I'd kill you."

"If you were a man," he said, just as rigidly, "my apologies would hardly be necessary." He bowed and went out, hoping the cold air would clear his head.

Chapter Four

She would have enjoyed killing him, Serena thought. With a sword. No, a sword was much too clean, much too civilized, for English vermin. Unless, of course, she used it to sever small pieces from him one at a time rather than end his worthless life with one thrust through the heart. She smiled to herself as she imagined it. A quick hack there, a slow, torturous slice here.

Her thoughts might have been gruesome, but no one would have guessed by looking at her. She was the picture of quiet feminine occupation as she sat in the warm kitchen and churned butter. It was true that when her thoughts darkened she brought the plunger down with unwarranted force, but the energy, whatever its source, only made the job go faster.

He'd had no right to kiss her that way, to force himself on her. And less right than that to make her like it. With her hands wrapped around the wooden staff, Serena sent the plunger dancing. Miserable English cur. And she had patched up his hurts with her own hands, served him a meal in her own house. Not willingly, perhaps not graciously, but she had done it nonetheless.

If she told her father what Brigham had dared to do... She paused for a moment as she dreamed of that possibility. Her father would rage and bellow and very likely whip the English dog within an inch of his miserable life. That made her smile again, the picture of the high-and-mighty earl of Ashburn groveling in the dirt, his arrogant gray eyes clouded with terror.

She began to churn faster as her smile turned into a snarl. The picture was right enough, but she'd prefer to hold the whip herself. She would make him whimper as he sprawled at her feet.

It was true, and perhaps sad, Serena thought, that she had such a love of violence. It concerned her mother. No doubt it was a pity she hadn't inherited her mother's temperament rather than her father's, but there it was. It was rare for a day to go by when Serena didn't lose her MacGregor temper and then suffer pangs of guilt and remorse because of it.

She wanted to be more like her mother—calm, steady, patient. The good Lord knew she tried, but it just wasn't in her. At times she thought God had made the tiniest mistake with her, forgetting the sugar and adding just a dab too much vinegar. But if God was entitled to a mistake, wasn't she then entitled to her temper?

With a sigh, she continued the monotonous chore of working the plunger up and down.

It was true enough that her mother would have known exactly the proper way to handle Lord Ashburn and his unwanted advances. She would have become frigidly polite when he'd gotten that look in his eyes. That look, Serena thought, that told a woman instinctively that he meant mischief. By the time Fiona MacGregor had been done with him, Lord Ashburn would have been putty in her hands.

For herself, she had no way with men. When they annoyed her, she let them know it—with a box on the ear or a sharp-tongued diatribe. And why not? she thought, scowling. Why the devil not? Just because she was a woman, did she have to act coy and pretend to be flattered when a man tried to slobber all over her?

"You'll be turning that butter rancid with those looks, lassie."

With a sniff, Serena began to work in earnest. "I was thinking of men, Mrs. Drummond."

The cook, a formidably built woman with graying black hair and sparkling blue eyes, cackled. She had been a widow these past ten years and had the hands of a farmer, thick fingered, wide palmed and rough as tree bark. Still, no one in the district had a better way with a joint of meat or a dainty fruit tart.

"A woman should have a smile on her face when she thinks of men. Scowls send them off, but a smile brings them around quick enough."

"I don't want them around." Serena bared her teeth and ignored her aching shoulders. "I hate them."

Mrs. Drummond stirred the batter for her apple cake. "Has that young Rob MacGregor come sniffing around again?"

"Not if he values his life." Now she did smile as she remembered how she had dispatched the amorous Rob.

"A likely enough lad," Mrs. Drummond mused. "But not good enough for one of my lassies. When I see you courted, wedded and bedded, it'll be to quality."

Serena began to tap her foot in time with her churning. "I don't think I want to be courted, wedded or bedded."

"Whist now, of course you do. In time." She gave a quick grin as her spoon beat a steady tattoo against the bowl. The muscles in her arms were as solid as mountain rock. "It has its merits. Especially the last."

"I don't want to find myself bound to a man just because of what happens in a marriage bed."

Mrs. Drummond shot a quick look at the doorway to be certain Fiona wasn't nearby. The mistress was kindness itself, but she would get that pinched look on her face if she heard her cook and her daughter discussing delicate matters over the butter churn.

"A better reason is hard to find—with the right man. My Duncan, now there was a man who knew how to do his duty, and there were nights I went to sleep grateful for it. Rest his soul."

"Did he ever make you feel—" Serena paused a moment, groping for the right words "—well, like you'd been riding fast over the rocks and couldn't get your breath?"

Mrs. Drummond narrowed her eyes. "Are you sure that Rob hasn't been around?"

Serena shook her head. "Being with Rob's like riding a lame pony uphill. You think it'll never be done with." Her own eyes were bright with laughter as she looked up at the cook.

That was the way Brigham saw her when he walked in. Her long fingers were wrapped around the plunger, her skirts were kilted up and her face was alive with laughter.

Damn the woman! He couldn't keep himself from staring at her. Damn her for making him want just by looking!

He made little sound, but Serena turned her head. Their eyes locked, briefly, almost violently, before Serena lifted her chin away and went back to her churning.

The look had lasted only an instant, but that had been long

enough to show Mrs. Drummond what had put Serena into a temper. Or rather who.

So that's the way of it? she mused, and couldn't prevent a small smile. Locked horns, without a doubt. It was as good a way to begin courting as she knew. She'd have to think on it, she decided. But the earl of Ashburn was certainly quality, as well as having a face and form that made even a widow's heart flutter.

"Can I serve you, my lord?"

"What?" Brigham turned to stare through Mrs. Drummond before his eyes slowly focused. "I beg your pardon. I've just come from Coll's room. He's complaining for food. Miss Gwen says a bit of your broth would do him."

Mrs. Drummond cackled and went to the pot by the fire. "I have my doubts he'd think so, but I'll spoon it up and have it sent. Would you mind me asking, my lord, how the lad does?"

He had made the mistake of looking at Serena again as she lazily stroked with the plunger. If anyone had told him that watching a woman churn butter could dry a man's mouth to dust, he would have laughed. Now he couldn't see the humor in it. He tore his eyes away, cursing himself. It would pay to remember that he had already spent one sleepless night because of her, two if he counted the one they had spent together nursing Coll.

"He seems to fare better today. Miss Gwen claims his color's good enough, though she'll have him stay in bed a while yet."

"She could do it. The good Lord knows no one else could deal as well with the lad." Mrs. Drummond tutted over the man she considered the oldest of her charges. She slanted a look at Serena and saw that she was watching Brigham from under her lashes. "Would you care for some broth yourself, my lord? Or a bit of meat pie?"

"No, thank you. I was on my way to the stables."

That had the color lifting into Serena's cheeks as she banged wood against wood. He lifted a brow. Though she set her chin and moved her bottom lip into a pout that had his stomach muscles clenching, she didn't speak. Nor did he as he gave a brisk nod and strode out.

"Now that's a man!" Mrs. Drummond exclaimed.

"He's English," Serena countered, as if that explained everything.

"Well, that's true, but a man's a man, kilt or breeches. And his fit him mighty true."

Despite herself, Serena giggled. "A woman's not supposed to notice."

"A blind woman's not supposed to notice." Mrs. Drummond set the bowl of broth on a tray and then, because her heart was soft, added a gooseberry tart. "Molly! Molly, you lazy wench, come fetch this tray to the young master." She set the tray aside and went back to her stirring. "The man Lord Ashburn brought with him from London, lassie, the proper-looking gentleman?"

"Parkins." Serena flexed her cramped hands and sneered. She found it odd that her heart rate had leveled almost to normal as soon as Brigham had swept out. "His English valet. Imagine, bringing a valet here to fuss with the cut of his coat and the shine on his boots."

"Quality's used to having things done a certain way," Mrs. Drummond said wisely. "I hear Mr. Parkins is an unmarried gentlemen."

Serena moved her shoulders. "Probably too busy starching Lord Ashburn's lace to have his own life."

Or he hasn't met a woman with life enough for two, Mrs.

Drummond mused. "Seems to me, Mr. Parkins could use a bit of fattening up." She grinned, then set the bowl aside to shout for Molly again.

Quality, Serena thought with a sniff a few hours later. Just because a man had a trace of blue blood in his veins didn't mean he was quality. It didn't make him a gentleman, either. All it made him was an aristocrat.

In any case, she wasn't going to waste her time thinking about the earl of Ashburn. For nearly two days she had been tied to the house, to the day-to-day chores, which were increased by Coll's needs. Now she had some time free. Perhaps she was stealing it, but she could make it all up later. The truth was, if she didn't get out and off by herself for just a little while she might burst.

Her mother probably wouldn't approve of her taking a ride in the forest so close to mealtime. Serena shrugged that off as she saddled her mare. Her mother would approve even less of the old work breeches she wore. Hanged if she had the patience to ride sidesaddle, she thought as she led the mare out of the stables. She would take care that her mother wouldn't see her so that her mother wouldn't have to be disappointed in her behavior. With luck, no one would see her.

Swinging astride, she led her mount to the rear of the stables, then over a low hill dotted with spindly briers and lichen. Surefooted, the mare picked her way over the uneven ground until they were almost out of sight of the house. Serena veered south, sending up a brief prayer that no one in her family would be looking out the window. The moment the forest swallowed her, she kicked the mare into a gallop.

Oh, God, she had needed this more than food, more than

drink. One wild ride through the naked trees with the wind on her face and a horse straining for speed beneath her. It might not be the proper thing, but she knew as well as she knew her name that it was the right thing for her. She didn't have to be a lady here, a daughter here, a sister here. She had only to be Serena. With a laugh, she spurred the horse on.

She startled small game and sent birds whirring upward. Her breath puffed out white, then vanished. The plaid she had wrapped around her shoulders held off the bite of the wind, and the exercise, the freedom, were enough to warm her. In fact, she welcomed the tingle on her skin from the cold winter air, and the sharp clean taste of it.

She had a fleeting wish, almost instantly blotted out by guilt, that she might continue to ride and ride and ride with never another cow to be milked, never another shirt to be washed, never another pot to be scrubbed.

It was probably an evil thought, she decided. There were those in the village who worked from dawn to dusk, who never had an hour they could set aside for dreaming. She, as daughter to the MacGregor, had a fine house to live in, a good table to eat from, a feather bed to sleep on. She was ungrateful, and would no doubt have to confess to the priest—as she had when she had secretly, then not so secretly, hated the convent school in Inverness.

Six months out of her life, Serena remembered. Six months wasted before her father had seen that her mind was made up and she would have none of it. Six months away from the home she loved to live with those simpering, giggling girls whose families had wanted them to learn about being ladies.

Bah.

She could learn everything there was about running a household from her own mother. As to being a lady, there wasn't a finer one than Fiona MacGregor. She was a laird's daughter herself, after all, and had spent time in Paris and, yes, even in England, long ago.

There were still times, when the chores were done and the fires burning low when Fiona played the spinet. Hadn't she taught Gwen, whose fingers were more clever and whose mind was more patient that her sister's, how to ply a fancy needle? Fiona could speak French and engage any visitor in polite conversation.

To Serena's mind, if she needed to be polished, she would be polished in her own home, where the talk was of more than hooped skirts and the latest coiffures.

Those giggling whey-faced girls were the kind of ladies Lord Ashburn preferred, she imagined. The kind who covered their faces with fans and fluttered their lashes over them. They drank fruit punch and carried vials of smelling salts and lace handkerchiefs in their reticules. Empty-headed twits. Those were the kind of women whose hands Brigham would kiss at fancy London balls.

As she neared the river, she slowed the horse to a walk. It would be pleasant to sit by the water for a little while. If she had had time, she would have ridden all the way to the loch. That was her special place when she was troubled or needed time by herself.

Today she wasn't troubled, Serena reminded herself as she slid from the saddle. She had only wanted to take a breath of air that was hers alone. She laid the reins loosely over a branch, then rested her cheek against the mare's.

Fancy London balls, she thought again, and sighed without
any idea that the sound was wistful. Her mother had told her
and Gwen what they were like. The mirrors, the polished floors,
the hundreds and hundreds of candles. Beautiful gowns sparkling. Men in curling white wigs. And music.

She closed her eyes and tried to see it. She'd always had a
weakness for music. Over the sounds of the rushing river she
imagined the strains of a minuet. There would be reels later,
Serena thought. But to start, it would be a slow, lovely minuet.

She began to move to the music in her head, her eyes still
closed, her hand held out to an invisible partner.

Lord Ashburn would give balls, she thought. All the beautiful women would come, hoping for just one dance with him.
Smiling a little, Serena executed a neat turn and imagined she
heard the sound of petticoats rustling. If she were there, she
would wear a dress of rich green satin, with her hair piled high
and powdered white so that the diamonds in it glittered like ice
on snow. All the men with their foaming lace and buckled shoes
would be dazzled. She would dance with them, one by one. As
long as the music played she would dance, twirling, stepping,
dipping into low, graceful curtsies.

Then he would be there. He would be dressed in black. It
suited him. Aye, he would wear black, black and silver, just what
he had worn that night he'd come into Coll's room, when there
had been only candle and firelight. It had made him look so
tall and trim. Now the light would be blinding, flashing in the
mirrors, shimmering on silver buttons and braid. As the music
swelled they would look at each other. He would smile, in the
way he did that softened his eyes and made her heart melt just
a little.

He would hold out his hand. She would lay hers on it, palm to palm. A bow from him, then her curtsy. Then... Giddy, Serena opened her eyes.

Her hand was caught in an easy grip. Her eyes were still clouded with the dream as she looked up at Brigham. The light was behind him, and as she stared up, dazed, it seemed to form a halo around his face. He was wearing black as she had imagined, but it was a simple riding coat, without the fancy silver work or the sparkle of jewels.

Slowly he raised her to her feet. Because she would have sworn she still heard music, she shook her head.

"Madam." Smiling, he lifted her hand to his lips before she could recover. "You seem to be without a partner."

"I was...." Dumbly she stared at their joined hands. Light glittered on his signet ring and reminded her of time and place and differences. Serena snatched her hand away and clasped it with the other behind her back.

"What are you doing here?"

"I was fishing." He turned and pointed to the pole he'd propped against a tree. Beyond it, his horse grazed lazily on the turf of the bank. "With Malcolm until a short time ago. He wanted to get back and look at Betsy."

She could already feel the color sting her cheeks as she thought how ridiculous she must have looked in her partnerless minuet. "He should have been about his lessons."

"I'm assured he did his duty by them this morning." Because he couldn't resist, Brigham stepped back to take a long, thorough study. "May I ask if you always dance alone in the wood— in breeches?"

Her eyes kindled as she chose anger over embarrassment. "You had no right spying on me."

"You quite took me by surprise, I promise you." He sat on a rock, crossed his ankles and smiled at her. "Here I was, contemplating how many more trout I might catch, when a rider comes barreling through the forest with enough noise to frighten every fish for miles." He didn't add that her wild approach had had him drawing his sword. Instead, he buffed his nails on his coat.

"If I had known you would be here," she said stiffly, "I would have ridden another way."

"No doubt. Then I would have missed the delightful sight of you in breeches."

With a sound of disgust, she whirled toward her horse.

"Such a fast retreat, Serena. One might think you were… afraid."

She spun toward him again, eyes flashing, and planted her feet. "I'm not afraid of you."

Magnificent. There was no other way to describe her as she stood, her body braced as though she held a sword in her hand, her eyes molten, her hair tumbling like firelight down her back. She had ridden through the forest with a speed too great for safety and with a skill few men could have matched. However much she aggravated him, Brigham could not deny her courage or her style.

Neither could he deny that the way she looked in breeches made him uncomfortable. However ill-fitting, they showed the enticing length of slim legs and the slender curve of waist and hip. With the homespun shirt tucked and cinched, he could see the gentle sweep of breasts that even now rose and fell in agitation.

"Perhaps you should be afraid," he murmured, as much to himself as to her. "As I find myself plagued with all manner of dishonorable intentions."

Her stomach quivered at that, but she held her ground. "You don't worry me, Lord Ashburn. I've dispatched better men than you."

"So I imagine." He rose and saw what he had wanted to see— the quick, and just as quickly controlled, flash of unease in her eyes. "However, you have yet to deal with me, Serena. I doubt you'll manage to box my ears."

She would have backed up a step if pride hadn't rooted her where she stood. "I'll do worse if you touch me again."

"Will you?" Why was it that the more the woman spit at him, the more he wanted her? "I've already apologized for what happened in the stables."

"The stables?" She lifted a brow, determined not to give an inch. "I fear whatever that might have been, my lord, was so unimportant as to be already forgotten."

"Cat," he said mildly, though not without admiration. "If you continue to sharpen your claws on me, you're bound to break them."

"I'll risk it."

"Then let me refresh your memory." He stepped closer. "You were as hot as I, as pleasured as I. It wasn't a swooning girl I held in my arms but a woman, ripe for loving, damned anxious for it."

"How dare you?" The words came out in a sputter. "No gentleman would speak to me so."

"Perhaps not. But no lady wears breeches."

That stung. It was true, she was not a lady, would never be one, though she wished constantly to find the way within her, to please her mother. "Whatever I choose to wear, I won't have you insult me."

"Won't you? By God, that's rich. You've done nothing but insult me since you first clapped eyes on me." Goaded past caution, he grabbed her arm. "Do you think because you're female I should tolerate your sneering comments about myself, my lineage, my nationality? Damn me if you can have it both ways, Serena. You dress like a man, talk like a man, then choose to hide behind your petticoats when it suits you."

"I hide behind nothing." She tossed back her head and glared at him. Through the bare branches of the ash trees the sunlight poured, turning her hair to molten gold. "If I insult you, it's no more than you deserve. You may have charmed my family, but not me."

"Charming you," he said between his teeth, "is the least of my concerns."

"Aye, your concern lies with the fall of your lace and the shine of your boots. You ride into my home with your talk of war and justice, but you do nothing."

"What I do, what I mean to do, is no business of yours."

"You sleep under my roof, eat at my table. Where were you when the English came to build their forts, to take our men off to their prisons and their gallows?"

"I can't change history, Serena."

"You can change nothing, nothing that has gone before, nothing that is yet to come."

His fingers tightened on her arm. "I won't discuss my plans with you, but I will tell you this—when the time comes, a change will be made."

"To benefit whom?"

He yanked her toward him. "Which means?"

"What does the fate of Scotland mean to you or any English nobleman? You came from England on a whim and can return as easily, depending on the way the wind blows."

His face paled with rage. "This time, my dear, you go too far."

"I'll say what I choose." She tried to wrench away but found her arm caught in viselike fingers. "You give me no reason why you align yourself with our cause, why you choose to raise your sword. Therefore I am free to think what I like."

"You may think as you choose, but words require payment."

She hadn't seen him truly angry before. She hadn't known his eyes could blaze or that his mouth could harden until it seemed as though his face were carved from granite. She nearly yelped when his fingers dug still more deeply into the tender flesh of her arm.

"What will you do," she managed, coolly enough, "run me through?"

"As you're unarmed, that pleasure is denied me. But I have a mind to throttle you." Whether the gesture was made in earnest or merely to frighten, Serena couldn't be sure. He lifted his free hand and circled her throat. His fingers pressed, not gently but not quite hard enough to cut off her air, and his eyes stayed on hers, dark and hard. "You have a very slender neck, Serena," he said silkily. "Very white, very easily snapped."

For a moment she froze, as a hare does when a hawk makes its killing dive. Her hand fluttered helplessly at her side, and her eyes widened. Her breath, when she managed to draw it in, was shallow.

Because her reaction was no more or less than what he had looked for, Brigham smiled. The wench needed to be taught her manners, and it pleased him very much to be her instructor. Then it was he who sucked in his breath as her boot caught him hard on the shin.

His grip relaxed as he stumbled back, swearing. Deciding against assessing the damage, Serena spun on her heels and dashed for her horse. Still swearing, he caught her in three strides.

He lifted her off the ground, his arms locked firmly around her waist, while she kicked and cursed. She didn't fight like a woman, with shrieks and scratches, but with hands knotted into fists and muttered oaths. He discovered she weighed next to nothing and could wriggle like a snake.

"Hold still, damn you. You'll pay for that."

"Let go of me!" She struggled and tossed her weight backward, hoping to unbalance him. "I'll kill you if I get the chance."

"Well I believe it," he said bitterly. Her struggles broke his grip, and his hand moved up and over her breast. The contact shocked both of them, and the combat took on a new desperation. "Be still, damn it." Out of breath and patience, he tried to find a purchase that was less arousing. Seeing her chance, Serena sank her teeth into the back of his hand. "Bloody viper," he managed before her heel connected with his still-tender shin and sent them both tumbling to the ground.

He told himself it was instinct, certainly not any concern for her welfare, that had him cushioning her fall. The impact knocked the breath from both of them and left them tangled together like lovers. The moment she had recovered, Serena brought her knee up, barely missing her mark.

They rolled over a bed of pine needles and dried leaves while she fought like a wildcat, pounding him with fists and spitting

Gaelic curses. Blinded by her hair, he made a grab for her and found himself gripping her bare flesh where her shirt had loosened.

"Name of God," he muttered as the blood stirred in his loins. She twisted, and her breast filled his hand. It was soft as water, hot as fire. "Bloody hell." Though it cost him, he drew his hand back and made a frantic grab for her arms.

Her breathing was shallow. A pulse had begun to thud in her throat when he had touched her. Her breast still tingled from his fingers. More than his threats, more than his anger, the unfamiliar reaction of her body frightened her. She was furious, she hated him. But oh, if he touched her like that again, she would melt like butter in high summer.

He scissored his legs until hers were trapped between them. Intimately, without the cushion of petticoats, they pressed center to center so that she felt for the first time the shock of a man's desire against her vulnerable womanhood. Heat flickered, then spread, in her stomach. The muscles of her thighs went lax. For an instant her vision blurred, giving him the advantage.

He braceleted her wrists in one hand and held them over her head. It was a movement meant as much to give him a moment for clear thinking as to allow him to protect himself. Her skin was glowing as the blood pounded hot beneath it. Tangled with leaves, her hair spread out like tongues of flame and melted gold.

His mouth dry, Brigham swallowed and tried to speak, but she was arching beneath him. Her continued struggles for freedom kindled fires in both of them that threatened to rage out of control.

"Rena, for God's sake, I'm only flesh and blood. Be still."

Her own movements were making her ears buzz and her limbs

weak. There was an excitement that had somehow become tangled with panic, making her all the more desperate to get away. In defense she twisted from side to side and pulled a moan from Brigham.

"You don't know what you're doing," he managed, "but if you continue, you'll find out soon enough."

"Let me go." Her voice was steady, and arousingly husky. As she watched him, her breasts rose and fell with each agitated movement.

"Not quite yet, I think. You'll still rip into me."

"If I had had a dirk—"

"Spare me the details. I can imagine." He had nearly caught his breath, and he let it out now, slowly, cautiously. "My God, you're beautiful. It tempts me to keep you on the edge of fury." With his free hand he traced a fingertip over her lips. "It simply tempts me."

When he started to lower his head, her lips warmed and parted. Stunned by her own reaction, she turned her head quickly to avoid the kiss. Brigham contented himself with the tender flesh just below her ear, and the slender line of her throat.

This was different from a kiss, she thought hazily as a moan escaped her. Less and more. It felt as though her skin were alive and yearning for him as he nuzzled and dampened and nibbled. Instinctively she lifted her hips and sent shock waves of pleasure and frustration through him. He felt her hands stiffen beneath his grip, then go limp with her shudder.

Her hair smelled of the forest, he discovered when he buried his face in it. Earthy, seductive. Her body was as taut as a bowstring one moment, pliant as warm tallow the next. Hungry, he

bit lightly at her ear, along her jaw, then slowly, almost trium-
phantly, at her waiting lips.

He tasted the breath that shuddered through them as he
teased the tip of her tongue into movement with his own. There
was so much he could teach her. Already he knew she would be
a student eager for knowledge, and skillful at applying it once
she learned. Her lips softened when they merged with his, then
parted with the gentlest of pressures. In the age-old rhythm, her
body moved shamelessly beneath his.

She hadn't known there was so much to feel, not just wind
and cold and heat, not simply hunger for food and fatigue. There
were hundreds, thousands of sensations to be discovered by the
merging of lips, the locking of bodies.

There was the scent of a man's skin and, she discovered as
she traced her tongue along the column of his throat, the taste
of it. There was the sound of her own name being murmured
thickly against her own mouth. There was the feel of strong
fingers on her face, tensing, stroking, the frantic beat of heart
against heart. Then the feel of those same fingers caressing her
breast, covering that heart and turning her muscles to jelly.

"Brigham." She thought she might float away, weightlessly,
painlessly, if only he would continue to touch her.

Her breast swelled in his hand. Unable to resist, he brushed
his thumb over the nipple and felt it go taut. He yearned to
draw the peak into his mouth, to experience the heat and the
flavor. Instead he crushed his mouth to hers, desperately, almost
brutally, as for the moment, just a moment, he let the wildness
take him.

Sharp points of passion replaced the languor, and she ached
with it, all but wept with it. Her hands were still trapped by

his. Though she pressed for freedom, she was unsure whether, if she gained it, she would use her hands to drag him closer or to thrust him aside.

It hurt. This grinding, overwhelming need clawed through her, pounding in her center, raging through her head until she feared she would be burned alive.

It pleasured. The sensations he brought to her, the promises he gave her glimpses of. If there was a border between heaven and hell, he had led her to it, and now he had her teetering on the edge.

When the trembling began she fought against it, against him, against herself.

At her muffled whimper, he lifted his head. It was there in her eyes, the fear, the confusion and the desire. The combination nearly undid him. He saw that his hand still locked her wrists where, undoubtedly, bruises would form. Cursing himself, he dragged himself from her and turned away until he could find some measure of control.

"I have no excuses," he managed after a moment. "Except that I want you." He turned back to see her scramble to her feet. "God knows why."

She wanted to weep. Suddenly, desperately, she wanted to weep, wanted him to hold her again, to kiss her as he had at first in that gentle, that patient way. She dragged a leaf from her hair and, after crumbling it in her fingers, tossed it aside. She might not have had any dignity left, but she had pride.

"Cows and goats mate, my lord." Her voice was cold, as were her eyes, as she was determined to make her heart. "They do not have to like each other."

"Well said," he murmured, knowing precisely how she felt

about him. He only wished he could be as certain at that moment of how he felt about her. "Let us hope we are a bit above the cattle. There's something about you, Serena, that tugs on my more primitive emotions, but I assure you I can restrain them under most circumstances."

His stiff manner only made her want to fly at him again. With what she felt was admirable control, she inclined her head. "I've yet to see it." Turning, she strode toward her horse. As she took the reins, she stiffened at the touch of Brigham's hand in her hair.

"You have leaves in your hair," he murmured, and fought back an urge to gather her close again, to just hold her in his arms.

"They'll comb out." When he put a hand on her arm, she braced herself to face him.

"Did I hurt you?"

That was almost her undoing, the regret in his eyes, the kindness in his voice. She was forced to swallow so that her answer could be steady and flat.

"I'm not easily broken, my lord." She shook off his offer of help and launched herself into the saddle. He stood back while she wheeled the horse and set off at a gallop.

Chapter Five

"If you think I'm keeping to my bed like an old man while you and my father ride out to do the Prince's work, you're a madman."

As Brigham watched, Coll pushed himself out of bed and uncertainly gained his feet. His head swam more than a little, but he braced himself against one of the bedposts and tugged off his nightshirt.

"Where in hell's name are my clothes?"

"My dear Coll," Brigham said dryly, "how should I know?"

"You must have seen what was done with them."

"I regret I can't help you there." Brigham flicked a speck of lint from his sleeve and continued in the mildest of tones, "Nor will I carry you back to your bed after you faint and fall from your horse."

"The day a MacGregor falls from his horse—"

"I hasten to remind you you've already done so once." When Coll merely swore and staggered to a chest to look for his clothing, Brigham clasped his hands behind his back. "Coll," he began, picking his way over tender ground, "I sympathize, believe me. I'm sure it's miserable to be tied to a sickbed day and night, but the simple fact is you're not well enough for the journey."

"I say I am."

"Gwen says not."

Frustrated at finding no more than linen and blankets, Coll slammed the chest shut again. "Since when does that slip of a girl run my life?"

"Since saving it."

That silenced Coll, who stood naked as a newborn in the early-morning sunlight. He had allowed his beard to grow since leaving London, and the roughness it gave his face suited him.

"I have no doubt she did," Brigham added. "And I wouldn't care to see all of her hard work go for nothing because you were too proud to rest until you were able to be of use."

"It's a black day when a Campbell stops me from riding with my father to gather the support of the clans for the Stuarts."

"Oh, there will be time yet. It's just beginning." Brigham smiled then, knowing that Coll's temper was easing, allowing him to see sense. He was much like his sister in the way that temper kindled as fast as dry wood. The pity was, Serena's didn't cool as quickly. "And I'll have you remember, we're riding out today for nothing more than an innocent hunting party. It wouldn't do for it to be rumored otherwise."

"I trust I can speak my mind in my own house," Coll muttered, but subsided. It was a bitter pill, but he knew he was far from ready for the journey west. Worse, if he insisted on going, he would slow the rest of the party down. "You'll meet with the MacDonalds and the Camerons?"

"So I'm led to believe. The Drummonds and Fergusons should be represented."

"You'll need to speak with the Cameron of Lochiel. He's always been a strong supporter of the Stuarts, and his voice is listened to." Coll dragged a hand through his mane of red hair. "Hell and damnation. I should be there, standing with my father, showing I stand for the Prince."

"No one will doubt it," Brigham began, then stopped when Gwen entered with a breakfast tray. She took one look at her brother, standing naked and furious, and clucked her tongue.

"I hope you haven't pulled any stitches out."

"Damn it, Gwen." Coll grabbed up a blanket and covered himself. "Have some respect."

With a gentle smile she set down the tray and curtsied to Brigham. "Good morning, Brig."

He touched a handkerchief to his lips in a futile effort to hide a grin. "Good morning."

"Brig, is it?" Coll sputtered. He knew that if he tried to stand five minutes more he'd embarrass himself. "You've become damn familiar with my sister, Ashburn."

Brigham nearly winced, thinking just how familiar he'd become with Coll's other sister. "We dispensed with formality shortly after we mopped up your blood." He picked up his greatcoat. "I fear you'll have trouble with your patient today, Gwen. He's in a foul temper."

Gwen smiled again and moved over to tidy Coll's bed linen. "Coll never gives me any trouble." She fluffed his pillows. "You may feel better after your breakfast, Coll. If you're up to taking a short walk, I'll go along with you. But I think you might dress first."

Stifling a chuckle, Brigham sketched a bow. She might not

have the bite of her sister, but Coll's little angel knew how to get her way. "Now that I see you're in good hands, I'll take my leave."

"Brig—"

Brigham merely laid a hand on Coll's shoulder. "We'll be back within a week."

Too weak to argue, Coll let himself be led back to bed. "God go with you."

Brigham left them with Gwen tugging a fresh nightshirt over Coll's shoulders. He started for the staircase, then stopped short when he saw Parkins waiting for him, stiff backed, thin lipped and carrying a valise.

"Decided to return to England, Parkins?"

"On the contrary, my lord, I mean to accompany you on your hunting trip."

Brigham gave him one brief, incredulous look. "I'm damned if you do."

Parkins's pointed chin came up, the only sign of his agitation. "I will accompany your lordship."

"Don't be daft, man. If I wanted to take someone along, I'd take Jem. At least he'd be of some use with the horses."

Though he gave an inward shudder at being compared to a lowly groom, Parkins remained resolute. "I'm convinced Lord Ashburn will have need of me."

"I'm convinced I won't," Brigham responded, and started past.

"Nonetheless, I will accompany you, my lord."

Slowly, almost certain he had misunderstood, Brigham turned to see Parkins standing, a figure of righteousness, at the top of the stairs. "You are ordered to remain," he said in a very quiet, very dangerous voice. Parkins's stomach lining turned to ice, but he remained unbroken.

"I regret that your orders fail to persuade me that my duties are not best carried out in your company, my lord. I will accompany you."

With his eyes narrowed, Brigham ascended a step. "I'm of a mind to dismiss you, Parkins."

The pointed chin quivered. "That is your lordship's prerogative. That being the case, I will accompany you still."

"Damn your eyes, Parkins." Exasperated, Brigham stormed down the steps. "Have it your own way then, but you won't care for the pace or the accommodations."

"Yes, my lord." Fully satisfied, Parkins smiled at Brigham's back.

Surly, Brigham strode out of the house and toward the stables to have a word with his groom. Barely dawn, he thought, and already he'd been engaged in two arguments. He flung on his greatcoat as he went, his long, purposeful strides eating up the frosty ground. God, it would be good to get in the saddle and ride. Away from here, he thought, glancing back and homing in unerringly on Serena's window. Away from her, he corrected, almost savagely.

She had managed to avoid him all through the evening. Or when she could not, Brigham remembered with some fury, she had spoken to him in a voice as frigid as the ground he was treading on.

He could hardly blame her, after his treatment of her.

He did blame her, completely.

It was she who had raged and ranted at him until his temper had snapped. It was she who had fought him like some kind of hellcat until his passions had torn loose. Never, never in his life had he treated a woman with any form of physical violence. In lovemaking he was known to be passionate but never harsh, thorough but never forceful.

With Serena he had barely restrained himself from ripping the clothes from her back and plunging into her like a man gone mad.

She was the cause. If he had managed to make it to midway through his third decade without ill-treating any woman save one, surely that woman was at fault. She goaded him, he thought viciously. She taunted him.

She fascinated him.

Damn her. He kicked a pebble out of his way—the mark on his lordship's gleaming boot would distress Parkins severely—and wished Serena could be dispatched as easily as the stone.

He would have the better part of a week away from her. When he returned, this madness that had taken hold of him would have passed. He would then treat her with cordial respect and disinterest, as befitted the sister of his closest friend.

He would not, under any circumstances, think of the way her body had felt, melting beneath his.

He would certainly not pause to reflect on the way her lips had tasted, warmed and swollen with his kisses.

And he would be damned if he would allow himself to remember the way his name had sounded when she had spoken it, just once, in the depths of passion.

No, he would do none of those things, but he might murder her if she got in his way again.

His mood filthy, his temper uncertain, he came to the stables. Before he could pull open the door it was pushed outward. Serena, all but swaying on her feet, stepped out. Her face was pale, her eyes were exhausted, and the bodice of her dress was smeared with blood.

"Rena, my God." He gripped her by the shoulders hard enough to make her cry out. Then he was gathering her tight against him. "What happened? Where are you hurt? Who did this to you?"

"What? What?" She found her face pressed into the folds of his greatcoat, and the hand that stroked her hair was trembling. "Brig—Lord Ashburn..." But it was difficult to think when she was being held as though he would never let her go. When she was being held, Serena realized dimly, as though she was someone to be protected and cherished. She fought back an urge to snuggle into him. "My lord—"

"Where is he?" he demanded, dragging her away again, one hand supporting her waist as he drew out his sword. "By God, he won't live longer than it takes me to kill him. How badly are you hurt, my love?"

Her mouth simply hung open. He was holding her gently, as though she might break, even as murder kindled in his eyes. "Are you mad?" she managed. "Who do you want to kill? Why?"

"Why? Why? You're covered with blood and you ask me why?"

Confused, Serena looked down at her dress. "Of course there's blood. There's always blood at a foaling. Jem and I have been working half the night with Betsy. She had twins, and the second didn't come as easily as the first. Malcolm is nearly beside himself with delight."

"Foaling," he said blankly while she stared at him.

Serena moistened her lips and wondered if he needed one of Gwen's potions. "Are you feverish?"

"I'm quite well." His voice was stiff as he stepped back and sheathed his sword. "I beg your pardon. I mistook the blood for your own."

"Oh." She looked foolishly down at her dress again, both warmed and confused by his explanation. So far as she knew, no one had ever raised a sword in her name before. She could think of nothing to say. He had leaped to her defense as though he would have fought an army for her. And he had called her his love. Serena pressed her lips together to moisten them. Perhaps he was feverish. "I should wash."

He cleared his throat and felt ten times the fool. "Do the mare and the foals do well?"

"Very well, though everyone but Malcolm is exhausted." She tucked her hands into the folds of her skirts, not knowing what to do next. Oddly enough, she wanted to laugh. It was laughable, after all—Brigham drawing his sword like an avenging angel. Or devil. And herself smeared with dirt and sweat and birthing blood. "I beg your pardon, my lord," she managed as a giggle escaped her. She might enjoy fighting him, but not for the world would she embarrass him deliberately.

"This amuses you, madam?" His voice was cold, cracking like ice on a pond.

"No. Yes." With a sigh, she wiped at her eyes. "I'm terribly sorry for laughing. I'm tired."

"Then I will leave you to find your bed."

She couldn't let him go that way, she thought as he put his hand on the door. If their parting words had been a shout, it would have contented her. But to have made him cringe when he had tried to protect her would keep her awake at night.

"My lord."

He turned back. His eyes were calm again and very cool. "Yes?"

Her tongue tied itself into knots. This wasn't the kind of man you could thank with a smile and a quick word. The other man would have understood—the one who had held her so gently. But not this one. "You, ah, ride with my father and his men today."

"Yes." The reply was curt as he drummed his fingers on the hilt of his sword.

"I will wish you luck…with your hunting."

He lifted a brow. So she knew, he thought. Then, that she would of course know, and being a MacGregor, would go to the grave with the knowledge if need be. "Thank you, madam. I shan't keep you longer."

She started to leave, then turned, the passion in her eyes again. "I would give so much to go with you today." Gathering up her skirts, she raced toward the house.

Brigham stood where he was, in the chill air of early morning, the light breeze ruffling his hair. It had to be madness. It had to be the gravest error of judgment, the sharpest of ironies.

He was in love with her.

Letting out a long breath, he watched her until she had scrambled over the rise. He was in love with her, he thought again, and she would sooner plunge a dagger into his heart than give hers to him.

It was a long, rough ride over land wilder than that he and Coll had traveled through on their way north. There were echoing hills and naked rock thrust like deeply gouged teeth from the bare ground. Gray peaks and crags glittered with snow and ice. For miles they would see hardly a hovel. Then they would come across a village where peat smoke rose thick and people clamored out for greetings and news.

It was very much the Scotland his grandmother had spoken of, hard, often barren, but always fanatically hospitable. They stopped at midday and were pressed into a meal by a shepherd and his family. There was soup, the makings of which Brigham didn't care to know, and bannock and black pudding. He might have preferred the supplies they had brought with them, but he ate what was offered, knowing it was as gracious a feast as could be afforded in the lonely hills. It was washed down with Ian's own ale.

There were a half-dozen children, all but naked, though happy enough, and the shepherd's wife, who sat near the fire working a spindle. The turf house smelled of the compost heap that lay just outside the door and of the cattle that were housed in the room beyond.

If the family considered their fate bitter, they didn't show it. The shepherd drank with gusto and pledged his loyalty to the Stuart king.

All the men were welcomed, and food was pressed on each, though the portions were meager. Brigham couldn't resist a grin at the sight of the proper Parkins struggling to swallow the mysterious soup while removing a pair of small, grimy hands from his spotless sleeve.

Dozens of excuses had to be made before the travelers could convince their hosts that business prevented them from remaining overnight. When they set out again the wind was rising, bringing with it the taste and the scent of snow.

"I feel as though we've caused them to starve for the next week," Brigham commented as they continued west.

"They'll do well enough. Their laird will see them provided for. That's the way of the clans." Ian rode like a man half his age, straight in the saddle, light wristed, tireless. "It's men like him darlin' Charlie will need to make Scotland thrive."

"And the Camerons?"

"Good fighters and true men." Ian settled into an easy, ground eating lope. "When we meet at Glenfinnan you'll judge for yourself."

"The Jacobites will need good fighters, and good generals, as well. The rebellion will only be as successful as the Prince's advisers."

Ian shot him a glittering look. "So you've thought of that."

"Yes." Brigham looked around him as they rode. The rocky, tumbled ground was a perfect field of war for the Highlanders. The men who rode behind them, the men who lived in it, would know its advantages and hardships well. "If we bring the battle here, we'll win. Britain will be united."

"It's my wish to see a Stuart on the throne," Ian mused. "But I'll tell you I've seen wars before. In '15, in '19. I've seen hopes raised and hopes dashed. I'm not so old that my blood doesn't warm at the thought of battle, at the hope of putting old wrongs right. But this will be the last."

"You'll live to see others, Ian."

"This will be the last," he said again. "Not just for me, lad, for all of us."

Brigham thought of those words as they neared Glenfinnan.

The waters of Loch nan Uamh were a dark, violent blue. As they arrived at the great stone fortress, the snow was just beginning. Overhead the sky had turned to a thick steel gray, and the wind whipped the waters of the lake into fury.

Their coming had been heralded by the playing of pipes, and the high, eerie music lifted into the thin air. Such music was used to celebrate, to mourn and to lead soldiers to battle. As he stood with the snow swirling about his feet, Brigham understood how a man could weep, or fight, to the sound of such notes.

Inside, servants were dispatched with what luggage had been carried on the journey west, fires blazed high and whiskey was pressed into every waiting hand.

"Welcome to Glenfinnan." Donald MacDonald held up his cup of whiskey. "Your health, Ian MacGregor."

Ian drank, and his eyes approved the caliber of MacDonald's whiskey. "And to yours."

"Lord Ashburn." MacDonald signaled for more whiskey to be poured. "I trust my old friend has made you comfortable?"

"Very. Thank you."

"To your successful stay at Glenfinnan." MacDonald toasted and drank again. Not for the first time, Brigham was grateful for his head for whiskey. When he noted how easily it was downed by his companions, he decided that he had inherited it from his grandmother. "So you're kin to Mary MacDonald of Sleat in Skye."

"Her grandson."

MacDonald was then compelled to offer a toast to her. "I remember her. She was a bonny lass, though I was hardly whelped when I visited her family. She reared you?"

"From the time my parents died. I would have been nearly ten."

"Since you're here, I can't doubt but she did a good job of

it. You'll be wanting food, gentlemen. We have a late supper for you."

"And the others?" Ian asked.

"Expected tomorrow." MacDonald glanced at the doorway, and his rather doughy face creased into a smile. "Ah, my daughter. Ian, you remember my Margaret."

Brigham turned and saw a small, dark-haired woman of about eighteen. She was dressed in a wide hooped gown of midnight blue that matched her eyes. She dropped into a curtsy, then came forward, hands extended to Ian, with a smile that brought out dimples in her cheeks.

"Why, here's a lass." With a great laugh, he kissed both of her cheeks. "You've grown up, Maggie."

"It has been two years." Her voice was soft, with a lilt.

"She's the image of her mother, Donald. Thank the Lord she didn't take her looks from you."

"Have a care when you insult me in my own home." But there was a ring of pride in MacDonald's warning. "Lord Ashburn, may I present my daughter Margaret."

Maggie dropped another curtsy and extended her fingertips to Brigham. "My lord."

"Miss MacDonald. It's a pleasure to see a flower on such a bitter night."

She giggled, spoiling the elegant curtsy. "Thank you, my lord. It's not often I hear flattery. You are a great friend of Coll's, are you not?"

"Yes, I am."

"I had thought..." She glanced from Brigham to Ian. "He did not accompany you, Lord MacGregor?"

"Not for lack of wanting, Maggie. And not so many years ago it was Uncle Ian."

She dimpled and kissed his bearded cheek. "It's still Uncle Ian."

He patted her hand as he turned to MacDonald. "Coll and Brigham ran into a bit of trouble on the road from London. Campbells."

"Coll?" Maggie spoke quickly, revealing more than she had intended. "Was he hurt?"

Ian's brows rose as her fingers curled into his. "He's on the mend now, lassie, but Gwen put her foot down and said he wasn't to travel."

"Please, tell me what happened. How badly was he wounded? Was he—"

"Maggie." With a little laugh, MacDonald cut off his daughter's rapid questions. "I'm sure Ian and Lord Ashburn will tell us the whole of it. Now I imagine they'd like to refresh themselves before dinner."

Though obviously impatient, she pulled herself back. "Of course. Forgive me. I'll show you to your rooms."

Gracefully she swept her skirts aside and led her father's guests out of the drawing room and up the staircase. "You've only to ask if there's anything you need. We dine in an hour, if it suits you."

"Nothing would suit me better," Ian told her, and pinched her cheek. "You've grown up nicely, Maggie. Your mother would be proud of you."

"Uncle Ian...was Coll badly hurt?"

"He's mending well, lass, I promise you."

Forced to be content with that, she left the men alone.

They dined leisurely and with elegance in the great dining

hall. There were oysters bigger than any Brigham could recall seeing anywhere before, and salmon in a delicate sauce, removed with roast duck. There were wild fowls and gooseberry sauce and joints of roast mutton. The claret was fine and plentiful. Their host pressed sweets upon them. Mince pie, tarts, stewed pears and sweetmeats.

Throughout, Maggie handled her duties as hostess with an ease and liveliness that became her well. By the time she had risen to leave the men to their port, she had charmed the entire table, from Ian down to his humblest retainer.

The talk turned to politics. Louis's intentions toward England and his support of Charles and the Jacobites were discussed, debated and argued over while servants brought fresh candles and stoked the roaring fire.

Here, in this dining hall in the wild western Highlands, there was unanimous support for the fair-faced Prince. Brigham saw that these men would not only fight behind him but had come to love him for the symbol of hope he had been almost from his birth.

He went late to bed but found sleep difficult. The fire burned red, and the plaid bedcurtains kept out any drafts, though he could hear the wind whistling against the window glazing. His thoughts, no matter how he struggled to discipline them, returned again and again to Serena.

Would she be in bed now, fast asleep, her mind at rest, her body relaxed? Or would she, like him, lie awake and restless, mind in turmoil, body tensed with needs that had been stoked like the flames of the night fire?

What kind of madness drew a man to a woman who detested him and everything he was? There had been prettier women in his life, and certainly there had been sweeter. There had been women who would laugh and frolic, in bed or out, without a care as to whether he was an English lord or a French peasant. There had been women, dignified and elegant, who had been delighted to receive him for tea or to accompany him on a leisurely ride through the park.

Why had none of them caused him to lie in bed and sweat with visions of slender white hands and tumbled red-gold hair? None of them had ever made him burn with just the thought of a name, a face, a pair of eyes. They had nothing in common but an allegiance to a deposed royal house. He could find no logic here, no reason for a man to lose his heart to a woman who would have delighted in crushing it beneath her heel.

But he did love her. It occurred to Brigham that he might pay more dearly for those feelings than he ever would for following his conscience and the Jacobite cause.

When he slept he slept poorly, and he was awakened shortly after dawn by the arrival of the Camerons.

By midday, the house was swarming with men. MacDonalds from the western isles, Camerons, Drummonds, more MacGregors from the outlying districts. It became a celebration with pipes playing and whiskey to be drunk. Rough manners were overlooked and laughter rang off stone.

Gifts had been brought—deer, rabbits and whatever game had been killed on the journey. They were served at dinner, and this time the great dining hall was packed with men. The company at this meal was varied, from the chiefs and lairds to their eldest sons and men of rank to the retainers. They were all served at the same table and served well, but with subtle distinctions.

At the head of the table was venison done to a turn and fine claret. At the middle there was ale and port with substantial dishes of mutton and rabbit. At the bottom, below the salt, beef and cabbage and table beer were offered. But at all levels the food was plentiful. No man seemed insulted by the arrangements, and all ate ferociously. Servants stood behind the chairs, many of them local villagers pressed into duty for the event.

Toasts were drunk, to the true king, to the Bonnie Prince, to each clan, to the wives and daughters of the chiefs, one after another, until bottles were drained and more opened. As a man, they lifted cups to the king across the water. There was no doubt that hearts were with him. But Brigham found as talk turned to the Stuarts and the possibility of war that the table was not of one mind.

There were some whose blood ran hot enough to make them yearn to make the march on Edinburgh immediately, swords raised and pipes playing. Old grudges festered, and like re-opened wounds their poison poured out. Proscriptions, executions, homes burned, kin sent to plantations and indentured, estates forfeited.

As Serena had once told him, it was not to be forgiven, it was not to be forgotten.

But others were less inclined to put their lives and their lands into the hands of the untried Prince. They had gone to war before and had seen their men and their dreams cut down.

Cameron of Lochiel, his clan's acting chief while his father remained in exile, pledged the Prince his heart, but with reservations. "If we fight without the support of French troops, the English will swarm over our land and drive us to the hills and the caves. Clan Cameron is loyal to the true king, but can the clans alone stand against the trained might of England? And a loss now will break the back of Scotland."

"So we do what?" James MacGregor, heir of Rob Roy, slapped his palm on the table. "Do we sit with our swords sheathed? Do we sit by our fires, growing old, waiting for retribution? I, for one, am sick of the elector and his German queen."

"If a sword is sheathed, it can't be broken," Lochiel returned quietly.

"Aye." A MacLeod chieftain nodded as he hunched over his port. "Though it goes against the grain to do nothing, it's madness to fight if there will be no victory. We have lost before, and paid a bitter price for it."

"The MacGregors stand behind the Prince to the man," James said with a dangerous light of battle in his eyes. "As we'll stand behind him when he takes his throne."

"Aye, lad." Keeping his voice soothing, Ian broke in. He knew James had inherited his father's loyalty, and a good deal of his guile and love of intrigue, but not his control. "We stand behind the Bonnie Prince, but there is more to be thought of than thrones and injustices. Lochiel is right. This is not a war to be waged rashly."

"Do we fight as women then?" James demanded. "With talk only?"

There had been whiskey enough drunk to bring tempers boiling. James's words had already stirred angry mutters. Before more could be said, Ian spoke again, drawing the men's attention to him.

"We fight as clansmen, as our fathers and their fathers. I fought beside your sire, James," he said quietly. "And at your side when we were both young," he added to Lochiel. "I am proud to pledge my sword and my son's to the Stuarts. When we fight, we should fight with cool heads and shrewdness, as well as sword and ax."

"But do we know the Prince means to fight?" someone at the table demanded. "We've gathered before, behind his father, and it came to nothing."

Ian signaled for his cup to be filled again. "Brigham, you spent time with the Prince in France. Tell us his mind."

The table quieted, so Brigham kept his voice moderate. "He means to fight for his rights and those of his house. Of that there can be little doubt." He paused to take stock of the faces around him. All listened, but not all seemed cheered by his words. "He looks to the Jacobites here and in England to fight with him, and hopes to convince King Louis to support his cause. With the French behind him, I think there is no doubt he could divide his enemies and cut through." He lifted his cup, taking his time. "Without them, it will take bold action and a united front."

"The Lowlanders will fight with the government army," Lochiel mused. He thought sadly of the death and destruction that would surely follow in their wake. "And the Prince is young, untried in battle."

"Yes," Brigham agreed. "He will need experienced men, advisers as well as fighting men. Don't doubt his ambition, or his resolve. He shall come to Scotland and raise his standard. He will need the clans behind him, heart and sword."

"He has both of mine," James stated, lifting his cup like a challenge.

"If the Prince's mind cannot be swayed," Lochiel said slowly, "the Camerons will fight behind him."

The talk continued into the night, and over the next day and the next. Some were convinced, their swords and their men at the ready. Others were far from encouraging.

When they took their leave of the MacDonalds, the sky was as gloomy as Brigham's thoughts. Charles's glittering ambition could all too easily be dulled.

Chapter Six

Serena sat before the crackling bedroom fire, wrapped in her night robe, while her mother brushed and dried her hair. For Fiona it brought back memories, both sweet and sad, of her eldest daughter's childhood. So many times she had stood like this, with her daughter bundled before the fire, her skin glowing from her bath. It had been simple then to ease a hurt or solve a problem.

Now the child was a woman, with, Fiona thought, a woman's needs and a woman's fears. There would come a time when her little girl would sit in front of a fire of her own.

Usually when they had this time together Serena was full of talk, questions, stories, laughter. Now she was strangely subdued, her eyes on the fire, her hands quiet in her lap. Through the open door they could hear Gwen and Malcolm entertaining Coll with some game. The laughter and crows of triumph came, muffled, into the room.

Of all her children, it was Serena who concerned Fiona most. Coll was headstrong, certainly, but enough like his father to content Fiona that he would find his way well enough. Gwen was mild and sweet-natured. Fiona had no doubt that her giving heart and fragile looks would bring her a kind man. And Malcolm... She smiled as she drew the brush through Serena's long, damp hair. He was full of charm and mischief, bright as a button, according to the good Father.

But it was Serena who had inherited the uncertain Mac-Gregor temper along with a heart easily bruised. It was Serena who hated as passionately as she loved, who asked questions that couldn't be answered, who remembered too well what should be forgotten.

It was that that concerned Fiona most of all. That one hideous incident had scarred her daughter as much as it had scarred her. Fiona still bore the marks of the English officer's use of her. Not on her body, but on her heart. And she was afraid that the marks would never fade from Serena's heart, any more than they would fade from her own. But while Fiona carried her shame secretly, Serena's hate too often burned from her eyes and fell unheedingly off her tongue.

Fiona would never forget the way her young daughter had washed her, comforted her, eased both her body and heart through the misery of that night. Nor could she forget that a wildness had been born in Serena as a result of it, a recklessness that caused her to ride off unattended into the forest, to flare up at any real or imagined slight to the family. As a mother, she worried at Serena's obvious disdain of the men who came courting.

Now it was Serena's uncharacteristic silence that troubled her. Fiona wondered, not for the first time, how to mother a grown child.

"You're so quiet, my love. Do you see dreams in the fire?"

Serena smiled a little. "You always said we could, if we looked hard enough." But she had looked tonight and had seen only flaming wood.

"You've kept to yourself so much the last few days. Are you feeling poorly?"

"No, I'm just…" She let her words trail off, not certain she could explain to herself, much less her mother. "Restless, I suppose. Wanting spring." She fell silent again, staring into the fire. "When do you think Papa will be back?"

"Tomorrow. Perhaps the day after." Fiona stroked the brush tirelessly through Serena's hair. Her daughter's pensive mood had come on the day the hunting party had left. "Do you worry about him?"

"No." She sighed, and her hands moved nervously in her lap. "Sometimes I worry where it will all end, but I don't worry for Papa." Abruptly she linked her fingers together to still them. "I wish I were a man."

The statement brought Fiona some measure of relief, as it was typical. With a little laugh, she kissed the top of Serena's head. "What foolishness is this?"

"I do. If I were a man I wouldn't forever be forced to sit and wait." And want, she thought, want something so nebulous she could never describe it.

"If you were a man you would rob me of one of the greatest pleasures of my life."

With another sigh, Serena quieted. "I wish I were more like you—more like Gwen."

"You are what you were born to be, love, and nothing pleases me more."

"I wish I did please you. I wish I could."

"What, more nonsense?"

"There are times I know you are disappointed with me."

"No, not disappointed, never that." For a moment, Fiona wrapped her arms around Serena and pressed cheek to cheek. "When you were born, I thanked God for giving you to me whole and safe. My heart was nearly broken from losing the two bairns between Coll and you. I feared I'd have no more children, then there you were, small as a minute, strong as a horse. What a time you gave me with the birthing. The midwife said you clawed your way into the world. Women don't go to war, Serena, but I tell you this, there would be no children in the world if men had to bring them into it."

That made Serena laugh. She tucked her legs up and settled more comfortably. "I remember when Malcolm came. Papa went to the stables and got drunk."

"So it was with all of you," Fiona said, smiling. "He's a man who would sooner face a hundred dragoons with only a dirk than set foot in a birthing room."

"How did you know— When you met him, how did you know you loved him?"

"I'm not sure I did." Dreaming herself, Fiona studied the fire. "The first time was at a ball. Alice MacDonald, Mary MacLeod and I were the best of friends. Alice MacDonald's parents were having a ball for her birthday. The MacDonalds of Glenfinnan. Your father's good friend Donald, as you know, is Alice's brother. Alice wore green, Mary blue, and I wore white with my grandmother's pearls. We had our hair powdered and thought we were very fashionable and beautiful."

"I know you were."

With a little sigh, Fiona stopped brushing to rest her hands on her daughter's shoulders. "The music was very gay, and the men so handsome. Your father had Donald introduce him, and he asked me to dance. I did, of course, but I was thinking— what do I want with this great beast of a man? He'll probably tread on my toes and ruin my new slippers."

"Oh, Mama, never say you thought Papa couldn't dance."

"I did, and was shown contrary, as you've witnessed time and time again. No one danced with more grace and lightness of foot than Ian MacGregor."

It pleased Serena, the mental picture she conjured up of her parents young and sharing their first dance. "So you fell in love with him for the way he danced."

"No, indeed. I flirted with him, I confess. Alice and Mary and myself had made a pact to flirt with all the men at the ball until we had a score of suitors. We had decided we would choose only the most handsome, the most elegant and the wealthiest for husbands."

With some astonishment, Serena looked over her shoulder. "You, Mama?"

"Aye, I was quite vain and full of myself." Fiona laughed and patted hair that was just beginning to show the first signs of graying. "My father had spoiled me miserably, you see. The next day, your father called on the MacDonalds, where I was staying. To ride out with Donald, he said, but he made certain I saw him striding around the house as if he owned it. Over the next weeks he put himself in my way more times than I could count. He wasn't the most handsome, the most elegant or the wealthiest of the men who called on me, but in the end, it was he I wanted."

"But how did you know?" Serena insisted. "How could you be sure?"

"When my heart spoke louder than my head," Fiona murmured, studying her daughter. So this was the problem, she realized, and wondered how she could have missed the signs. Her little one was falling in love. Rapidly Fiona ran through the names and faces of the young men who had come calling. She could not recall Serena sparing even one of them a second glance. In fact, Fiona thought with a frown, Serena had sent most of them off with their tails between their legs.

"There has to be more than that." As confused as she was unsatisfied, Serena plucked at the folds of her skirts. "There has to be a rightness to it, a sense to it. If Papa had been different, if you hadn't had the same beliefs, the same backgrounds, your heart would never have spoken at all."

"Love doesn't account for differences, Rena," Fiona said slowly. A sudden thought had intruded, one that made her uncertain whether to laugh or weep. Had her daughter, her fiery, headstrong daughter, fallen in love with the English lord?

"My sweet." Fiona touched a hand to Serena's cheek. "When love happens it's most often right, but it rarely makes sense."

"I'd rather be alone," Serena said passionately. Her eyes glowed in the firelight, showing as much confusion as determination. "I'd rather play aunt to Coll's and Gwen's and Malcolm's children than find myself pining after a man I know would make me unhappy."

"That's your head talking, and your temper." Fiona's hand was as gentle as her voice. "Falling in love is frightening, especially for a woman who tries to fight it."

"I don't know." She turned her cheek into her mother's hand. "Oh, Mama, why don't I know what I want?"

"When the time's right, you will. And you, the most courageous of my children, will take it."

Her fingers tightened suddenly on Serena's cheek. They both heard the rumble of horses approaching. For a moment, in the light of the fire, both remembered another time, another night.

"Papa's back early." Serena rose to take her mother's hand.

"Aye." Degree by degree, Fiona forced herself to relax. "He'll be wanting something hot."

The men had ridden hard in their desire to sleep in their own beds. They had indeed hunted, and came home laden with fresh-killed deer and rabbit and wild duck. The house, which had been so quiet, erupted with Ian's shouts and commands. Clad in her night robe, Serena had decided to remain upstairs until she heard her father bellowing for her.

She began smoothing her hair and skirts, then stopped herself in disgust. It hardly mattered what she looked like. She came down to see her father, his face still reddened by the bite of wind, giving Gwen a hearty kiss. Coll sat near the fire, a lap robe covering his knees and Malcolm perched laughing on the arm of his chair.

With a full cup already in his hand, his other dug into his breeches pocket, Brigham stood in front of the hearth. His hair was ruffled by the ride, his boots splashed with mud. Despite her resolve not to, she found her eyes drawn to his. For the space of three heartbeats, there was nothing and no one else.

Nor was there for him. He watched her enter, her dark green robe flowing down her, her hair glowing like firelight. Brigham's fingers tightened so quickly, so violently, on the pewter cup that he thought they might leave dents. Deliberately relaxing them, he sketched her a bow. Her chin shot up, making him want more than anything else to stride across the room and crush her against him.

"There she is, my little Highland wildcat." Ian threw open his arms. "Have you got a kiss for your Papa?"

She gave him a saucy smile. "I might." Crossing to him, she gave him a very demure peck on the cheek. Then, with a laugh, she threw her arms around his neck and gave him a loud, smacking one. He responded by lifting her off her feet and twirling her twice.

"Now here's a likely lass," he told the room in general. "If a man can survive the claws, he'll have a prize worth keeping."

"I'll not be a prize for any man." She gave his beard a hard, disrespectful tug that earned her a slap on the bottom and a grin.

"You see I speak the truth, Brig. She's a lively one. I've a good mind to give you to Duncan MacKinnon, as he asks me nigh on every week."

"And so you may, Father," she said mildly. "He'll be less of a nuisance once I slice him in two."

He laughed again. Though all his children delighted him, Serena held the tightest grip on his heart. "Fill my cup, brat, and the rest besides. Young Duncan's not the match for you."

She did as he bade, passing the cup to him before walking over to add to Brigham's. It was impossible to resist raising her gaze to his, or allowing the challenge to glow in her eyes. "Nor, perhaps, is any man," she responded.

When a gauntlet was thrown down, Brigham was honor bound to pick it up. "It may be, my lady, that none has yet taught you to sheathe your claws."

"In truth, my lord, none who tried have survived."

"It would seem you're in need of a man made of tougher stuff."

She lifted a brow as if assessing him. "Believe me, I'm not in need of a man at all."

His eyes warned her he could prove her wrong, but he only smiled. "Forgive me, madam, but a high-strung mare rarely understands the need for a rider."

"Oh, please." Coll choked on his own laughter and held up a hand. "Don't encourage him, Rena. The man can go on like that for hours, and you'll never win. Have pity and bring that jug here. My cup's empty."

"As your head is," she muttered, and poured whiskey into the cup her brother held out.

"Easy, lass, don't flay me. I'm still a sick man."

"Are you now?" With a smile, she snatched the cup from him. "Then you'll be wanting one of Gwen's brews and not whiskey." She tossed it off herself before he could grab it.

"Wench." Grinning, he pulled her down in his lap. "Pour me some more and I'll keep your secrets."

"Hah! What secrets?"

He put his mouth to her ear and whispered only one word. "Breeches."

Serena swore under her breath and filled the cup again. "So you haven't been so sick you couldn't spy out your window," she muttered to him.

"A man takes what weapons he can."

"If you children would stop your bickering…" Ian waited until all eyes were on him. "We found the MacDonalds well. Donald's brother Daniel is a grandfather again. His third, which shames me." He sent a look at his two oldest children, who forgot their annoyance with each other long enough to give their father identical smiles. "Well you should grin like a couple of simpletons while neglecting your duties to the clan. A better father would have had you both married off and breeding, willing or not."

"There is no better father than our own," Serena said, and watched him soften.

"We'll pass over that. I've invited Maggie MacDonald to visit."

"Oh, good Lord," Coll moaned. "Talk of nuisances."

The comment earned him a cuff on the ear from his sister. "She's a great friend of mine, I'll remind you. When does she come?"

"Next week." Ian sent Coll a stern look. "And I'll remind you, my lad, that no guest in my home is a nuisance."

"They are when they're forever underfoot so that you can't walk but trip over them." Then he relented, knowing that hospitality was a matter of honor and tradition. "No doubt she'll have outgrown that by now and be happy in Rena's and Gwen's company."

The next days passed in a flurry of activity in preparation for the expected company. As was Fiona's wont, wood and silver were polished, foods prepared, floors scrubbed. Serena welcomed the diversion and was too used to work to resent the extra labor. She looked forward to the company of a girl her own age who had been her friend since childhood.

Now that Coll had mended, he and Brigham rode out often, sometimes in the company of Ian and other men, sometimes alone. There were discussions nightly debating the Jacobite cause and the Prince's next move. Rumors flew from hill to glen, from burn to forest. The Prince was on his way. The Prince was in Paris. The Prince was never coming at all.

Once, a messenger had been hustled into the drawing room with a dispatch for Brigham. The doors had remained shut on the men for hours, and the rider had left again after dark. Whatever news he had brought had not been passed on to the women, a fact Serena bitterly resented.

In the kitchen, with the fire blazing, Serena dealt with the washing, her share and Gwen's. She had exchanged her polishing duties for Gwen's help with the laundry. It suited her. She preferred stamping on linen in the big tub to cramping her hands with beeswax.

With her skirts kilted up, she waded in water up to her calves. She enjoyed the energy it took, just as now she enjoyed the solitude of the kitchen. Mrs. Drummond was visiting a neighbor for an exchange of recipes and gossip. Malcolm was about his lessons, and their mother was supervising the preparation of a guest room.

Serena high-stepped like a pony in the cooling water, humming to herself to make the chore less monotonous and to keep the rhythm steady.

She wondered if Brigham had found Maggie MacDonald pretty and if he had kissed her hand the way he had once kissed her own.

Why should it matter? she asked herself, and began to stamp on the wash with more vigor. The man had barely spared her a glance since he had returned, and that was precisely the way she preferred it. He meant nothing to her, at least no more than any prickly thorn in her side.

She wished he would go away. Serena began to stamp harder,

until water rose to the lip of the tub. She wished he would take his cool voice and hot eyes back to London—or to hell, for that matter. She wished he would fall in the river and catch a chill, then waste slowly, painfully, away. Better yet, she wished he would come in, fall on his knees and beg her for one smile.

Of course, she would sneer.

She wished—

She stopped wishing, stopped washing, stopped thinking, when he strode into the room. Brigham was brought up short, just as she was. He had thought she was busy upstairs with her mother, or in the dining hall with her sister. For days he had made a science out of avoiding her and the discomfort and pleasure being in her company brought him.

Now she was here, alone in the overheated kitchen, her face flushed with exercise, her hair escaping from its pins, and her skirts— Dear God.

Her legs were pale and wet and as shapely as any man could dream of. Before he controlled himself, he watched a drop of water slide down from her knee, along one smooth calf and into the tub. His breath hissed out softly between his teeth.

"Well, this is an unexpected and charming domestic scene."

"You've no business in the kitchen, Lord Ashburn."

"Your father persuaded me to make myself at home. As everyone is occupied, I thought it would be less trouble for me to come in and charm Mrs. Drummond out of some soup."

"It's there in the pot." She indicated the steaming kettle. "Help yourself to it and take it away. I've got too much to do to wait on you."

"So I see." He recovered enough to walk closer. She smelled of soap and made his stomach quiver. "Madam, I assure you,

I will never sleep quite the same again knowing how my bed linen was washed."

She swallowed a chuckle and began to stamp in the water again. "It does the job, *Sassenach*, and does it well. Now, if you'll be about your business, I'll be about mine before the water goes cold." Inspired perhaps by the devil, she brought her foot down hard and sent water splashing over his breeches. "Oh, I beg your pardon, my lord." Unable to prevent it, she snickered.

Brigham looked down at his breeches and gave a wry shake of his head. "Perhaps you think these need washing, as well."

"Toss them in," she invited recklessly. "I've had a mind to plant my foot on your breeches before."

"Have you?" He reached down toward the fastening and had the satisfaction of watching her eyes widen. Flushing to the roots of her hair, she stepped back and nearly tumbled down in the water.

"Brigham—"

He caught her before she could send herself and the wash-water all over the kitchen. "There, I knew I would have it out of you again."

He had an arm around her waist, another on her hair. The remaining pins plopped into the water and sunk. Serena stood, flustered, with her arms trapped between their bodies. "What?"

"My name," he murmured. "Say it again."

"I've no need to." She moistened her lips, unwittingly stirring his blood all the more. "And you've no need to hold me. I have my balance now."

"But I do have a need, Rena. I've told myself three days running that I cannot, I should not, I shall not touch you." As he spoke he ran his hand up her back, down her hair, as if he could take as he chose. "But I have a need. The same one I see now in your eyes."

She hated herself for lowering them. "You see nothing."

"Everything," he corrected, pressing a kiss to her hair. "Oh, God, I haven't been able to get the scent of you out of my mind, the taste of you off my palate."

"Stop." If she could have freed her hands, she would have covered her ears with them. "I won't listen."

"Why?" The hand on her hair tightened so that she was forced to lift her head. "Because I'm English?"

"No. Yes. I don't know." Her voice rose, roughened by the beat of her pulse. "I only know I don't want this. I don't want to feel the way you make me feel."

He felt a moment of triumph as he dragged her closer. "How do I make you feel, Rena?"

"Weak, afraid, angry. No, don't," she whispered as his lips hovered above hers. "Don't kiss me."

"Then kiss me." He brushed his lips lightly over hers.

"I won't."

His lips curved as hers met them. "You already are."

With a shuddering moan, she clutched at him, taking what her heart wanted and blocking out the warning in her head. He wasn't for her, could never be for her, and yet when he held her it seemed as though he had always been for her.

His lips teased and retreated, seduced and tormented, until she was driven to take possession. Had she told him he made her feel weak? That was a lie, she thought dimly. She felt strong, incredibly strong, with energy coursing through her and pumping through her blood until it ran hot. A woman could fear weakness, but not power.

She wrapped her arms around him, let her head fall back and her lips part as she all but dared him to try to sap her strength.

It was like holding a lightning bolt, he thought. Full of fire and flash and dangerous power. One moment he was coaxing, the next he was bombarded with the heat that seemed to radiate from her. Murmuring her name, he lifted her from the water. He held her aloft for a moment, then slowly let her slide down his body until her feet hit the floor.

Then her lips were racing over his face. She slipped her hands beneath his coat to run them impatiently over the linen of his shirt. Her body was arched against his, begging to be touched. Her breasts yielded temptingly against his chest.

Knowing his only choices were to pull her to the floor and pleasure them both or stop, Brigham dragged himself away.

"Serena." He took both of her hands and brought them to his lips. "We must talk."

"Talk?" Thoughts couldn't surface in a head that swam so thickly.

"Yes, and soon, before I abuse the trust of your father and my friend more than I already have."

She stared at him a moment, and then her mind began to clear. Pulling her hands away, she pressed them to her cheeks. How could she have thrown herself at him in that way? "I don't want to talk, I want you to go away."

"Want or not, we will talk." He grabbed her hands again before she could turn away. "Serena, we can't pretend that something doesn't happen between us every time we're together. I may not want this any more than you, but I'm not fool enough to say it doesn't exist."

"It will pass," she said, desperate to believe it. "Desires come, and they go."

He lifted a brow. "Such cool and worldly talk from a woman in bare feet."

"Oh, leave me be, will you?" She shoved at him. "I was fine and happy before you came here. I'll be fine and happy when you leave."

"The hell you will." He pulled her against him again. "If I were to leave now, you'd weep."

Pride stiffened her spine. "I'll never shed a tear over you. Why should I? You're not the first man I've kissed, and you won't be the last."

His eyes narrowed to slits, darkened like onyx. "You live dangerously, Serena."

"I live as I please. Now let me go."

"So I'm not the first you've kissed," he murmured. He had a desperate and vivid desire to know the names and faces of each one so he could murder them. "Tell me, did the others make you tremble?" He kissed her again, hard enough to make her gasp. "Did they make your skin go hot and soft?" His mouth came to hers again, and this time she could do nothing but sigh against his lips and let him have his way. "Did you look at them the way you look at me now?" he demanded. "With your eyes dark and clouded?"

She clutched at his shoulders, almost afraid she would dissolve and slide through his hands. "Brigham—"

"Did you?" he demanded, his eyes dark and bright.

Her head was reeling, and she shook it. "No."

"Serena, I've finished in—" Gwen pushed open the door, then stood, her mouth forming a surprised O as she stared at her sister caught in a close embrace with their guest. Serena stood on the toes of her bare feet, gripping Brigham's beautiful coat. And he—Gwen's young imagination caused her blush to deepen.

"I beg your pardon," she managed, and continued to stand, looking from one to the other without the least idea what to do.

"Gwen." With more force than dignity, Serena pulled out of Brigham's arms. "Lord Ashburn was just—"

"Kissing your sister," he finished coolly.

"Oh." Gwen watched Serena send Brigham a furious glance. "I do beg your pardon," she repeated, wondering if it would be best to go or stay.

Amused, Brigham watched Gwen wrestle with propriety while Serena whirled to the cupboard and rattled crockery. "There's no need to beg anyone's pardon," she said testily. "Lord Ashburn wanted soup."

"So I did, but as it happens I've had all my appetite can handle at the moment. If you ladies will excuse me…" He strolled out, wincing only slightly as a bowl hit the floor.

Chapter Seven

"King Louis will not intervene." Brigham stood in front of the fire, his hands clasped behind his back. Though his eyes were calm and his stance relaxed, his voice was grim. "It becomes less and less likely as time passes that he will support the Prince with gold or with men."

Coll tossed the letter that had come earlier by messenger onto a table and rose to pace. Unlike Brigham's, his impatience needed room and movement. "A year ago, Louis was more than ready to lend support. Ready? Damn, he was eager to lend it."

"A year ago," Brigham pointed out, "Louis thought Charles might be of use to him. Since the French invasion was abandoned last March, the Prince is largely ignored by the French court."

"Then we'll do without the French." Coll turned to glare first at Brigham, then at his father. "The Highlanders will fight for the Stuarts."

"Aye," Ian agreed. "But how many?" He held up a hand to prevent his son from launching into a passionate speech. "My mind and my heart remain unchanged. When the time comes, the MacGregors fight for the rightful king. But it's unity we need, as well as numbers. To win, the clans must fight as one."

"As we have fought before," Coll said with a slap of his fist. "And will again."

"Would that were true." Ian's voice was quiet, one of reason and regret. And of age, he thought with an inward sigh. Growing old was the damnedest thing. "We can't pretend that every chief in Scotland stands behind the true king or will rally his clan for the Prince. How many, Brig, will stand against us in the government army?"

Brigham picked up the letter from the table and, after glancing at it once more, tossed it into the fire. "I expect word from my contacts in London any day."

"How much longer do we wait?" Coll took his seat again to stare into the fire. "How many more months, how many more years do we only sit and talk while the elector grows fat on the throne?"

"I think the time of rebellion comes sooner than you might think," Brigham murmured. "Sooner than we might be prepared for. The Prince is impatient."

"The Highland chiefs will meet again." Ian drummed his fingers on the arm of his chair. Like any wise general, he preferred to plan his war before raising his sword. "Care must be taken to keep such meetings from raising the suspicions of the Black Watch."

Coll swore roundly at the mention of the Highlanders recruited by the English to maintain order in Scotland.

"Another hunting party?" Brigham asked.

"I had in mind something a bit different." At the sound of approaching carriage wheels, Ian smiled and tapped out his pipe. "A ball, my lads. It's time we did a spot of entertaining. And the lass who comes visiting is, I believe, a very pretty reason for dusting away cobwebs."

Brigham twitched the curtains aside in time to see Serena dash down the steps toward the waiting carriage. A dark-haired girl descended and launched herself into Serena's arms. "Maggie MacDonald."

"Aye. She's of marriageable age, as is my own first daughter." He set his gaze on Brigham's back a moment. A man would have to be blind, he thought, not to see that there was a tune playing between his young guest and his daughter. "Nothing more reasonable than to hold a ball to introduce them to a few suitable young bucks."

Fighting back annoyance, Brigham let the curtain fall into place. He didn't want to look at Serena now, with the sun falling on her face and her eyes dark with laughter. "It will do well enough, I suppose."

Coll only scowled at the toe of his boot. "I don't care for it. Bringing another giggling female into the house now. Damned if I'm going to find myself cornered into taking her for sedate rides and listening to talk of the latest bonnets when we should be polishing our swords."

Ian merely rose to open the salon doors. "I've no doubt that Rena and Gwen will entertain her well enough without you." The moment the doors were opened, women's voices and laughter poured through. Coll grumbled and stayed stubbornly in his seat. "There's the lass." Ian's voice rumbled to the ceiling. "Come here and give your Uncle Ian a kiss."

Smiling, Maggie danced across the hall. She laughed when

he lifted her off her feet, but Fiona scolded him. "The girl's already been bumped enough on the journey. Go in and warm yourself by the fire, Maggie."

With her arm still tucked in Ian's, Maggie stepped into the room.

Manners prevented Coll from scowling, and he began to rise reluctantly. Then, manners or not, his mouth fell open. She still looked hardly bigger than a doll beside his broad-shouldered father, but the skinny, smudge-faced pest he remembered had miraculously been replaced by a slender vision in dark blue velvet. Her hair, dark as midnight, fell in curls beneath a hat that framed her face. Had her eyes always been that beautiful, like the loch at twilight? he wondered as he managed to close his mouth. Had her skin always looked like fresh cream?

Maggie smiled at him. Then, because she had planned her moves carefully during the journey, she turned to curtsy to Brigham. "Lord Ashburn."

"It's a pleasure to see you again, Miss MacDonald." He took her offered hand and brushed his lips over her fingers. Behind Ian, Serena's breath came out in a quiet hiss. "I trust your journey wasn't too taxing."

"Not at all."

Because Maggie's hand was still in Brigham's, Serena couldn't prevent herself from stepping forward. "You remember Coll, don't you, Maggie?" With a little more force than was necessary, she pulled Maggie away from Brigham and toward her brother.

"Of course I do." Maggie had practiced a friendly, almost impersonal smile in front of her mirror night after night in preparation for this first meeting. Though her heart was pounding, she put her practiced smile to use now. He was even more handsome than she remembered, taller, broader, even more exciting. Growing up had taken so long, but now, at this moment, it seemed worth it. "I'm happy to see you again, Coll. I hope your wound is healed."

"Wound?" He took her hand, feeling unbearably clumsy.

"Your father explained that you were wounded on the way from London." Her voice was mild as a spring morning. She wondered he couldn't hear the furious thundering of her heart. "I trust you've recovered?"

"It was nothing."

"I'm persuaded it was a great deal more than nothing, but it's good to see you up and about again." Because she was afraid that if her hand stayed in his another moment she would faint with delight, Maggie drew herself away and twirled around. There was a blush in her cheeks now that she prayed everyone would take for excitement from the journey. "It's wonderful to be here again. I can't thank you enough, Uncle Ian, Aunt Fiona, for asking me to come."

Refreshments were brought in, seats were taken. Rather than making the excuses he had prepared, Coll found himself jockeying for the chair nearest Maggie. Brigham took advantage of the situation and leaned close to Serena as he passed a plate of cakes.

"Will you try one of these, Miss MacGregor?" he asked. Then, in a quiet voice that was covered by the conversation: "You've been avoiding me, Rena."

"That's ridiculous." She took a cake and wondered how she had been maneuvered to the fringes of the party with him.

"I agree completely. Avoiding me is ridiculous."

Her cup rattled in its saucer. "You flatter yourself, *Sassenach*."

"It's gratifying to see I make you nervous," he said quietly, then turned and continued in a normal tone, "Gwen, I must tell you how charming you look in pink."

He never tells me I look charming, Serena thought as she bit, almost viciously, into her cake. He never gives me gallant bows and pretty compliments as he did with Maggie. With me it's barbs and snarls. And kisses, she remembered with an inward shiver. Deep, dark kisses.

She wouldn't think of it—or of him. When a man treated a woman that boldly, he wanted only one thing. She might have been raised in the Highlands, but she was no fool when it came to the ways of the English aristocracy.

She would be no man's mistress. Certainly she would be no Englishman's mistress. No matter what magic he could make her feel, no matter what wonders he could make her dream of, she would never shame herself or her family. If she avoided him, it wasn't that she was afraid, it was that she was being sensible.

"Daydreams, my love," Brigham murmured, making her jump. "I hope they are of me."

"They are of cows to be milked," she said between her teeth. When he chuckled, she put up her chin and prepared to speak to Maggie. Her friend, at that moment, was bubbling with laughter and smiling beautifully at Coll. Her brother, Serena noted, was flushed and glassy-eyed.

"Apparently Coll doesn't find Miss MacDonald a nuisance after all," Brigham commented.

"He looks as though he's been hit on the head with a rock."

"Or struck through the heart with Cupid's arrow."

Her eyes widened at that, then narrowed consideringly. In a moment she had to smother a chuckle of her own. "Who would have thought it?" Too amused to do otherwise, she leaned closer to Brigham. "Do you suppose he'll start spouting poetry?"

He caught a whiff of her hair and imagined bury-ing his face in it. The woman was made to drive him mad, snapping one moment, smiling the next. "Men have been known to do worse when so afflicted."

"But Coll? Coll and Maggie! A few years ago he couldn't wait to dust Maggie off his boots."

"And now she is a beautiful woman."

A little pang of jealousy warred with friendship. "Aye," Serena murmured, and wondered fleetingly what it would be like to be tiny and fragile. "You certainly seem to think so."

His brow lifted at that, and then a smile ghosted around his lips. "For myself, I've come to prefer green eyes and a sharp tongue."

She looked at him then and blushed despite herself. "I have no way, my lord, with drawing room flirtations."

"Then that is perhaps one more thing I shall teach you."

Choosing to retreat rather than fight with a dull sword, Serena rose. "Let me take you up, Maggie, and show you your room."

Maggie's company was precisely the distraction Serena needed. It had been nearly two years since they had been together, but time and distance were swept away. They talked late into the night, rode out together into the forest, walked for miles in the hills. As always, Maggie spoke whatever was in her heart, while Serena kept her innermost thoughts close. The fact that her friend was still in love with Coll didn't surprise her. The fact that Coll seemed equally besotted with Maggie did.

It pleased her. Though Serena had never believed, as Mag-

gie always had, that Coll would fall in love with her friend, she
couldn't deny what was happening in front of her eyes. He made
dozens of excuses to be in their company, when just two years
before he had made twice as many to be out of it. He listened
to Maggie's cheerful ram-blings as though she were the most
fascinating person on earth. And with the sharp and always
critical eye of a sister, Serena noted that Coll was taking great
pains with his appearance.

She even had it from Mrs. Drummond that Coll was asking
Parkins's advice on his wardrobe.

She would have laughed about it if she had not felt constant
prickings of jealousy. More than once she had caught herself
sulking when she thought of how rosy and dreamy being in
love had made her friend. And how nervous and unhappy falling in love was making her. The weakness infuriated her, and
made her only more determined to see that Coll and Maggie
had their hearts' desire.

Coll accompanied them on some of their rides, which meant
they more often than not rode as a foursome, including Brigham.
The new situation gave Serena as much pleasure as it did discomfort.

The weather was brisk, but the bite of winter was easing. In
another month, Serena thought, the trees would be greening
and the first hardy wildflowers would brave their way out to the
sun. For now, there was the slap of a March wind on her face as
she rode. The spring thaws had not yet come, and the ground
still rang hard under the horses' hooves, but there were birdcalls
and occasional bright flashes of wings as the horses disturbed
the midmorning quiet. Ice and frost had melted from the trees,
leaving them wet and glistening.

They kept to a sedate canter that caused Serena to rein in her impatience, as well as her horse. She knew Maggie could ride as well as anyone, but her friend seemed to prefer picking her way daintily along the path.

"You would prefer a run?" Brigham asked as he came up beside her.

"I would," she said feelingly.

He shot a look over his shoulder while his own mount danced beneath him. "Let them catch up."

Though she was tempted, she shook her head. Her mother would never approve of their going in pairs rather than in a group. "It wouldn't be right."

"Afraid you can't keep up with me?" He was rewarded by a flash in her eyes.

"There isn't an Englishman alive a MacGregor can't beat on horseback."

"Easy talk, Rena," he said mildly. "The lake's less than a mile."

She hesitated, knowing proper manners dictated she remain with her guest. But a challenge was a challenge. Before she could stop herself, she pressed in her heels and sent her mount leaping forward.

She knew the way as well as she knew the corridors of her own home. With a light hand, she guided the horse through the curves and twists, whipping under low-hanging branches, leaping over or skirting fallen limbs. The path was barely wide enough for two, but neither gave way, so they rode all but shoulder-to-shoulder. She glanced over to see Brigham's face alive with laughter as he spurred his mount forward. The forest rang with her own as she leaned forward to coax more speed out of her mare.

There was a pleasure here that came as much from the company as the race. There was a freedom she experienced only with him, but one that, for now, she didn't question Brigham's part in. She only wished that the lake were ten miles away rather than one, so that they could continue to ride fast and reckless, with the sun shooting beams through bare trees.

She rode like a goddess, he thought. Brilliantly, with a careless disregard for life and limb. With another woman he would have held back, slowed the pace out of concern for her safety, and perhaps her pride. With Serena he only pushed harder, out of the sheer pleasure of seeing her fly along the path, her plaid streaming over her dove-gray riding habit. With a grin he watched her gallop half a length ahead, regretting only that she had chosen the habit over breeches.

Not so easy, he murmured to himself as he spotted the sun striking the lake's surface in the distance. With a kick of his heels they were neck and neck again, thundering down the rise toward the water.

They reached the bank together, and his heart stopped as Serena waited until the last possible instant to rein in. With a ringing whinny, her mare reared. She was laughing in the moment she hung suspended between sky and earth, her eyes dark and reckless, her body fluid. If Brigham hadn't already been in love, he would have fallen then, as quickly and as dangerously as a man hurled from a cliff.

"I won, *Sassenach*."

"The devil you did." Breathless, he patted his horse's neck and grinned at her. "I had you by a head."

"Head be damned," she said, forgetting herself. "I won, and you're not man enough to admit it." She took a deep, greedy breath of air that tasted of pine and water. "If I hadn't been hampered by riding sidesaddle, I'd have left you in my dust." Then she was laughing at him, her eyes greener than any of the lush lawns he knew in England, her flirty little hat tilted askew from the race. "You've nothing to be ashamed of," she said with her tongue in her cheek. "You're as good a horseman as any Englishman might be, and nearly as good as a lame Scot with a blind eye."

"Your compliments put me to the blush, my lady. Regardless, the race was mine, but you're too vain—or too mulish—to concede."

She tossed her head so that the hat fell off to hang by its ribbons. The hair that Maggie had labored over that morning tumbled down in a mass of sunset curls. "I won. A gentleman would have the grace to admit it."

"I won." Reaching over, he loosened her ribbons and snatched the hat away. "A lady would never have raced in the first place."

"Oh." If it had been possible, she would have stamped her foot. Instead, she swung her horse around until they were face-to-face. She didn't mind being called vain and mulish, but to have her lack of ladylike graces tossed in her face was too much. "Isn't that just like a man! The race was your idea. If I had refused, I would have been a coward. But I accept, and win, so I'm not a lady."

"Accepted, and lost," Brigham corrected, enjoying the way temper flushed her cheeks. "You've no need to be a lady for me, Rena. I prefer you as you are."

Her eyes kindled. "Which is?"

"A delightful wildcat who wears breeches and fights like a man." She hissed at him and, on impulse, gave his mount a slap that had it leaping forward. If Brigham hadn't reacted quickly enough, or had his skill been less sharp, he would have landed headfirst in the icy waters of the lake.

"Vixen," he murmured, half in amazement, half in admiration. "Have you a mind to drown me now?"

"It would hardly be my fault if you sank to the bottom. You have a head like a stone." But she was biting her lip to keep from laughing. Tossing her head again, she looked up at the sky. It was a glorious day, perhaps the most beautiful she would ever see. Annoyance with him faded easily when she remembered that he had given her the chance for a run.

"I'll call a truce," she decided. "Coll and Maggie will be here soon. If I'm angry with you, I'll have no one to talk to while they make moon eyes at each other."

"So, I have my uses." Brigham slipped from his horse. "You warm my heart, madam."

"The race, and winning it, put me in a pleasant mood." She unhooked her knee from the saddle and laid her hands on his shoulders as he stood to assist her to the ground.

"I'm delighted to hear it." Before she had an inkling of his purpose, he had tossed her over his shoulder. "But I'll remind you, I won."

"Are you mad?" She thudded a fist against his back, not certain if she wanted to laugh or swear. "Set me down, you oaf."

"I've a mind to do just that." He took a few easy strides to the verge of the lake. Serena's eyes widened. Rather than beat against him, she dug her fingers into his jacket.

"You wouldn't dare."

"My dear, have I told you that a Langston never, absolutely

never, refuses a dare?" She kicked and gave a passing thought to biting as his hand slid up her calf. "Can you swim?"

"Better than you, *Sassenach*, I'll swear. If you don't let me—" Her threat was cut off by her squeal as he feinted a toss. "Brigham, don't! It's freezing!" She began to laugh, even as she kicked and strug

gled. "I swear I'll murder you the moment I'm free."

"That's hardly incentive for me to release you. Now if you'll concede that I won the race…"

"I will not."

"Well, then." He had started to step closer to the water when Serena landed a blow with the toe of her boot close enough to a sensitive area to make him wince. In defense, Brigham stepped back and tripped over a root. They went down in a flurry of petticoats and curses. For propriety's sake, and his own sake of mind, he removed his hand from the taut curve of her bottom.

"We've been here before, I believe," he managed as they both struggled to catch their breath.

Serena shoved herself off him and remembered, belatedly, to cover her legs. "Damn you. You've stained my skirts."

"My lady, you came a great deal too close to unmanning me."

She grinned and pushed the hair out of her eyes. It was a glorious day, and she felt too alive to remember to be a lady. "Did I? I'll do better at the next opportunity." After a glance at the dirt on his breeches, she snickered. "Parkins will undoubtedly scold you for ruining those."

"My valet does not scold." But Brigham rubbed at the streak of dirt. "He simply looks mortally offended, which causes me to feel as though I were a schoolboy again."

Serena plucked at the turf. "What is he like, your Parkins?"

"Steady as a rock, infuriatingly proper. Stubborn. Why?"

"Mrs. Drummond has decided he would make a likely husband."

"Mrs. Drummond?" Brigham turned his head to stare. "*Your* Mrs. Drummond, and Parkins?"

Family honor brought the light of battle to Serena's eyes. "And why not? Mrs. Drummond is a fine woman."

"You'll get no argument from me. But Parkins?" Brigham leaned back on his elbows and laughed. He could do nothing else when he thought of the scarecrow-framed Parkins and the prodigiously built cook. "Does he know?"

"She'll get around to letting him." Because she had found the pairing funny herself, Serena lay back on the grassy bank and smiled at the sky. "She'll charm him with her tarts and sauces, just as Maggie is charming Coll with her pretty eyes and shy smiles."

"Does that bother you?"

"Maggie and Coll?" Serena cushioned her head with her arm and thought it through. "No. She's been in love with him for as long as I can remember. I'd be more than happy for them if they make a match, and since she's already my friend I wouldn't have to worry about hating the woman Coll chose for a wife. But—"

"But?"

"Seeing them together has made me think. Things are changing, and there's nothing to be done to stop it." She closed her eyes, content to have the chilly breeze dance over her face. "When spring comes, love comes. So they say." If her voice was wistful, she blamed it on the air. "When this spring comes, war comes. There will be nothing to stop that, either."

"No." He reached over to toy with the ends of her hair. "Would you have it stopped, Serena?"

She sighed, opening her eyes to watch the wispy clouds chased by the wind. "Part of me hates not being able to take a sword and fight myself. Yet another part, a part that seems to have just begun, wishes there was no need to fight at all. That part of me wishes we could go on living as we have been, watching the flowers come up in the spring."

He took her hand. It was too fragile to hold a sword, he thought, however strong her heart. "There will still be flowers. And there will be other springs."

She turned her head to look at him. It hadn't occurred to her that she was relaxed with him, content, even happy to be alone with him on the banks of the lake. It was her favorite place, one she came to when she was deeply troubled or very happy. Now she was there with him, and it seemed so right, somehow—the gentle call of birds, the smell of the water and damp earth, the almost harsh light of the sun.

Her fingers curled into his in a move so instinctive that she didn't know she had done it until it was too late, until the change had come into his eyes, the subtle darkening, the sharpening of intensity. It was as if in one instant the rest of the world had slipped out of its orbit and only they were left, hands linked, eyes only for each other.

"No." Quickly she pushed herself up so that she was sitting rather than lying on the bank. It had seemed a move of self-preservation, but it was a poor one, as it only put them closer together. Brigham reached out to trace the line of her jaw.

"I could let you go, Rena. It wouldn't change what's between us."

"There can be nothing between us."

"Stubborn." He nipped her lower lip. "Willful." Then he traced the ache with his tongue. "Beautiful."

"I'm none of those things." She lifted a hand, thinking to push him away, but somehow she was clutching his jacket.

"You're all of them." He bit gently at her jaw, making her eyes widen in confused desire. His lips curved at her reaction. She would be a joy in bed. Slowly, almost leisurely, he shifted to nibble her earlobe.

"Don't."

"I've waited for days to have five minutes alone with you and do just this." He dipped his tongue into her ear so that both pleasure and heat rippled through her. "There is nothing more I want than to make love with you, Serena. Every inch of you."

"I can't. You can't."

"You can," he murmured. "We will." He teased her lips apart with his.

For a moment she luxuriated in it, the feel of his lips on hers. The rightness of it. But it couldn't be right. It would never be right. "Please, stop. It's wrong for you to speak that way to me. It's wrong to— I can't think."

"Don't think." Suddenly he gripped her by the shoulders so that they were again face-to-face. "Feel. Just feel. And show me."

Her head was spinning, with longings, with warnings. With a moan, she dragged his mouth to hers. It was wrong. It was madness. But she couldn't resist. When he touched her, she wanted only for him to go on touching her. When he kissed her, she felt she might die from the pleasure of it. To be wanted like this was its own kind of torment. She could feel his desire for her in the way his fingers gripped, in the way his mouth devoured. With each passing second she could feel her will drain until she knew there would come a time when she would give everything to him.

He covered her heart with his hand, aroused to desperation by its pounding. For him. Unable to resist, he traced his fingers over her curves, trailing his lips down her throat, then up again, to find her lips warmed and waiting for his.

"My God, Serena, how I want you." His breath ragged, he pushed her away to stare at her flushed face. "Can you understand?"

"Aye." Her hand was shaking as she lifted it to her throat. "I need time to think."

"We need time to talk." Very carefully he released her, only just realizing how hard his fingers had dug into her arms. He heard the sound of approaching horses and swore. "Every time I'm alone with you I end up kissing you. We won't get any talking done this way. I need you to understand how I feel, and what I want for us."

She thought she did. And to her shame, and her excitement, she knew she was close to agreeing. He wanted her, and she would be his lover. It would be the most precious moment of her life. And then he would offer to make an arrangement. As his mistress, she would be well provided for, well housed, well clothed, well attended. And miserable. If she found the strength to refuse him, she would retain her pride, and she would be even more miserable.

"There's no need to talk. I understand." She rose to brush off her skirts. "I simply need time to think about it."

He took her hand, knowing they had only moments to be alone. "Do you love me?"

She closed her eyes, wishing she could hate him for asking

what he must already know. "That isn't the only question to be answered, Brigham."

He dropped her hand and stepped back, his eyes cold again. "We're back to that, are we? I'm English, and no matter what you may feel for me, no matter what we can bring to each other, you won't forget it."

"Can't," she corrected, and wanted to weep. "No, I can't forget who you are, what you are, any more than I can forget who and what I am. I need time to see if I can live with what you want from me."

"Very well." He inclined his head. "You'll have time. But remember this, Serena. I won't beg you."

Chapter Eight

"It's going to be a beautiful ball." Maggie balanced on the rung of a ladder and polished the topmost corner of a mirror. The servants, under Fiona's eagle eye, were turning the house inside out. Family was expected to do no less. "Everything will be perfect, Rena. You'll see. The music, the lights—"

"And Coll," Serena added, rubbing her cloth over the arm of a chair.

"Especially Coll." Smiling, Maggie looked down over her shoulder. "He's already asked me for the first dance."

"That comes as no surprise."

"He was so sweet when he asked," Maggie murmured, peering closer to the mirror to give her face a careful study. She was terrified that the long, sunny rides she had indulged in would bring out freckles that Coll would despise. "I wanted to tell him there was no one else I wanted to dance with at all, but I knew that would make him go red and stutter."

"I don't remember ever hearing Coll stutter until you came to visit."

"I know." Maggie bit her lip in delight. "Isn't it wonderful?"

A sarcastic response faded from her mind when Serena looked up at Maggie's beaming face. "Aye. He's fallen in love with you, and I've no doubt it's the finest thing that has ever happened to him."

"Not just because you're my friend?" Maggie asked anxiously.

"No, because he looks happier whenever you're in the room."

Maggie felt tears sting her eyes, then blinked them away. She didn't want them red and puffy if Coll happened in. She was still floating in the fantasy that her love should see her as nothing less than perfect.

"Remember years ago when we promised each other we'd be sisters one day?"

"Of course. You would marry Coll and I would marry whichever of your cousins I—" With the cloth dangling from her fingers, Serena looked up. "Oh, Maggie, never say Coll has made an offer?"

"Not yet." Maggie tucked a loose curl back in her cap. For a moment she got the stubborn line between her brows her father would have recognized very well. "But he will. Rena, it can't just be wishful thinking. I love him so much."

"Are you certain?" Rising, Serena crossed over to lay a hand on Maggie's skirt. "We were only children when we talked that way. I know you had your heart set on him, but you're not a child anymore, and Coll's a man."

"It *is* different." With a sigh, Maggie rubbed at a spot on the mirror. "When we were children I would think of him as a prince."

"Coll?" Serena couldn't prevent a sisterly snort.

"He was so tall and bonny. I imagined him fighting duels over me, sweeping me up on his horse and carrying me off." Laughing a little, she stepped down a rung. "But now, these past few weeks, being around him has made me see him in a whole new way. He's a steady man, dependable, gentle, even shy in his way. Oh, I know he has a temper and can be reckless, but that's the part that makes him exciting, as well as steady. He's not a prince, Rena, and I love him more than I ever knew I could."

"Has he kissed you?" Serena asked, thinking that Brigham was more like Maggie's childhood vision of Coll. The earl of Ashburn was a man for duels and carrying off.

"No." Maggie pouted for a moment over it, knowing it was wrong to wish he had just once taken command of her. "I think he was about to once, but Malcolm came in." Maggie fluttered her hands. "Do you think it's wrong for me to want him to?"

"No." Serena's answer was flat and honest, but Maggie was dreaming and didn't notice the tone.

"I miss my mother more now than when she died," Maggie mused. "Not being able to talk to her about all of this. To ask her if being with my father ever made her feel as though her heart had turned upside down. Tell me the truth, Serena, do you really think he loves me?"

"I've never seen him act so stupid around anyone else. Stammering, going around dreamy eyed and slack mouthed. Whenever he looks at you he either goes pale or colors up."

"Truly?" Maggie clapped her hands in delight. "Oh, but the man's slow. I'll go mad soon if he doesn't stop looking and take."

"Maggie!" Though her laughter was scandalized, Serena gave her friend a careful study. "You wouldn't, well, agree to more than a kiss?"

"I don't know." Her color was high as she stepped down another rung. "The only thing I'm sure of is, if he doesn't declare himself soon, I'll take matters into my own hands."

Fascinated, Serena tilted her head. "How?"

"I—" Maggie stopped at the sound of approaching footsteps. Her heart fluttered once, making her certain it was Coll even before he swung into the room. On impulse, she let her foot slip off the rung and gasped in alarm as she tumbled the last few feet toward the polished floor.

Serena reached out, but Coll took the distance in a leap and caught Maggie around the waist. He had only a fleeting sensation of how tiny she was before he was swamped with concern.

"There now, lassie, have you hurt yourself?"

"How clumsy of me," she managed over the lump in her throat as she stared up into his wide, rugged face. If Serena had asked her now if she would agree to more than a kiss, her answer would have been yes, a hundred times yes.

"Nonsense." Overwhelmed by tenderness, he held her gently. "A little slip of a girl like you shouldn't be climbing ladders."

Suddenly afraid he might bruise her with his big, clumsy hands, he started to set her down. Drastic desires called for drastic measures, Maggie thought, and she let out a muffled cry as her foot touched the ground. Instantly she was gathered in Coll's arms again. She nearly swooned in earnest when she felt the rapid beat of his heart against hers.

"You have hurt yourself? Shall I call Gwen?"

"Oh, no! If I could just sit for a moment..." She fluttered her lashes and was rewarded when Coll swept her up and carried her to a chair. It took him only six steps, but he had never felt more of a man.

"You're a bit pale, Maggie. A little water should help." He

was up and striding out before she could think of an excuse to keep him.

"How badly does it hurt?" Serena had already knelt by her feet. "Oh, Maggie, it would be so unfair if you couldn't dance tomorrow."

"I'll dance. And I'll dance with Coll."

"But if you've sprained your ankle—"

"There's not a thing wrong with my ankle. Don't be silly." To prove it, she sprang up and did a quick, laughing dance step.

"Why, Margaret MacDonald. You lied to him."

"No such thing." She sat again, careful to arrange her skirts in their most flattering folds. "He assumed I'd hurt myself, I never said so. Oh, Rena, how is my hair? It must be a mess."

"You fell on purpose."

"Aye." Maggie's face glowed with triumph. "And it worked."

Disgusted, Serena sat back on her heels. "That's nothing but a trick, and a demeaning one at that."

"It's not a trick, or only a small one, and there's nothing demeaning about it." She touched a hand to her cheek where Coll's beard had tickled her. "It was simply a way to make him feel as though I needed tending. A man doesn't fall in love with a woman who's a packhorse, you know. If it makes him feel good to think of me as a bit helpless and fragile, what's the harm?"

Serena chewed over that one, remembering the time Brigham had raised his sword for her when he'd thought she had been attacked. If she had acted a little more…fragile… With a shake of her head, she told herself that was for Maggie, not for her.

"None, I suppose."

"When a man's shy, he needs a bit of a push. There, he's coming back." She gripped Serena's hands and squeezed. "If you could leave us alone for just a little while."

"I will, but… It almost seems as though he hasn't a chance."

Her smile spread. "I hope not."

"Here now." Coll knelt beside her and offered a cup. "Drink a little."

"Perhaps I'll go fetch Gwen," Serena said as she rose. Neither Maggie nor Coll spared her a glance. "And perhaps I won't," she murmured, and left them alone.

Coll took Maggie's hand in his. It seemed so soft, so tiny. He felt like a bear hulking over a dove. "Are you in much pain, Maggie?"

"No, it's nothing." She looked at him from under her lashes, amazed to find herself as stricken with shyness as he. "You don't need to fuss, Coll."

Looking at her, he was reminded of one of the beautiful porcelain dolls he had seen in Italy. His need to touch her was as great as his fear that he would bruise her. "I was afraid I wouldn't be quick enough to catch you."

"So was I." Daringly, she laid her hand on his. "Do you remember, years ago, I fell in the forest and tore my dress?"

"Aye." He had to swallow. "I laughed at you. You must have hated me."

"No, I could never hate you." Her fingers curled into his. "I must have been a dreadful nuisance." She drew together her courage and looked up. "Am I still?"

"No." His throat was dry as dust. "You're the most beautiful woman in Scotland, and I—" Now his throat was not only dry but seemed to have swollen to twice its size, and his collar threatened to strangle him.

"And you?" Maggie prompted.

"I should find Gwen."

She nearly screamed with frustration. "I don't need Gwen, Coll. Can't you—don't you see?"

He did, the moment he braced himself to look into those dark blue eyes. He was thunderstruck for a moment, then terrified, and then he was lifting her out of the chair and into his arms. "You'll marry me, Maggie?"

"I've waited all my life for you to ask." She tilted her face up for his kiss.

"Coll!" Fiona stepped into the room. Her voice was ripe with warning and disapproval. "Is this how you treat a young female guest in our home?"

"Aye." He laughed and carried Maggie forward. "When she's agreed to be my wife."

"I see." She looked from one to the other. "I won't pretend I'm surprised, but—I think you'd best refrain from carrying Maggie around until after the wedding."

"Mother—"

"Set the lass down."

Stiff with annoyance, he complied. Maggie gripped her hands together, then relaxed when Fiona opened her arms. "Welcome to the family, Maggie. I can only be grateful my son is finally showing good sense."

She still couldn't believe it. As she finished up the morning milking, Serena thought over Maggie's breathless announcement. Coll was getting married.

"What do you think of that?" she asked the placid cow as milk squirted into the pail.

No one was supposed to know yet, of course. Fiona had insisted that Coll approach MacDonald with an offer first, as was proper, but Maggie hadn't been able to hold the news inside. In fact, Serena's eyes were gritty this morning because Maggie hadn't let her sleep until it had been nearly time to rise again.

There was little doubt that when MacDonald arrived later that day with many of the other guests he would agree to the betrothal. Maggie was nearly delirious at the thought of announcing the engagement at the ball that night.

Ready to dance out of her shoes, Serena thought as she squeezed and pulled the last of the milk from the bored cow. Then there was Coll, strutting around like a rooster with two tails. With a shake of her head, Serena set the milking stool aside and lifted her two pails.

Of course she was happy for them. As long as she could remember, Maggie had dreamed of marrying Coll. She would be a good and loving wife to him, calming his more radical impulses, indulging the harmless ones. She would be content to spin, ply her needle and raise a brood of raucous children. And Coll, like their father, would be devoted to his family.

For herself, she had reaffirmed her decision never to marry. She would make a poor wife. It wasn't that she minded the work, or that she wouldn't dearly love to have children of her own, but she hadn't the patience or the biddable nature to sit and wait, to nod and obey.

In any case, how often did anyone find a mate to both love and respect? She supposed she'd been spoiled by being a part of her parents' marriage. Settling for less would make her feel like a failure.

How could she marry anyone, she asked herself as she came

out of the cow shed, when she had fallen in love with Brigham? How could she give herself to a man when she would always wonder what it would have been like with another? Knowing she could never be a part of Brigham's life, or he a part of hers, didn't change what was in her heart. Until she could convince herself that the love she had for him was dead, she would remain alone.

It would be harder now, watching Coll and Maggie. Serena balanced herself with the pails as she started down the rise. The sun was struggling to brighten the sky and melt the last of the winter's snow. The path was slick, but manageable for one who had made the trip day after day all her life. She moved without hurry, not for caution's sake but because her mind was elsewhere.

No, she wouldn't begrudge them their happiness because she could never have the same. That would be mean-hearted, and she loved them both too much for that. But she had to wonder at the way Maggie had claimed her heart's desire simply by tumbling off a ladder.

The way Coll had looked at Maggie! As if she were a piece of precious glass that might shatter at a touch, Serena remembered with a quick shake of her head. How would it be to have a man look at you that way? Of course, it wasn't what she wanted, Serena reminded herself. Still, just once it might be nice.

She heard the sound of boots ringing on rock and glanced up to see Brigham striding toward the stables. Without giving herself time to think, she changed directions so that they would pass each other. Offering a silent apology for the spilled milk, Serena let out what she hoped was a convincing gasp of alarm and slid to the ground.

Brigham was beside her instantly, his hands on his hips, his face already darkened by his black mood.

"Have you hurt yourself?"

It was more an accusation than a question. Serena bristled, then forced herself to play the part. She wasn't precisely sure how it was done, but Maggie had used her lashes. "I'm not sure. I may have twisted my ankle."

"What the devil are you doing hauling milk?" Disgusted, he bent down to examine her ankle. The communication that had been brought to him late the previous night was weighing on his mind. But for that, he might have seen the thunder come into her eyes. "Where's Malcolm or that scatterbrained Molly or one of the others?"

"The milking's not Malcolm's job, and Molly and everyone else are busy preparing for the guests." All thoughts of being fragile and feminine were whisked away. "There's no shame in hauling milk, *Lord* Ashburn. Perhaps your dainty English ladies wouldn't know a cow's teat from a bull's—"

"This has nothing to do with my English ladies, as you call them. The paths are slippery and the pails are heavy. So it has to do with you doing more than you're able."

"More than I'm able?" She knocked his hand away from her ankle. "I'm strong enough to do as much as you and more. And I've never in my life slipped on this path."

He sat back on his heels and let his gaze sweep over her. "Sturdy as a mule, aren't you, Rena?"

That was it. A woman could take only so much. Serena sprang up and emptied the contents of one bucket over his head. It was done before either of them could prevent it. She stood, swinging an empty bucket, while he swallowed a mouthful of very fresh milk.

"There's a warm milk bath for your soft English skin, *my lord.*"

She grabbed the other bucket, but before she could toss it in his face, his hands closed over hers on the handles. His grip was very firm, very steady, but there was smoke from a volatile fire in his eyes.

"I should thrash you for that."

She tossed her head back and watched with growing satisfaction as milk dripped down his cheeks. "You can try, *Sassenach.*"

"Serena!"

The challenging gleam in her eyes turned to one of distress when she heard her father call her name. She braced herself as she waited for him to rush the last few feet toward her.

"Father." There was nothing to do but hang her head before his glowering eyes and wait for the worst.

"Have you lost your mind?"

She sighed. Because she was looking at the ground, she didn't notice that Brigham shifted just enough to put himself between Serena and her father's wrath. "My temper, Father."

"There was a slight accident, Ian," Brigham began. Taking out his handkerchief, he wiped milk from his face. "Serena lost her footing while she was carrying the milk."

"It wasn't an accident." It would not have occurred to Serena to claim it as one and save herself. "I poured the pail of milk on Lord Ashburn deliberately."

"I had eyes to see that for myself." Ian planted his feet. At that moment, with the sun rising behind his back, his plaid tossed over one shoulder and his face hard as granite, he looked fierce and invincible. "I'll apologize for the miserable behavior of this brat, Brigham, and promise you she'll be dealt with. Into the house, girl."

"Yes, Father."

"Please." Brigham put a hand on her shoulder before Serena could make her humiliated retreat. "I can't in good conscience allow Serena to take the full blame. I provoked her, also deliberately. I called you a mule, I believe, did I not, Serena?"

Her eyes kindled as she lifted her head. She was careful to lower it again quickly lest her father see she was unrepentant. "Aye."

"I thought that was it." Brigham wrung out his sodden handkerchief. What Parkins would say to this, Brigham couldn't even surmise. "The incident was as unfortunate as the insult, and as regrettable. Ian, I would take it as a favor if you would let the matter drop."

Ian said nothing for a moment, then made an impatient gesture toward Serena. "Take what's left of that milk into the house and be quick about it."

"Yes, Father." She sent a quick look at Brigham that was a mixture of gratitude and frustration, then ran, milk slopping at the lip of the pail.

"She deserved a whipping for that," Ian commented, though he knew he would laugh later at the memory of his little girl dumping milk all over the young English buck.

"That was my first thought." Brigham glanced idly at the ruined sleeve of his coat. "Unfortunately, on further consideration, I'm forced to admit I quite deserved it. Your daughter and I seem unable to maintain a polite demeanor with each other."

"So I see."

"She is stubborn, sharp-tongued, and has a temper that flares faster than a torch."

Ian rubbed a hand over his beard to hide a smile. "She's a curse to me, Brigham."

"To any man," Brigham murmured. "She makes me wonder if she was put here to complicate my life, or to brighten it."

"What do you intend to do about it?"

It was only then Brigham realized he had spoken his last thoughts aloud. He glanced back to see Serena disappear into the kitchen. "I intend to marry her, with your permission."

Ian let out a long breath. "And without it?"

Brigham gave him a level look. "I shall marry her anyway."

It was the answer Ian wanted, but still he hedged. He would know his daughter's mind first. "I'll think on it, Brigham. When do you leave for London?"

"The end of the week." His mind returned to the letter and his duty. "Lord George Murray believes my presence will help gain more support from the English Jacobites."

"You'll have my answer when you return. I won't deny that you're a man I would be content to give my daughter to, but she must be willing. And that, lad, I can't promise you."

A shadow came over Brigham's eyes as he dug his hands into his pockets. "Because I'm English."

Ian saw that this ground had been crossed before. "Aye. Some wounds run deep." Because he had a generous heart, he clapped a hand on Brigham's damp shoulder. "Called her a mule, did you?"

"I did." Brigham flicked his sodden lace. "And should have moved more quickly."

With a rumbling laugh, Ian gave Brigham's shoulder another slap. "If you've a mind to marry her, you'd best be a fast learner."

* * *

She wished she were dead. She wished Brigham were dead. She wished fervently that he had never been born. Setting her teeth, Serena scowled at her reflection as Maggie fussed with the curling irons.

"Your hair is so thick and soft. You'll never have to sleep in papers all night."

"As if I would," Serena mumbled. "I don't see why any woman goes to so much fuss and bother just for a man."

Maggie smiled the wise smile of a woman in love and engaged. "What other reason is there?"

"I wish I could wear mine up." Gwen scooted around to the mirror to study her own hair. "You did make it look so pretty, Maggie," she said, afraid of seeming ungrateful. "But Mother said I couldn't pin it up until next year."

"It looks like sunbeams," Serena told her, then went immediately back to frowning.

"Yours looks more like candlelight." Gwen sighed and tried a few dance steps. This would be her first ball, and her first gown. She could hardly wait to put it on and feel grown-up. "Do you think anyone will ask me to dance?"

"Everyone will." Maggie tested the iron.

"Perhaps someone will try to kiss me."

"If they do," Serena said grimly, "you're to tell me. I'll deal with them."

"You sound like Mother." With a light laugh, Gwen twirled in her petticoats. "It's not as though I would let anyone kiss me, but it would be so nice to have someone try."

"Keep talking like that, my lass, and Father will lock you up for another year."

"She's just excited." Expertly Maggie threaded a green riband edged in gold through Serena's hair. "So am I. It feels like my very first ball. There." She patted Serena's hair before she stepped back to study her handiwork. "You look beautiful. Or would, if you'd smile."

In answer, Serena bared her teeth in a grimace.

"That should send the men scurrying to the hills," Maggie commented.

"Let them run." Serena almost smiled at the thought. "I'd as soon see the back of them."

"Brigham won't run away," Gwen said wisely, earning a glare from her sister.

"It's of no concern to me what Lord Ashburn does." Serena flounced away to snatch her gown from the bed. Behind her back, Gwen and Maggie exchanged delighted grins.

"Well, he is rather stuffy, isn't he?" Maggie put her tongue in her cheek, then moved over to check her own gown for creases. "Handsome, certainly, if one likes dark, brooding looks and cool eyes."

"He isn't stuffy at all." Serena turned on her. "He's—" She caught herself, warned by Gwen's giggle. "Rude is what he is. Rude and annoying, and English."

Dutifully Gwen began hooking Maggie's gown. "He was kissing Rena in the kitchen."

Maggie's eyes went as round as saucers. "*What?*"

"Gwen!"

"Oh, it's just Maggie," Gwen said with a move of her bare shoulder. "We always tell her everything. He was kissing her right in the kitchen," Gwen continued, turning dreamy circles as she remembered it. "It was so romantic. He looked as though he might swallow her right up, like a sugarplum."

"That's enough." Hot and flushed, Serena struggled to step into her gown. "It wasn't romantic at all, it was infuriating and, and—" She wanted to say unpleasant, but couldn't get her tongue around the lie. "I wish he would go to the devil."

Maggie lifted a brow. "If you wished him to the devil, why didn't you tell me he had kissed you?"

"Because I'd forgotten all about it."

Gwen started to speak, but was hushed by a quick gesture from Maggie. "Well, I daresay there wasn't anything special about it, then." Calmly she began to hook Serena's gown. "My cousin Jamie is coming tonight, Rena. Perhaps you'll find him more to your taste."

Serena only groaned.

By the time Brigham escaped from Parkins's perfecting hands, he was frazzled and impatient. With the rumors and the unrest in both Scotland and England he felt little like partnering a bunch of simpering girls and plump matrons at a country ball. His summons back to London weighed on him. The support the Prince expected from his English followers wasn't as immediately forthcoming as he had hoped. There was a chance that adding his own voice would sway those who were straddling the political fence, but it would be a dangerous mission.

He had no way of knowing how long he would be gone, how successful he might be or, if he were found out, what would be the fate of his lands and title.

There would be dozens of Highland chiefs under the same roof that night. Loyalties would be tested, oaths would be sworn.

What he learned here he would take with him to London in hopes of stirring fighting blood among those English loyal to the Stuarts. It was a war that still dealt more in talk than in the sword. Like Coll, he was growing weary of it.

As he descended the steps toward the ballroom, he was the picture of the fashionable aristocrat. His lace was snowy, foaming from his throat, falling over his wrists. His buckles gleamed, as did the emerald on his finger. A matching one winked out of the lace at his throat. His black waistcoat was threaded with silver, topped by a silver-buttoned coat that fitted without a wrinkle over his shoulders.

At a glance, it would have appeared that he was a young, wealthy man, used to the finer things and unhampered by any care. But his thoughts were as bright and as dangerous as his dress sword.

"Lord Ashburn." Fiona curtsied as he entered. Since that morning she had been fretting over what her husband had told her of Brigham's feelings for her oldest daughter. More than Ian could, she understood the warring emotions Serena must be experiencing.

"Lady MacGregor. You look stunning."

She smiled, noting that his gaze was already sweeping the room. And she thought as she softened that the love in it was unmistakable. "Thank you, my lord. I hope you will enjoy the evening."

"I shall, if you promise me a dance."

"It would be a pleasure. But all the young ladies will be angry if I monopolize your time. Please, let me introduce you."

She laid her hand on his arm and led him into the room. It was already scattered with people, dressed in their best. Satin

162 of the hundreds

gowns glimmered and silk shimmered in the light of the hundreds of candles that floated in the chandeliers overhead or rose from high stands. Jewels gleamed and winked. Men were wrapped in dress kilts, plaids of bright reds and greens and blues contrasting with doublets of calfskin. Buckled brogues and silver buttons caught the light, vying for brilliance with the shine of women's jewels.

For the ladies' part, it was apparent that in the Highlands French fashions were watched closely. The more opulent styles were preferred, with an abundance of tinsel and silver lace in evidence. Hoops swished and swayed like bells. Heavy brocades in vivid shades were worn by both men and women, with thick gold ornamentation worked into dress coats and huge cuffs that covered the elbows. Stockings were white or clocked and worn with dressy garters.

Glenroe might have been remote, with the nearest shop half a day's ride away, but the Scots' love of fashion was no less than that of the Frenchman or the Englishman.

Brigham was introduced to the pretty and the plain by his hostess. When the music began, he would do his duty. For now, he curbed his impatience as he continued to scan the room for the one face he wanted to see. Willing or not, he was determined to lead her out in the first dance, and for as many others as he could manage.

"The little MacIntosh lass has the grace of a bullock," Coll confided in his ear. "If you find yourself shackled with her, best to offer to fetch her a drink and sit out the dance."

"I appreciate the warning." Brigham turned to examine his friend. "You look quite self-satisfied. Shall I take it that your interview with MacDonald went as you wished?"

Coll's chest puffed out. "You may take it that Maggie and I will be wed by May Day."

"My felicitations," Brigham said with a bow. Then he grinned. "I shall have to find someone else to drink under the table."

Coll snorted and fought off a blush. "Not likely. I wish I could ride with you to London."

"Your place is here now. I'll be back in a matter of weeks."

"With cheering news. We'll continue to work here, but not tonight. Tonight's for celebrating." He clapped a hand on Brigham's shoulder. "There's my Maggie now. If you want a turn with someone light on her feet, ask Serena to stand up with you. A foul temper she might have, but the lass can dance."

Brigham could only nod as Coll strode away to claim his betrothed. Beside the demure Maggie MacDonald, Serena stood like a flame, her hair dressed high, the rich green silk of the dress trimmed in gold and cut square at the neck to reveal the smooth swell of her breasts. There were pearls around her throat, gleaming dully, no whiter, no creamier, than her skin. Her skirts flared out, making her slender waist seem impossibly small.

Other women were dressed more opulently, some with their hair powdered, others with jewels glistening. They might have been hags dressed in burlap. Serena looked up at Coll and laughed. Brigham felt as though he'd taken a stroke of the broadsword across his knees.

As the strains of the first dance began, several young ladies cast a hopeful look in his direction. Brigham found his feet and moved across the room to Serena.

"Miss MacGregor." He made her an elegant bow. "Might I have the honor of this dance?"

She had made up her mind to refuse him, should he ask. Now

she found herself wordlessly offering her hand. The strains of a minuet floated through the room. Skirts rustled as ladies were led to their places by their partners. Suddenly she was certain she would never remember even the most basic steps. Then he smiled at her and bowed again.

It seemed her feet never touched the floor, and her eyes refused to leave his. She had dreamed of this once, standing in the chill air of the forest. There had been lights there, too, and music. But it hadn't been like this. This was like floating, like feeling beautiful, like believing in dreams.

His hand held hers lightly, fingertips to fingertips. It made her feel weak, as though she were caught up in his arms. They stepped together sedately, moved apart. Her heart thundered as though they were wrapped together, tumbling into an intimate embrace. His lips curved as she sank into her final curtsy. Hers warmed as if they had been kissed.

"Thank you." He didn't release her hand, as they both knew was proper, but brought her fingers to his lips. "I've wanted that dance since I found you alone by the river. Now, when I think of it, the only difficulty will be deciding whether you look more lovely in your green gown or in your breeches."

"It's Mother's. The gown—" she said quickly, and cursed herself for stammering. When he led her off the floor, she felt like a queen. "I want to apologize for this morning."

"No, you don't." Boldly he kissed her hand again. More than one murmur arose because of it. "You only think you should."

"Aye." She shot him a quick, amused look. "It's the least I can do after you saved me from the threat of a beating."

"Only the threat?"

"Father only has the heart to threaten. He's never taken a strap to me in my life, which is probably why I'm unmanageable."

"Tonight, my dear, you're only beautiful."

She flushed and lowered her eyes. "I don't know what to say when you speak like that."

"Good, Rena—"

"Miss MacGregor." Both Brigham and Serena looked impatiently at the intruder, a young son of one of the neighboring Highland lairds. "Would you honor me with this dance?"

She would have preferred honoring him with a kick in the shins, but she knew her duty too well. She laid a hand on his arm, wondering how soon it would be proper to dance with Brigham again.

The music played on—reels, country dances, elegant minuets. Serena danced with elderly gentlemen, sons, cousins, the portly and the dashing. Her love of dancing and her skill kept her in constant demand. She had one other set with Brigham, then was forced to watch him lead out one after another of the pretty guests.

He couldn't keep his eyes off her. Damn it, it wasn't like him to resent watching a woman dance with another man. Did she have to smile at them? No, by God, she didn't. And she had no business flirting with that skinny young Scot in the ugly coat. He fingered the hilt of his dress sword and fought back temptation.

What had her mother been thinking of to allow her to wear a dress that made her look so... delectable? Couldn't her father see that that young rake was all but drooling on his daughter's neck? Her bare neck. Her soft, white, naked skin, just at the point where the fragile line of her collarbone swelled into her breast.

He swore under his breath and earned a wide-eyed stare from Gwen. "I beg your pardon, Brig?"

"What?" He dragged his eyes away from Serena long enough to focus on her sister. He had no notion that his stormy looks had prevented half a dozen young swains from approaching Gwen for a dance. "Nothing, Gwen. It was nothing." He drew a deep breath and struggled for a casual tone. "Are you enjoying yourself?"

"Very much." She smiled up at him and secretly wished he would ask her to dance again. "I suppose you go to many balls and parties."

"In London, in the season, you can barely turn around without one."

"I would love to see London and Paris."

She looked very young at that moment, and he was reminded of how devotedly she had nursed her brother back to health. Some man, one day, he thought, and delighted her by kissing her fingers. "You, my dear, would be all the rage."

She was young enough to giggle without simpering. "Do you think so, really?"

"Without a doubt." Offering his arm, he led her onto the floor again and told her as many stories as he could recall about balls and assemblies and routs. Even as he spoke, his eyes were locked on Serena as she danced with her skinny partner. When the dance was over, Gwen had enough to dream on for years. Brigham had worked himself into a fine, shining, jealous rage.

He led her off the floor, watching as Serena was led in a different direction by her partner. One who was wearing, in Brigham's opinion, a particularly hideous yellow brocade. While the coat might have offended him, the possessive manner in which the man clutched Serena's hand did a great deal more.

"Who is that Serena's talking with?"

Gwen followed the direction Brigham was scowling into. "Oh, that's only Rob, one of Serena's suitors."

"Suitors?" He said between his teeth. "Suitors, is it?" Before Gwen could elaborate, he was striding across the room. "Miss MacGregor, a word with you?"

Her brow lifted at his tone. "Lord Ashburn, may I present Rob MacGregor, my kinsman."

"Your servant," he said stiffly. Then, taking Serena's elbow, he dragged her off toward the first convenient alcove.

"What do you think you're doing? Have you lost your senses? You'll have everyone staring."

"To hell with them." He stared down at her mutinous face. "Why was that popinjay holding your hand?"

Though she privately agreed that Rob MacGregor was a popinjay at his best, she refused to accept any slur on a kinsman. "Rob MacGregor happens to be a fine man of good family."

"The devil take his family." He had barely enough control left to keep his voice low. "Why was he holding your hand?"

"Because he wanted to."

"Give it to me."

"I will not."

"I said give it to me." He snatched it up. "He's no right to it, do you understand?"

"No. I understand that I'm free to give my hand to whomever I choose."

The cool light of battle came into his eyes. He preferred it, much preferred it, to the grinding heat of jealousy. "If you want your fine young man of good family to live, I wouldn't choose him again."

"Is that so?" She tugged at her hand and got nowhere. "Let me go this instant."

"So you can return to him?"

She wondered for a moment if Brigham was drunk, but decided against it. His eyes were too sharp and clear. "If I choose."

"If you choose, I promise you you will regret it. This dance is mine."

Moments before, she had longed to dance with him. Now she held her ground, equally determined not to. "I don't want to dance with you."

"What you want and what you'll do may be different matters, my dear."

"I will remind you, Lord Ashburn, only my father can command me."

"That will change." His fingers tightened on hers. "When I return from London—"

"You're going to London?" Her anger was immediately eclipsed by distress. "When? Why?"

"In two days. I have business there."

"I see." Her hand went limp in his. "Perhaps you had planned to tell me when you saddled your horse."

"I only just received word that I was needed." His eyes lost their fire, his voice its roughness. "Would you care that I go?"

"No." She turned her head away, to stare toward the music. "Why should I?"

"But you do." With his free hand he touched her cheek.

"Go or stay," she said in a desperate whisper. "It matters nothing to me."

"I go on behalf of the Prince."

"Then Godspeed," she managed.

"Rena, I will come back."

"Will you, my lord?" She pulled her hand away from his. "I wonder." Before he could stop her, she rushed back into the ballroom and threw herself into the dancing.

Chapter Nine

Perhaps she had been more unhappy in her life. But she couldn't remember when tears had seemed so miserably and inescapably close. Perhaps she had been angrier. But she could think of no time in her life when fury had raged quite so high or burned so hot.

And the fury and misery were all with herself, Serena thought as she kicked the mare into a gallop. With herself, for dreaming, even for a moment, that there could be something real, something lovely, between herself and Brigham.

He was going back to London. Aye, and London was where he belonged. In London he was a man of wealth and means and lineage. He was a man with parties to attend, ladies to call on. A line to continue. Swearing, she pushed the horse harder.

He might stand behind the Prince. She was coming to believe he was dedicated to the cause and would fight for it. But he would fight in England, for England. Why should he not? Why should a man like the earl of Ashburn waste a thought on her once he was back in his own world?

Just as she would waste no thought on him, she promised herself, once he was gone.

She knew he had met with her father and many of the other chiefs early that morning. Oh, women weren't supposed to know or bother themselves with plans of war and rebellions, but they knew. France would move on England, and when she did, Charles hoped to sway the French king to his cause.

The previous winter, Louis had planned to invade England with Charles in attendance as his father's representative. If the fleet had not been wrecked in a storm and the invasion abandoned... Well, that was another matter. It was clear that Louis had supported Charles because he wanted a monarch on the English throne who would be dependent on France. Just as it was clear Charles would use France or any means to gain his rightful place. But the invasion had been abandoned, and the French king was now biding his time.

Just because a body had to busy herself with sewing and cleaning didn't mean she had no head for politics.

So Brigham would go to London and beat the drum for the young Prince. It had become more important than ever to rally the Jacobites for the Stuarts, English and Scottish. The time for rebellion was ripe. Charles was not his father, and would not be content, as James had been, to while away his youth in foreign courts.

When the time came, Brigham would fight. But come back to the Highlands? Come back to her? No, she couldn't see it. A man didn't leave his home and country for a mistress. Desire her he might, but she already knew a man's desire was easily fanned, and easily cooled.

For her it was love. Her first. Her only. Without ever having taken her innocence, he had ruined her. There would never be another man for her. The only one she wanted was preparing even now to ride out of her life.

If he stayed, what difference would it make? she asked herself. There would always be too much between them. Had he loved her... No, even that would have changed nothing. Her beloved books had shown her time and time again that love did not necessarily conquer all. Romeo and Juliet. Tristan and Isolde, Lancelot and Guinevere. Serena MacGregor was no weak-moraled Guinevere, nor was she a starry-eyed Juliet. She was a Scot, hot-blooded perhaps, but tough-minded. She knew the difference between fantasy and fact. There was one fact that could not be ignored, now or ever.

Brigham would always be tied to England, and she to Scotland.

So it was best that he was going. She wished him well. She wished him to the devil.

"Serena?"

She whipped her head around to see Brigham racing up behind her. It was then she realized there were tears in her eyes. The shame of them, the need to keep them hers alone, had her wheeling back to drive her mount yet faster. Cursing the cumbersome sidesaddle, she made for the lake in a mad dash she hoped would leave Brigham behind. She planned to pass the water and ride up into the hills, into the rougher land where he would never be able to track her. Then she was swearing at him as he thundered to her side and snatched the reins from her hands.

"Hold up, woman. What devil's in you?"

"Leave me be." She kicked her horse, nearly unseating

Brigham as he struggled to hold both mounts. "Oh, damn you to hell. I hate you."

"Well you may after I take a whip to you," he said grimly. "Are you trying to kill both of us?"

"Just you." She sniffled, and despised herself for it.

"Why are you crying?" He drew her mount in closer to his as he studied her face. "Has someone hurt you?"

"No." Her hysterical laugh shocked her enough to make her swallow another. "No," she repeated. "I'm not crying. It's the wind in my eyes. Go away. I rode here to be alone."

"Then you'll have to be disappointed." She was crying, however much she denied it. He wanted to gather her close and comfort her, but he knew her well enough by now to know her response would be to sink her teeth into his hand. Instead, realizing it might be just as foolish, he tried reason. "I leave at first light tomorrow, Serena. There are things I wish to say to you first."

"Say them, then." She began searching her pockets for a handkerchief. "And go away to London, or to hell for all I care."

After casting his eyes to the heavens, Brigham offered her his handkerchief. "I would prefer dismounting."

She snatched the cloth to dry the hated tears. "Do what you want. It doesn't matter to me." She blew her nose heartily.

He did, taking care to keep her reins in his hand. After he had secured the horses, he reached up to help her down.

After a last defiant sniff, she stuffed the handkerchief into her pocket. "I don't want your help."

"You'll have more than that before I'm done with you." So saying, he plucked her with more speed than style from the saddle. He'd finished with reason. "Sit."

"I will not."

"Sit," he repeated, in a tone dangerous enough to have her chin jerking up. "Or, before God, you will wish you had."

"Very well." Because his eyes warned her it was no idle threat, she chose a rock, deliberately taking her time, smoothing her skirts, folding her hands primly in her lap. Perversely, now that he was growling she was determined to be proper. "You wished to converse with me, my lord?"

"I wish to throttle you, my lady, but I trust I have enough control left to resist."

She gave a mock shudder. "How terrifying. May I say, Lord Ashburn, that your visit to my home has broadened my perception of English manners."

"I've had enough of that." He moved so quickly she had only time to stare. Grasping the front of her riding jacket, he dragged her to her feet. "I am English, and not ashamed of it. The Langstons are an old and respected family." The way he held her, she was forced to stand on tiptoe, eye-to-eye with him. And his eyes were dark as onyx, with a heated fury in them only a few had seen and lived. "There is nothing in my lineage to make me blush, and much to make me proud to bear the name. I've had my fill of your slurs and insults, do you understand?"

"Aye." She thought she had understood what it was to be truly frightened. Until this moment, she hadn't known at all. Still, frightened didn't mean cowed. "It's not your family I mean to insult, my lord."

"Only me, then? Or perhaps the whole of England? Damn it, Rena, I know what your clan has suffered. I know that even now your name is so proscribed that many of you are forced to take others. It's a cruelty that's already gone on too long. But it wasn't I who brought the persecution, nor was it all of England. Insult me if you will, scratch or bite, but I'm damned if I'll take either for something that wasn't of my doing."

"Please," she said very quietly. "You're hurting me."

He let her go and curled his hands into fists at his sides. It was rare, very rare, for him to come that close to losing control of both thoughts and actions. As a result, his voice was ice.

"My apologies."

"No." She reached out tentatively, to touch his arm. "I apologize. You're right, it is wrong of me to lash out at you for many things that were done before either of us were born." She was no longer afraid, she realized, but shamed, deeply shamed. She would have done more than shout if anyone had slashed so at her family. "It's wrong to blame you because English dragoons raped my mother. Or because they put my father in prison for over a year so that even that dishonor went unavenged. And it's wrong," she continued after a long, cleansing breath, "to want to blame you because I'm afraid not to."

"Why, Rena? Why are you afraid?"

She started to shake her head and turn away, but he took her arms to hold her still. His grip wasn't fierce this time, but it was just as unbreakable.

"I hope you will forgive me, my lord. And now I would prefer to be alone."

"I shall have your answer, Serena." His voice was nearly calm again, but there was a thread of hot steel through it. "Why are you afraid?"

Raising her head, she sent him a damp, desperate look. "Because if I don't blame you I might forget who you are, what you are."

"Does it have to matter?" he demanded, shaking her a little.

"Aye." She discovered she was frightened again, but in a wholly different way. Something in his eyes told her that no matter what she said, no matter what she did, her fate was already sealed. "Aye, it has to. For both of us."

"Does it matter?" He dragged her against him. "Does it matter when we're like this?" Before she could answer, he closed his mouth over hers.

She didn't fight him. The moment his lips covered hers she knew she was through fighting him, and herself. If he was to be her first, her only, she needed to take whatever could be given. Now his mouth was hot and desperate on hers, his body taut as wire and straining against hers. Part was still temper, yes, she knew it. But there was more. It was the more she was ready to answer. If she had ever had a choice, she made it now, and caution flew to the winds.

"Does it matter?" he said again as he rained kisses over her face.

"No, no, it doesn't matter now, not today." She threw her arms around him and clung. "Oh, Brig, I don't want you to go. I don't want you to leave me."

With his face buried in her hair, he memorized her scent. "I'll come back. Three weeks, four at the most, I'll come back." When he received no response, he drew her away. Her eyes were dry now but solemn. "I will be back, Serena. Can't you trust even that?"

"I trust you more than I thought I would ever trust any man." She smiled a little and lifted a hand to his face. Oh, God, if this was love, why should it hurt so? Why couldn't it bring her the joy she saw in Maggie's eyes? "No, I don't trust you'll come back to me. But we'll not speak of that." She moved her hand to cover his lips when he would have spoken. "We'll not think of it. Only of today."

"Then we'll talk of other things."

"No." She kissed both of his hands, then stepped back. "We won't talk at all." Slowly she began to unfasten the buttons of her riding habit.

"What are you doing?"

He reached out to stop her, but she slipped the snug jacket from her shoulders, revealing a simple chemise and small, high breasts. "Taking what both of us want."

"Rena." He managed her name, though the pulse beating at his throat made the word low and rough. "Not like this. This isn't right for you."

"How could it be more right?" But her fingers trembled slightly as she unhooked her skirt. "Here, with you."

"There are things that need to be said," he began.

"I want you," she murmured, halting his words and his thoughts. "I want you to touch me the way you touched me before. I want—I want you to touch me the way you've made me dream of." She stepped closer. "Do you not want me any longer?"

"Not want you?" He closed his eyes and dragged an unsteady hand through his hair. "There is no one and nothing I've ever wanted more than I want you at this moment. God help me, there may never be again."

"Then take me here." She reached for her laces, watching in a kind of dazed wonder as his gaze dipped down. "And give me something of yourself before you leave me." Taking his hand, she pressed her lips to his palm. "Show me what it is to be loved, Brigham."

"Rena—"

"You're leaving tomorrow," she said, suddenly desperate. "Will you leave me with nothing, then?"

He let his fingers trail along her cheek. "I would not leave at all if the choice were mine."

"But you will go. I want to belong to you before you do."

Her shoulders were cool to his touch. "Are you certain?"

"Aye." With a smile, she laid his hand on her heart. "Feel how fast it beats? Always when I'm close to you."

"You're cold," he said unsteadily, and pulled her closer.

"There's a plaid on the mare." With her eyes closed, she drew in his scent. As he had with her hair, she committed it to memory. "If we spread it in the sun we'll be warm enough."

"I won't hurt you." He lifted her face, and she saw that the intensity was back in his eyes. "I swear it."

She trusted him for that, trusted him to be gentle. It was in his eyes as they spread the plaid on the bank of the lake and knelt upon it. It was in his lips as he lowered them to her bare white shoulder. It was in his hands as they clasped hers, communicating care as much as need.

She knew what she was about to do, what she was about to give him—the innocence a woman could give to only one man, and only once in her life. As they knelt face-to-face with the sun warm overhead and the waters cool beside them, she knew she hadn't offered the gift on impulse or in the madness of passion, but almost quietly, with a confidence that it would be accepted with tenderness. And remembered.

She had never looked more beautiful, he thought. Her eyes were brilliant, steady. Her hands didn't tremble as they locked with his, but he thought he could almost feel the nervous beating of her heart through his fingertips. Her cheeks were pale, as smooth and white as porcelain.

He thought of the shepherdess, of how he had wanted to touch it as a child but had been afraid, lest his hands grow clumsy. He brought her hands to his lips. He would not be clumsy with Serena.

He kissed her and filled himself with the flavor alone. Though their time together now would be short, he treated the moment as if it could last for hours. With slow, tortuous nibbles he had her breath quickening. His tongue moistened and traced, then lured hers into a lazy duel that made her heart swell and thunder in her breast. Tentatively at first, she ran her hands along his coat, as if making certain his body was warm and real beneath. Murmuring something against her mouth, he began to shrug out of it. Her own shyness surprised her. She fought it back as she helped him strip it off, and as she fumbled with the buttons of his waistcoat.

He found it almost unbearably arousing to have her inexperienced hands undress him. With his eyes closed he traced kisses over her brow, her temples, her jaw, while his body tensed and hardened from the hesitant movements of her fingers. It was torture of the most exquisite kind. He realized that he was moving slowly not only for Serena and her innocence but for himself. Every instant, every heartbeat they shared here would be remembered.

She tugged off his shirt, her gaze skimming down over his bare flesh as delicately as her fingertips did. Slowly, almost afraid her hand might pass through him, she reached out to touch.

They were still kneeling, their bodies swaying closer, their breath mingling as mouth was drawn to mouth. Her mind began to whirl as she stroked her hands over him. His skin was smooth, while the muscles beneath were hard. She felt awe, as well as excitement, wonder, as well as nerves. Who would have thought a man could feel beautiful?

The sun warmed his skin as it poured over the little patch of ground they had chosen. Birds trilled in the wood beyond. On the far side of the lake, deer came quietly to drink.

As he nuzzled her neck, she felt herself go weak. She thought she knew what was to follow, but the pleasure was more than she had ever dreamed it could be.

His hands were very sure as they cupped her breasts, dragging a moan out of her as the rough material shifted and rubbed over her skin. In submission, in acceptance, in demand, her back arched and her head fell back, leaving him free to plunder. She felt his mouth cover her, nipping and sucking through the material. The tingling started deep within her stomach and spread until her body seemed alive with nerves. Then what had gone before vanished from her mind as he peeled the chemise aside and found her flesh.

She cried out in surprise and pleasure, her hands reaching for his shoulders and gripping for balance. Yet she felt as though she were falling still.

She shuddered against him, strained against him, confused, delighted, desperate for more. What she had offered, she had offered of her own free will. What she gave now, she gave without thought, without reason. When she tumbled back on the blanket, she was stripped of defenses and open to whatever commands he might give.

He had to fight back the first sharp-edged need to take. It was like a knife turning slowly in his gut. Her arms were wrapped around him, her breasts, small and white, shivering at each touch. He saw that her eyes were clouded, not with fear, no longer with confusion, but with newly awakened passions. If he were to take her now, as his body begged to, she would open for him.

But the need in his heart beat as strong as the need in his loins. He would give her more than she had asked, perhaps more than either of them could understand.

"I've dreamed of this, Serena." His voice was low as he bent his head for the next kiss. "I've dreamed of undressing you like this." He slipped the chemise from her. Now only the breeze and Brigham caressed her. "Of touching what no man has touched." He skimmed a fingertip up her thigh and watched her mouth tremble open in speechless pleasure.

"Brigham. I want you."

"And you shall have me, my love." He circled the rigid point of her breast with his tongue, then drew it slowly, almost painfully, into his mouth. "Before you do, there is much, much more."

If she could have spoken again, she would have said it was impossible. Her body seemed sated already, sensation rolling over sensation, shudder racked by shudder. Then he began.

The eyes that had begun to close flew open in stunned awakening. Her hips arched up, meeting his questing lips just before the first flood of terrifying pleasure poured through her. Gasping, she groped for him, only to find her damp palms sliding off his skin as he moved over her, lighting fires where he willed.

The roaring in her ears prevented her from hearing herself call his name again and again. But he heard. Nothing he had heard before or would hear again would ever sound quite so sweet. She moved under him, bucking, twisting, trembling as he found and exploited new secrets. The dark taste of passion filled his mouth, driving him to find more, to give more.

Her skin was hot and damp wherever he touched, making him mad with thoughts of how she would be when he filled her. Could she know how weak she made him, how completely she satisfied him? His mind teemed with thoughts of her, memories he knew would follow him until he died. Each time he took a breath he drew in the scent of her skin, sheened now with her passion and his. No other woman would ever tempt him again, because no other woman would be Serena.

She wanted to beg him to stop. She wanted to beg him never to stop. Each breath she dragged into her lungs seemed to clog there until she feared she would die from lack of air or the surplus of it. Her eyes filled with tears, not from sorrow or regret but from the ache of a beauty so great she knew she could never describe it. Her strength ebbed and flowed, rushing into her like wildfire, then pouring out like a waterfall. But weak or strong, she had never known pleasure so huge. In some corner of her brain she wanted to know if he felt the same. But each time she began to ask, he would touch her again and send her thoughts spinning into a void of sensation.

When his lips came back to hers, she tasted desperation on them. Wanting to soothe, she answered with her heart, pulling him close.

He slipped into her, fighting with every fiber of his being to take her gently, struggling against every urge to plunge in to his own satisfaction. Sweat pooled at the base of his spine. The muscles in his arms quivered as he braced over her and watched, as he had dreamed of watching, her face as he made her his.

She cried out, but not in pain. Perhaps there was pain, but it was so smothered in pleasure that she couldn't feel it. Only him. She could feel only him as he moved into her, became part of her. With her eyes open and focused on his, she matched his rhythm. Slow…beautifully, gloriously slow. The moment when they joined would be savored, like the finest of old wines, the purest of promises.

He bent to take her lips again and swallowed her sigh. He could feel her pulse around him as clearly as he could feel her hands stroke down his back. When he thrust deep inside her, she arched and the sigh became a moan. Now it was she who changed the rhythm and he who followed. It no longer mattered who was rider, who was ridden, as they raced together. His last thought as his pleasure burst into her was that he had found home.

She wasn't certain she would ever move again, or that she would ever wish to. Her skin was cooling now that the heat of passion had faded into a softer glow of contentment. They lay tangled in the blanket, with the shadows growing long around them. His face was buried in her hair, his hand cupped loosely at her breast.

How much time had passed she couldn't be sure. She knew the sun was no longer high overhead, but there was a timelessness she needed to cling to for just a little longer.

It was almost possible, if she kept her eyes closed and refused to think, to believe it would always be like this. With the afternoon shimmering around them, the woods quiet but for the call of birds, it was difficult to believe that politics and war could pull them apart.

She loved as she had never thought to love, in a way she

hadn't known was possible. If only it could all be as simple as a blanket spread beside the water.

"I love you, Rena."

She opened her eyes to see that he was watching her. "Aye. I know you do. And I love you." She traced her fingers along his face as if to memorize it. "I wish we could stay like this."

"We'll be like this again. Soon."

She shifted away from him to reach for her chemise.

"Can you doubt that? Now?"

It was more important than ever to keep her voice steady. She loved him too much, much too much, to beg him to stay. She began to lace up her bodice. "I know that you love me, and that you wish it could be so. I know that what we shared here will never be shared with anyone else."

"You don't think I'll come back." He dragged his shirt on and wondered how any one woman could pull so many emotions from his heart.

She touched his hand. She had no regrets, and she needed him to understand that. "I think if you come back, you'll come for the sake of the Prince. It's right that you should."

"I see." He began to dress methodically. "So you believe what happened here between us will be forgotten when I reach London."

"No." She stopped struggling with her own buttons and reached for him. "No, I believe what happened here will be remembered always. When I'm very old and I feel the first hint of spring I'll think of today and of you."

The anger came quickly, making him dig his fingers into her arms. "Do you think that's enough for me? If you do, you're either very stupid or mad."

"It's all there can be—" she began, but her words slipped down her throat as he shook her.

"When I come back to Scotland, I come for you. Make no mistake, Serena. And when this war is over, I'll take you with me."

"If I had only myself to think of, I would go." She clutched at his coat, willing him to understand. "Can't you see that I would die slowly with the shame to my family?"

"No, by God, I can't see that being my wife would bring your family shame."

"Your wife?" She could barely whisper the words, then jerked back as if he had slapped her. "Marriage?"

"Of course marriage. What did you think—?" Then he saw, and saw clearly, just what it was she believed he was asking her. His anger turned inward until it was a dull heat in the pit of his stomach. "Is this what you thought I meant the last time we were here?" he demanded. "Is this what you needed to think through?" His laugh was quick and humorless. "You think highly of me, Serena."

"I…" Because her legs were weak, she sank limply onto a rock. "I thought…I understood that men took mistresses, and…"

"And so they do," he said curtly. "And so I have, but only a dim-witted fool would have thought I was offering you anything but my heart and my name."

"How was I supposed to know you meant marriage?" She sprang up to face him again. "You never said so."

"I've already spoken with your father." His voice was stiff as he snatched up the plaid.

"You've spoken with my father?" she repeated, measuring each word. "You spoke with my father without ever speaking to me?"

"It's proper to ask your father's permission."

"The devil with proper." She grabbed the blanket from him. "You had no right going behind my back to him without ever saying a word to me."

He took a long look at her tumbled hair, at her lips, still swollen from his. "I believe I did more than say a word to you, Serena."

She flushed, then marched over to toss the blanket over her horse. "I'm not so green that I think what has passed here always leads to marriage." She might have struggled into the saddle if Brigham hadn't whirled her around.

"Do you think I'm in the habit of seducing virgins and then making them my mistresses?"

"I don't know your habits."

"Then know this," he began as the horse danced skittishly aside. "I intend you for my wife."

"You intend. *You* intend." She shoved him away. "Perhaps in England you can bully, my lord, but here I have some say in my life. And I say I won't marry you, and you must be mad to think it."

"Did you lie when you said you love me?" he demanded.

"No. No, but—" The words were lost as his lips crushed down on hers.

"Then you lie when you say you won't be my wife."

"I can't be," she said desperately. "How can I leave here and go with you to England?"

His fingers tensed on her arms. "So, it comes down to that once more."

"You must see, you must, how it would be." She began to speak very fast, taking his arms, as well, willing him to understand. "I would live there because I loved you, because you asked it of me, and end by bringing shame on both of us. You would hate me before a year had passed. I'm not meant to be an earl's wife, Brigham."

"An English earl," he corrected.

She took the time to draw a deep breath. "I'm a laird's daughter, it's true, but I'm not fool enough to believe that's enough. I would hate being trapped in London when I want to ride through the hills. You yourself have told me more than once that I'm not a lady. I'll never be one. I would make a poor wife for the earl of Ashburn."

"Then you will make a poor one, but you will be my wife."

"No." She dried her cheeks with her knuckles. "I will not."

"You'll have no choice, Rena, when I go to your father and tell him I've compromised you."

The tears stopped, to be replaced by shock, then fury. "You wouldn't dare."

"I would," he said grimly.

"He would kill you."

Brigham only raised his brow. Beneath them, his eyes were dark and growing cold. Men he had faced in battle would have recognized the look. "I believe the father is not quite so blood-thirsty as the daughter." Before she could speak again, he lifted her into the saddle. "If you refuse to marry me because you love me, then you will marry me because you are commanded."

"I would rather marry a two-headed toad."

He launched himself into his saddle beside her. "But you will marry me, my dear, smiling or weeping. My journey to London should give you time to think sensibly. I will speak with your father and make arrangements when I return."

After sending him a furious look, Serena kicked her heels. She hoped he broke his neck on the ride to London.

And when he left the following morning, she wept her own broken heart into her pillow.

Chapter Ten

He had missed London, the pace of it, the look of it, the smell of it. Most of his life had been spent there or at the graceful old manor home of his ancestors in the country. He was well-known in polite society and had no trouble finding company for a game of cards at one of the fashionable clubs or interesting conversation over dinner. Mothers of marriageable daughters made certain to include the wealthy earl of Ashburn on their guest lists.

He had been six weeks in town, and spring was at its best. His own garden, one of the finest in the city, boasted vistas of lush lawns and colorful blossoms. The rain that had drummed almost incessantly as April had begun had worked its magic and was now replaced by balmy golden days that lured pretty women in their silk dresses and feathered hats into the parks and shops.

There were balls and assemblies, card parties and levees. A man with his title, his reputation and his purse could have a comfortable life here with little inconvenience and much pleasure.

He had indeed missed London. It was his home. It had taken

him much less than six weeks to discover that it was no longer his heart.

That was in Scotland now. Not a day passed that he didn't think of the hard Highland winter or of how Serena had warmed it. As he looked out at the crowded streets and the strollers in their walking coats and hats of the latest fashion, he wondered what spring was like in Glenroe. And whether Serena ever sat by the lake and thought of him.

He would have gone back weeks earlier, but his work for the Prince was taking longer than had been thought, and the results were less satisfactory than anyone had foreseen.

The Jacobites in England were great in number, but the number among them who showed eagerness to raise their sword for the untried Prince was much less. On Lord George's advice, Brigham had spoken to many groups, giving them an outline of the mood of the Highland clans and conveying what communications he had received from the Prince himself. He had ridden as far as Manchester, and had held a council as close as his own drawing room.

Each was as risky as the other. The government was uneasy, and the rumor of war with France louder than ever. Stuart sympathizers would not be suffered gladly, and active supporters would be imprisoned, at best. Memories of public executions and deportations were still fresh.

After six weeks he had the hope, but only the hope, that if Charles could act quickly, and begin his campaign, his English followers would join him.

They had so much to lose, Brigham thought. How well he knew it. Homes, lands, titles. It was a difficult thing to fight for something as distant as a cause when you gambled your name and your fortune, as well as your life.

Turning, he studied the portrait of his grandmother. His decision had already been made. Perhaps it had been made when he had still been a schoolboy, his head on her knee as she wove tales of exiled kings and a fight for justice.

It was dangerous to tarry much longer in London. The government had a way of uncovering rebels and dealing with them with nasty efficiency. Thus far, Brigham's name had kept him above suspicion, but he knew rumors were flying. Now that war with France was once more inevitable, so was talk of a new Jacobite uprising.

Brigham had never hidden his travels to France, to Italy, to Scotland. If anyone decided to shift the blocks of his last few years around, they would come up with a very interesting pattern.

So he must leave, Brigham thought, kicking a smoldering log in the dying fire. This time, he would go alone and under the cover of night. When he returned to London next, it would be with Serena. And they would stand where he stood now and toast the true king and his regent.

He returned to Scotland for the Prince, as Serena had said. But he also returned to claim what was his. Rebellion aside, there was one battle he was determined to win.

Hours later, as Brigham was preparing to leave for a quiet evening at his club, his sober-faced butler intercepted him.

"Yes, Beeton?"

"Your pardon, my lord." Beeton was so old one could almost hear the creak of his bones as he bowed. "The earl of Whitesmouth requests a word with you. It seems to be a matter of some urgency."

"Then show him up." Brigham grimaced as Parkins fussed over his coat, looking for any sign of lint. "Leave off, man. You'll drive me to a fit."

"I only desire my lord to show himself to his best advantage."

"Some of the female persuasion would argue that to do that I must strip." When Parkins remained stone-faced, Brigham merely sighed. "You're a singularly humorless fellow, Parkins. God knows why I keep you."

"Brig." The earl of Whitesmouth, a small, smooth-faced man only a few years Brigham's senior, strode into the room, then pulled up short at the sight of the valet. It only took a glance to see that Whitesmouth was highly agitated.

"That will be all for this evening, Parkins." As if he had all the time in the world, Brigham crossed to the table by the bedroom fire and poured wine into two glasses. He waited until he heard the adjoining door click quietly shut. "What is it, Johnny?"

"We have trouble, Brig." He accepted the glass, and downed the contents in one swallow.

"I surmised as much. Of what nature?"

Steadier for the drink, Whitesmouth continued. "That pea-brained Miltway drank himself into a stupor with his mistress this afternoon and opened his mouth too wide for any of us to be comfortable."

After taking a long breath, Brigham sipped and gestured to a chair. "Did he name names?"

"We can't be sure, but it seems likely he spilled at least a few. Yours being the most obvious."

"And his mistress… She's the redheaded dancer?"

"The hair on her head's red," Whitesmouth stated crudely. "She's a knowing little package, Brigham, a bit too old and too experienced for a stripling like Miltway. Trouble is, the young idiot has more money than brains."

Miltway's romantic liaisons were the last of Brigham's concerns. "Will she keep quiet, for a bribe?"

"It's too late for that. That's why I've come. She's already passed on some of the information, enough that Miltway's been arrested."

Brigham swore viciously. "Young fool."

"The odds are keen that you'll be questioned, Brigham. If you have anything incriminating—"

"I am not that young," Brigham interrupted as he began to think ahead. "Nor such a fool." He paused a moment, wanting to be certain his decision was made logically and not on impulse. "And you, Johnny? Will you be able to cover yourself?"

"I have urgent business on my estate." The earl of Whitesmouth grinned. "In fact, I have been en route several hours already."

"The Prince will do well with men like you."

Whitesmouth poured a second drink and toasted his friend. "And you?"

"I'm for Scotland. Tonight."

"Flight now will show your hand, Brig. Are you ready for that?"

"I'm weary of pretense. I stand for the Prince."

"Then I'll wish you a safe journey, and wait for word from you."

"God willing, I shall send it soon." He picked up his gloves again. "I know you've run a risk by coming to tell me when you could have been on your way. I shan't forget it."

."The Prince has my pledge, as well," Whitesmouth reminded him. "I pray you won't tarry too long."

"Only long enough. Have you told anyone else about Miltway's indiscretion?"

"That's a cool way of putting it," Whitesmouth muttered. "I thought it best to come to you directly."

Brigham nodded. "I'll spend a few hours at the club as I had planned and make certain word is passed. You'd best get out of London before someone notes that you are not indeed en route to your estate.

"On my way." Whitesmouth picked up his hat. "One warning, Brig. The elector's son, Cumberland. Don't take him lightly. It's true he's young, but his eyes are cold and his ambition hot."

The club held many faces familiar to Brigham. Games were being played, bottles already draining. He was greeted cheerfully enough and invited to join groups at cards or dice. Making easy excuses, he strolled over to the fire to share a bottle of burgundy with Viscount Leighton.

"No urge to try your luck tonight, Ashburn?"

"Not at cards." Behind them, someone complained bitterly about the fall of the dice. "It's a fair night," Brigham said mildly. "One well suited for traveling."

Leighton sipped, and though his eyes met Brigham's, they gave away nothing. "Indeed. There is always talk of storms to the north."

"I have a feeling there will be a storm here sooner." The dice game grew noisier. Brigham took advantage of the noise to lean forward and pour more wine in the glasses. "Miltway confided his political leanings to his mistress and has been arrested."

Leighton said something unflattering about Miltway under his breath, then settled back. "How loose a tongue has he?"

"I can't be sure, but there are some who should be put on guard."

Leighton toyed with the diamond pinned to the lace at his throat. He was fond of such trinkets, and was often taken for a man who preferred a soft life. Like Brigham, he had made his decision to back the Prince coolly and without reservation.

"Consider it done, my dear. Do you wish for company on your journey?"

Brigham was tempted. Viscount Leighton, with his pink waist-coats and perfumed hands, might have looked like a self-indul-gent fop, but there was no one Brigham would have chosen over him in a fight. "Not at the moment."

"Then shall we drink to fair weather?" Leighton lifted his glass, then gave a mildly annoyed glance over Brigham's shoul-der. "I believe we should patronize another club, my dear Ash-burn. This establishment has begun to open its doors to anyone."

Brigham glanced around idly to the game. He recognized the man holding the bank, and most of the others. But there was a thin man leaning on the table, a sulky look in his eyes, a half-filled glass by his elbow. He was not taking his losses in a man-ner acceptable to polite society.

"Don't know him." Brigham sipped again, thinking that he might never again sit cozily by the fire in this club and drink with a friend.

"I've had the dubious pleasure." Leighton took out a snuffbox. "An officer. I believe he's off to cross swords with the French quite soon, which should make the ladies sigh. However, I am told that he is not in favor with our ladies any longer, despite the romantic figure he attempts to cut."

With a laugh, Brigham prepared to take his leave. "Perhaps it has something to do with his lack of manners."

"Perhaps it has something to do with his treatment of Alice Beesley when she was unfortunate enough to be his mistress."

Brigham raised a brow, but was still only vaguely curious. The game was growing louder yet, the hour later, and he still needed Parkins to pack his bag. "The lovely Mrs. Beesley is a dim-witted piece, but from what I'm told, quite amiable."

"Standish apparently thought she wasn't amiable enough and took a riding crop to her."

Brigham's eyes registered distaste as he glanced over again. "There is something particularly foul about a man who…" He trailed off and his fingers tightened on his glass. "Did you say Standish?"

"I did. A colonel, I believe. He earned a particularly nasty reputation in the Porteous scandal in '35." Leighton flicked a flake of snuff from his sleeve. "It seems he quite enjoyed sacking and burning and looting. I believe that's why he was promoted."

"He would have been a captain in '35."

"Possibly." Interest flickered in Leighton's eyes. "Do you know him after all?"

"Yes." Brigham remembered well Coll's story of Captain Standish and the rape of his mother, the houses burned, the defenseless crofters routed. And Serena. He rose, and though his eyes were cold, there was nothing of his temper in his voice. "I believe we should become better acquainted. I fancy a game after all, Leighton."

"It grows late, Ashburn."

Brigham smiled. "Indeed it does."

Nothing was easier than joining the game. Within twenty minutes he had bought the bank. His luck held, and as fate or justice would have it, so did Standish's. The colonel continued to lose and, egged on by Brigham's mild disdain, he bet heavily. By midnight, there were only three left in the game. Brigham signaled for more wine as he sprawled easily in his chair. He had deliberately matched drink for drink with Standish. Brigham had no intention of killing a man whose faculties were less sharp than his own.

"The dice appear to dislike you this evening, Colonel."

"Or they like others too well."

Standish's words were blurred by drink and bitterness. He was a man who required greater sums of money than his soldier's pay to back his lust for gambling, and his equal lust for a place in society. Tonight his bitterness stemmed from a failure to achieve either. His offer for a well-endowed—both physically and financially—young lady had been turned down only that afternoon. Standish was certain the bitch Beesley had gone whining to whomever would listen. She'd been a whore, he thought as he swilled down more wine. A man had a right to treat a whore however he chose.

"Get on with it," he ordered, then counted the fall of Brigham's dice. Snatching up the dice box, he threw and fell short.

"Pity." Brigham smiled and drank.

"I don't care to have the bank switched so late in the game. It spoils the luck."

"Yours seemed poor all evening, Colonel." Brigham continued to smile, but the look in his eyes had driven more than one man away from the game. "Perhaps you consider it unpatriotic that I'm fleecing a royal dragoon, but here we are only men, after all."

"Did we come to play or to talk?" Standish demanded, signaling impatiently for more wine.

"In a *gentlemen's* club," Brigham replied, coloring his words with contempt, "we do both. But then Colonel, perhaps you don't often find yourself in the company of gentlemen."

The third player decided the game was a bit too uneasy for his taste. Several of the other patrons had stopped what they were doing to look, and to listen. Other games were abandoned as men began to loiter around the table. Standish's face reddened. He wasn't certain, but he thought he had been insulted.

"I spend most of my time fighting for the king, not lounging in clubs."

"Of course." Brigham tossed again, and again topped the colonel's roll. "Which explains why you are inept at polite games of chance."

"You seem a bit too skilled, my lord. The dice have fallen for you since you took your seat."

"Have they?" Brigham glanced up to raise a brow at Leighton, who was idly swirling a drink of his own. "Have they indeed?"

"You know damn well they have. It seems more than luck to me."

Brigham fingered the lace at his throat. Behind them the club fell into uncomfortable silence. "Does it? Perhaps you'll enlighten me by telling me what it seems to you."

Standish had lost more than he could afford to, drunk more than was wise. He looked across at Brigham and hated him for being what and who he was. Aristocrats, he thought, and wanted to spit. It was for wastrels like this that soldiers fought and died.

"Enlighten everyone. Break the dice."

The silence roared into murmurs. Someone leaned over to tug on Brigham's sleeve. "He's drunk, Ashburn, and not worth it."

"Are you?" Still smiling, Brigham leaned forward. "Are you drunk, Standish?"

"I am not." He was beyond drunk now. As he sat he felt every eye on him. Staring at him, he thought. Popinjays and fops with their titles and smooth manners. They thought him beneath them because he had taken a whip to a whore. He'd like to take a whip to all of them, he thought, tossing back the rest of his wine. "I'm sober enough to know the dice don't fall for only one man unless they're meant to."

Brigham waved a hand toward the dice, but his eyes were sharp as steel. "Break them, by all means."

There was a rush of protests, a flurry of movements. Brigham ignored both and kept his eyes on Standish. It pleased him a great deal to see the sweat begin to pearl on the colonel's forehead.

"My lord, I pray you won't act rashly. This isn't necessary." The proprietor had brought the hammer as requested, but stood casting worried glances from Brigham to Standish.

"I assure you it's quite necessary." When the proprietor hesitated, Brigham whipped his rapier gaze up. "Break them."

With an unsteady hand, the proprietor did as he was bid. There was silence again as the hammer smashed down, showing the dice to be clean. Standish only stared at the pieces that lay on the green baize. Tricked, he thought. Somehow the bastards had tricked him. He wished them dead, all of them, every one of the pale-faced, soft-voiced bastards.

"You seem to be out of wine, Colonel." And Brigham tossed the contents of his glass in Standish's face.

Standish leaped up, wine dripping down his cheeks like blood. Drink and humiliation had done its work well. He would have drawn his sword if others hadn't stepped in to hold his arms. Brigham never moved from where he sat sprawled in his chair.

"You will meet me, sir."

Brigham examined his cuff to be certain none of the wine had spattered it. "Naturally. Leighton, my dear, you will stand for me?"

Leighton took a pinch of snuff. "Of course."

Just before dawn they stood in a meadow a few minutes' ride from the city. There was a mist nearly ankle high, and the sky was purple and starless, as it was caught between night and day. Leighton let out a weary sigh as he watched Brigham turn back his lace.

"You have your reasons, I suppose, dear boy."

"I have them."

Leighton frowned at the rising sun. "I trust they are good enough to delay your trip."

He thought of Serena, of the look on her face when she had spoken of her mother's rape. He thought of Fiona, with her small, slender hands. "They are."

"The man is a pig, of course." Leighton frowned again, this time down at the moisture the dew had transferred to his gleaming boot. "Still, it hardly seems reason enough to stand about in a damp field at this hour. But if you must, you must. Do you intend to kill him?"

Brigham flexed his fingers. "I do."

"Be quick about it, Ashburn. This business has postponed my breakfast." So saying, he strolled off to confer with Standish's second, a young officer who was pale with both fear and excitement at the idea of a duel. The swords were judged acceptable. Brigham took one, letting his hand mold to the hilt, weighing it as though he had a mind to purchase it rather than draw blood.

Standish stood ready, even eager. The sword was his weapon. Ashburn wouldn't be the first he had killed with it, nor would he be the last. Though he might, Standish thought as he remembered the stares and murmurs of the night, be the most pleasurable. He had no doubt that he would cut down the young prig quickly and ride home in triumph.

They made their bows. Eyes locked. Sword touched sword in salute. Then the quiet meadow rang with the crash of steel against steel.

Brigham measured his opponent from the first thrust. Standish was no fool with a sword, had obviously been well-trained and had kept himself in fighting trim. But his style was a bit too aggressive. Brigham parried, putting Serena out of his mind. He preferred to fight emotionlessly, using that as a weapon, as well as his blade.

The ground was rich with dew, and the mist silenced the slide and fall of boots. There was only the song of metal slicing over metal as the birds quieted. Their swords slid from tip to hilt as they came in close. Their breath mingled like that of lovers through the deadly cross of blades.

"You are handy with a sword, Colonel," Brigham said as they drew apart to circle. "My compliments."

"Handy enough to slice your heart, Ashburn."

"We shall see." The blades kissed again, once, twice, three

times. "But I don't suppose you required a sword when you raped Lady MacGregor."

Puzzlement broke Standish's concentration, but he managed to block Brigham's thrust before the sword could run home. His brow darkened as he realized he had been led to this duel like a mongrel on a leash.

"One doesn't rape a whore." He attacked, fueled by a drumming rage. "What is the Scots bitch to you?"

Brigham's wrist whipped the sword up. "You shall die wondering."

They fought in silence now, Brigham cold as Highland ice, Standish hot with rage and confusion. Blades hissed and rang, competing now with the sound of labored breathing. In a daring move, Standish feinted, kissed his sword off Brigham's, sliced in *contre écart*. A red stain bloomed on Brigham's shoulder.

A cooler head might have used the wound to his advantage. Standish saw only the blood, and with the smell of it scented victory. He came in hard, judging himself moments away from triumph. Brigham countered thrust after thrust, biding his time as the blood dripped down his arm and into the thinning mist. He pulled back a fraction, an instant, laying his chest bare. The light of victory came into Standish's eyes as he leaped forward to open Brigham's heart.

With a bright flash of metal, Brigham knocked the sword aside moments before it pierced him. With a speed Leighton would claim later made the blade a blur, he twisted and plunged the point into the colonel's chest. Standish was dead before Brigham had pulled the point free.

Beside the pale-faced soldier, Leighton examined the body.

"Well, you've killed him, Ashburn. Best be on your way while I deal with the mess."

"My thanks." Brigham handed Leighton the sword, hilt first. "Shall I bind up your hurts, as well?"

With faint amusement, Brigham glanced over to his horse. Beside it, the estimable Parkins sat on another. "My valet will see to it."

Serena awoke just before dawn. She hadn't slept well for the past week, ever since a dream from which she had woken with her heart hammering. She had been sure then, somehow, that Brigham was in danger.

Even now, the moment of fear haunted her, adding to the ache she had lived with since he'd left. But that was foolish, she told herself. He was in London, safe. With a sigh, she sat up, knowing sleep was impossible. He was in London, she repeated. He might as well have been worlds away.

For a little while she had allowed herself to believe he would come back, as he'd said he would. Then the weeks had passed and she had stopped looking down the path at the sound of horses. Coll and Maggie had been married more than a week. It had been at their wedding that Serena had finally allowed hope to die. If he hadn't come back for Coll's wedding, he wasn't coming back.

She had known it, Serena reminded herself as she washed and dressed. When she had given herself to him on the banks of the loch, she had known it. And had sworn there would be no regrets. She had known, she told herself now as she bound back her hair. She had known, and she had been given everything she could have wanted.

Except that the afternoon she had spent in Brigham's arms hadn't made her quicken. She had hoped, though she had known it mad, that she would find herself with Brigham's child.

That wasn't to be. All she had left were her memories.

Still, she had her family, her home. It helped fill the gaps. She was strong enough to live her life without him. She might never be truly happy again, but she would live and she would be content.

The morning chores eased her mind and kept it from drifting. She worked alone, or with the women of her family. For them, and for the sake of her own pride, she kept her spirits up. There would be no moping, no pining, for Serena MacGregor. Whenever she was tempted to fall into depression, she reminded herself that she had had one golden afternoon.

It was early evening when she slipped away. Her mother and Maggie were sorting thread and Gwen was visiting one of the sick in the village. Dressed in her breeches, she avoided everyone but Malcolm, whom she bribed with a piece of hard candy.

She rode for the loch. It was an indulgence, right or wrong, that occasionally she allowed herself. Whenever time allowed, she went there to sit on the bank and dream a little. And remember. It brought Brigham closer to her. As close, Serena knew, as he would ever be. He was gone. Back to London, where he belonged.

Now spring was here in all its glory. Flowers waved in the gentle breeze, trees were ripe with green, green leaves. The sunlight dappled through, making pretty patterns on the soft path. Young deer walked through the forest.

By the loch the ground was springy and warm, though the water would be frigid for weeks yet, and would carry a chill all through the summer. Content from the ride, she lay on the grassy knoll to read a little, and dream. It was solitude she had wanted, and it was serenity she found. From somewhere to the west, like mourning, came the haunting call of a greenshank.

Dog violets grew, pale blue and delicate, beside her. She plucked a few, threading them idly through her hair while she studied the glassy calm of the lake. On the rocks above, heather grew like purple stars. Its fragile scent drifted to her. Farther up, the crags had been worn sheer by rain and time. There was little that could grow there, and to Serena, their very starkness made them beautiful. They were like fortresses, guarding the eastern verge of the loch.

She wished Brigham could see this spot, this very special spot, now, when the wind was kind and the water so blue it made your eyes sting.

Pillowing her head on her arm, she closed her eyes and dreamed of him.

It felt as though a butterfly had landed on her cheek. Dozing, Serena brushed it lazily away. She didn't want to wake, not just yet, and find herself alone. Soon enough she would have to go back and give up the hours she had stolen for herself. Not yet, she thought as she curled into her self. For just a little while longer, she would lie here and dream of what might have been.

She sighed, groggy with sleep, as she felt something—the butterfly—brush over her lips. She smiled a little, thinking how sweet that was, how it warmed her. Her body stretched against the gentle fingers of the breeze. Like a lover's hands, she thought. Like Brigham's. Her sigh was quiet and drowsily aroused. Her breasts tingled under it, and seemed to fill. All along her body, her blood seemed to rush to the surface. In response, her lips parted.

"Look at me, Serena. Look at me when I kiss you."

She obeyed automatically, her mind still trapped in the dream, her body heating from it. Dazed, she saw Brigham's eyes looking into hers as her mouth was captured in a kiss that was much too urgent, much too powerful, for any dream.

"My God, how I've missed you." He dragged her closer. "Every day, I swear it, every hour."

Could this be real? Her mind swam as fiercely as her blood as she wrapped her arms tight around him. "Brigham?" She held on, terrified to let go and find him vanished. "Is it really you? Kiss me again," she demanded before he could speak. "And again and again."

He did as she asked, his hands dragging through her hair, streaming down her body until they were both shuddering. He wanted to tell her how he had felt when he had stopped his horse and had seen her sleeping, sleeping where they had first come together. No one had ever looked more beautiful than his Serena, lying in her men's breeches with her head pillowed on her arm and flowers scattered in her hair.

But he couldn't find the words, and if he had, she would never have let them be spoken. Her mouth was hungry as it fused to his. When he had loved her before she had been fragile, a little afraid. Now she was all passion, all demand. Her fingers pulled and dragged at his clothes as if she couldn't bear to have anything between them. Though he murmured to her, wanting to show some gentleness on this, their first meeting in so many long weeks, she burned like a fire in his arms.

Unable to resist, he tugged the men's clothes aside and found his woman.

It was as it had been before, she thought. And more, so much more. His hands and mouth were everywhere, torturing, delighting. Her skin was covered with a moist sheen and nothing else as he pleasured both of them. Whatever shyness she had felt when she had first given herself to him was eclipsed now by a need so sharp, so desperate, that she touched and tasted in places that made him gasp in amazement and passion. She drew him down to her, reveling in the scent of him—in some way the same as it had been on their very first meeting. Sweat, horse, blood. It spun in her head, touching off primitive urges, the darkest desires.

"Name of God, Rena." He could barely speak. She was taking him places he had never been, places he had never known existed. No other woman had mastered him in this way, not the most experienced French courtesan, not the most worldly British flower. He was learning from the Scots wildcat more of love and lust than he had thought possible.

The blood was hammering in his brain. There was pain, exquisite, terrifying pain. The control with which he lived his life, with which he raised a sword or fired a pistol, was gone as if it had never existed. He dragged her against him, his fingers raking through her hair, bruising her soft flesh.

"Now, for pity's sake." He plunged into her, going deep. Her nails dug into his back as she cried out, but she was moving with him, driving her hips up to meet each thrust. With her head thrown back, she gasped for air. In some part of her brain she knew this was something like dying. Then there was no thought at all. Though her eyes flew open, she saw nothing, nothing but a white flash as her body went rigid.

The aftershocks of pleasure racked her body even as her hands fell limply to the ground. Her vision was misted—it seemed only more of the dream. But Brigham lay, warm and solid, over her. And he was…he was trembling, she realized with a kind of wonder. It was not only she who was left weak and vulnerable, but he, as well.

"You came back," she murmured, and found the strength to lift her hand to his hair.

"I said I would." He shifted to kiss her again, but softly now. "I love you, Serena. Nothing could have stopped me from coming back to you."

She framed his face with her hands to study it. He meant it, she realized. Seeing the truth only made her more uncertain of what to do. "You were gone so long. No word."

"Sending word would have put too many at risk. The storm's coming, Rena."

"Aye. And you'll—" She broke off as she noted blood on her fingers. "Brig, you're hurt." She scrambled up to her knees to fret over the soaked bandage on his shoulder. "What happened? You were attacked? Campbells!"

"No." He had to laugh at the way she snarled the rival clan's name. "A little business in London before I left. It's nothing, Serena."

But she was already ripping the cuff from his shirt to make a fresh bandage. Brigham sighed, knowing Parkins would make him pay, but he sat meekly and let her tend his wound.

"A sword," she said.

"A scratch. We won't talk of it now. The sun's going down."

"Oh." She blinked, noting for the first time how much time had passed. "I have to go back. How did you find me here?"

"I could say I followed my heart, which I would have. But Malcolm told me you'd ridden out."

A few flowers clung yet to her hair, and her hair was all that covered her breasts. She looked like a witch or a queen or a goddess. He could only be certain that she was all he needed. He grabbed her hands. The intensity was back in his eyes, dark, demanding.

"Tell me, Rena."

"I love you, Brigham." She brought his hand to her cheek. "More than I can say."

"And you'll marry me." When her eyes dropped from his, he erupted. "Damn it, woman. You say you love me, you all but kill me with passion, then you go skittish when I speak of making you my wife."

"I have told you I cannot."

"I have told you you will." He picked up his ruined shirt and slipped it gingerly over his shoulder, which was just beginning to ache. "I shall speak with your father."

"No." Her head shot up quickly. Trying to think, she pushed the hair back from her face. How could they have come so far and be back where they had begun? "I beg you not to."

"What choice do you leave me?" He pulled her shirt down over her head, struggling for patience when she jerked away from him to dress herself. "I love you, Rena, and I have no intention of living my life without you."

"Then I'll ask for time." She looked at him then and knew she had to resolve what was in her heart and what was in her head. "There is so much to be done, Brigham. So much that will be happening around us, to us. When the war begins, you'll go, and I shall only wait. Give me time. Give us both time to deal with what has to be."

"Only so much, Serena. And only because, in the end, I'll leave you no choice."

Chapter Eleven

Serena was right. Things were happening around them that would shape the destiny not only of two lovers, but of the whole of Scotland.

Within days of Brigham's arrival at Glenroe, the French dealt the English a crushing defeat at Fontenoy. Though Charles's, and many of the Jacobites' hopes rose with it, Louis of France still withheld his support from the rebellion. Charles had hoped to ride on the glory that surrounded the French victory, to gain much-needed impetus for his cause; once again, however, he was left to his own devices.

But this time he moved. Brigham was both confidant and informer. He knew to the day when Charles, with money raised by the pawning of his mother's rubies, fitted out the frigate *Doutelle* and a ship of the line, the *Elizabeth*. While the push in the Highlands, and in England, went on for support, Charles Edward, the Bonnie Prince, set sail from Nantes for Scotland and his destiny.

It was high summer when word came that the Prince was on

his way. The *Elizabeth*, with its store of men and weapons, was chased back to port by British pursuers, but the *Doutelle*, with Charles aboard, sailed on toward the Scottish coast, where preparations were being made to greet him.

"My father says I cannot go." Malcolm, sulking in the stables, frowned up at Brigham. "He's says I'm too young, but I'm not."

The boy had just passed his eleventh birthday, Brigham thought, but prudently held back from mentioning it. "Coll goes, as do I."

"I know." Malcolm glared at the toe of his grubby boot and thought it the height of injustice. "Because I'm the youngest, I'm treated like a bairn."

"Would your father trust his home and his family to a bairn?" Brigham asked gently. "When your father leaves with his men, there will be no MacGregor in MacGregor House, but for you. Who will protect the women if you ride with us?"

"Serena," he said easily, and he spoke no less than the truth.

"Would you leave your sister alone to protect the family name and honor?"

The boy moved a shoulder, but began to think on it. "She is a better shot with a pistol than I, or Coll, really, though he wouldn't like to say so." This news brought Brigham's brow up. "But I'm better with a bow."

"She will need you." He dropped a hand on Malcolm's tousled hair. "We will all need you. With you here, we needn't worry that the women are safe." Because he was still young enough to know what it was to be a boy, he sat on the mound of hay beside Malcolm. "I can tell you this, Malcolm, a man never goes easily to war, but he goes with a lighter heart if he knows his women are protected."

"I won't let harm come to them." Idly Malcolm fingered the dagger at his belt. For a moment, Brigham thought he looked too much a man.

"I know, as your father knows. If the time comes when Glenroe is no longer safe, you will take them up into the hills."

"Aye." The idea made Malcolm brighten a bit. "I'll see that they have food and shelter. Especially Maggie."

"Why especially Maggie?"

"Because of the bairn." His fingers slid away from his dagger. "She's to have one, you know."

For a moment, Brigham only stared. Then, with a laugh, he shook his head. "No, I didn't. How do you?"

"I heard Mrs. Drummond say so. She said Maggie's not sure she's increasing yet, but Mrs. Drummond was sure and there'd be a new wee bairn by next spring."

"Keep your ear to the ground, do you, my lad?"

"Aye." This time Malcolm grinned. "I know Gwen and Maggie are always talking about how you'll be marrying Serena. Will you be marrying her, Brig?"

"I will." He ruffled the boy's hair. "But she doesn't know it yet."

"Then you'll be a MacGregor."

"To an extent. Serena will be a Langston."

"A Langston. Will she like it?"

Brigham's eyes lost their amusement. "She'll grow used to it. Now, if you've a mind to take that ride, we'd best be off."

Always cheered by the idea of his horses, Malcolm jumped up. "Did you know that Parkins is courting Mrs. Drummond?"

"Good God." Brigham stopped in the act of leading out his horse and turned to the boy. "Someone should plug those ears of yours." Malcolm only laughed, and Brigham, unable to do otherwise, put a hand on the boy's shoulder again. "Is he really?"

"Brought her flowers yesterday."

"Sweet Jesus."

From the window of the parlor she was supposed to be dusting, Serena watched them ride off. How wonderful he looked, so tall, so straight. She leaned out the window so that she could watch him until he was out of sight.

He wouldn't wait much longer. Those had been his words the last time they had stolen an hour together by the loch. He wanted her wedded, and properly bedded. He wanted to make her Lady Ashburn of Ashburn Manor. Lady Ashburn of London society. The idea was nothing less than terrifying.

She looked down at herself now, at her dress of pale blue homespun and at the dusty apron that covered it. Her feet were bare—something Fiona would have sighed over. Lady Ashburn would never run over the moors or through the forest in bare feet. Lady Ashburn would probably never run.

Her hands. Serena turned them this way and that, examining the backs and the palms critically. They were smooth enough, she supposed. Because her mother insisted she rub lotion into them every night. But they weren't lady's hands any more than hers was a lady's heart.

But God, she loved him. She understood now that the heart could indeed speak louder than the head. English or not, she would be his. She had even come to know that she would leave her beloved Scotland behind for his England rather than live without him. And yet...

How could she marry a man who deserved the finest of ladies? Even her mother had thrown up her hands at Serena's attempts

to learn the spinet. She couldn't do fancy work with her needle, only the most basic stitches. She could run a home, to be
sure, but she knew from Coll that Brigham's house in London
and his manor in the country were a far cry from what she was
used to. She would make a mess of it, but even that she could
almost bear. It was knowing how poorly she had dealt with her
one brush with society—the brief months she had spent in the
convent school.

She had nothing to say to the kind of women who spent their
days shopping for the right shade of ribbon and making social
calls. A few weeks of that life and she would go not-so-quietly
mad, and once she had, Brigham would hate her.

We can't change what we are, she thought. Brigham could
no more stay here in the Highlands and live her life than she
could go with him to England and live his.

And yet... She had begun to see that living without him
would be no life at all.

"Serena."

She turned quickly to see her mother in the doorway.

"I'm nearly done," she said, flourishing her dusting cloth again.
"I was daydreaming."

Fiona shut the doors at her back. "Sit down, Serena."

Fiona used that quiet but concerned tone of voice rarely. Usually it meant that she was worried or annoyed. As Serena moved
to comply, she searched her mind for any infraction. True, she'd
been wearing the breeches a bit too freely on her rides, but
her mother usually overlooked that. She had torn the skirt of
the new gray dress, but Gwen had mended it so that it hardly
showed at all.

Serena sat, pulling the cloth between her fingers. "Have I done something to upset you?"

"You're troubled," Fiona began. "I had thought it was because Brigham had gone and you were missing him. But he's been back for several weeks now and you're troubled still."

Serena tucked her bare feet under the hem of her skirt as her fingers knotted and unknotted the cloth. "I'm not troubled really. It's only that I'm thinking about what will happen after the Prince comes."

That was true, Fiona thought, but not all the truth. "There was a time you would talk to me, Serena."

"I don't know what to say."

Gently Fiona laid a hand on hers. "What's in your heart."

"I love him." Serena slid to the floor to lay her head in her mother's lap. "Mama, I love him and it hurts so terribly."

"I know it does, my darling." She stroked Serena's hair and felt the pang in her own heart that only a mother understands. "To love a man is great misery and great joy."

"Why?" There was passion in Serena's eyes and voice as she lifted her face. "Why must it bring misery?"

Fiona gave a little sigh and wished there could be a simple answer. "Because once the heart opens, it feels everything."

"I didn't want to love him," Serena murmured. "Now I can do nothing else."

"And he loves you?"

"Aye." She closed her eyes, comforted by the familiar scent of lavender in the folds of her mother's skirts. "I don't think he wanted to, either."

"You know he has asked your father for your hand?"

"Aye."

"And that your father, after long thought and consideration, has given his consent."

This she hadn't known. Serena lifted her head, and her cheeks were pale. "But I can't marry him. Don't you see? I can't."

With a frown in her eyes, Fiona caught Serena's face in her hands. From what source did this fear written so plainly on her daughter's face spring? "No, I don't see, Rena. You know well your father would never force you to marry a man you didn't want. But did you not just tell me you loved Brigham and that your love is returned?"

"I do love him, too much to marry him, too much not to. Oh, Mama, how much I would give him frightens me."

Fiona saw a bit clearer now, and she smiled. "Poor wee lamb. You're not the first to have these fears, nor will you be the last. I understand when you say you love him too much *not* to marry him. But how can you love him too much to marry him?"

"I don't want to be Lady Ashburn."

Fiona blinked, surprised by the vehemence in her daughter's words. "Because he's English?"

"Aye— No. No, because I don't want to be a countess."

"It's a good family. An honorable one."

"It's the title, Mama. Even the sound of it frightens me. Lady Ashburn would live in England, grandly. She would know how to dress fashionably, how to behave with dignity, how to serve beautiful dinners and laugh at the cleverest wits."

"Well. I never thought to see the day that Ian MacGregor's wildcat cowered in a corner and whined."

The color rose sharply in Serena's cheeks. "I am afraid, I'll admit it." She rose, locking her fingers tightly together. "But I'm not only afraid for my own sake. I would go, I would try, I would be determined to be the kind of wife Brigham needs, to be the best Lady Ashburn ever to rule in Ashburn Manor. And I would hate it. Never to be free, never to have a moment with the space to breathe. But there's more." She paused a moment, wanting to choose her words so that she would be understood. "If Brigham loves me, he loves *me*, as I am. Would he love the woman I would have to become to be his wife?"

Fiona was silent for a long moment. The girl had surely become a woman, with a woman's mind, a woman's heart and a woman's fears. "You've given this a great deal of thought."

"I've hardly thought of anything else for weeks. He will have his way, of that I'm sure. But I've come to wonder if we might not both be sorry for it."

"Think of this. If he loves you, for yourself, then he would not want you to pretend to be what you are not, nor would he ask you to."

"I would rather lose him than shame him."

"I could tell you you will do neither," Fiona said wearily as she rose. "But you must learn it for yourself. But I want to tell you one more thing." Now it was Fiona who linked her hands together. "There's been gossip in the kitchen." Her mouth twitched slightly at Serena's expression. "Aye, Parkins and Mrs. Drummond. I chanced to overhear while working in the kitchen garden."

"Aye, Mother?" Serena managed, barely able to smother a giggle. The idea of her mother eavesdropping on the valet and the cook was almost too ludicrous.

"It seems on the morning he left London, Brigham fought a duel with an officer of the government army. An officer called Standish."

At this, all humor drained from Serena's face, along with all her color. "Brigham." She remembered the wound on his shoulder, the one he had steadfastly refused to discuss. "Standish," she said in a whisper as the name came home. She saw him, as she had seen him almost ten years before, bringing his hand against her mother's face. "Dear God, how did it happen? Why did it happen?"

"I know only that the duel was fought and Standish is dead. God help me, I'm glad of it. The man you love avenged my honor, and I will never forget it."

"Nor will I," Serena murmured.

She went to him that night. The hour was late, the house quiet. After pushing open his door, she saw him with the moonlight and the candlelight tangled around him while he sat at the desk by the window penning a letter. The air coming through the open window was hot and still, so he had stripped to his breeches, leaving his shirt hung casually over the back of the chair.

It was only an instant before he glanced up and saw her, only an instant that she could look at him unobserved. But the instant flashed into her mind and was sealed there to make a memory as precious as a kiss.

The light fell over his skin, making her think of the marble statues Coll had described from his trip to Italy. Statues of gods and warriors. His hair, thick and dark, was tied back from his face and mussed a bit, as though he had worried it with his hand. His eyes were dark, as well, holding a combination she recognized as concentration and concern.

Her heart began to dance in her breast as she stood in the

doorway. This was the man she loved, a man of action and loyalty. A man both reckless and deliberate, a man of arrogance and of compassion. A man of honor.

He looked up, and saw her. In the woods beyond an owl hooted, the sound rising on the air and fading like a ghost. He set the quill down and rose even as she shut the door at her back. The movement stirred the air and sent the flame and its shadow wavering.

"Serena?"

"I needed to see you alone."

He released a difficult knot of breath. It took great care and great restraint not to cross to her and gather her up. She wore only a thin white linen nightdress, and had left her hair unbound to fall in a wild mass over her shoulders and down her back. "You should not have come here like this."

"I know." She moistened her lips. "I tried to sleep, but couldn't. You are leaving tomorrow."

"Yes." The intensity in his eyes softened, as did his voice. "My love, do I have to tell you again that I'll come back?"

Tears threatened, but she willed them away. She would not leave him with the image of a weak, weeping woman. "No, but I have a need to tell you that I will wait. And I would be proud to be your wife when you come back to me."

For a moment he said nothing, only stared, as if trying to read her face and be certain he had not misheard her. She stood, her hands folded. But she wasn't meek. Her eyes held fire, her chin was up. Now he crossed to her to take one of her hands in his.

"Has your father commanded you?"

"No, the decision is mine, only mine."

It was the answer he wanted, the one he had hoped for. Gently he brushed his lips over her knuckles. "I will make you happy, Rena. On my honor."

"I will be the wife you need." Somehow, she thought within her heart. "I swear it."

He bent to kiss her brow. "You *are* the wife I need, my love. And the woman." Stepping back, he drew the emerald from his finger. "This ring has been worn by a Langston for more than a hundred years. I ask you to keep it for me until I return and give you another." He slipped it onto her finger. Serena curled her hand automatically to keep it there. "I shall give you another ring as soon as God allows, and my name, as well."

"Oh, Brigham, be safe." She threw herself into his arms. It was harder, much harder, to fight these tears than any others she had known. "If I lost you now, I couldn't bear to live. Know that if you bleed, I bleed, and take care."

"What's this?" With a light laugh he caressed her hair, but it was difficult to ignore the press of her thinly clad body against his. "Never say you worry about me, Rena."

"I will say it," she murmured against his shoulder. "If you allow yourself to be killed, I shall hate you forever."

"Then I will take great care to stay alive. Go now, before you make me feel too much alive."

She gave a weak laugh. "I fear I have done that already, my lord." She shifted wantonly to prove there were no secrets between them. She had only to rise to her toes to fit herself unerringly against him. Desire to desire. "Does being near me do that to you?"

"All too often." His own laugh was strained as he fought off the drugging power of her scent, of her shape.

"I'm glad." She lifted her head to look up at him, and her smile was wicked. "Very glad."

She made him laugh again. "You've flowered in front of my eyes, Rena. Under my hands." He kissed her, gently, though her lips tempted him. "I wonder if there is a more precious gift a woman can give a man."

"I would give you another tonight." She drew his head down to hers. Her kiss was not so gentle. With it, she felt his body tense. "I would share your bed, Brig, your love and your sleep. No," she murmured against his lips before he could speak. "Don't tell me why it should not be, only show me why it must." She dragged her hands up his back to tangle her fingers in his hair while her lips moved restlessly on his. "Love me, Brigham. Love me so that I can live on it in all the empty days to come."

He couldn't deny her. He could no longer deny himself. Her body trembled against his, no longer from fear, no longer from doubt, but only from need. With a muffled oath, he swept her into his arms. He would be leaving at dawn. Between then and now he could give her, give them, a few perfect hours.

Her body was fluid in his arms, cool, soft, languid. Her eyes were as rich, as hot, as the flash of emerald that had passed from his finger to hers. She kept her arms around his neck as he lowered her to the bed, so that he came down with her. Then, with his hands braced on either side of her head, he began to make love to her face with his mouth alone.

She thought she could float away on this kind of sweetness. It was like a cloud, delicate and dreamy. Her body felt light and free as her lips met his again and again in a slow, luxurious dance. Another minuet, she thought. Elegant, harmonious and beautiful. With a sigh she felt him slip the nightdress from her, then heard his quick intake of breath as he discovered for himself that she wore nothing beneath it.

"You are so lovely." He touched his lips to the pulse of her throat. "Here," he murmured as his fingertips brushed her breasts. "Here." And again, as his light, clever hands moved over her: "Here."

Giddiness speared through the languor. Giddiness and delight. "Is that why you fell in love with me, *Sassenach*? For my body?"

He drew himself up far enough for a long, lazy study. "It was a great influence."

Flushed, she laughed and pinched him. Then her laughter turned into a moan as he dipped his head and streaked his tongue over a hardening nipple.

"I love all of you, Serena. Your temper, your mind, your heart, and oh, yes…" His teeth closed teasingly over the peak. "Your body."

"Show me," she demanded breathlessly.

He showed her, with tenderness, with ardor, with restraint and with desperation. Every emotion they had shared became part of that endless night of loving. There were new ways. He guided her, delighted by the eagerness with which she learned, the passion with which she gave and received. There was no shyness in her. She came to him with a trust so complete that that alone nearly dragged him over the edge.

Skin grew slick in the airless night. Not a breeze stirred through the window. High above the hills, thunder rumbled. Closer, in the forest, the owl hunted. Its scream of triumph melded with the scream of its prey. The candle flickered and guttered out.

They were aware of nothing but each other, nothing but the world they made on the soft mattress.

She made him weak, and then she made him strong. She made him laugh, and then she made him groan. He was breathless, sated, then as eager to devour her as a man starving.

In the deepest part of the night they slept briefly, only to wake with the need spiraling high once more.

There was no part of her he couldn't make ache or tremble. She could only hear her skin sing as he touched. Her body grew heavy with pleasure as it built and built to roll through her like the thunder in the distant hills. Then she was light, weight-less, agilely skimming over him like a fantasy. Energy poured through her, molten.

She rose over him, her hair silvered with dying moonlight, her skin sheened with damp, her face pale with an exhaustion she had yet to feel. She took him into her, arching her back as pleasure raced through her like delirium. The fever of it boiled under her skin until her hips moved like lightning. His name sobbed through her lips as she drove them both higher. Lost, she dragged her hands up her body, over her trembling stomach, up to her breasts, then down again until they met his.

At last she slid bonelessly down, her breath shuddering out, to lie in his arms.

"I wonder," she said when she could speak again, "if it is always like this. It makes me see how one might kill for love."

"For love." He shifted so that he could hold her yet closer. "It is not always like this. For me, it has only been like this with you."

She turned her head so that she could see his face. The light was nearly gone in that hour before day begins to break through. "Truly?"

He brought their joined hands to his lips. "Truly."

She smiled a little, pleased. "If you take a mistress after we wed, I will kill her. Then you. But I will kill you more horribly."

He laughed, then took a quick bite at her lower lip. "Well I believe it. Even if I were tempted, you leave me too exhausted for a mistress."

"If I believed you were too tempted, I would leave you inadequate for a mistress." She slid a hand up his thigh meaningfully.

He started to laugh again, but her bland expression had him lifting a brow. "By God, I think you would. Should I remind you that your pleasure would be, ah, cut off, as well?"

"The sacrifice would be great." She trailed her fingers over him, delighted when he shuddered. "The satisfaction is greater."

"Perhaps I should think twice about taking a jealous hellcat to wife."

The humor fled from her eyes. "You should. But I have come to know you will not."

"No. There is only one woman for me." He kissed her again before shifting her comfortably into the crook of his arm. "One day I will take you to Ashburn Manor and show you what is mine, what is ours, what shall be our children's. It's beautiful, Rena, graceful, timeless. Already I can picture you in the bed where I was born."

She started to protest, but her fingers grazed over the pucker of skin on his shoulder where his wound was still healing. "Then our first child will be born there." She turned her face into his throat. "Oh, Brigham, I want your child inside me soon."

Stunned, and deeply moved, he lifted her face to his again. "My God, you humble me. We shall have a dozen children if you like, be they all as bad-tempered as their mother."

That made her smile again. "Or as arrogant as their father." She relaxed against him again. Their time was nearly at an end. Already she could sense a faint lessening of the darkness. There had been a time for loving. Now was the time for truths.

"Brigham, there is something I need to ask you."

"At this moment, you could ask me anything."

"Why did you fight the English soldier, the one called Standish?"

The surprise came first, then the quick realization that Parkins and Mrs. Drummond gossiped as well as courted. "It was a matter of honor… He accused me of using weighted dice."

She said nothing for a moment, then braced herself on her elbow to watch his face. "Why do you lie to me?"

"I don't lie. He lost, lost more, then decided there must have been a reason for it other than his lack of luck."

"Are you telling me you didn't know who he was? What he was…to me?"

"I knew who he was." He had hoped to keep the matter to himself. Since that was not to be, he decided to make his explanations quickly and be done with it. "One might say I encouraged him to make an accusation so that a duel would be fought."

Her eyes were very intense. "Why?"

"It was also a matter of honor."

Serena closed her eyes. Then, lifting his sword hand, she kissed it, almost reverently. "Thank you."

"Thanks are not necessary for killing a vicious dog." But he tensed even as she held his hand against her cheek. "You knew of this. Is that why you came to me tonight, why you agreed to be my wife?"

"Aye." When he started to pull away, she held him only tighter. "Don't. Let me say it all. It wasn't for gratitude that I came, though I am grateful. It wasn't for obligation, though I owe you a debt that can never be paid."

"You owe me nothing."

"Everything," she said passionately. "When I dream now of that night, when I see my mother's eyes after he had done with her, when I hear in my mind the way she wept, I will know that he is dead, and that he died by your hand. Knowing that, there is nothing I would deny you."

"I didn't kill him for your gratitude or to put you under obligation." His voice was stiff. "I want you as my wife, Serena, intend to have you, but not because you feel you owe a debt."

"I know that." She knelt beside him and putting her arms around him, buried her face in his neck. "Did I not tell you already that I come to you willingly? Can you doubt it after what we've shared?" She pressed her lips against his skin, then skimmed them up to his. "When I was told of the duel, of his death, I was glad, afraid, confused. Tonight, I lay in bed and it all came so clear. It was not your fight, my love, not your family, not your mother. But you made it so. He might have killed you."

"You have a poor opinion of my skill with a sword."

Shaking her head, she drew back a little. He could see by her face that she would not be put off lightly. "I bound your wound. Your blood was on my hand, as my mother's was that night so many years ago." She held it, palm out. "You bled for my family. I will remember that until the day I die. I loved you before, Brigham. I had already accepted I would love no other. But tonight I came to see that you had honored my family as a man honors his own. I shall honor yours, if you'll let me."

He took the hand she held out to him and turned it over so that the emerald lay dark upon her finger. "I leave you with my heart, Serena. When I return, I'll give you my name, as well."

She opened her arms to him. "For tonight, give me your love once more."

Chapter Twelve

Prince Charles set his royal feet on the thin soil of Scotland in high summer, but not, as he and many others had hoped, in triumph. He was advised by MacDonald of Boisdale as he landed on the island of Eriskay to go home. His reply was terse, and telling.

"I am come home."

From Eriskay, he and the seven men who had sailed with him traveled to the mainland. There, too, the Jacobites were filled more with concern than enthusiasm. Support was slow in coming, but Charles sent out letters to the Highland chiefs. Cameron of Lochiel was among them, and though his support was given reluctantly, and perhaps with a heavy heart, it was given.

So it passed that on August 19, in the year 1745, before some nine hundred loyal men, the standard was raised at Glenfinnan. Charles's father was proclaimed James VIII of Scotland and James III of England, with the young Prince as regent.

The small force moved eastward, gathering strength. The

clans rallied, words were pledged, and men bade goodbye to their women and joined the march.

Brigham's journeys through Scotland with Ian and with Coll had given him a knowledge of the land. They were able to make good time, ironically enough on one of the roads built to discourage Highland rebellion. Using this, and the rugged hills for cover, they avoided the government garrisons at Fort William and Fort Augustus.

Spirits were high, the men as rough and ready as their land. It had only taken, as Brigham had always imagined, the energy and force of the young Prince to bind them together. When men thought of the battles ahead, they thought not of their mortality but of victory, and of a justice that had been denied them too long.

Some were young; Brigham saw the future in their eager faces, in the way they laughed and looked at the Prince, who wore the dress of the Highlands and had fastened a white cockade, the symbol of his house, on his blue bonnet.

Some were old, and there the past could be seen, the ageless pride, the battles already lost and won. They looked to the Prince, with his fresh Stuart blood, as the glue that would hold the clans together.

But old or young, eager or heavyhearted, Charles swept them along by the force of his personality alone. This was his time, and his place. He meant to make his mark.

The weather held fine, the breezes warm. It was said by some that God Himself had blessed the rebellion. For a time, it seemed so. The men and weapons that had been lost to the Jacobites when the *Elizabeth* had turned back were forgotten. Peat was plentiful for fires, and the water was fresh from icy mountain streams. The pipes were played, whiskey was drunk, and by night the men slept the good sleep men do when they begin an adventure.

It was to Brigham that word came that a government army had been dispatched north, headed by General Sir John Cope. Brigham took the news directly to the Prince as the men broke camp and prepared for the day's march. Brigham watched the full, almost girlish mouth curve up into a smile that was very much a man's.

"So we shall fight, at last."

"It appears so, Your Highness."

The morning was warm, with the soft, watery light of Scotland gaining strength. The camp carried the scent of horses and soldiers and smoke. The rugged hills were softened now by a springy spread of heather. A golden eagle, early to the hunt, crested overhead.

"It seems a good day to fight," Charles murmured as he studied Brigham's face. "You would prefer we had Lord George with us."

"Lord George is an excellent field commander, Your Highness."

"Indeed. But we have O'Sullivan." Charles gestured toward the Irish soldier of fortune who was organizing the men for the day's journey.

Brigham already had doubts in that quarter. He didn't question the Irishman's loyalty to the Prince, but he felt there was more flash than caution. "If we are engaged, we shall fight."

"I look forward to it." Charles fingered the hilt of his sword as he gazed around him. He felt something for this land, something deep and true. When he was king, he would see that Scotland

and her people were rewarded. "It's been a long journey, Brigham, a far distance from Louis's court and all those pretty faces."

"A long journey, Your Highness," Brigham agreed. "But one well worth the making."

"I should tell you that there were tears on some of those pretty faces when you left. Have you taken time to break hearts in Scotland, as well?"

"There is only one face for me now, sire, and one heart I will take great care not to break."

The Prince's dark eyes were alight with amusement. "Well, well, it appears the dashing Lord Ashburn has fallen for a High-land lassie. Tell me, *mon ami*, is she as pretty as the luscious Anne-Marie?"

Brigham managed a wry grin. "I would beg Your Highness to make no comparisons, particularly in front of the Highland lassie. She has a rare temper."

"Does she?" With a delighted laugh, Charles signaled for his mount. "I am most anxious to meet her and see what manner of woman snared the most sought-after man at the French court."

The pipes sounded along the road, but Cope's troops were never seen. Word came that he had detoured to Inverness. The road to Edinburgh lay open to the rebels. Three thousand strong, they captured Perth after a short, vicious battle. Victorious, they continued their drive south, engaging and routing two regiments of dragoons.

The fighting seemed to fuel the rebels. Here at last was action instead of talk, deeds instead of plans. With sword and pipe, shield and ax, they were like a fury. Survivors would spread tales of their maniacal skill and daring that themselves would serve as a weapon.

Joined by Lord George Murray at Perth, they entered Edinburgh and took it for their own.

The city was in a panic. News of the invasion had preceded the Highland forces, and rumors flew about barbarians, cannibals and butchers. The city guard had fled, and while Edinburgh slept a party of Camerons rushed the sentries, and control was gained.

Under the Prince's command, there was no looting, no pillaging. The people of Edinburgh were given justice and compassion, as was due the subjects of the true king.

It was only a month after the standard had been raised at Glenfinnan and James had been proclaimed king, and his son and regent was preparing to open a royal court at Holyrood House.

Coll was beside Brigham when the Prince rode his gray gelding into Holyrood Park. A crowd had gathered to watch him. Shouts and cheers followed them, for the people saw their heart's delight in the young man in his tartan shortcoat and blue bonnet. Perhaps he was not yet England's Prince, but he was theirs.

"Listen to them." Coll leaned forward in the saddle and grinned. "Here is our first real victory, Brigham, and by God, it has a good feel."

Brigham steadied his mount as he maneuvered through the narrow, crowded streets. "I'll swear he could drive them to London now with only a word. I can only hope the supplies and men we need will arrive before it comes time."

"We could be outnumbered ten to one today and never taste defeat. It would be as it was at Perth and, aye, at Coltbridge." The early-autumn breeze drifted, making Coll grimace. "But in God's name, this place is filthy. Give me the open Highlands and the hills. How does a man breathe," he wondered, "without the room to draw air?"

Edinburgh was packed with houses and shops, some still fashioned of mud and wood. The stone buildings rose high, like aeries, with the fronts four or five stories high, and the backs often stretching nine or ten stories down the perilously steep hills.

"Worse than Paris," Brigham agreed. The stench drifted out from crowded lanes, and waste and garbage clogged the alleys, but the people, cheering the Prince, seemed oblivious to it all.

Above the slums, the filth of the alleys and the dirt of the streets was the Royal Mile. Edinburgh Castle, majestic, already glamorous with age and history, guarded one end of that great street. Where its slope ended was Holyrood House, where palace and abbey stood together elegantly poised before the rough crags. It had already been the scene, time after time, of turbulence and passion. Mary, Queen of Scots, had been its most famous and doomed inhabitant. She had lived there, marrying her cousin Henry Stuart of Darnley in Holy-rood Abbey, and seeing her lover Rizzio murdered by him in the little supper room of her own apartments. Her son James had been born in the castle, and had survived a troubled and turbulent boyhood to become king of England, as well as Scotland.

It was here, at this site of pomp and intrigue that James's great-great grandson Charles would hold his court, bringing Holyrood House to life once more.

He rode toward the palace that had once housed his ancestors. Dismounting, he walked slowly under the archway, to appear moments later in the window of his new apartments, waving to the shouts of the crowd.

Edinburgh held the Prince, and he held Edinburgh.

He was to prove this only days later, when Cope moved his troops south.

Primed, even eager, the Jacobites met the government army east of the city at Prestonpans. Red-coated dragoons faced the Highlanders, who were dressed for battle in kilts or close-fitting trews. Brigham, with a leather shield in one hand and his sword in the other, joined the MacGregors. For a moment the field was eerily silent, with only the hollow sound of the pipes rising into the misty air. Like the heartbeats of men, Brigham thought, men who were willing to die. Opposing standards waved, caught by the early breeze.

The first charge sent birds wheeling and screaming up the sky. Men on foot met with a thunderous crash of sword and ax. Here, as they had on the route south, the Scots fought like demons, hacking with blades, pressing on even when bloody. As had happened before, the English infantry couldn't withstand the violence of the Highland charge. The red line wavered and broke.

The cavalry surged forward, vicious hooves striking, claymores glinting. Brigham ignored the cries and curses around him as he met his man. A shot rang whistling past his ear, but his eyes never lost their icy determination. The Campbell on the road from London would have recognized it. Brigham was a man who was willing to die but confident he would not.

Smoke from cannon and mortar grew thick, so that men on both sides fought in a fog. The heat of battle set sweat pouring as freely as blood so that the stench of both stung the air. Already carrion birds circled overhead, lured by the battle sounds.

As Brigham maneuvered his mount through what was left of the English lines, he could see the white cockades of the Jacobites and the plaids of MacGregors, MacDonalds, Camerons. Some fell around him, victims of bayonets or swords. Again and again the ground exploded where mortars struck, flinging out rock and dirt and deadly metal. Men screamed as they were struck down. Others died in silence.

Within ten minutes, the battle was over. Dragoons sought safety in flight and raced to the concealing hills on horse or on foot. Blood streaked the thin grass and stained the gray rock. The bodies of the dead and wounded lay sprawled on the ground. That day the pipes played in victory, and the standard of the House of Stuart was held high.

"Why do we stay snug in Edinburgh when we should be marching toward London?" Coll demanded as he strode out into the courtyard at Holyrood, a plaid wrapped around his shoulders to ward off the chilly dusk.

For once Brigham could only agree with Coll's impatience to be doing. They had been nearly three weeks at Charles's newly established court. The court itself was very glamorous, with levees and councils in the palace, but the Prince had not forgotten his men and so divided his time between Holyrood and the camp at Duddingston. Morale was good, though there was more than one man among them who would have agreed with Coll's sentiments.

Balls and receptions could wait.

"Victory at Prestonpans earned us more support." Brigham flicked his cloak back, welcoming the damp evening air. "I doubt we tarry here much longer."

"Councils," Coll grumbled. "Every blessed day we have another council. If there's a problem here, my lad, it's between Lord

George and O'Sullivan. I'll swear, if one says black, the other before God will vow it to be white."

"I know." It was a matter that caused Brigham no little concern. "I'll tell you true, Coll, O'Sullivan worries me. I prefer a commander a bit steadier, one who is less interested in routs than in overall victory."

"We can have neither if we dally here in court."

Brigham smiled, but he was looking out into the lowering night. "You miss your Highlands, Coll, and your wife."

"Aye. It's been barely two months since we left Glenroe, but we had little time together. With the bairn coming, I worry."

"A man's entitled to worry about the ones he loves."

"There's many a man with us who knows once the march south begins it could be a year before we see our homes and families again." Because he had no wish to fall into a black mood, Coll slapped Brigham on the shoulder. "At least there's plenty here for you to enjoy. The women are bonny. I wonder that you don't pick out a wench to charm. I'd swear you've broken a dozen hearts with your indifference these past few weeks."

"You could say I've something on my mind." Someone, Brigham thought. The only one. "What do you say we crack a bottle and find a game?" He turned at Coll's nod of assent, and together they started back across the courtyard.

Brigham noticed the woman step through the shadowy archway, but his gaze skimmed over her and passed without interest. He had taken only three steps when he stopped, turning slowly, deliberately, to stare. The light was fading quickly, and he could see only that she was tall and very slender. A plaid was draped over her head and shoulders. She might have been a servant, or one of the ladies of the court taking the air. He wondered why a stranger should remind him so achingly of his porcelain shepherdess.

And though he couldn't see her face, he was certain she was staring at him as intently as he stared at her.

The leap of attraction was unexpected. Annoyed with himself, Brigham turned again and continued on. Inexplicably, he was compelled to stop, to turn yet again. She was still there, standing in the fading light, her hands folded, her head held high.

"What the devil's wrong with you?" Coll stopped and turned himself. Spotting the figure in the archway, he grinned. "Well, if that's all. I don't suppose you'll want to dice with me now."

"No, I..." Brigham let his words trail off as the woman lifted her hands to slip the plaid from her head. The last of the light fell over her hair. Like sunset, it gleamed.

"Serena?" He could only stare. She took a step toward him, and he saw her face, and that she was smiling. His boots rang against stone as he strode across the courtyard. Before she could say his name, he swept her up into his arms, then around and around in dizzying circles.

"So that's the way of it," Coll murmured as he watched his friend drag his sister close for a long, bruising kiss.

"Why are you here? How did you come?" Then Brigham kissed her again and swallowed her answer.

"Give way, man." Coll plucked Serena from Brigham's arms, kissed her hard, then set her on her feet. "What are you doing in Edinburgh, and where's Maggie?"

"She's here." Breathless, Serena found herself swung back against Brigham's side. "And Mother and Gwen and Malcolm, as well." She reached out to give Coll's beard a sisterly tug. "The

Prince invited us to court. We arrived almost an hour ago, but didn't know where to find you."

"Maggie's here? Is she well? Where is she?" With his usual impatience, Coll turned on his heel and strode off to see for himself.

"Brigham—"

"Say nothing." He combed his hands through her hair, delighted with the feel of it, the scent of it. "Say nothing," he repeated, and lowered his head.

He held her like that, mouth to mouth, body to body, while the shadows deepened. The weeks of separation melted away. Restless, his hands moved down her back, over her hips, up to her face, while his lips, heated with desire, had her moaning and straining against him.

"Beautiful, always more beautiful, Serena. A man could die from missing you."

"I thought of you every day, and prayed. When we heard of the battles, I nearly went mad waiting for your letters telling me you were safe." At last she drew away to look at him. Because he and Coll had ridden in from camp, he had yet to change to his court dress. With some relief, Serena noted that he was the same man who had ridden away from Glenroe nearly three months before.

"I was afraid you'd change somehow, being here." She moistened her lips as she looked back toward the buildings. Nothing she had ever seen was more magnificent than the palace, with its towers and steeples with lights flickering behind its tall windows. "Everything here is so splendid. The palace, the abbey."

"Wherever I am, nothing changes between us, Rena."

She moved back into his arms to rest her head on his shoulder. "I was afraid it would. I prayed every day for you to be safe. And I prayed every day that you wouldn't seek comfort in the arms of another woman."

He laughed and kissed her hair. "I shan't ask which you prayed for with more fervor. My love, there is no one else. Can be no one else. Tonight I shall find more than comfort in your arms."

She smiled as she turned her lips to his cheek. "Would that we could. In truth, next to finding you safe, my dearest desire was to spend a night loving you."

"Then I shall see to it that you have both your desires."

She kissed him again and chuckled. "I'm to share a chamber with Gwen. It would be as unseemly, my lord, for you to come to my bed as it would for me to search the corridors for yours."

"Tonight you share my chamber, as my wife."

Her mouth opened in surprise as she stepped out of his arms. "That's impossible."

"It is very possible," he corrected. "And it shall be." Without giving her a chance to speak, he pulled her through the archway.

The Prince was in his apartments, preparing for that evening's entertainment. Though Brigham's request for an audience at that hour surprised him, he granted it.

"Your Highness." Brigham bowed as he entered Charles's sitting room.

"Good evening, Brigham. Madam," he said as Serena sank into a curtsy. She would kill Brigham, she thought, for dragging her before the Prince without even a chance to wash off the travel dirt or take a comb to her hair. "You would be Miss MacGregor." Charles drew Serena to her feet and kissed her hand. "It is easy to see why Lord Ashburn no longer notices the ladies at court."

"Your Highness. It was good of you to allow me and my family to come."

"I owe the MacGregors a great deal. They have stood behind my father, and behind me. Such loyalty is priceless. Will you sit?" He led her to a chair himself.

She had never seen a room like this one. The high ceiling was festooned with swirls and clusters of fruits and flowers, and from its center hung a dripping chandelier. Murals ran along the walls depicting Stuart victories in battle. A fire crackled in the hearth beside her chair. Music lay open on a harpsichord in the center of the room.

"Sire, I have a favor I would ask."

Charles sat, then gestured Brigham to a chair. "I am sure I owe you more than one."

"There is no debt for loyalty, Your Highness."

Charles's eyes softened. Serena saw then why he was called the Bonnie Prince. It wasn't just his face and form, it was his heart. "No, but there can be gratitude. What would you ask of me?"

"I would wed Miss MacGregor."

Charles's smile spread as he tapped his fingertips on his knee. "I had already surmised as much. Shall I tell you, Miss Mac-Gregor, that in Paris Lord Ashburn was very generous with the ladies at court? At Holyrood House he has proved most selfish."

Serena kept her hands folded primly in her lap. "I believe Lord Ashburn is a wise warrior, sir. He has some knowledge of the fierce and terrible temper of Clan MacGregor."

Highly entertained, Charles laughed. "So, I shall wish you well. Perhaps you would care to be married here, at court."

"Yes, sir, and tonight," Brigham said.

Now Charles's pale brows rose. "Tonight, Brigham? Such haste is..." He let his words trail off as he glanced at Serena again. The firelight played seductively over her hair. "...understandable," he decided. "Do you have the MacGregor's permission?"

"Yes, sir."

"Well, then. You are both Catholic?" Receiving nods, he thought it through. "The abbey is convenient. There is a matter of the banns and so forth, but I believe if a man cannot deal with such matters, he can hardly hope to win a throne." He rose, bringing both Serena and Brigham to their feet. "I will see you wed tonight."

Pale, not at all certain she wasn't dreaming, Serena found her parents in their chamber.

"Serena." Fiona sighed over the fact that her daughter still wore her traveling suit. "You must change. The Prince's court is no place for muddy boots and soiled skirts."

"Mama, I am to be wed."

"Devil, lass." Ian kissed her tumbled hair. "We're aware of that."

"Tonight."

"Tonight?" Fiona rose from her chair. "But how—?"

"Brigham went to the Prince. He took me, like this." Serena spread her muddy skirts, knowing her mother would understand her feelings on the matter.

"I see," Fiona murmured.

"And he, they..." She looked from her mother to her father, then back again. "Mama."

"Is it your wish to marry him?"

She hesitated, feeling the old doubts well up. Instinctively she lifted a hand to her breast. On a heavy chain under her bodice was the emerald Brigham had given her. "Aye," she managed.

"But it has all happened so fast." He would be leaving again, she thought. Leaving to fight. "Aye," she said, her voice stronger. "There is nothing I want more than to belong to him."

Fiona slipped an arm around Serena's shoulders. "Then we have much to do. Leave us, please, Ian, and send a servant for Maggie and Gwen."

"Tossing me out, are you, my lady?"

Fiona held out a hand to him, even as Serena reached for his other. "I fear you would have a strong dislike for the woman's work that must be done in the next few hours."

"Aye, I'll go willingly." He paused a moment to draw Serena close. "You have always made me proud. Tonight I give you to another man, and you will take his name. But you will always be a MacGregor." He kissed her. "Royal is our race, Serena, and rightly."

There was no time to think, and certainly no time to dwell on the enormity of what she would do before the night was over. Servants rushed in and out of the chambers with jugs of hot water that Fiona scented delicately for her daughter's bath. Gwen and Maggie chattered as they took out seams and sewed new ones on the dress Serena would wear to be married.

"It's romantic," Gwen said as she scanned her stitches with a critical eye.

"It's madness." Maggie glanced over, knowing Serena was soaking behind the screen. "Rena must have woven strong magic to make Brigham hurry so. He must not be so stuffy as I once thought."

"Imagine." Gwen shifted the ivory satin delicately. "Going to the Prince. We never had a chance to unpack from the journey before we're changing Mother's ball gown into Serena's wedding gown."

Maggie sat back, touching a hand to the mound of her belly. The baby she carried always became more active at night. The unpacking would have to wait, she thought, just as she and Coll would have to wait to have a proper reunion. She stifled a giggle as she remembered how he had roared when they had been interrupted just as they had started to become reacquainted. She looked over as Serena emerged, wrapped in towels, her skin and hair dripping.

"The dress will be beautiful," Maggie told her, blinking back tears at the thought of the wedding. "And so will you."

"By the fire," Fiona ordered, armed with a brush. Knowing the trembles had nothing to do with a chill, Fiona began to soothe her daughter as she dried her hair. "A woman's wedding is one of her most precious memories. Years from now, when you look back, what seems now like a dream will be very clear."

"Should I be so afraid?"

Fiona reached over Serena's shoulder to take her hand. "I almost think the more you love, the sharper the fear."

Serena gave a weak laugh. "Then I must love him more than I knew."

"I could not wish a better man for you, Rena. When the fighting is done, you will have a good life together."

"In England," Serena managed.

Fiona began to stroke with the brush as she had so many times before. Her hands were gentle as she thought of this small pleasure that would soon be denied her.

"When I married your father, I left my family and my home. I had grown up with the sound of the sea, the smell of it. As a girl I would climb the cliffs and watch the waves break on the rocks below. The forest of Glenroe was foreign to me, and frightening. I wasn't sure I could bear being so far away from everything I had known and loved."

"How did you?"

"By loving your father more."

They left her hair loose so that it streamed like candlelight down her back. The bodice of the gown was snug, skimming her breasts, leaving them to rise softly above as a resting place for a rope of pearls. The sleeves belled out, sheening down to her wrists. There was a glimmer of pearls on the skirt where it flared over hoops and petticoats. At the waist was a sash gathered up with a clutch of the palest pink wild roses. With her heart hammering, Serena stepped into the abbey.

It was a place of legends, of joy and despair, and of miracles. There she would be wed.

He was waiting for her. In the wavering light of lamps and candles, she walked to him. She had always thought he was at his most elegant in black, but she had never seen him look more handsome. Silver buttons glinted, adding richness to the severe cut of his coat. For the first time since she had known him, he wore a wig. The soft white added romance to his face, contrasting royally with the dark gray of his eyes.

She didn't see the Prince, or the pews filled with the lords and ladies who had come to watch the ceremony. She only saw Brigham.

When her hand touched his, it stopped trembling. Together, they faced the priest and pledged.

The clock struck midnight.

The Prince had decided that a wedding, however hurried,

deserved a celebration. Within minutes after becoming Lady Ashburn, Serena found herself being led to the picture gallery of the palace, where Charles had given his first grand ball on the night he had taken the city.

The long, wide room was already filled with music. Serena was kissed and congratulated by strangers, envied by the ladies, studied by the men. Her head was reeling by the time she was handed her first glass of champagne. She sipped and felt the bubbles burst on her tongue.

Exercising his privilege, Charles claimed her for a dance. "You make a lovely bride, Lady Ashburn."

Lady Ashburn.

"Thank you, Your Highness. How can I thank you for making this possible?"

"Your husband is of great value to me, my lady, as a soldier and as a friend."

Her husband.

"You have his loyalty, sir, and mine, both as a Langston and as a MacGregor."

Brigham claimed her when the dance had ended, fending off complaints by others who would have partnered the new bride.

"You are enjoying yourself, my love?"

"Aye." Ridiculous to be shy, she thought, but she felt herself color as she smiled at him. He looked different in the wig, with the flash of jewels, she thought. Not at all like a man who would toss her over his shoulder and threaten to dump her in a loch. He looked as glamorous as the Prince himself. And nearly as much a stranger. "It's a beautiful room."

"You see the portraits?" he asked, leading her gently by the elbow for a closer look. "There are eighty-nine, Scottish monarchs all. I'm told they were commissioned by Charles II, though he never once entered Holyrood House, in fact never returned to Scotland after the Restoration."

She knew her history, she thought irritably, but tried to show an interest. "Aye. This is Robert the Bruce, a fierce soldier and well-loved king."

"I should have known a woman as well-read as you would know her history and her politics." He leaned close to her ear. "What do you know about military strategy?"

"Military strategy?"

"Ah, so there is something yet I might teach you." Before she could answer, he pulled her roughly through a doorway. She had only time for a muffled squeal before he swept her into his arms and began to race along a corridor.

"What are you doing? You've gone mad again."

"I'm escaping." As the music faded behind them, he slowed his pace. "And I went mad from the moment you walked into the abbey. Let them dance and drink. I'm taking my wife to bed."

He mounted a staircase, not even bothering to nod at a servant who, wide-eyed, bowed himself out of the way. With Serena still in his arms, he kicked the door to his chamber open, then kicked it closed again behind them. Without ceremony, he dropped Serena on the bed.

She tried to look indignant. "Is that a way to treat your new bride, my lord?"

"I haven't even begun." Turning he shot the bolt on the door.

"I might have wanted another dance or two," she said, smoothing her palm over the bed.

"Oh, I intend to dance with you, be sure of it. From now till dawn and after."

She gave him a cheeky grin. "There's dancing, *Sassenach*, and there's dancing."

"Aye," he said, mocking her. "It's not the minuet I have in mind."

She smoothed the rumpled skirt of her gown. "What is it you have in mind, then?" She lifted her brow as she assessed him and wondered that he didn't hear how fast and loud her heart was beating. "Gwen thinks you're romantic. I doubt she'll continue to think so when I tell her how you dropped me on the bed like a sack of meal."

"Romance?" He lighted the candles that stood beside the bed. "Is that what you want, Rena?"

She moved a nearly bare shoulder. "It's what Gwen dreams of."

"But not you?" With a little laugh, he shrugged out of his coat and tossed it over a chair in a manner that would have made Parkins shudder. "A woman's entitled to romance on her wedding night." He surprised her by kneeling on the bed and slipping off her shoes. "I had no chance to tell you how magnificent you looked standing beside me in the lamplight of the abbey. Or of how, when I saw you there, every dream I have ever had came true."

"I thought you looked like a prince," she murmured, then shivered when he ran his fingertips along the arch of her foot.

"Tonight I'm only a man in love with his wife." He brushed his lips over her ankle. The scent of her bath clung to it and spun seductively in his head. "Bewitched by her." Slowly he skimmed his mouth along her calf to trace the pulse at the back of her knee. "Enslaved by her."

"I was afraid." She reached for him, gathering him close. "From the moment I stepped inside the nave I was afraid." Then she sighed as he ran kisses along the edge of her bodice, moistening and heating her skin.

"Are you still?" With sure fingers he unfastened her gown, then watched as it dropped silently to her waist.

"No. I stopped being afraid when you picked me up and ran with me through the corridors." She smiled, and her hands were as confident as his as she pushed the waistcoat from his shoulders. "That was when I knew you were my Brigham again."

"I am always yours, Rena." He lowered her gently to the bed and showed her how true his words were.

Chapter Thirteen

They were three more weeks at court. Nothing could have been more splendid than Prince Charles's Holyrood. The food was sumptuous, as was the music, the entertainment, the people. It was a gold and gleaming time, when the great halls echoed with laughter and dancing, when frivolous games and affairs of the heart were played with equal abandon.

From all over the country came elegantly dressed men in their powdered wigs, and glamorously gowned women to flirt with them. Holyrood was gay and glittering, and in it Charles lived those weeks a true prince. It was a place and a time that would never be forgotten.

Serena watched Brigham meld into this world he had been born for, while she, fueled by determination more than by confidence, adjusted to the life of beauty and glamour.

There were new rules to learn, a new pattern to the days and the nights. Here, at the first court to grace Scotland in many years, Serena discovered what it was to be Lady Ashburn. There were servants to attend her whether she wanted them or not.

Because of Brigham's position, they were given a gracious chamber hung with tapestries and appointed with elegant furnishings. She met more people in a matter of weeks than she had in the whole of her life, many of whom had come out of curiosity, but more still who had come out of loyalty.

Court life continued to make her uneasy, and often impatient, but the people who comprised it made her proud of her heritage, and her husband.

Serena had the first true inkling of Brigham's wealth when he presented her with the Langston emeralds. With the help of his contacts in London he had them transported from Ashburn Manor and gave them to Serena less than a week after they had exchanged vows.

The necklace was as stately as its name and glimmered with stones as green as the lawns of his estate. It was matched with a bracelet and ear bobs that made Maggie's jaw drop. To accent them, Brigham commissioned a dressmaker. Serena found herself gowned in silks and satins, in soft lawns and wispy lace. She discovered what it was like to wear diamonds in her hair and scent her skin with the finest of French perfumes.

She would have given it all for a week alone with Brigham in a Highland croft.

It was impossible not to enjoy the splendor, impossible not to revel a little in the envious glances of other ladies as she was escorted into a room by Brigham. She wore the gowns and the jewels, dressed her hair and felt beautiful. But as the days passed, she couldn't shake the sensation that it was all like a dream. The lights, the glamour, the tinkling laughter of women, the sweeping bows of men, her own easy relationship with the Prince.

But the nights were real. Serena clung to them as tightly as she clung to Brigham in the privacy of their marriage bed. She knew it was temporary, and that its continuation was in God's hands. It was only a matter of time before Brigham would leave. They did not speak of it. There was no need to speak of what they both understood. If force of will alone could bring him back safely to her, she could be content.

At night she could be his wife freely, in heart, mind and body. By day she often felt like an impostor, masquerading in fashionable gowns as a lady while in her heart she remained a product of the Highlands, longing to kilt up her skirts and race through the autumn trees surrounding the park as the wind tore the leaves from the branches for a dizzying dance. Instead, she walked sedately with the other women while the men held council or rode to the camp.

Because she loved, she put her heart and soul into being the kind of wife she thought Brigham should have. She sat, desperately struggling to be attentive, through musical evenings. Though she found it absurd, she never complained about the necessity to change from a morning dress to an afternoon dress, then again for evening. Only once, when she was sure she wouldn't be noticed, did she accompany Malcolm to the stables to admire the horses.

She envied her young brother the freedom to take wild rides, but set her teeth and determined to enjoy her own demure ones.

"Do this, do that," she muttered as she paced alone in her bedchamber. "Don't do this, don't do that." Swearing, she kicked a chair with the toe of the pretty slipper that matched her violet morning dress. "A body could go mad trying to remember the rules, then madder still trying to live by them."

With a hiss of breath she dropped down into the chair, skirts billowing. She wanted the loch, the peace of it. She didn't just want to look out at the hills and crags. She wanted to climb them. She wanted her breeches, she thought, and her boots. She wanted...

Sighing, she braced her elbows on her knees and cupped her face in her hands. Not an attitude suitable for Lady Ashburn, but Serena didn't feel like Lady Ashburn at the moment. She was being selfish and ungrateful, she told herself. Brigham was giving her things many another women would have swooned over. He was promising her the kind of life only a fool would toss aside.

And she was a fool, Serena decided, because she would have done just that if it wouldn't have meant losing Brigham, as well. Living with dignity and propriety was a small price to pay for love. But oh, she had nearly botched it a dozen times already, and they had only been married three weeks.

She heard the door open and popped up like a spring, smoothing her skirts. A breath of relief escaped when she saw that it was Brigham. She would have hated for a servant to gossip below stairs about how Lady Ashburn sulked in her room with her elbows on her knees.

Brigham lifted a brow when he saw her. He would have sworn she grew more beautiful each day, though he did wish from time to time that she could wear her hair loose and free so that he could bury his hands in it at will.

"I thought you were going for a walk with your sister and Maggie."

"I was just getting ready." Automatically she reached up to pat her hair, afraid her pacing had loosened the careful arrangement. "I didn't expect you back until much later. Is the council over?"

"Yes. You look exquisite, Rena. Like a wild violet."

With a laugh that was half sob, she raced into his arms. "Oh, Brig, I love you. I love you so much."

"What's this?" he murmured as she pressed her face against his neck. "Are you crying?"

"No—aye, a little. It's only that whenever I see you I love you more than the last time."

"Then I'll take care to leave and come back several times each day."

"Don't laugh at me."

"And risk fatal injury?" He tilted her head back so that he could kiss her properly. "No, my dear, I shan't laugh at you."

She saw it in his eyes, and knew then that she had seen it the moment he had come into the room. The courage she had promised herself she would show wavered, but she willed it back. "It's time, isn't it?"

He brought her hand to his lips. "Come, sit."

"There is no need," she said steadily. "Just tell me."

"We march in a matter of days. Tomorrow you must leave for Glenroe."

Her cheeks paled, but her voice remained strong. "I would stay until you go."

"I would go with an easier mind if I knew you were safe at Glenroe. The journey will take longer because of Maggie."

She knew he was right, knew it was necessary, and tried to live with it. "You march to London?"

"God willing."

With a nod, she stepped back, but she kept his hand in hers. "The fight is mine, as well as yours, doubly so now that I am your wife. I would go with you, if you would let me."

"No. Do you think I see my wife as a camp follower?" The look, the very familiar look, in her eyes warned him to change tactics. "Your family needs you, Serena."

What of my needs? The words sprang to her tongue and were bitten back. She would do him no good by following him into battle. She looked at her hand and cursed the fact that it was too weak to wield a sword, to protect him as he would protect her.

"You're right. I know. I will wait for you."

"I take you with me. Here." He brought their joined hands to his heart. "There is something I would ask of you. If things go wrong—" She shook her head, but a look from him stopped her urgent protest. "There is a chest in my chamber, and a strong-box. In the box is gold and enough jewels to buy your safety and that of your family. In the chest is something more precious that I would have you keep."

"What is it?"

He traced a fingertip along her cheekbone, remembering. "You will know when you see it."

"I won't forget, but there will be no need. You will come back." She smiled. "Remember, you have promised to show me Ashburn Manor."

"I remember."

Lifting her hands, she began to undo the tiny buttons at her bodice.

"What are you doing?

Smiling still, she let the dress open. "What I am not doing

is going for a walk with my sister." She undid the satin sash at her waist. "Is it improper to seduce one's husband at this hour?"

"Probably." He grinned as she tugged the coat from his shoulders. "But we shall keep it our secret."

They made love on the elegantly skirted bed, under the high canopy, with the sun coming strong through the windows. The proper morning dress lay discarded in billows of violet. She knelt beside him, slender, with the light playing over her skin as she drew the pins from her hair. Heavily, in a glory of flame-tipped gold, it fell over her naked shoulders and breasts. Brigham reached for it, wrapped it once, twice, around his wrists as if to imprison himself, then drew her slowly down to him.

Their bodies fit.

They both remembered the loch, and another sun-drenched morning filled with love and passions. The memory of it, and thoughts of the cloudy, uncertain future brought them gently together. Selflessly they gave to each other, beautifully they received.

With a sigh, he slipped into her. With a murmur, their lips met and clung. Together they showed one another a new level of pleasure, one that could be reached only through the purity and the passions of unconditional love.

It was the first of November when the march finally began. Many, Brigham among them, had urged the Prince to begin the campaign earlier, moving on the advantage they had gained by taking Edinburgh. Instead, Charles had continued to hope for active support from France. Money had indeed come, and supplies, but no men. Charles put his own strength at eight thousand, with three hundred horses. He knew that he must make one decisive stroke, bringing victory or defeat in a short time. As before, he decided the best strategy was a bold one.

Charles had a high opinion of his troops, as did the English. A few months before, the young Prince's ambitions and his rag-tag troops of rugged Highlanders had been laughed at. Then he had swept down on Edinburgh. His early victories, and the flair with which he had brought defeat to the English had the uneasy government recalling more and more troops from Flanders, sending them to Field Marshal Wade in Newcastle.

Still, as the Stuart army marched into Lancaster under the leadership of Lord George Murray, they met with little resistance. But the celebration there might have been was offset by the disappointing number of English Jacobites who had rallied.

Near a hot fire on a cold night, Brigham sat with Whitesmouth, who had ridden from Manchester to join the cause. Men warmed themselves with whiskey and wrapped themselves in plaids against the keening wind.

"We should have attacked Wade's forces." Whitesmouth tipped his flask. "Now they've called the elector's fat son Cumberland in haste, and he's advancing through the Midlands. How many are we, Brig? Four, five thousand?"

"At best." Brigham accepted the flask but only stared into the fire. "The Prince is pushed two ways by Murray and O'Sullivan. Each decision comes only after agonizing debate. If you want the truth, Johnny, we lost our momentum in Edinburgh. We may never get it back."

"But you stay?"

"He has my oath."

They sat another moment in silence, listening to the wind

crying over the hills. "You know that some of the Scots are drifting off, going quietly back to their glens and hills."

"I know it."

Only that day, Ian and other chiefs had spoken together. They meant to hold their men. Brigham wondered if they, or anyone, fully understood that the brilliant victories of their outnumbered and ill-equipped army had been won because the men hadn't simply been ordered to fight, but had fought with their hearts. Once the heart was lost, so would be the cause.

With a shake of his head, he shifted his thoughts to practical matters. "We reach Derby tomorrow. If we hit London quickly, thoroughly, we could still see the king on the throne." He sipped then, as someone began to play a mournful tune on the pipes. "We've yet to be beaten. From what news you bring, there is panic in the city and the elector prepares to leave for Hanover."

"There may he stay," Whitesmouth mumbled. "My God, it's cold."

"In the north the wind has an edge as sharp and as sweet as a blade."

"If luck is with us, you'll be back to your wife and her Highlands by the new year."

Brigham drank again, but in his heart he knew it would take more than luck.

In Derby, with London only 130 miles away, Charles held his council of war.

Snow fell fitfully outside as the men rounded the table. A gloom was in the room, both from the leaden light and on the faces of men. There was a good fire, but over its crackle and hiss the sound of the icy wind could still be heard.

"Gentlemen." Charles spread his fine hands in front of him. "I

seek advice from you who have pledged to my father. It is bold-
ness we need, and unity."

His dark eyes scanned the room, lighting briefly on each
man. Murray was there, and the man whom Murray considered
a thorn in his side, O'Sullivan. Brigham watched, holding his
silence, as the Prince continued to speak.

"We know that three government troops threaten to con-
verge on us, and morale among the men is suffering. A thrust,
rapier-sharp, at the capital—now, while we still remember our
victories—is surely our move."

"Your Highness." Murray waited, then was given permission
to speak. "The advice I must offer is caution. We are poorly
equipped and greatly outnumbered. If we withdraw to the Highlands, take the winter to plan a new campaign that would launch
in spring, we might rally those men we have already lost and
draw fresh supplies from France."

"Such counsel is the counsel of despair," Charles said. "I can
see nothing but ruin and destruction coming to us if we should
retreat."

"Withdraw," Murray corrected, and was joined by the assent
of other advisers. "Our rebellion is young, but it must not be
impulsive."

Charles listened, shutting his eyes a moment as one after another of the men who stood with him echoed Murray's sentiments. Prudence, patience, caution. Only O'Sullivan preached
attack, using flattery and reckless promises in his attempt to
sway the Prince.

All at once, Charles sprang up from his chair, scattering the
maps and documents spread out in front of him. "What say
you?" he demanded of Brigham.

Brigham knew that, militarily, Murray's advice was sound. But he remembered his own thoughts as he had sat with Whitesmouth by the fire. If they withdrew now, the heart of the rebellion would be lost. For once, perhaps for the only time, his thoughts marched in step with O'Sullivan's.

"With respect, Your Highness, if the choice was mine I would march to London at daybreak and seize the moment."

"The heart says to fight, Your Highness," one of the advisers put in, closely echoing Brigham's thoughts. "But in war, one must heed the head, as well. If we ride to London as we are, our losses could be immeasurable."

"Or our triumph great," Charles interrupted passionately. "Are we women who cover our heads at the first sign of snow or who think of only warming our tired feet by the fire? Withdraw, retreat." He swung back toward Murray, eyes furious. "It is one and the same. I wonder if you have a mind to betray me."

"I have only a mind to see you and our cause succeed," Murray said quietly. "You are a prince, sire. I am but a soldier and must speak as one who knows his troops and the way of war."

The argument continued, but long before it was finished, Brigham saw how it would be. The Prince, never strong of purpose when faced with dissension among his advisers, was being forced to heed Murray's words of caution. On December 6, the decision to retreat was taken.

The road back to Scotland was long, and the men dispirited. It was as Brigham had feared. When a halt was called to the exuberant, aggressive advance that had given the clans such power since the previous summer, the heart went out of the rebellion. Men might still talk of another invasion in the following year, but all believed in their secret hearts that they would never march south again.

They fell back behind the Scottish border and took Glasgow, though the city was openly hostile. The men, frustrated and disillusioned, might have taken that Christmas day to loot and sack, had not Cameron of Lochiel's cool head and compassion dissuaded them.

Stirling surrendered just as reinforcements, men, stores and ammunition arrived from France. It started to seem as if the right decision had been made, but if Charles now believed Lord George had been correct, he never spoke of it.

The Prince's numbers were again on the increase as more clans came to him, pledging heart and sword and men. But there were MacKenzies and MacLeods, MacKays and Munroes who followed the elector's colors.

They fought again, south of Stirling, in the purple winter's dusk, Scot fighting Scot, as well as English. Again they tasted victory, but with it came grief, as Ian MacGregor fell to an enemy blade.

He lingered through the night. Men who ride in battle need not be told when wounds are mortal. Brigham knew it as he sat beside the old man with the night wind flapping at the tent.

He thought of Serena and how she had laughed when the big bear of a MacGregor had swung her around and around in her night robe. He thought of riding with Ian through the winter wind and of sharing a bottle of port near a great fire. Now, approaching death seemed to have stolen both size and strength so that he was only an old, fragile man. Still, his hair glowed rich and red in the pale glow of the lamp.

"Your mother..." Ian began, reaching for Coll's hand.

"I'll care for her." They were men who loved each other too well to pretend there would be a tomorrow.

"Aye." Ian's breath hissed in and out, like wind through an empty husk of wheat. "The bairn—my only regret is I won't see the bairn."

"He shall carry your name," Coll vowed. "He shall know the man who was his grandsire."

There was a faint smile on Ian's mouth, though his lips were the color of ashes. "Brigham."

"I'm here, sir."

Because his vision was fading, Ian concentrated on the voice. "Don't tame my wildcat. She would die from it. You and Coll will tend to little Gwen and Malcolm. Keep them safe."

"My word on it."

"My sword—" Ian struggled for another breath. "My sword to Malcolm. Coll, you have your own."

"He shall have it." Coll bent over Ian's hand. "Papa."

"We were right to fight. It will not be for naught." He opened his eyes for the last time. "Royal is our race, lad." He managed a final fierce grin. "We are MacGregors despite them."

There were men dispatched to bear the body back to Glenroe, but Coll refused to go with them. "He would have me stay with the Prince," Coll told Brigham as they stood out in the bitter sleet. "That he died here, with our backs turned to London."

"It's not finished, Coll."

Coll turned his head. There was grief in his eyes, and also a bright anger. "No, by God, it's not."

The men of the clans grew dispirited, as it seemed ever clearer that the invasion of England was fast petering out into a holding action. Desertions had become frequent, and the decision was made to consolidate forces in the north of Scotland. But the leaders continue to bicker, even after the rebels forded the icy waters of the Forth and marched north up the Great Glen. For seven weeks that winter, Charles made his base in Inverness. Inactivity again took its toll, dwindling the numbers of the so recently replenished troops. There were short, sporadic, often bitter little battles during those weeks. The Jacobites were again victorious in the taking of Fort Augustus, that hated English stronghold at the heart of the Highlands, but the men longed for a decisive victory and for home. Meanwhile, Cumberland massed his forces. It seemed the winter would never end.

It was snowing when Serena stood by her father's grave. He had come back to them nearly a month before, and all Glenroe had wept. Her own tears fell freely as she longed for him, for the thunderous sound of his voice, for the crushing strength of his arms and the laughter in his eyes.

She wanted to cry out. Serena much preferred fury to tears, but the anger had drained out of her. There was only a sorrow, a deep, abiding grief that stirred in her heart even as the child she now carried stirred in her womb.

It was the helplessness, she thought, that made a body weak and the heart brittle. No amount of work or temper or love could bring her father back or take the dull pain out of her mother's eyes. Men fought, and women grieved.

She closed her eyes and let the snow fall stinging to her cheeks. There must be more, she thought, more than waiting and mourning. She had already lost one man she loved. How would she go on if she lost another?

The rebellion, she thought with the first flash of fire she had felt in weeks. The damned rebellion was…was right, she realized, pushing the heels of her hands over her face to dry them. It was right and it was just. If people believed strongly, they should be willing to fight, and to die. Her father had said so, and had stood unwaveringly by his words. How could she do less?

"I miss you so," she murmured. "And I'm afraid. There's the child now, you see. Your grandchild." She smoothed a hand over the slight slope of her belly. "There was nothing I could do to save you, just as there's nothing I can do to protect Brigham or Coll. I wish— Oh Papa, I'm with child and part of me still wishes I could be a man so I could pick up a sword for you." She searched in her pockets until her fingers closed over the handkerchief Brigham had given her so many months before. She laid it on her cheek, using it as a talisman to bring him clearly to mind. "Is he safe? He doesn't even know we made a child between us. I would go to him." She felt the baby quicken. "But I can't. I can't protect and fight for him, but I can protect and fight for the child."

"Rena?"

She turned to see Malcolm standing a little way off. Snow fell in sheets between them, but she could see the quiver of his lips and the sheen of tears in his eyes. Wordlessly she opened her arms to him.

While he wept, she held him, finding comfort somehow in comforting another. He had been so brave, she remembered, standing so straight, holding their mother's arm while the priest had said the last words over their father's grave. He'd been a man then. Now he was a little boy.

"I hate the English." His voice was muffled against her shawl.

"I know. Mother would say hate is not Christian, but sometimes I think there is a time for hate, just as there is a time for love. And there is a time, my love, to let go of it."

"He was a fierce warrior."

"Aye." She was able to smile now as she drew him back to study his tear-streaked face. "Do you not think, Malcolm, that a fierce warrior might prefer to die fighting for what he believes?"

"They had retreated," Malcolm said bitterly, and Serena saw a glimpse of Coll in his eyes.

"Aye." The letter she had received from Brigham had explained the maneuver, his dissatisfaction with it and the growing dissent in the ranks. "I don't understand the strategy of generals, Malcolm, but I do know that whether the Prince is victor or vanquished, nothing will ever be the same."

"I want to go to Inverness and join."

"Malcolm—"

"I have Father's sword," he interrupted, passion darkening his eyes. "I can use it. I will use it to avenge him and support the Prince. I am not a child."

She looked at him then. The little boy who had run weeping into her arms was a man again. He stood as high as her shoulder, his jaw firm, his hand clenched on the hilt of his dagger. He could go, Serena realized with a flutter of fear.

"No, you are not a child, and I believe you could raise Father's sword like a man. I will not stop you if your heart tells you to go, but I would ask that you think of Mother, of Gwen and Maggie."

"You can care for them."

"Aye, I would try, but every day the child within me grows." She took his hand in hers. It was stiff and cold and surprisingly strong. "And I'm afraid. I can't tell Mother or the others, but I'm afraid. When I grow as big as Maggie, how will I be able to keep them safe if the English come? I don't ask you not to fight, Malcolm, nor do I tell you you're a child. But I will ask you to be a man and fight here."

Torn, he turned back to stare down at her father's grave. The snow lay over it in a soft white blanket. "Father would have wanted me to stay."

Relief coursed through her, but she only touched his shoulder. "Aye. There is no disgrace in staying behind, not when it's the right thing."

"It's hard."

"I know." Now she slipped her arm around him. "Believe me, Malcolm, I know. There are things we can do," she murmured, thinking aloud. "When the snow stops. If the Prince's troops are as close as Inverness, the English will not be far behind. We cannot fight in Glenroe, there are too few of us, and almost all women and children."

"You think the English will come here?" he demanded, half eager, half terrified.

"I begin to believe it. Did word not come to us that there was a battle at Moy Hall?"

"And the English were routed," Malcolm reminded her.

"But it is too close. If we cannot defend, then we protect. You and I will find a place in the hills and prepare it. Food, supplies, blankets, weapons." She thought of the strongbox. "We will plan, Malcolm, as warriors plan."

"I know a place, a cave."

"You will take me there tomorrow."

* * *

Brigham rode hard. Though it was nearly April, the weather remained cold, with snow often whipped up by the hateful wind. He commanded a handful of weary, hungry men. This foraging party, like others that had been sent out from Inverness, went in search of much-needed food and supplies. One of their greatest hopes, a captured government sloop renamed *Prince Charles*, had been retaken by the enemy off the Kyle of Tongue, and her desperately looked-for funds were now in the hands of the enemy.

Brigham's party had found more than oats and venison. They had discovered news. The duke of Cumberland, the elector's second son, lay in Aberdeen with a well-armed, well-fed army of twice their strength. He had received a powerful reinforcement of five thousand German soldiers, who remained in Dornoch, blocking the route south. The word came that Cumberland was beginning his advance on Inverness.

Hooves thudded on the layer of snow still covering the road. The men rode mostly in silence, edgy with hunger and fatigue. They wanted a meal and the cold comfort of sleep.

Redcoats were spotted to the west. With a quick signal, Brigham halted his troops and scanned the distance. They were outnumbered nearly two to one, and the dragoons looked fresh. He had a choice. They could run, or they could fight. Turning his horse, he took a hard look at his men.

"We can make the hills and lose them, or we can meet them here on the road, with the rocks to their backs."

"We fight." One man fingered his sword. Then another and another added his voice. The dragoons had already spurred into a gallop. Brigham flashed a grin. It was the answer he'd wanted.

"Then let's show them the faces of king's men." Wheeling his horse, he led the charge.

There was something fierce and chilling about a Highland charge. They rode as if they rode into hell, screaming in Gaelic and brandishing blades. Wall met wall, and the lonely hills echoed with the fury. Around Brigham men fought like demons and fell dying from the slice and hack of steel. Snow ran red.

It was unlike him to allow his emotions to surface in battle. Here, after weeks of frustration and anger, he let himself go, cutting through the line of oncoming dragoons like a man gone mad. He saw no faces, only that nameless entity known as the enemy. His sword whipped out, severing flesh as he dragged his horse right, then left, then right again.

They drove the dragoons onto the rocks, pursuing them mercilessly. Weeks of waiting had worked like a cancer that came rising to the surface to eat away at the civilized veneer.

When they were done five Jacobites lay dead or dying alongside a dozen dragoons. The rest of the government troop had fled over the rocks like rabbits.

"After them, lads," one of the Highlanders shouted. Brigham swung his horse to block the next charge.

"For what purpose?" He dismounted to clean his blade in the snow. "We've done what we've done. Now we tend to our own." A foot away, a man moaned. Sheathing his weapon, Brigham went to him. "The English dead will be buried. Our own dead and wounded will be taken back to Inverness."

"Leave the English for the kites."

Brigham's head whipped around. His eyes had lost their fever and were cold again as they studied the blood-spattered face of the hefty Scot who had spoken. "We are not animals. We bury the dead, friend or enemy."

In the end, the English dead were given cairns. The ground was too hard for graves.

The men were still weary, still hungry, when they turned their mounts toward Inverness. They rode slowly, burdened by their wounded. With each long mile, Brigham thought of how close the dragoons had been to Glenroe.

Chapter Fourteen

In the chill of April, the drums sounded and the pipes were played. In Inverness, the army readied for battle. Only twelve miles away, Cumberland had pitched camp.

"I do not like the ground." Once more, Murray stood as Charles's adviser, but the rift between them that the retreat had caused had never fully healed. "Drumossie Moor is well suited to the tactics of the English army, but not to ours. Your Highness…" Perhaps because he knew Charles had yet to forgive him for the retreat north, Murray chose his words with care. "This wide, bare moor might as well have been designed for the maneuvers of Cumberland's infantry, and I tell you there could never be a more improper ground for Highlanders."

"Do we withdraw again?" O'Sullivan put in. He was as loyal as Murray, as brave a soldier, but he lacked the hardheaded military sense of the Englishman. "Your Highness, have not the Highlanders proved themselves fierce and fearsome warriors, as you have proven a canny general? Again and again you have beaten back the English."

"Here we are not simply outnumbered." Murray turned his back on O'Sullivan and appealed to the Prince. "The ground itself is the most terrible weapon. If we withdraw north again, across Nairn Water—"

"We shall stand to meet Cumberland." Charles, his eyes cool, his hands neatly folded, watched his most trusted men. "We shall not run again. Through the winter we have waited." And the wait, he knew, had disillusioned and disgruntled his men. It might have been that more than O'Sullivan's flattery or his own impatience that swayed him. "We wait no longer. Quartermaster-General O'Sullivan has chosen the ground, and we shall fight."

Murray's eyes met Brigham's briefly. They had already discussed the Prince's decision. "Your Highness, if your mind is made up, may I propose a maneuver that may strengthen our advantage?"

"If it does not include a retreat, my lord."

Color stained Murray's cheeks, but he continued. "Today is the duke's birthday, and his men will celebrate it. They will be drunk as beggars. A surprise night attack could turn the tide."

The Prince considered. "I find this interesting. Continue."

"Two columns of men," Murray began, using candlesticks to illustrate. "They would close in in a pincer movement, coming into camp from both sides and cutting down the size of Cumberland's army while they sleep off the effects of the birthday brandy."

"A good plan," the Prince murmured, excitement once more kindling his eyes. "The duke should celebrate well, for the celebration will be short-lived."

They marched. Men with no more than a single biscuit in their bellies set out to cover the twelve miles in the dark and

the unrelieved cold. The plan was a good one, but the men sent
to accomplish it were tired and hungry. Once, twice, then yet
again, they lost direction and heart, until they were no more
than a group wandering.

On horseback, the sun newly up, Brigham and Coll watched
them return to camp.

"My God," the Scot muttered. "We've come to this."

With his own fatigue weighing on him, Brigham shifted in
the saddle. Men exhausted from the march and grinding hunger
dropped to the ground, many nodding off to sleep in the park
of Culloden House or near the road. Others grumbled, even as
the Prince rode among them.

Turning his head, Brigham looked out on Drumossie Moor.
It was wide and bare, skimmed now with early frost and a thin,
shifting mist. To Brigham, it might have been a parade ground
for Cumberland's infantry. To the north, across the river called
Nairn, the ground was broken and hilly. There Murray would
have chosen to stand. And there, Brigham thought, there would
have been a chance for victory.

But O'Sullivan had the Prince's ear now, and there was no
turning back.

"It ends here," Brigham said softly. "For better or worse." In
the east, the sun struggled sluggishly to life, trapped behind
churning clouds. Spurring his horse, he rode through the camp.
"On your feet!" he shouted. "Will you sleep until you wake with
your throats cut? Can you not hear the English drums beating
to arms?"

Dragging themselves up, men began to gather in their clans.
Artillery was manned. What rations were left were passed among
the troops, but they served only to leave stomachs edgy and

empty. With pike and ax, gun and scythe, they rallied under the standard. MacGregors and MacDonalds, Camerons and Chisholms, Mackintoshes and Robertsons and more. They were five thousand, hungry, ill-equipped, held only by the cause that still bound them together.

Charles looked every bit the prince as he rode up and down their lines in his tartan coat and cockaded bonnet. They were his men, and the oath he had sworn to them was no less than that they had sworn him.

Across the moor, they watched the enemy advance. They were in three columns that slowly and smoothly swung into line. As Charles had done, the duke, pudgy in his red coat, a black cockade pinned to his tricorn, rode along encouraging his men.

There was the sound of drum and pipe, and the empty hum of wind that whipped sleet into the faces of the Jacobites. The first shots were fired by Jacobite guns. They were answered, and devastatingly.

As the first cannon exploded near Culloden House, Maggie arched against a contraction. They were coming quickly, powerfully. Her body, weakened by the full night of labor, was racked with pain her mind no longer registered. Over and over she cried out for Coll.

"Poor lass, poor lass." Mrs Drummond brought fresh water and linen to the bedchamber. "Such a wee thing she is."

"There, darling, there." Fiona bathed Maggie's streaming face. "Mrs. Drummond, another log on the fire, please. We need it warm when the baby comes."

"Wood's nearly gone."

Fiona only nodded. "We'll use what we have. Gwen?"

"The babe's breech, Mother." Gwen straightened a moment to ease the strain in her back. "Maggie's so small."

Serena, one hand holding Maggie's, laid the other protectively over the child growing inside her own womb. "Can you save them, save them both?"

"God willing." Gwen wiped the sweat from her face with the sleeve of her dress.

"Lady MacGregor, I can tell Parkins to find more wood." Mrs. Drummond's wide face creased with concern as Maggie cried out with the next pain. She had birthed and lost two babies of her own. "A man ought to be good for something other than planting a seed in a woman."

Too tired to disapprove of the sentiment, Fiona nodded. "Please, Mrs. Drummond. Tell him we'd be grateful to him."

"Coll." Maggie sobbed, turning her head from side to side. Her eyes focused on Serena. "Rena?"

"Aye, my love, I'm here. We're all here."

"Coll. I want Coll."

"I know. I know you do." Serena kissed Maggie's limp hand. "He'll be back soon." Her own baby kicked, making her wonder if in a few months she would find herself confined, calling out Brigham's name over waves of pain, all the while knowing he wasn't there to answer. "Gwen says you must rest between the pains, gather your strength back."

"I try. Should it take so long?" Weakly she turned her head back to Gwen. "Tell me the truth, please. Is something wrong with the babe?"

For a split second Gwen debated lying. But though she was young still, she had already seen that women dealt best with the truth, no matter how frightening. "He's turned wrong, Maggie. I know what to do, but it won't be a simple birth."

"Am I going to die?" There was no desperation in Maggie's question, only a need for truth. As difficult as it was, Gwen had already made her decision. If she had to choose, she would save Maggie and lose the child. Before she could speak, the next contraction hit, bringing Maggie, exhausted as she was, rearing up.

"Oh, God. My baby, don't let my baby die. Swear it to me. Swear it."

"No one's going to die." Serena squeezed her hand hard, so hard it cut through the other pain and had Maggie quieting. "No one's going to die," she repeated. "Because you're going to fight. When the pain comes you're going to scream it out if need be, but you're not going to give up. MacGregors don't give up."

The round shot of the government artillery cut huge holes in the Jacobite lines. Their own guns could only answer ineffectually as men fell like slain deer. Wind blew smoke and sleet back in their faces while they stood and suffered the slaughter of their ranks. Even with their lines running six deep, the cannonfire broke through and brought writhing, miserable death.

"Sweet Jesus, why won't they give the order to charge?" Coll, his face blackened with smoke, looked with desperate eyes at the carnage. "Will they have us stand here and be cut down to the last man before we raise a sword?"

Brigham swung around and galloped for the right wing, driving hard through the smoke and fire. "In the name of God," he cried when he faced the Prince, "give us the command to charge. We die like dogs."

"What are you saying? We wait for Cumberland to attack."

"You can't see what the cannons have done to your front lines. If you wait for Cumberland, you wait in vain. He won't attack as long as his guns can murder from a distance. We haven't their range, and sweet Lord, we're dying."

Charles began to dismiss him, for indeed his position was such that he had no clear view of the murderous skill of Cumberland's artillery, but at that moment, Murray himself rode to the Prince with the request.

"Give the command," Charles agreed.

The messenger was sent, but was felled by a cannonball before he could reach the ranks. Seeing it, Brigham continued the drive himself, shouting the order "Claymore" over the cheers and oaths of the men.

The center of the line moved first, racing like wild stags across the moor, and fell upon the dragoons, swinging broadsword and scythe. It would be written that the Highlanders came like wolves, desperate for blood, fearless in spirit. But they were only men, and many were cut down by bayonet and dagger.

If the English had run in front of a Highland assault before, they had now learned. In a canny and merciless maneuver, the dragoons shifted lines to catch the charging Scots in a sweeping and deadly rifle volley.

The Highland charge continued, but the ground itself, as predicted, served the English. A hail of bullets split the line. Still, it seemed for an instant as though their combined strength would crumble Cumberland's ranks, as the English were forced back to the next line of defense. But that second line held, pouring devastating fire onto the raging Highlanders. They fell, men heaping onto men so that those who still stood were forced to crawl over the bodies of their comrades.

Still the guns thundered, scattering grapeshot now—canisters full of nails and lead balls and iron scrap—like hideous rain.

The well-trained dragoons held their ground, one rank firing while the next reloaded so that the hail of bullets was unending. But still the clansmen pressed on.

Grapeshot blasted against Brigham's shield, scoring his arm and shoulder as he fought his way over the dead and wounded and through the duke's line. He saw James MacGregor, Rob Roy's impetuous son, driving his men through the living wall of English troops. His own eyes stung from the smoke that blurred his vision. Ice was in his veins as he hacked and sliced his way toward the back of Cumberland's line. Through the fog, he saw that Murray had preceded him, his hat and wig blown off during the battle. Only then did the confusion surrounding them start to come clear.

True, their right wing had cut through, taking down the dragoons in the press of their charge. But elsewhere, the Jacobites were in tatters. The MacDonalds had taken fearful punishment as they tried to lure the dragoons into attack with short, daring rushes, for the men facing them down had stood their ground and fired unrelentingly.

In a desperate move, Brigham wheeled back, determined to fight his way through yet again and rally what men he could.

He saw Coll, legs planted, claymore and dirk whistling viciously as he fought off three red-coated English. Without hesitation, Brigham went to his aid.

This was no romantic duel at dawn, but a sweaty, grunting fight for life. The wound Brigham had already received was oozing blood, and his dagger hand was slippery. Smoke billowed, clogging the lungs, even as the sleet continued to fall.

Only small, sporadic skirmishes remained in the area around them. The Jacobites were still fighting wildly but were being forced back over the moor, which was already strewn with dead and wounded. The wall of men that had once been strong on the right wing had been broken, allowing the red-coated cavalry to storm through and threaten the retreating men.

But the bigger defeat meant little at that moment to Coll and Brigham, who fought back-to-back, outnumbered in their personal war as surely as the whole of the Prince's army had been outnumbered by Cumberland's. Coll took a hit to the thigh, but the gash went almost unfelt as he continued to lash out with his weapon. Behind him, Brigham whirled and struck before another blow hit home. With this small personal victory, both men turned and began the race over the littered, smoke-covered moor.

"My God, they've destroyed us." Breathless and bleeding, Coll scanned the carnage. It was a picture a man would never forget, a glimpse of hell steaming with smoke and stinking of blood. "There must have been ten thousand of them." He saw, as they broke into a pocket of clear air, a dragoon brutally mutilating the body of an already-dead clansman. With a lionlike roar, Coll fell on him.

"Enough. Sweet Jesus." Brigham dragged him off. "There's nothing more we can do here but die. The cause is lost, Coll; the rebellion is over." But Coll was like a madman, sword raised, ready to use it on the first man who crossed his path. "Think. Glenroe is close, too close. We have to get back, get the family out."

"Maggie." Only at his father's death had Coll felt so much like weeping. "Aye, you've the right of it."

They began again, swords at the ready. Here and there could still be heard the volley of shots and the screams. They had nearly reached the hills when a chance twist of his head showed Brigham the wounded dragoon lifting his musket and taking unsteady aim.

There was time only to shove Coll out of the line of the fire. Brigham felt the ball slam into his body, felt its roaring, hideous pain.

He fell on the edge of Drumossie Moor, in the place that came to be known as Culloden.

Numb, nearly asleep on her feet, Serena burst out of the house to drag in cold, fresh air. There were wars only women knew, and she had fought such a war. They had been nearly two nights in the desperate battle to bring Maggie's child out of her womb and into the world. There had been blood and sweat and pain she had never imagined. The boy had come, feet first, into the world, leaving his mother wavering between life and death.

Now it was nearly dusk, and Gwen had said that Maggie would live. Serena could only remember those first thin, wailing cries. Maggie had heard them, too, before she had fainted from exhaustion and loss of blood.

Here, outside, the light was soft with approaching evening. To the west the first stars had shivered themselves into life, luring a lone owl. Serena felt its call pierce through her.

"Oh, Brigham." She wrapped her arms around the slope of her own belly. "I need you."

"Serena?"

She turned, narrowing her eyes to focus as a figure limped out of the shadows. "Rob? Rob MacGregor?" Then she saw him fully, his doublet streaked with blood, his hair matted with dirt and sweat, and his eyes, his wild eyes. "What happened to you? My God." She reached for him as he stumbled at her feet.

"The battle. The English. They've killed us, Serena. Killed us."

"Brigham." She snatched at his torn shirt. "Brigham. Where is he? Is he safe? In the name of pity, tell me, where is Brigham?"

"I don't know. So many dead, so many." He wept into her skirts, broken. He had once been young, idealistic, fond of fancy waistcoats and pretty girls. "My father, my brothers, all dead. I saw them fall. And old MacLean, too, and young David Mackintosh. Slaughtered." The horror of it showed in his eyes when he lifted his face. "Even when we ran they slaughtered us like pigs."

"Did you see Brigham?" she said desperately, shaking him as he sobbed against her. "And Coll. Did you see them?"

"Aye. I saw them, but there was smoke, so much smoke, and the guns never stopped. Even when it was over it didn't stop. I saw—I saw them killing women, and children. There was a farmer and his son plowing. The dragoons rode over them, stabbing and stabbing. I was hiding, and I saw the wounded on the field. They murdered them with clubs."

"No." Again she wrapped her arms around her unborn child as she began to rock back and forth. "No."

"A man would put down his weapons in surrender and still be shot down like a dog. They came after us. There were bodies along the road, hundreds, we couldn't even bury our dead."

"When? When was the battle fought?"

"Yesterday." With a choked sob, he wiped his eyes. "Only yesterday."

He was safe. She had to believe that Brigham was safe. How could she move, how could she act, if she thought him dead?

He was not dead, she told herself as she slowly rose. She would not let him be dead. She looked to the house, where the candles were already lighted for evening. She had a family to protect.

"Will they come here, Rob?"

"They are hunting us down like animals." Recovered, he spit on the ground. "My shame is that I did not kill a dozen more instead of running."

"Sometimes you run so you can fight again." She remembered him as he had been, and knew that he would never be that way again. In pity, she put her arms around him. "Your mother?"

"I haven't gone to her yet. I don't know how I can tell her."

"Tell her that her men died bravely in the service of the true king, then get her and the other women into the hills." She looked down the path to where the shadows fell over a thin frost. "This time, when the English come to burn, there will be no women to rape."

Inside the house, she sought out Gwen. The fear she felt for Brigham was trapped in the back of her mind. For her own sanity, and for the sake of her family, she wouldn't allow it to break free. Over and over, like a chant, her thoughts ran on.

He was alive. He would come back.

"Gwen." Taking her sister's hand, Serena drew her from Maggie's bedside. "How is she?"

"Weak." Gwen was teetering on the brink of exhaustion herself. "I wish I knew more. There is still so much to learn."

"No one could have done more than you. You saved her, and the bairn."

Gwen, her eyes still clouded with fatigue, looked back toward the bed where Maggie slept. "I was afraid."

"We all were."

"Even you?" Gwen smiled and pressed her sister's hand. "You seemed so fearless, so confident. Well, the worst is over. The bairn is healthy, miraculously so." She sighed, allowing herself to think for the first time of her own bed. "A few weeks of rest and care and Maggie will regain her strength."

"How soon can she be moved?"

"Moved?" Gwen paused in the act of adjusting the fillet that held back her hair. "Why, Serena?"

Maggie murmured in her sleep. With a gesture, Serena brought Gwen outside into the hallway. "I've just seen Rob MacGregor."

"Rob? But—"

"There was a battle, Gwen. It was bad, very bad."

"Coll?" Gwen managed after a moment. "Brigham?"

"Rob didn't know. But he told me that our troops were routed and that the English are pursuing the survivors."

"We can hide them. Rob, and whoever else comes. Surely if the English come and find us only women alone they will leave again."

"Do you forget what happened before when we were only women and the English came?"

"That was only one man," Gwen said in a desperate whisper.

"Listen to me." Serena put her hands on Gwen's shoulders and struggled to speak calmly. "Rob told me. He said it was like madness. He said the dragoons murdered the wounded, that they struck down women and children. If they come here before the madness is passed they will kill us all, even Maggie and the bairn."

"We may kill her if we move her."

"Better that than have her butchered at the hands of the

English. Gather together what she and the child will need. We daren't wait to move longer than first light."

"Rena, what of you and your child?"

A light came into her eyes that had nothing to do with fear. Had her father seen it, he would have smiled. "We will survive, and we will remember."

With her own words drumming in her ears, she walked downstairs. In the kitchen, her mother was preparing a tray of broth and bread.

"Serena, I thought you would rest. Go now, get to your bed. As soon as I have seen Gwen eat this, I shall be certain she does the same."

"Mama, we must talk."

"Maggie?" Fiona said immediately. "The babe?"

"No, Gwen tells me they do well enough." She turned her head so that her eyes met Mrs. Drummond's, then Parkins's. "We must all talk. Where is Malcolm?"

"In the stables, my lady," Parkins told her. "Tending the horses."

With a nod, Serena led her mother to a chair at the table. "Is there tea, Mrs. Drummond? Enough for all of us?"

"Aye." Silently she poured the cups, then took a seat when Serena gestured.

"There is news," Serena said, and told them.

At first light, they took what they could carry. Parkins laid Maggie as gently as he could in the litter he had fashioned. She bit back her moans, and though she tried, she was too weak yet to hold the baby. The journey into the hills was slow and nearly silent, with Malcolm leading the way.

At the top of a ridge, where the first early flowers were pushing their way through the thin soil, Fiona stopped. The forest where she had come as a bride spread beneath, shimmering behind a thin, morning mist. At the top of the rise stood the house where she had lived with Ian, given birth to her children.

As she stood, the breeze rippled her plaid but left her cheeks colorless and her eyes dull.

"We will come back, Mother." Serena slipped an arm around her mother's waist and laid her head on Fiona's shoulder. "They will not take our home."

"So much of my life is there, Serena, and my heart. When they brought your father back, I thought my life had ended, as well. But it has not." She took a long breath. Her slender shoulders straightened. Her head came up. "Aye, the MacGregors will come back to Glenroe."

They stood a moment longer, watching the blue slate house glimmer in the strengthening sunlight.

They reached the cave two hours later. Malcolm and Serena had already laid by wood and peat for the fire. They had blankets and stores from the kitchen, medicines and milk drawn fresh that morning. Hidden behind rocks was the chest that held Brigham's shepherdess and a miniature of his grandmother, and his strongbox. Serena set her grandfather's claymore at the entrance to the cave and checked the pistols and ammunition.

Gwen tended Maggie while Fiona soothed the baby they already called young Ian.

"Can you fire a pistol, Parkins?" Serena asked.

"Yes, Lady Ashburn, should it become necessary."

Despite her fatigue, she grinned. He had used the same tone of voice he might have if she had asked him if he knew how to re-move a wine stain from lace. "Perhaps you would take this one?"

"Very well, my lady." He took the pistol with a slight bow.

"You are more than you seem, Parkins." She thought of the competent manner with which he had fashioned the litter, and of the way he had pulled it and its fragile burden over the rough ground. "I begin to see why Lord Ashburn keeps you close. You have been with him long?"

"I have been in service with the Langstons for many years, my lady." When she only nodded and stared at the mouth of the cave, he softened. "He will come back to us, my lady."

Tears threatened, but only one managed to escape before she blinked them back. "I would give him a son this first time, Par-kins. What was his father's given name?"

"It was Daniel, my lady."

"Daniel." She was able to smile again. "We shall name him Daniel, and he will be brave enough to walk into the lion's den." She turned her smile up to Parkins. "He shall be the next earl of Ashburn, and one day he shall walk through Glenroe."

"Will you rest now, Lady Ashburn? The journey has tired you more than you know."

"Aye, in a moment." She turned to be certain the others were busy. "When Brigham and my brother return, they will not know where to find us. It will be necessary for one of us to go down every few hours and watch for them. You and Malcolm and I will take shifts."

"No, my lady."

Her mouth opened, then shut, then opened again. "No?"

"No, my lady, I could not in good conscience permit you to travel again. My master would not hear of it."

"Your master has nothing to say about it. Both he and Coll will need to be led to this place."

"And so they shall be. Young Malcolm and I will arrange it. You and the other women will remain here."

Her face, pale and bruised with fatigue, set into stubborn lines. "I will not sit in this bloody cave and wait when I can be of use to my husband."

Parkins merely spread a blanket over her. "I fear I must insist, Lady Ashburn. My lord would demand it."

Serena merely scowled at him. "I wonder that Lord Ashburn didn't dismiss you years ago."

"Yes, my lady," Parkins said comfortably. "So he has said himself many times. I will bring you a cup of milk."

She slept. She had the pistol at one hand and the sword at the other, but her dreams were peaceful and filled with Brigham. She could see him clearly, almost clearly enough to touch him as he smiled at her. Her hand was in his, and she could all but feel the warmth of his flesh as they danced together under dappled sunlight near the riverbank. He wore the gleaming black and silver, and she the ivory satin seeded with pearls.

They were alone, gloriously alone, with only the rippling rush of water and the call of the birds for music. Their faces were close, then closer, then close enough to kiss as they continued to step and sway with the dance.

He was so handsome, her tall English lover with the dashing rebel's heart. His kiss was so sweet, so gentle, like one of greeting or of farewell.

Then she saw the blood staining his coat, seeping through it to dampen her hand as she reached for him. The blood was real, real enough that she could feel the warmth of it on her skin. But when she tried to take him into her arms, he faded until she stood alone on the banks of the river, with the only sound the high call of a warbler searching for its mate.

She woke with Brigham's name on her lips and her heart thundering. Fighting for air, she lifted her trembling hand and found no blood. Slowly, struggling to separate dream from reality, she pressed the hand to her heart. It wasn't a warbler she heard, but an eagle. It wasn't the song of the river, but the moan of the wind.

He was alive, she told herself, and laid a hand over the mound of her stomach as if to reassure her child that its father was safe. Almost immediately she heard the whimper of the baby already born. Wearily she rose to make her way to the back of the cave. With Fiona's help, Maggie held young Ian to her breast, where he sucked lustily.

"Serena." Maggie's voice was thin and her cheeks still deathly pale, but her smile was sweet. "He grows stronger every hour," she murmured, and lifted a hand to stroke his downy head. "Soon you'll have your own."

"He's beautiful." With a little sigh, Serena sat beside her. "God was good enough to give him your looks instead of his father's."

Maggie laughed, settled comfortably in the crook of Fiona's arm. "I didn't know I could love anyone as much as Coll. But now I do."

"I know the journey was difficult for you. How do you feel?"

"Weak. I hate feeling so weak and helpless."

Serena stroked her cheek. "A man doesn't fall in love with a packhorse, you know."

This time Maggie's laugh was a little stronger. "If some girl tries that trick with my little Ian, I'll scratch her eyes out."

"Of course, but you'll be sure to teach it to your daughters."

"Oh, aye." Maggie shut her eyes. "I'm so tired."

"Just sleep," Fiona murmured. "When the bairn's had his fill, we'll tend him."

"Will Coll come soon?"

Over Maggie's drooping head, Fiona's eyes met Serena's. "Aye." Fiona's voice was soothing. "Very soon. He'll be so proud of you for giving him a son."

Serena gathered up the dozing baby as Fiona settled Maggie among the blankets. "So tiny." Serena swaddled Ian and laid him to sleep. "It always seems a miracle."

"It is." Fiona looked to the far side of the cave to where Gwen lay curled in exhausted sleep. "Each child is a miracle. There is always death, Serena; there is always grief and loss. Without the promise of new life, we couldn't bear it."

Serena asked now what she had not been brave enough to ask before. "Do you think they're dead?"

"I pray they live." Fiona took Serena's hands in hers. "And I will pray every moment until we know. You must eat," she said briskly. "For yourself and the child."

"Aye, but..." She let her words trail off as she glanced around the cave. "Where is Malcolm?"

"With Parkins. They left soon after you went to sleep. Down for more supplies."

Frowning, Serena started to accept the bowl Mrs. Drummond offered.

"Don't you fret about them, lassie, my Parkins knows what he's about."

"Aye, he is a good man, Mrs. Drummond, a steady one."

A becoming blush glowed in the widow's cheeks. "We are to be wed."

"I am happy for you." She stopped, her fingers tightening on the bowl. "Do you hear that?" she whispered as she set the bowl down.

"I hear nothing." But Fiona's heart had risen into her throat.

"Someone's coming. Stay to the back of the cave. See that Ian makes no sound."

"Serena."

But even as Fiona reached for her, Serena was moving quietly to the cave opening. Ice ran through her veins, freezing her fear and making her strong. She would kill if God showed her no other way, and she would kill well.

With a steady hand, she picked up the pistol, then the sword. If the English had come, they would find women alone, but they would not find women defenseless. Behind her, Mrs. Drummond gripped a carving knife.

As the footsteps came closer, there could be no doubt the cave would be seen. Holding both weapons, Serena stepped out of the cave and prepared to do battle. The sun fell over her, striking her eyes so that she narrowed them even as she leveled the pistol.

"Still a hellcat, I see."

Brigham, supported by Coll and Parkins, managed to grin at her as he was half carried over the broken ground. The light shone over his blood-streaked coat and breeches.

"Oh, sweet God." Laying the weapons down, Serena ran to him.

Her face swam in front of his eyes as he struggled to speak again. He could only manage her name before darkness closed in on him and smothered the pain.

Chapter Fifteen

"How bad is it?" Serena knelt on the floor of the cave beside Brigham while Gwen examined his wounds. The fear had returned, drying her mouth to dust.

Wordlessly Gwen probed Brigham's side where the ball was lodged. A few feet away, Fiona dressed the gash in Coll's leg while he stared in wonder at his son.

"The shot was meant for me." Coll clung to Maggie's hand. The fire in his leg was a dull, almost dreamy pain beneath his exhaustion. He was alive, beside his beloved wife and firstborn son while his friend lay bleeding from a bullet that had been meant for him. "He stepped in front of it, took it. We were trying to fight our way into the hills. We'd lost, everything was lost. We were separated from our regiment. I thought—at first I thought him dead."

"You brought him back." Serena looked up, gripping a blood-soaked cloth.

"Aye." Coll turned his face into his wife's hair. Wanting to smell only the sweetness of it and not the stench of death and battle.

He would never be able to describe the events of the last day and night. But he would always remember the desperation he had felt when he had carried Brigham into the hills. He would remember hiding like a wild dog and binding the wounds as best he could while the English searched the rocks and heather. He had hidden in the lee of a rock, too weak to cross the stretch of moor to a barn. There, lying in scrub with Brigham unconscious beside him, he had seen the soldiers come and set fire to the building. And he had heard the screams of the wounded who had hidden within.

He had made the rest of the miles to Glenroe mostly at night, supporting Brigham when he was conscious, carrying him when he was not.

"We were afraid for you," he managed after a moment. "Afraid the English would come before we could warn you."

"The bullet must come out right away." Gwen pressed a cloth against the wound as all eyes turned toward her. "We must find a doctor."

"There is no doctor." Serena felt the hysteria bubbling up and fought to control it. Had he been given back to her only so that she could watch him die? "If we searched for one, we would only bring the English down on us."

"I know the risk," Gwen began.

"They would kill him." Serena spoke flatly. "As an English nobleman, they would be doubly harsh. They would heal his wound only to keep him alive for execution. You must take it out."

"I've never done anything like this." Gwen closed a hand over

Serena's arm. "I lack the skill and the knowledge. I would kill him in trying to save him."

Panic fluttered. Beneath her hands, Brigham moaned and stirred. "Better he die with us, here." Her eyes were grim as she looked down at Brigham. "If you won't try, I will do it myself."

"My lady." Parkins's voice was as expressionless as ever as he stepped forward. "I will remove the ball, with Miss MacGregor's assistance."

"You? Can you?" Serena gave a brittle laugh. "We're not talking about starching lace, man."

"I have done it once before, my lady. That is once more than you. And Lord Ashburn is my master," he said stiffly. "I will tend him. He will need to be held." Parkins turned his gaze to Coll.

"I will hold him." Serena leaned over Brigham's body, as if to shield him. "And God help you if the knife slips."

They built a fire and turned a blade in it until the tip glowed red. When Brigham surfaced, Gwen held a bowl of medicine heavily laced with poppies to his lips. Sweat poured down his face no matter how diligently Serena wiped his skin with a cool cloth.

"Sit with Maggie and Mother, Rena," Coll said quietly. "Let me hold him down."

"No. This is for me to do." She braced herself over Brigham, clasping her hands on his arms, then lifted her face to Parkins. "I know you will have to hurt him, but for mercy's sake, be quick."

The valet had stripped off his coat and rolled back his sleeves to reveal thin, spindly arms. Serena closed her eyes a moment. She was putting her love, her life, into the hands of a man who looked able to do no more than shine boots. Opening them again, she studied the valet's face. Steady. She had called him so herself. Loyal. More than loyal, she realized. As a man could love another, he loved Brigham. With a prayer, she nodded for Parkins to begin. And watched the knife cut into her husband's flesh.

Even dazed by the drug, Brigham stiffened. Serena used all her strength to press him down even as she murmured to him, nonsense, endearments, promises. She watched the knife go deeper and ignored the rolling of her stomach.

As the pain of the knife sliced through the swoon and the drug, Brigham began to fight. Coll tried to take Serena's place, but she snarled him away and summoned all her strength.

There was no sound in the cave but for Brigham's harsh breathing and the low crackle of the fire. But the air was charged with silent prayers, said with a unity that made them as strong as a novena. Serena watched her husband's blood stain the floor of the cave and his face go ashen. In her prayers, she begged to take some of his pain into herself and spare him.

"I've found it." Sweat streamed down Parkins's face as he probed for the ball. In his heart he prayed that his master would faint and escape the pain. But his thin hand was steady. Slowly, terrified of causing more damage, he began to guide the bullet out. "Keep him still, my lady."

"Get the damn thing out." She shot a furious look at Parkins as Brigham moaned and struggled under her confining hands. "He suffers."

She watched, her breathing harsh and unsteady, as Parkins pried the small ball of metal from Brigham's flesh. Before Parkins could release the breath he had been holding, Gwen was taking over.

"We must stop the bleeding. He can't lose much more and

live." Competently she began to pack the wound. "Mama, will you see to his arm and shoulder? They are less severe, but look ugly. Mrs. Drummond, my medicines."

As Brigham went limp again, Serena leaned back. Her arms and back were trembling with the pressure. Carefully, mindful now of the child, she made herself relax. "How can I help?"

Gwen glanced up only briefly from her work. Serena's face was as pale as Brigham's. "By getting air. Please, leave this to me."

With a nod, Serena rose and moved slowly to the mouth of the cave. It was nearly dusk again, she noted. How quickly the time had passed. And how strangely. A year before it had been Brigham, carrying a wounded Coll. Now it was Brigham who lay near death. The time between seemed like a dream, filled with love and passion, laughter and weeping.

She could see the hills going purple in the lowering light. The land, she thought. Would they now lose even that? They had fought, they had died. Coll had told her that their father's last words had been "It will not be for naught." But the man she loved lay wounded and the land they had fought for was no longer hers.

"Lady Ashburn?"

Blinking, Serena brought herself back. She was Lady Ashburn. She was a MacGregor. She laid a hand over her stomach as the child within kicked. A new life. A new hope. No, she thought, she would not say it had been for naught.

"Aye?"

"I thought you might enjoy a hot drink."

She turned, nearly smiling at the formal tone of Parkins's voice. He was wearing his coat again, and the perspiring, intense man who had removed a bullet might never have been. "Thank you, Parkins." She took the cup and let the liquid soothe her raw throat. "I would like to apologize for speaking to you as I did."

"Pray do not consider it, my lady. You were distraught."

Serena lifted her hand to her face as she was caught between tears and laughter. "Aye. Distraught. You have a steady hand, Parkins. A steady heart."

"I have always strived to, my lady."

She let out a long breath, swiping at her face with her knuckles. "Have you a handkerchief, as well?"

"Of course, Lady Ashburn." With a slight bow, Parkins offered one of sensible cloth.

"Parkins, you have served Lord Ashburn today, and you have also served me. There may be a time when you require a favor of me. You have only to ask."

"My service was given without condition, my lady."

"Aye." She took his hand, causing him to color a bit. "I know it. The boon is still yours when you need it." She offered him back the damp handkerchief. "I will go sit with my husband now."

The wind picked up and howled like a wild beast. It fought its way through the blanket over the cave opening and sent the flames of the low fire dancing. In its shrieks, Serena heard what her ancestors would have called the spirits in the hills. They laughed and moaned and mumbled. She felt no fear of them.

She watched Brigham through the night, unable to sleep even when Gwen pleaded with her. The fire burned through him, so hot at times Serena feared it would eat him alive. Sometimes he spoke, in rambling sporadic sentences that told her he was reliving the battle. Through his words, she saw more clearly than ever how complete the slaughter had been. Once he spoke to his grandmother, telling her despairingly of the dreams that had been shattered by the English guns.

He called for Serena, and would be soothed for a time by her murmurs and by her hand, cool on his brow. He would wake again, delirious, certain that the English had found her.

"I will sit with him, Serena." Fiona knelt beside her, laying a comforting arm over her shoulders. "You need rest, for yourself and your child."

"I cannot leave him, Mama." Serena wrung out a cool cloth and stroked it over Brigham's pale face. "I am easier here than I would be if I tried to sleep. Just looking at him helps somehow. Sometimes he opens his eyes and looks at me. He knows I'm with him."

"Then sleep here, for just a little while. Put your head in my lap as you did when you were a girl."

With Fiona's gentle persuasion, Serena curled up on the floor of the cave. Reaching out, she covered Brigham's hand with her own.

"He is beautiful, is he not, Mama?"

With a little smile, Fiona stroked her daughter's hair. "Aye, he is beautiful."

"Our baby will look like him, with those fine gray eyes and strong mouth." She closed her eyes and listened to the fearless song of the wind. "I loved him, I think, almost from the first. I was afraid. That was foolish."

Fiona continued to soothe and stroke as Serena's words grew slurred with sleep. "Love is often foolish."

"The child is moving," she murmured, smiling as she drifted off. "Brigham's child."

Brigham's dreams were unrelenting. Sometimes he was back on the moor, trapped in the smoke and fury of battle. Men died agonizing deaths around him, some by his own hand. He could smell the blood and the acrid scent of gunpowder. He could hear the pipes and drums and the unrelenting boom of artillery.

Then he was limping through the hills, the fire in his side and the mist over his brain. He thought he smelt burning—wood and flesh—and heard screams echoing in his head.

Just when he knew he would scream himself from the sound of it, it stopped. Serena stood beside him, wearing a white dress that glittered over her skin, her hair falling like melted gold.

Sometimes when he opened his eyes he would see her, so clearly that he could make out the smudges of sleeplessness under her eyes. Then his weighted lids would close again and he would be pitched back onto the battlefield.

For three days he drifted between consciousness and unconsciousness, often delirious. He knew nothing of the little world that had been conceived within the cave, or of the comings and goings of its people. He heard voices, but had not the strength to understand or to answer. Once, when he floated to the surface, it was dark and he thought he heard a woman's quiet weeping. Another time, he heard the thin cry of a baby.

At the end of three days he fell into a deep, dreamless sleep, a sleep as peaceful as death.

Waking was something like being born, confusing, painful, helpless. The light burned his eyes, though it was dim in the rear of the cave. Weakly he shut them again and tried to orient himself with sounds and smells.

There was earth and smoke and, oddly, a smell of cooking

food. There was also the sickly scent of poppies that spoke of sickness. He heard murmurs. With the patience of the weak he lay still until he began to make them out.

Coll. Gwen. Malcolm. Relief poured through him nearly as strongly as the delirium. If they were here and safe, so was Serena. He opened his eyes again, wincing at the light. He was gathering his strength to speak when he heard a rustle beside him.

She was there, sitting with her knees curled up close, her back against a wall of rock. Her hair had fallen forward, almost curtaining her face. A wave of love all but drained him.

"Rena," he murmured, and reached to touch.

She woke immediately. Emotions raced across her face as she shifted close to run her hands over his face. It was cool, blessedly cool. "Brigham." She lowered her lips to his. "You've come back to me."

There was so much to tell him, so much to hear. At first Brigham was only strong enough to stay awake for an hour at a time. The memory of the battle was clear, but that of the aftermath was, mercifully, a blur to him. There had been pain, a hotter, sharper one than the throbbing ache he felt now. He remembered being dragged and lifted and carried. There had been cool water poured down his burning throat. Once he remembered coming out of a half swoon when he and Coll had stumbled across six bodies.

Gradually, at his insistence, the gaps were filled in. He listened grimly, his fury and disgust at Cumberland's atrocities offset only by the joy of having Serena and his unborn child close to him.

"This place won't be safe for long." Brigham sat braced against the wall of the cave, his face still pale in the dim light. It had been two days since he had come out of that fever. "We need to move as soon as possible, toward the coast."

"You're not strong enough." Serena kept his hand in hers. A part of her wanted to stay snug in the cave and forget there was a world outside.

In answer, he brought their joined hands to his lips. But his eyes were hard and focused. He would be damned if he would see her forced to give birth in a cave. "I think we could seek help from my kin on Skye." He looked at Gwen. "How soon will Maggie and the baby be fit enough to travel?"

"In a day or two, but you—"

"I'll be ready."

"You'll be ready when we say you are," Serena cut in.

A trace of the old arrogance flickered into his eyes. "You've grown tyrannical since I last saw you, madam."

She smiled and touched her lips to his. "I have always been a tyrant, *Sassenach*. Rest now," she urged as she settled a blanket over him. "When your strength returns we shall go anywhere you choose."

His eyes became very intense, and her smile wavered. "I may hold you to that, Rena."

"Just rest." The weariness in his voice made her ache. He had left her a strong, seemingly invincible man. He had come back to her inches from death. She would not risk losing him to his own stubbornness. "Perhaps Coll and Malcolm will bring back meat." She lay beside him, stroking his brow as he drifted off, and wondering why her brothers tarried so long.

* * *

They had seen the smoke from the ridge. Sprawled on their bellies, Coll and Malcolm looked down at Glenroe. The English had come again, bringing their fire and their hate. Already the crofts lay in ruins, their thatched roofs gone. MacGregor House was alight, and flames flickered out of broken windows.

"Damn them," Coll murmured over and over as he pounded a fist against the rock. "Damn them all."

"Why do they burn our houses?" Malcolm was ashamed of the tears and hastened to wipe them away. "What need is there to destroy our homes? The stables," he said suddenly, and would have risen up if Coll hadn't restrained him.

"They would have taken the horses, lad."

Malcolm pressed his face to the rock, caught between childish tears and a man's fury. "Will they go now, and leave us?"

Coll remembered the carnage surrounding the battlefield. "I think they will hunt the hills. We must get back to the cave."

Serena lay quietly, listening to the comforting domestic sounds. Young Ian was suckling again, and Maggie hummed to him. Mrs. Drummond and Parkins murmured over the preparation of a meal, easily as if they were still gossiping in the kitchen. Near Maggie, Fiona worked with a spindle, peacefully spinning what would one day be made into a blanket for her grandchild. Gwen fussed with her jars and pots of medicine.

They were all together at last, together and safe. One day, when the English grew tired of raping Scotland and returned over the border, they would go back down to Glenroe. She would make Brigham happy there somehow, make him forget the glittering life he had led in London. They would build a house of their own near the loch.

Smiling, Serena shifted away to let Brigham sleep. She had a passing thought to look out and see if she could spot her brothers returning, but even as she stood, she heard the sound of someone moving near the mouth of the cave. Words of greeting were on the tip of her tongue, but then she stopped. Neither Coll nor Malcolm would have a need to come so cautiously. With a hand that had gone suddenly cold, she reached for the pistol.

A shadow blocked out the light at the mouth of the cave. Then she saw with a sickening lurch of her heart the glint of metal and the telling red of the coat.

The soldier straightened, his sword raised, as he took quick stock of his find. Serena noted that his coat and his face were streaked with dirt and soot. There was a look of triumph in his eyes, and an unmistakable glint in them when he spotted Gwen.

Without a word, and with no thought of mercy, he advanced on Parkins. Serena lifted the pistol and fired. He stumbled back, blank surprise showing in his face the instant before he crumpled to the ground. Thinking only of defending what was hers, Serena gripped the hilt of her grandfather's claymore. Another soldier broke in. Even as she raised the sword, she felt a hand close over hers. Brigham was beside her. The soldier, teeth bared, charged forward, leading with his bayonet. Another shot rang out, felling him. Parkins stood, his rail-thin body shielding Mrs. Drummond's, the pistol still smoking in his hand.

"Reload," Brigham ordered, thrusting Serena behind him as another dragoon pushed into the cave. The redcoat didn't advance, only stood stiffly for an instant before falling headfirst. There was an arrow quivering in his back.

Breathing through his teeth, Brigham rushed out of the cave. There were two more. Coll was fighting one, sword to sword, as he maneuvered desperately to shield Malcolm with his body. The other dragoon advanced on the young boy, who held an empty bow as a useless defense.

With a shout, Brigham lunged. The pain exploded afresh in his side, almost blinding him. The dragoon swung around, but raised his sword again over Malcolm's head.

Serena fired the freshly loaded pistol from the mouth of the cave and sent a ball into his heart.

It was over in minutes. Five dragoons lay dead, but the sanctuary of the cave was ended.

They moved at dusk, heading west. Two of the horses the dragoons had tethered were Malcolm's own. They took shifts, riding, walking. When it was possible, they sheltered in mud huts or with the cattle. Highland hospitality was as it had always been. Through the people they met they learned of Cumberland, who was already known as the Butcher. The persecution was unbearable, and the search for the Prince through the heather unrelenting.

Houses were in ruin; cattle and horses and sheep had been driven off. The Highlanders, never rich, faced starvation. Still, they hid their Prince and any fugitive who asked for shelter.

Progress was slow, with each day bringing its own dangers. Thousands of troops had been engaged to find the Prince. It was June before they were able to sail from the mainland to Skye, where they were taken in by the MacDonalds of Sleat.

"It's as beautiful as she said it was," Brigham murmured as he stood with Serena on the lush green grass of a small slope and looked out at Uig Bay. "My grandmother told me how she ran through the grass as a girl and watched the boats."

"It is beautiful." The breeze was kind against her face. "Everything is beautiful now that we're all together and safe."

For how long? Brigham wondered. There were troops here, as well. The sea was being patrolled. There were rumors that the Prince was near. If he was, the English would be on his heels. A way had to be devised for the Prince to return to France or Italy. But more personally, and more importantly, Serena and the child had to be kept safe.

He had thought of little else during the days of his recovery, during the nights they had traveled like outcasts through the hills of Scotland. He could not now return to England and give Serena what was rightfully hers as Lady Ashburn. Nor could he, though she had yet to accept it, return to Glenroe for years to come.

"Sit with me, Serena."

"Gladly." She laughed a little as he helped her settle what had become a cumbersome weight. "I shall never be able to face a cow again."

"You've never looked more beautiful."

"You lie." She grinned and turned her face for a kiss. "But the truth wouldn't earn you a kiss." With her head on his shoulder, she looked out at the bay. The sun scattered over it, edging the blue with gold, like a lady's ball gown. "It is beautiful here, Brig. I'm glad you had the chance to see the land where your grandmother grew up. That we had the chance to see it together." With a little sound of discomfort, she rested a hand on her stomach.

"Do you feel unwell?"

"No, better every day since we've come here." It was true, spiritually. She didn't want to tell him how poorly she had begun to feel physically. Only that morning the ache in her back, and the pressure, had nearly kept her in bed. "Your grandmother's people have been so kind to us."

"I know. I shall always be grateful to them, and all the others who gave us shelter." His eyes clouded as he looked down over the water. "It is difficult to understand how they could give shelter so freely to an Englishman."

"How can you speak so?" There was genuine anger in her voice as she gripped his arm. "It was not your England that has murdered Scotland. It was, is, Cumberland and his thirst for blood, his need to destroy. It is he who has laid waste to the glens."

"And in London he is cheered like a hero."

"Listen to me." Her grip gentled as she reached for his hand. "There was a time I blamed all for the wrongs of a few. As you love me, don't do the same." With a smile, she moved his hand over her belly. "Our child carries English blood. I am proud of it."

He brought her close a moment, just to hold her. "Again you humble me." They remained as they were, sitting close, clinging to the hope that had come even out of loss. "You know, if I am found here, what will happen to the MacDonalds?"

It was cowardly, but she didn't want to think of it. "You will not be found."

"I cannot run forever, Rena, nor continue to endanger friend and stranger."

She plucked nervously at the turf. It was so green and smelled so sweet. "I know, but what choice do we have? The Prince is still hunted. I know you worry for him."

"I do, but I also worry for you and our child." When she started to reassure him, he gripped her hands. "I will never forget that last day in the cave, the way you were forced to defend me, to kill for me and your family."

"I did what needed to be done, what you would have done. All those months I felt useless because I could do nothing. That day, things changed. A woman might not join the rebellion on a battlefield, but a woman can protect what she loves."

"I will tell you in truth that I have never loved you more than I did that day, when you held a sword and a pistol in your hands." He kissed them, then looked steadily into her eyes. "Can you understand that I wanted to give you beauty, not a life of fear and running? I wanted to give you what was mine, but is mine no longer."

"Brigham—"

"No, wait. There is something I must ask you. You said you would go with me wherever I chose. Will you?"

She felt a little pain ripple through her, but nodded. "Aye."

"Will you leave Scotland, Rena, and travel with me to the New World? I cannot give you all that I once promised, though we won't be poor. So many of the things I wanted for you will be left behind. You will be only Mrs. Langston, and the land and the people will be strange to you, to both of us. I know what I ask you to give up, but perhaps one day we can return."

"Ssh." Overcome, she wrapped her arms around him. "Don't you know I would ride into hell with you if you asked?"

"I don't ask you to ride into hell, but I know what I ask you and what promises I break."

"You promised only to love me, and to come back to me. You have done both." She shook her head before he could speak.

"You must listen, and try to understand. The weeks I had with you at court were beautiful, but only because we were together. I have never needed such things, Brigham. The title means nothing to me, nor do the balls or the gowns. Only you." With a watery laugh, she pulled back. "Every day at Holyrood I worried that I would make a mistake and embarrass you, that you would see you had made a grave error in judgment in taking me for Lady Ashburn."

"What nonsense is this?"

"I shall never be an easy aristocrat, Brigham. I was afraid you would ask me to go to France, to court."

His eyes narrowed as he studied her. "Your life would be easier there, as it was in Edinburgh."

"And I would have to pretend to be a lady while I longed for my breeches and a fast ride."

"You would rather go to America with only a chest of gold and a dream?"

She framed his face with her hands. "England was yours and Scotland mine. We've lost them. Together we will make our own."

"I love you, Rena. More than my life."

"Brigham, the child—"

"Shall be happy. I swear it."

"Sooner than we think," she managed. At his expression, she managed another laugh, then winced. "Oh, I think he has my impatience. I need Gwen, Brigham, and Mother."

"But you said it would be a few weeks yet."

"It's not what I say." She held a hand over her belly as it hardened with a contraction. "It's what he says."

She caught her breath, then giggled when he swept her awkwardly into his arms. "Brigham, there is no need. I'll break your back."

At that moment she felt weightless. "Madam," he said with a trace of mockery. "Have a little faith."

Epilogue

Near the last day of June, fourteen months after he had raised his standard, Prince Charles landed near Mugston House on the Isle of Skye. He was disguised as the lady's maid of Flora Mac-Donald, a young woman who risked her life to travel with him and see him to safety.

He had missed capture by a hairbreadth, but had lost neither his ambition nor his eagerness. Nor had he lost his air of romance. He left Flora with a lock of his hair and the wish that they might meet again, at the Court of St. James.

Brigham saw him briefly. They spoke as they had often spoken in the past, with ease and mutual respect. Charles did not, though the hope was in his heart, ask Brigham to join him on the journey to France.

"You will miss him," Serena said as they stood in their bed-chamber at Mugston House.

"I will miss him as a man, and I will grieve for the loss of what might have been." He gathered her close, holding her newly slim body against his. "It was he and his cause that brought me to

you. We did not win, Rena, but I have only to look at you, and
my son, to know that neither did we lose." With his arm around
her, he turned to look down at the child they had christened
Daniel. "It is as your father said, love. It has not been for naught."
He pressed his lips to hers, lingering over the kiss, drawing out
the passion, the love and the trust. "Are you ready?"

With a nod, she picked up her traveling cloak. "If only Mother
and Coll and Maggie would go with us."

"They need to stay, as we need to go." He waited as she gathered up the child. "You will have Gwen and Malcolm."

"I know. I only wish..."

"There will be a MacGregor in Glenroe again, Serena. And
we will come back."

She looked at him. The sun was streaming through the window at his back. He was as he had been when she had first
seen him, dark, stunningly handsome, a little reckless. It made
her smile even as the baby stirred against her. "There will be a
Langston at Ashburn Manor again. Daniel will come back, or
his children will. They will have their place there, and in the
Highlands."

He lifted the chest that held the little Dresden shepherdess.
One day he would give it to his son. He had bent to kiss her
again when there was a knock on the door.

"Your pardon, my lord."

"What is it, Parkins?"

"We will lose the tide."

"Very well." He gestured to the other cases. "And Parkins,
must I remind you that you are to address me as Mr. Langston
now?"

Parkins hefted the cases in his thin arms. He had asked his

favor of his lady, and he and the new Mrs. Parkins were traveling to America. "No, my lord," he said mildly, and proceeded them.

Over Brigham's oath, Serena laughed and walked out with the baby. "You will always be Lord Ashburn, *Sassenach*. Come." She held out a hand to him. "We are going home."

* * * * *

Storm Warning

To Michael and Darlene,
good friends.

Chapter One

The Pine View Inn was nestled comfortably in the Blue Ridge Mountains. After leaving the main road, the meandering driveway crossed a narrow ford just wide enough for one car. The inn was situated a short distance beyond the ford.

It was a lovely place, full of character, the lines so clean they disguised the building's rambling structure. It was three stories high, built of brick that had been weathered to a soft rose, the facade interspersed with narrow, white-shuttered windows. The hipped roof had faded long ago to a quiet green, and three straight chimneys rose from it. A wide wooden porch made a white skirt around the entire house and doors opened out to it from all four sides.

The surrounding lawn was smooth and well tended. There was less than an acre, house included, before the trees and outcroppings of rock staked their claim on the land. It was as if nature had decided that the house could have this much and no more. The effect was magnificent. The house and mountains stood in peaceful coexistence, neither detracting from the other's beauty.

As she pulled her car to the informal parking area at the side of the house, Autumn counted five cars, including her aunt's vintage Chevy. Though the season was still weeks off, it appeared that the inn already had several guests.

There was a light April chill in the air. The daffodils had yet to open, and the crocuses were just beginning to fade. A few azalea buds showed a trace of color. The day was poised and waiting for spring. The higher, surrounding mountains clung to their winter brown, but touches of green were creeping up them. It wouldn't be gloomy brown and gray for long.

Autumn swung her camera case over one shoulder and her purse over the other—the purse was of secondary importance. Two large suitcases also had to be dragged from the trunk. After a moment's struggle, she managed to arrange everything so that she could take it all in one load, then mounted the steps. The door, as always, was unlocked.

There was no one about. The sprawling living room which served as a lounge was empty, though a fire crackled in the grate. Setting down her cases, Autumn entered the room. Nothing had changed.

Rag rugs dotted the floor; hand-crocheted afghans were draped on the two patchworked sofas. At the windows were chintz priscillas and the Hummel collection was still on the mantel. Characteristically, the room was neat, but far from orderly. There were magazines here and there, an overflowing sewing basket, a group of pillows piled for comfort rather than style on the windowseat. The ambience was friendly with a faintly distracted charm. Autumn thought with a smile that the room suited her aunt perfectly.

She felt an odd pleasure. It was always reassuring to find that something loved hasn't changed. Taking a last quick glance around the room, she ran a hand through her hair. It hung past her waist and was tousled from the long drive with open windows. She gave idle consideration to digging out a brush, but promptly forgot when she heard footsteps down the hall.

"Oh, Autumn, there you are." Typically, her aunt greeted her as though Autumn had just spent an hour at the local supermarket rather than a year in New York. "I'm glad you got in before dinner. We're having pot roast, your favorite."

Not having the heart to remind her aunt that pot roast was her brother Paul's favorite, Autumn smiled. "Aunt Tabby, it's so good to see you!" Quickly she walked over and kissed her aunt's cheek. The familiar scent of lavender surrounded her.

Aunt Tabby in no way resembled the cat her name brought to mind. Cats are prone to snobbishness, disdainfully tolerating the rest of the world. They are known for speed, agility and cunning. Aunt Tabby was known for her vague meanderings, disjointed conversations and confused thinking. She had no guile. Autumn adored her.

Drawing her aunt away, Autumn studied her closely. "You look wonderful." It was invariably true. Aunt Tabby's hair was the same deep chestnut as her niece's, but it was liberally dashed with gray. It suited her. She wore it short, curling haphazardly around her small round face. Her features were all small-scaled—mouth, nose, ears, even her hands and feet. Her eyes were a mistily faded blue. Though she was halfway through her fifties, her skin refused to wrinkle; it was smooth as a girl's. She stood a half-foot shorter than Autumn and was pleasantly round and soft. Beside her, Autumn felt like a gangly toothpick. Autumn hugged her again, then kissed her other cheek. "Absolutely wonderful."

Aunt Tabby smiled up at her. "What a pretty girl you are. I always knew you would be. But so awfully thin." She patted Autumn's cheek and wondered how many calories were in pot roast.

With a shrug, Autumn thought of the ten pounds she had gained when she'd stopped smoking. She had lost them again almost as quickly.

"Nelson always was thin," Aunt Tabby added, thinking of her brother, Autumn's father.

"Still is," Autumn told her. She set her camera case on a table and grinned at her aunt. "Mom's always threatening to sue for divorce."

"Oh well." Aunt Tabby clucked her tongue and looked thoughtful. "I don't think that's wise after all the years they've been married." Knowing the jest had been lost, Autumn merely nodded in agreement. "I gave you the room you always liked, dear. You can still see the lake from the window. The leaves will be full soon though, but... Remember when you fell in when you were a little girl? Nelson had to fish you out."

"That was Will," Autumn reminded her, thinking back on the day her younger brother had toppled into the lake.

"Oh?" Aunt Tabby looked faintly confused a moment, then smiled disarmingly. "He learned to swim quite well, didn't he? Such an enormous young man now. It always surprised me. There aren't any children with us at the moment," she added, flowing from sentence to sentence with her own brand of logic.

"I saw several cars. Are there many people here?" Autumn stretched her cramped muscles as she wandered the room. It smelled of sandalwood and lemon oil.

"One double and five singles," she told her. "One of the singles is French and quite fond of my apple pie. I must go check on my blueberry cobbler," she announced suddenly. "Nancy is a marvel with a pot roast, but helpless with baking. George is down with a virus."

She was already making for the door as Autumn tried to puzzle out the last snatch of information.

"I'm sorry to hear that," she replied with what she hoped was appropriate sympathy.

"I'm a bit shorthanded at the moment, dear, so perhaps you can manage your suitcases yourself. Or you can wait for one of the gentlemen to come in."

George, Autumn remembered. Gardener, bellboy and bartender.

"Don't worry, Aunt Tabby. I can manage."

"Oh, by the way, Autumn." She turned back, but Autumn knew her aunt's thoughts were centered on the fate of her cobbler. "I have a little surprise for you—oh, I see Miss Bond is coming in." Typically, she interrupted herself, then smiled. "She'll keep you company. Dinner's at the usual time. Don't be late."

Obviously relieved that both her cobbler and her niece were about to be taken care of, she bustled off, her heels tapping cheerfully on the hardwood floor.

Autumn turned to watch her designated companion enter through the side door. She found herself gaping.

Julia Bond. Of course, Autumn recognized her instantly. There could be no other woman who possessed such shimmering, golden beauty. How many times had she sat in a crowded theater and watched Julia's charm and talent transcend the movie screen? In person, in the flesh, her beauty didn't diminish. It sparkled, all the more alive in three dimensions.

Small, with exquisite curves just bordering on lush, Julia Bond was a magnificent example of womanhood at its best. Her cream-colored linen slacks and vivid blue cashmere sweater set off her coloring to perfection. Pale golden hair framed her face like sunlight. Her eyes were a deep summer blue. The full, shapely mouth lifted into a smile even as the famous brows arched. For a moment, Julia stood, fingering her silk scarf. Then she spoke, her voice smoky, exactly as Autumn had known it would be. "What fabulous hair."

It took Autumn a moment to register the comment. Her mind was blank at seeing Julia Bond step into her aunt's lounge as casually as she would have strolled into the New York Hilton. The smile, however, was full of charm and so completely unaffected that Autumn was able to form one in return.

"Thank you. I'm sure you're used to being stared at, Miss Bond, but I apologize anyway."

Julia sat, with a grace that was at once insolent and admirable, in a wingback chair. Drawing out a long, thin cigarette, she gave Autumn a full-power smile. "Actors adore being stared at. Sit down." She gestured. "I have a feeling I've at last found someone to talk to in this place."

Autumn's obedience was automatic, a tribute to the actress's charm.

"Of course," Julia continued, still studying Autumn's face, "you're entirely too young and too attractive." Settling back, she crossed her legs. Somehow, she managed to transform the wingback chair, with the small darning marks in the left arm, into a throne. "Then your coloring and mine offset each other nicely. How old are you, darling?"

"Twenty-five." Captivated, Autumn answered without thinking.

Julia laughed, a low bubbling sound that flowed and ebbed like a wave. "Oh, so am I. Perennially." She tossed her head in amusement, then left it cocked to the side. Autumn's fingers itched for her camera. "What's your name, darling, and what brings you to solitude and pine trees?"

"Autumn," she responded as she pushed her hair off her shoulders. "Autumn Gallegher. My aunt owns the inn."

"Your aunt?" Julia's face registered surprise and more amusement. "That dear fuzzy little lady is your aunt?"

"Yes." A grin escaped at the accuracy of the description. "My father's sister." Relaxed, Autumn leaned back. She was doing her own studying, thinking in angles and shadings.

"Incredible," Julia decided with a shake of her head. "You don't look like her. Oh, the hair," she corrected with an envious glance. "I imagine hers was once your color. Magnificent. I know women who would kill for that shade, and you seem to have about three feet of it." With a sigh, she drew delicately on her cigarette. "So, you've come to pay your aunt a visit."

There was nothing condescending in her attitude. Her eyes were interested and Autumn began to find her not only charming but likable. "For a few weeks. I haven't seen her in nearly a year. She wrote and asked me to come down, so I'm taking my vacation all at one time."

"What do you do?" Julia pursed her lips. "Model?"

"No." Autumn's laughter came quickly at the thought of it. "I'm a photographer."

"Photographer!" Julia exclaimed. She glowed with pleasure. "I'm very fond of photographers. Vanity, I suppose."

"I imagine photographers are fond of you for the same reason."

"Oh, my dear." When Julia smiled, Autumn recognized both pleasure and amusement. "How sweet."

"Are you alone, Miss Bond?" Her sense of curiosity was ingrained. Autumn had already forgotten to be overwhelmed.

"Julia, please, or you'll remind me of the half-decade that separates our ages. The color of that sweater suits you," she commented, eyeing Autumn's crewneck. "I never could wear gray. Sorry, darling," she apologized with a lightning-quick smile. "Clothes are a weakness of mine. Am I alone?" The smile deepened. "Actually, this little hiatus is a mixture of business and pleasure. I'm in between husbands at the moment—a glorious interlude." Julia tossed her head. "Men are delightful, but husbands can be dreadfully inhibiting. Have you ever had one?"

"No." The grin was irrepressible. From the tone, Julia might have asked if Autumn had ever owned a cocker spaniel.

"I've had three." Julia's eyes grew wicked and delighted. "In this case, the third was *not* the charm. Six months with an English baron was quite enough."

Autumn remembered the photos she had seen of Julia with a tall, aristocratic Englishman. She had worn tweed brilliantly.

"I've taken a vow of abstinence," Julia continued. "Not against men—against marriage."

"Until the next time?" Autumn ventured.

"Until the next time," Julia agreed with a laugh. "At the moment, I'm here for platonic purposes with Jacques LeFarre."

"The producer?"

"Of course." Again, Autumn felt the close scrutiny. "He'll take one look at you and decide he has a new star on the horizon. Still, that might be an interesting diversion." She frowned a moment, then shrugged it away. "The other residents of your aunt's cozy inn have offered little in the way of diversions thus far."

"Oh?" Automatically, Autumn shook her head as Julia offered her a cigarette.

"We have Dr. and Mrs. Spicer," Julia began. One perfectly shaped nail tapped against the arm of her chair. There was something different in her attitude now. Autumn was sensitive to moods, but this was too subtle a change for her to identify. "The doctor himself might be interesting," Julia continued. "He's very tall and nicely built, smoothly handsome with just the right amount of gray at the temples."

She smiled. Just then Autumn thought Julia resembled a very pretty, well-fed cat.

"The wife is short and unfortunately rather dumpy. She spoils whatever attractiveness she might have with a continually morose expression." Julia demonstrated it with terrifying skill. Autumn's laughter burst out before she could stop it.

"How unkind," Autumn chided, smiling still.

"Oh, I know." A graceful hand waved in dismissal. "I have no patience for women who let themselves go, then look daggers at those who don't. He's fond of fresh air and walking in the woods, and she grumbles and mopes along after him." Julia paused, giving Autumn a wary glance. "How do you feel about walking?"

"I like it." Hearing the apology in her voice, Autumn grinned.

"Oh well." Julia shrugged at eccentricities. "It takes all kinds. Next, we have Helen Easterman." The oval, tinted nails began to tap again. Her eyes drifted from Autumn's to the view out the window. Somehow, Autumn didn't think she was seeing mountains and pine trees. "She says she's an art teacher, taking time off to sketch nature. She's rather attractive, though a bit overripe, with sharp little eyes and an unpleasant smile. Then, there's Steve Anderson." Julia gave her slow, cat smile again. Describing men, Autumn mused, was more to her taste. "He's rather delicious. Wide shoulders, California blond hair. Nice blue eyes. And he's embarrassingly rich. His father owns, ah…"

"Anderson Manufacturing?" Autumn prompted and was rewarded with a beam of approval.

"How clever of you."

"I heard something about Steve Anderson aiming for a political career."

"Mmm, yes. It would suit him." Julia nodded. "He's very well-mannered and has a disarmingly boyish smile—that's always a political asset."

"It's a sobering thought that government officials are elected on their smiles."

"Oh, politics." Julia wrinkled her nose and shrugged away the entire profession. "I had an affair with a senator once. Nasty business, politics." She laughed at some private joke.

Not certain whether her comment had been a romantic observation or a general one, Autumn didn't pursue it. "So far," Autumn said, "it seems an unlikely menagerie for Julia Bond and Jacques LeFarre to join."

"Show business." With a smile, she lit another cigarette, then waved it at Autumn. "Stick with photography, Autumn, no matter what promises Jacques makes you. We're here due to a whim of the last and most interesting character in our little play. He's a genius of a writer. I did one of his screenplays a few years back. Jacques wants to produce another, and he wants me for the lead." She dragged deep on the cigarette. "I'm willing—really good scripts aren't that easy to come by—but our writer is in the middle of a novel. Jacques thinks the novel could be turned into a screenplay, but our genius resists. He told Jacques he was coming here to write in peace for a few weeks, and that he'd think it over. The charming LeFarre talked him into allowing us to join him for a few days."

Autumn was both fascinated and confused. Her question was characteristically blunt. "Do you usually chase writers around this way? I'd think it would be more the other way around."

"And you'd be right," Julia said flatly. With only the movement of her eyebrows, her expression turned haughty. "But Jacques is dead set on producing this man's work, and he caught me at a weak moment. I had just finished reading one of the most appalling scripts. Actually," she amended with a grimace, "three of the most appalling scripts. My work feeds me, but I won't do trash. So..." Julia smiled and moved her hands. "Here I am."

"Chasing a reluctant writer."

"It has its compensations."

I'd like to shoot her with the sun at her back. Low sun, just going down. The contrasts would be perfect. Autumn pulled herself back from her thoughts and caught up with Julia's conversation. "Compensations?" she repeated.

"The writer happens to be incredibly attractive, in that carelessly rugged sort of way that no one can pull off unless he's born with it. A marvelous change of pace," she added with a wicked gleam, "from English barons. He's tall and bronzed with black hair that's just a bit too long and always disheveled. It makes a woman itch to get her fingers into it. Best, he has those dark eyes that say 'go to hell' so eloquently. He's an arrogant devil." Her sigh was pure feminine approval. "Arrogant men are irresistible, don't you think?"

Autumn murmured something while she tried to block out the suspicions Julia's words were forming. It had to be someone else, she thought frantically. Anyone else.

"And, of course, Lucas McLean's talent deserves a bit of arrogance."

The color drained from Autumn's face and left it stiff. Waves of almost forgotten pain washed over her. *How could it hurt so much after all this time?* She had built the wall so carefully, so laboriously—how could it crumble into dust at the sound of a name? She wondered, dully, what sadistic quirk of fate had brought Lucas McLean back to torment her.

"Why, darling, what's the matter?"

Julia's voice, mixed with concern and curiosity, penetrated. As if coming up for air, Autumn shook her head. "Nothing." She shook her head again and swallowed. "It was just a surprise to hear that Lucas McLean is here." Drawing a deep breath, she met Julia's eyes. "I knew him…a long time ago."

"Oh, I see."

And she did see, Autumn noted, very well. Sympathy warred with speculation in both her face and voice. Autumn shrugged, determined to treat it lightly.

"I doubt he remembers me." Part of her prayed with fervor it was true, while another prayed at cross-purposes. Would he forget? she wondered. Could he?

"Autumn, darling, yours is a face no man is likely to forget." Through a mist of smoke, Julia studied her. "You were very young when you fell in love with him?"

"Yes." Autumn was trying, painfully, to rebuild her protective wall and wasn't surprised by the question. "Too young, too naive." She managed a brittle smile and for the first time in six months accepted a cigarette. "But I learn quickly."

"It seems the next few days might prove interesting, after all."

"Yes." Autumn's agreement lacked enthusiasm. "So it does." She needed time to be alone, to steady herself. "I have to take my bags up," she said as she rose.

While Autumn stretched her slender arms toward the ceiling, Julia smiled. "I'll see you at dinner."

Nodding, Autumn gathered up her camera case and purse and left the room.

In the hall, she struggled with her suitcases, camera and purse before beginning the task of transporting them up the stairs. Throughout the slow trek up the stairs, Autumn relieved tension by muttering and swearing. *Lucas McLean,* she thought and banged a suitcase against her shin. She nearly convinced herself that her ill humor was a result of the bruise she'd just given herself. Out of breath and patience, she reached the hallway outside her room and dumped everything on the floor with an angry thud.

"Hello, Cat. No bellboy?"

The voice—and the ridiculous nickname—knocked a few of her freshly mortared bricks loose. After a brief hesitation, Autumn turned to him. The pain wouldn't show on her face. She'd learned that much. But the pain was there, surprisingly real and physical. It reminded her of the day her brother had swung a baseball bat into her stomach when she had been twelve. *I'm not twelve now,* she reminded herself. She met Lucas's arrogant smile with one of her own.

"Hello, Lucas. I heard you were here. The Pine View Inn is bursting with celebrities."

He was the same, she noted. Dark and lean and male. There was a ruggedness about him, accented by rough black brows and craggy, demanding features that couldn't be called handsome. Oh, no, that was much too tame a word for Lucas McLean. Arousing, irresistible. Fatal. Those words suited him better.

His eyes were nearly as black as his hair. They kept secrets easily. He carried himself well, with a negligent grace that was natural rather than studied. His not-so-subtle masculine power drifted with him as he ambled closer and studied her.

It was then that Autumn noticed how hellishly tired he looked. There were shadows under his eyes. He needed a shave. The creases in his cheeks were deeper than she remembered—and she remembered very well.

"You look like yesterday." He grabbed a handful of her hair as he fastened his eyes on hers. She wondered how she could have ever thought herself over him. No woman ever got over Lucas. Sheer determination kept her eyes level.

"You," she countered as she opened her door, "look like hell. You need some sleep."

Lucas leaned on the doorjamb before she could drag her cases inside and slam the door. "Having trouble with one of my characters," he said smoothly. "She's a tall, willowy creature with chestnut hair that ripples down her back. Narrow hipped, with legs that go right up to her waist."

Bracing herself, Autumn turned back and stared at him. Carefully, she erased any expression from her face.

"She has a child's mouth," he continued, dropping his glance to hers a moment. "And a small nose, somewhat at odds with high, elegant cheekbones. Her skin is ivory with touches of warmth just under the surface. Her eyes are long lidded and ridiculously lashed—green that melts into amber, like a cat's."

Without comment, she listened to his description of herself. She gave him a bored, disinterested look he would never have seen on her face three years before. "Is she the murderer or the corpse?" It pleased Autumn to see his brows lift in surprise before they drew together in a frown.

"I'll send you a copy when it's done." He searched her face, then a shutter came down, leaving his expression unreadable. That, too, she noted, hadn't changed.

"You do that." After giving her cases a superhuman tug, jettisoning them into her room, Autumn rested against the door. Her smile had no feeling. "You'll have to excuse me, Lucas, I've had a long drive and want a bath."

She closed the door firmly and with finality, in his face.

Autumn's movements then became brisk. There was unpacking to do and a bath to draw and a dress to choose for dinner. Those things would give her time to recover before she allowed herself to think, to feel. When she slipped into lingerie and stockings, her nerves were steadier. The worst of it had been weathered. Surely, she mused, the first meeting, the first exchange of words were the most difficult. She had seen him. She had spoken to him. She had survived. Success made her bold. For the first time in nearly two years, Autumn allowed herself to remember.

She had been so much in love. Her assignment had been an ordinary one—a picture layout of mystery novelist Lucas McLean. The result had been six months of incredible joy followed by unspeakable hurt.

He had overwhelmed her. She'd never met anyone like him.

She knew now that there was no one else like him. He was a
law unto himself. He had been brilliant, compelling, selfish and
moody. After the first shock of learning he was interested in
her, Autumn had floated along on a cloud of wonder and admiration. And love.

His arrogance, as Julia had said, was irresistible. His phone
calls at three in the morning had been treasured. The last time
she had been held in his arms, experiencing the wild demands
of his mouth, had been as exciting as the first. She had tumbled
into his bed like a ripe peach, giving up her innocence with the
freedom that comes with blind, trusting love.

She remembered he'd never said the words she wanted to hear.
She'd told herself she had no need for them—words weren't
important. There were unexpected boxes of roses, surprise picnics on the beach with wine in paper cups and lovemaking
that was both intense and all consuming. What did she need
with words? When the end had come it had been swift—but
far from painless.

Autumn put his distraction, his moodiness down to trouble
with the novel he was working on. It didn't occur to her that he'd
been bored. It was her habit to fix dinner on Wednesdays at his
home. It was a small, private evening, one she prized above all
others. Her arrival was so natural to her, so routine, that when
she entered his living room and found him dressed in dinner
clothes, she only thought he had decided to add a more formal
atmosphere to their quiet dinner.

"Why, Cat, what are you doing here?" The unexpected words
were spoken so easily, she merely stared. "Ah, it's Wednesday,
isn't it?" There was a slight annoyance in his tone, as though

he had forgotten a dentist appointment. "I completely forgot. I'm afraid I've made other plans."

"Other plans?" she echoed. Comprehension was still a long way off.

"I should have phoned you and saved you the trip. Sorry, Cat, I'm just leaving."

"Leaving?"

"I'm going out." He moved across the room and stared at her. She shivered. No one's eyes could be as warm—or as cold—as Lucas McLean's. "Don't be difficult, Autumn, I don't want to hurt you any more than is necessary."

Feeling the tears of realization rush out, she shook her head and fought against acceptance. The tears sent him into a fury.

"Stop it! I haven't the time to deal with weeping. Just pack it in. Chalk it up to experience. God knows you need it."

Swearing, he stomped away to light a cigarette. She had stood there, weeping without sound.

"Don't make a fool of yourself, Autumn." The calm, rigid voice was more frightening to her than his anger. At least anger was an emotion. "When something's over, you forget it and move on." He turned back with a shrug. "That's life."

"You don't want me anymore?" She stood meekly, like a dog who waits to feel the lash again. Her vision was too clouded with tears to see his expression. For a moment, he was silent.

"Don't worry, Cat," he answered in a careless, brutal voice. "Others will."

She turned and fled. It had taken over a year before he had stopped being the first thing in her mind every morning.

But she had survived, she reminded herself. She slipped into a vivid green dress. And I'll keep right on surviving. She knew she was basically the same person who had fallen in love with Lucas, but now she had a more polished veneer. Innocence was gone, and it would take more than Lucas McLean to make a fool of her again. She tossed her head, satisfied with the memory of her reception to him. That had given him a bit of a surprise. No, Autumn Gallegher was no one's fool any longer.

Her thoughts drifted to her aunt's odd assortment of guests. She wondered briefly why the rich and famous were gathering here instead of at some exclusive resort. Dismissing the thought with a shrug, she reminded herself it was dinnertime. Aunt Tabby had told her not to be late.

Chapter Two

It was a strange assortment to find clustered in the lounge of a remote Virginia inn: an award-winning writer, an actress, a producer, a wealthy California businessman, a successful Cardiovascular surgeon and his wife, an art teacher who wore St. Laurent. Before Autumn's bearings were complete, she found herself enveloped in them. Julia pounced on her possessively and began introductions. Obviously, Julia enjoyed her prior claim and the center-stage position it gave her. Whatever embarrassment Autumn might have felt at being thrust into the limelight was overridden by amusement at the accuracy of Julia's earlier descriptions.

Dr. Robert Spicer was indeed smoothly handsome. He was drifting toward fifty and bursting with health. He wore a casually expensive green cardigan with brown leather patches at the elbows. His wife, Jane, was also as Julia had described: unfortunately dumpy. The small smile she gave Autumn lasted about two seconds before her face slipped back into the dissatisfied grooves that were habitual. She cast dark, bad-tempered glances at her husband while he gave Julia the bulk of his attention.

Watching them, Autumn could find little sympathy for Jane and no disapproval for Julia—no one disapproves of a flower for drawing bees. Julia's attraction was just as natural, and just as potent.

Helen Easterman was attractive in a slick, practiced fashion. The scarlet of her dress suited her, but struck a jarring note in the simply furnished lounge. Her face was perfectly made-up and reminded Autumn of a mask. As a photographer, she knew the tricks and secrets of cosmetics. Instinctively, Autumn avoided her.

In contrast, Steve Anderson was all charm. Good looks, California style, as Julia had said. Autumn liked the crinkles at the corners of his eyes and his careless chic. He wore chinos easily. From his bearing, she knew he would wear black tie with equal aplomb. If he chose a political career, she mused, he should make his way very well.

Julia had offered no description of Jacques LeFarre. What Autumn knew of him came primarily from either the gossip magazines or his films. He was smaller than she had imagined, barely as tall as she, but with a wiry build. His features were strong and he wore his brown hair brushed back from his forehead where three worry lines had been etched. She liked the trim moustache over his mouth, and the way he lifted her hand to kiss it when they were introduced.

"Well, Autumn," Steve began with a smile. "I'm playing bartender in George's absence. What can I fix you?"

"Vodka Collins, easy on the vodka," Lucas answered. Autumn gave up the idea of ignoring him.

"Your memory's improved," she said coolly.

"So's your wardrobe." He ran a finger down the collar of her dress. "I remember when it ran to jeans and old sweaters."

"I grew up." Her eyes were as steady and as measuring as his. "So I see."

"Ah, you have met before," Jacques put in. "But this is fascinating. You are old friends?"

"Old friends?" Lucas repeated before Autumn could speak. He studied her with infuriating amusement. "Would you say that was an accurate description, Cat?"

"Cat?" Jacques frowned a moment. "Ah, the eyes, *oui*." Pleased, he brushed his index finger over his moustache. "It suits. What do you think, *chérie?*" He turned to Julia, who seemed to be enjoying herself watching the unfolding scene. "She's enchanting, and her voice is quite good."

"I've already warned Autumn about you," Julia drawled, then gave Robert Spicer a glorious smile.

"Ah, Julia," Jacques said mildly, "how wicked of you."

"Autumn works the other side of the camera," Lucas stated. Knowing his eyes had been on her the entire time, Autumn was grateful when Steve returned with her drink. "She's a photographer."

"Again, I'm fascinated." Autumn's free hand was captured in Jacques's. "Tell me why you are behind the camera instead of in front of it? Your hair alone would cause poets to run for their pens."

No woman was immune to flattery with a French accent, and Autumn smiled fully into his eyes. "I doubt I could stand still long enough to begin with."

"Photographers can be quite useful," Helen Easterman stated

suddenly. Lifting a hand, she patted her dark, sleek cap of hair. "A good, clear photograph is an invaluable tool…to an artist."

An awkward pause followed the statement. Tension entered the room, so out of place in the comfortable lounge with its chintz curtains that Autumn thought it must be her imagination. Helen smiled into the silence and sipped her drink. Her eyes swept over the others, inclusively, never centering on one.

Autumn knew there was something here which isolated Helen and set her apart from the rest. Messages were being passed without words, though there was no way for Autumn to tell who was communicating what to whom. The mood changed swiftly as Julia engaged Robert Spicer in bright conversation. Jane Spicer's habitual frown became more pronounced.

The easy climate continued as they went in to dinner. Sitting between Jacques and Steve, Autumn was able to add to her education as she observed Julia flirting simultaneously with Lucas and Robert. She was, in Autumn's opinion, magnificent. Even through the discomfort of seeing Lucas casually return the flirtation, she had to admire Julia's talent. Her charm and beauty were insatiable. Jane ate in sullen silence.

Dreary woman, Autumn mused, then wondered what her own reaction would be if it were her husband so enchanted. Action, she decided, not silence. I'd simply claw her eyes out. The image of dumpy Jane wrestling with the elegant Julia made her smile. Even as she enjoyed the notion, she looked up to find Lucas's eyes on her.

His brows were lifted at an angle she knew meant amusement. Autumn turned her attention to Jacques.

"Do you find many differences in the movie industry here in America, Mr. LeFarre?"

"You must call me Jacques." His smile caused the tips of his moustache to rise. "There are differences, yes. I would say that Americans are more...adventurous than Europeans."

Autumn lifted her shoulders and smiled. "Maybe because we're a mixture of nationalities. Not watered down. Just American-ized."

"Americanized." Jacques tried out the word and approved it. His grin was younger than his smile, less urbane. "Yes, I would say I feel Americanized in California."

"Still, California's only one aspect of the country," Steve put in. "And I wouldn't call L.A. or southern California particu-larly typical." Autumn watched his eyes flick over her hair. His interest brought on a small flutter of response that pleased her. It proved that she was still a woman, open to a man—not just one man. "Have you ever been to California, Autumn?"

"I lived there...once." Her response to Steve, and the need to prove something to herself, urged her to turn her eyes to Lucas. Their gazes locked and held for one brief instant. "I relocated in New York three years ago."

"There was a family here from New York," Steve went on. If he'd noticed the look that had passed, he gave no sign. Yes, a good politician, Autumn thought again. "They just checked out this morning. The woman was one of those robust types with energy pouring out of every cell. She needed it," he added with a smile that was for Autumn alone. "She had three boys. Trip-lets. I think she said they were eleven."

"Oh, those beastly children!" Julia switched her attention from Robert and looked across the table. She rolled her summer blue eyes. "Running around like a pack of monkeys. Worse, you could never tell which one of them it was zooming by or leaping down. They did everything in triplicate." She shuddered and lifted her water glass. "They ate like elephants."

"Running and eating are part of childhood," Jacques commented with a shake of his head. "Julia," he told Autumn with a conspirator's wink, "was born twenty-one and beautiful."

"Anyone with manners is born twenty-one," Julia countered. "Being beautiful was simply a bonus." Her eyes were laughing now. "Jacques is crazy about kids," she informed Autumn. "He has three specimens of his own."

Interested, Autumn turned to him. She'd never thought of Jacques LeFarre in terms other than his work. "I'm crazy about them, too," she confessed and shot Julia a grin. "What sort of specimens do you have?"

"Boys," he answered. Autumn found the fondness in his eyes curiously touching. "They are like a ladder." With his hand, he formed imaginary steps. "Seven, eight and nine years. They live in France with my wife—my ex-wife." He frowned, then smoothed it away. Autumn realized how the worry lines in his brow had been formed.

"Jacques actually wants custody of the little monsters." Julia's look was more tolerant than her words. Here, Autumn saw, affection transcended flirtation. "Even though I hold your sanity suspect, Jacques, I'm forced to admit you make a better father than Claudette makes a mother."

"Custody suits are sensitive matters," Helen announced from the end of the table. She drank from her water glass, peering over the rim with small, sharp eyes. The look that she sent Jacques seemed to brush everyone else out of her line of vision. "It's so important that any...unsuitable information doesn't come to light."

Tension sprang back. Autumn felt the Frenchman stiffen beside her. But there was more. Undercurrents flowed up and down the long pine table. It was impossible not to feel them, though there was nothing tangible, nothing solid. Instinctively, Autumn's eyes sought Lucas's. There was nothing there but the hard, unfathomable mask she had seen too often in the past.

"Your aunt serves such marvelous meals, Miss Gallegher." With a puzzling, satisfied smirk, Helen shifted her attention to Autumn.

"Yes." She blundered into the awful silence. "Aunt Tabby gives food a high rating of importance."

"Aunt Tabby?" Julia's rich laugh warred with the tension, and won. The air was instantly lighter. "What a wonderful name. Did you know Autumn has an Aunt Tabby when you christened her Cat, Lucas?" She stared up at him, her eyes wide and guileless. Autumn was reminded of a movie Julia had been in, in which she played the innocent ingenue to perfection.

"Lucas and I didn't know each other well enough to discuss relatives." Autumn's voice was easy and careless and pleased her very much. So did Lucas's barely perceptible frown.

"Actually," he replied, recovering quickly, "we were too occupied to discuss family trees." He sent her a smile which sneaked through her defenses. Autumn's pulse hammered. "What did we talk about in those days, Cat?"

"I've forgotten," she murmured, knowing she had lost the edge before she'd really held it. "It was a long time ago."

Aunt Tabby bustled in with her prize cobbler.

There was music on the stereo and a muted fire in the hearth when they returned to the lounge. The scene, if Autumn could have captured it on film, was one of relaxed camaraderie. Steve and Robert huddled over a chessboard while Jane made her discontented way through a magazine. Even without a photographer's eye for color, Autumn knew the woman should never wear brown. She felt quite certain that Jane invariably would.

Lucas sprawled on the sofa. Somehow, he always managed to relax in a negligent fashion without seeming sloppy; there was always an alertness about him, energy simmering right under the surface. Autumn knew he watched people without being obvious—not because he cared if he made them uncomfortable, he didn't in the least—it was simply something he was able to do. And in watching them, he was able to learn their secrets. An obsessive writer, he drew his characters from flesh and blood. With no mercy, Autumn recalled.

At the moment, he seemed content with his conversation with Julia and Jacques. They flanked him on the sofa and spoke with the ease that came from familiarity; they shared the same world.

But it's not my world, Autumn reminded herself. I only pretended it was for a little while. I only pretended he was mine for a little while. She had been right when she told Lucas she had grown up. Pretend games were for children.

Yet, Autumn thought as she sat back and observed, there was a game of some sort going on here. There was a faint glistening of unease superimposed over the homey picture. Always attuned to contrasts, she could sense it, feel it. They're not letting me in on the rules, she mused, and found herself grateful. She didn't want to play. Making her excuses to no one in particular, Autumn slipped from the room to find her aunt.

Whatever tension she had felt evaporated the moment Autumn stepped into her aunt's room.

"Oh, Autumn." Aunt Tabby lifted her glasses from her nose and let them dangle from a chain around her neck. "I was just reading a letter from your mother. I'd forgotten it was here until this minute. She says by the time I read this, you'll be here. And here you are." Smiling, she patted Autumn's hand. "Debbie always was so clever. Did you enjoy your pot roast, dear?"

"It was lovely, Aunt Tabby, thank you."

"We'll have to have it once a week while you're with us." Autumn smiled and thought of how she liked spaghetti. Paul probably gets spaghetti on his visits, she mused. "I'll just make a note of that, else it'll slip right through my mind." Autumn recalled that Aunt Tabby's notes were famous for their ability to slip into another dimension, and felt more hopeful. "Where are my glasses?" Aunt Tabby murmured, puckering her impossibly smooth brow. Standing, she rummaged through her desk, lifting papers and peering under books. "They're never where you leave them."

Autumn lifted the dangling glasses from her aunt's bosom, then perched them on her nose. After blinking a moment, Aunt Tabby smiled in her vague fashion.

"Isn't that strange?" she commented. "They were here all along. You're just as clever as your mother."

Autumn couldn't resist giving her a bone-crushing hug. "Aunt Tabby, I adore you!"

"You always were such a sweet child." She patted Autumn's cheek, then moved away, leaving the scent of lavender and talc hanging in the air. "I hope you like your surprise."

"I'm sure I will."

"You haven't seen it yet?" Her small mouth pouted in thought. "No, I'm quite sure I haven't shown you yet, so you can't know if you like it. Did you and Miss Bond have a nice chat? Such a lovely lady. I believe she's in show business."

Autumn's smile was wry. There was no one, she thought, absolutely no one like Aunt Tabby. "Yes, I believe she is. I've always admired her."

"Oh, have you met before?" Aunt Tabby asked absently as she shuffled the papers on her desk back into her own particular order. "I suppose I'd better show you now while I have it on my mind."

Autumn tried to keep up with her aunt's thought processes, but it had been a year since her last visit and she was rusty. "Show me what, Aunt Tabby?"

"Oh now, it wouldn't be a surprise if I told you, would it?" Playfully, she shook her finger under Autumn's nose. "You'll just have to be patient and come along with me." With this, she bustled from the room.

Autumn followed, deducing they were again discussing the surprise. She had to shorten her gait to match her aunt's. Autumn usually moved in a loose-limbed stride, a result of leanness and lengthy legs, while her aunt scuttled unrhythmically. Like a rabbit, Autumn thought, that dashes out in the road then can't make up its mind which way to run. As they walked, Aunt Tabby muttered about bed linen. Autumn's thoughts drifted irresistibly to Lucas.

"Now, here we are." Aunt Tabby stopped. She gave the door an expectant smile. The door itself, Autumn recalled, led to a sitting room long since abandoned and converted into a storage room. It was a convenient place for cleaning supplies, as it adjoined the kitchen. "Well," Aunt Tabby said, beaming, "what do you think?"

Searching for the right comment, Autumn realized the surprise must be inside. "Is my surprise in there, Aunt Tabby?"

"Yes, of course, how silly." She clucked her tongue. "You won't know what it is until I open the door."

With this indisputable logic, she did.

When the lights were switched on, Autumn stood stunned. Where she had expected to see mops, brooms and buckets was a fully equipped darkroom. Every detail, every piece of apparatus stood neat and orderly in front of her. Her voice had been left outside the door.

"Well, what do you think?" Aunt Tabby repeated. She moved around the room, stopping now and again to peer at bottles of developing fluid, tongs and trays. "It all looks so technical and scientific to me." The enlarger caused her to frown and tilt her head. "I'm sure I don't understand a thing about it."

"Oh, Aunt Tabby." Autumn's voice finally joined her body. "You shouldn't have."

"Oh dear, is something wrong with it? Nelson told me you developed your own film, and the company that brought in all these things assured me everything was proper. Of course..." Her voice wavered in doubt. "I really don't know a thing about it."

Her aunt looked so distressed, Autumn nearly wept with love. "No, Aunt Tabby, it's perfect. It's wonderful." She enveloped the small, soft body in her arms. "I meant that you shouldn't have done this for me. All the trouble and the expense."

"Oh, is that all?" Aunt Tabby interrupted. Her distress dissolved as she beamed around the room again. "Well, it was no trouble at all. These nice young men came in and did all the work. As for the expense, well..." She shrugged her rounded shoulders. "I'd rather see you enjoy my money now than after I'm dead."

Sometimes, Autumn thought, the fuzzy little brain shot straight through to sterling sense. "Aunt Tabby." She framed her aunt's face with her hands. "I've never had a more wonderful surprise. Thank you."

"You just have a good time with it." Aunt Tabby's cheeks grew rosy with pleasure when Autumn kissed them, and she eyed the chemicals and trays again. "I don't suppose you'll blow anything up."

Knowing this wasn't a pun, and that her aunt was concerned about explosions in her vague way, Autumn assured her she would not. Satisfied, Aunt Tabby then bustled off, leaving Autumn to explore on her own.

For more than an hour, Autumn lost herself in what she knew best. Photography, started as a hobby when she had been a child, had become both craft and profession. The chemicals and complicated equipment were no strangers to her. Here, in a darkroom, or with a camera in her hands, she knew exactly who she was and what she wanted. This was where she had learned control—the same control she knew she had to employ over her thoughts of Lucas. She was no longer a dewy-eyed girl, ready to follow the crook of a finger. She was a professional woman with a growing reputation in her field. She had to hang on to that now, as she had for three years. There was no going back to yesterday.

Pleasantly weary after rearranging the darkroom to her own preference, Autumn wandered into the kitchen to fix herself a solitary cup of tea. The moon was round and white with a thin cloud drifting over it. Unexpectedly, a shudder ran through her, quick and chilling. The odd feeling she had sensed several times that evening came back. She frowned. Imagination? Autumn knew herself well enough to admit she had her share. It was part of her art. But this was different.

Discovering Lucas at the inn had jolted her system, and her emotions had been strained. That, she decided, was all that was wrong. The tension she had felt earlier was her own tension; the strain, her own strain. Dumping the remaining tea into the sink, she decided that what she needed was a good night's sleep. No dreams, she ordered herself firmly. She'd had her fill of dreams three years before.

The house was quiet now. Moonlight filtered in, leaving the corners shadowed. The lounge was dark, but as she passed, Autumn heard muted voices. She hesitated a moment, thinking to stop and say good-night, then she detected the subtle signs that told her this wasn't a conversation, but an argument. There was anger in the hushed, sexless voices. The undistinguishable words were quick, staccato and passionate. She walked by quickly, not wanting to overhear a private battle. A brief oath shot out, steeped in temper, elegant in French.

Climbing the stairs, Autumn smothered a grin. Jacques, she concluded, was probably losing patience with Lucas's artistic stubbornness. For entirely malicious reasons, she hoped the Frenchman gave him an earful.

It wasn't until she was halfway down the hall to her room that Autumn saw that she'd been wrong. Even Lucas McLean couldn't be two places at once. And he was definitely in this one. In the doorway of another room, Lucas was locked in a very involved embrace with Julia Bond.

Autumn knew how his arms would feel, how his mouth would

taste. She remembered it all, completely, as if no years had come between to dull the sensations. She knew how his hand would trail up the back until he cupped around the neck. And that his fingers wouldn't be gentle. No, there were no gentle caresses from Lucas.

There was no need for her to worry about being seen. Both Lucas and Julia were totally focused on each other. Autumn was certain that the roof could have toppled over their heads, and they would have remained unmoving and entwined. The pain came back, hatefully, in full force.

Hurrying by, she gave vent to hideous and unwelcome jealousy by slamming her door.

Chapter Three

The forest was morning fresh. It held a tranquility that was full of tangy scents and bird song. To the east, the sky was filled with scuttling rags of white clouds. An optimist, Autumn put her hopes in them and ignored the dark, threatening sky in the west. Streaks of red still crowned the peaks of the mountains. Gently, the color faded to pink before it surrendered to blue.

The light was good, filtering through the white clouds and illuminating the forest. The leaves weren't full enough to interfere with the sun, only touching the limbs of trees with dots of green. Sometimes strong, the breeze bent branches and tugged at Autumn's hair. She could smell spring.

Wood violets popped out unexpectedly, the purple dramatic against the moss. She saw her first robin marching importantly on the ground, listening for worms. Squirrels scampered up trees, down trees and over the mulch of last year's leaves.

Autumn had intended to walk to the lake, hoping to catch a deer at early watering, but when her camera insisted on planting itself in front of her face again and again, she didn't resist. She ambled along, happy in the solitude and in tune with nature.

In New York, she never truly felt alone—lonely sometimes, but not solitary. The city intruded. Now, cocooned by mountains and trees, she realized how much she'd needed to feel alone. To recharge. Since leaving California and Lucas, Autumn hadn't permitted herself time alone. There had been a void that had to be filled, and she'd filled it with people, with work, with noise—anything that would keep her mind busy. She'd used the pace of the city. It had been necessary. Now, she wanted the pace of the mountains.

In the distance, the lake shimmered. Reflections of the surrounding mountains and trees were mirrored in the water, reversed and shadowy. There were no deer, but as she drew closer, Autumn noticed two figures circling the far side. The ridge where she stood was some fifty feet above the small valley which held the lake. The view was spectacular.

The lake itself stretched in a wide finger, about a hundred feet in length, forty in width. The breeze that caught at Autumn's hair where she strode didn't reach down to the water; its surface was clear and still. The opaque water gradually darkened towards the center, warning of dangerous depths.

Autumn forgot the people walking around the lake, her mind fully occupied with angles and depths of field and shutter speeds. The distance was too great for her to make them out even if she had been interested.

The sun continued its rise, and Autumn was content. She stopped only to change film. As she replaced the roll, she noted that the lake was now deserted. The light was wrong for the mood she wanted and, turning, she began her leisurely journey back to the inn.

This time, the stillness of the forest seemed different. The sun was brighter, but she felt an odd disquiet she hadn't experienced in the paler light of dawn. Foolishly, she looked back over her shoulder, then told herself she was an idiot. Who would be following her? And why? Yet the feeling persisted.

The serenity had vanished. Autumn forced herself to put aside an impulsive desire to run back to the inn where there would be people and coffee brewing. She wasn't a child to take flight at the thought of ogres or gnomes. To prove to herself that her fantasies hadn't affected her, she forced herself to stop and take the time to perfect a shot of a cooperative squirrel. A faint rustle of dead leaves came from behind her and terror brought her scrambling to her feet.

"Well, Cat, still attached to a camera?"

Blood pounding in her head, Autumn stared at Lucas. His hands were tucked comfortably into the pockets of his jeans as he stood directly in front of her. For a moment, she couldn't speak. The fear had been sharp and real.

"What do you mean by sneaking up behind me that way?" When it returned, her voice was furious. She was annoyed that she'd been foolish enough to be frightened, and angry that he'd been the one to frighten her. She pushed her hair back and glared at him.

"I see you've finally developed the temper to match your hair," he observed in a lazy voice. He crossed the slight distance between them and stood close. Autumn had also developed pride and refused to back away.

"It gets particularly nasty when someone spoils a shot." It was a simple matter to blame her reaction on his interference with her work. Not for a moment would she amuse him by confessing fear.

"You're a bit jumpy, Cat." The devil himself could take lessons on smiling from Lucas McLean, she thought bitterly. "Do I make you nervous?"

His dark hair curled in a confused tangle around his lean face, and his eyes were dark and confident. It was the confidence, she told herself, that she cursed him for. "Don't flatter yourself," she tossed back. "I don't recall you ever being one for morning hikes, Lucas. Have you developed a love of nature?"

"I've always had a fondness for nature." He was studying her with deep, powerful eyes while his mouth curved into a smile. "I've always had a penchant for picnics."

The pain started, a dull ache in her stomach. She could remember the gritty feel of sand under her legs, the tart taste of wine on her tongue and the scent of the ocean everywhere. She forced her gaze to stay level with his. "I lost my taste for them." She turned in dismissal, but he fell into step beside her. "I'm not going straight back," she informed him. The chill in her voice would have discouraged anyone else. Stopping, she took an off-center picture of a blue jay.

"I'm in no hurry," he returned easily. "I've always enjoyed watching you work. It's fascinating how absorbed you become." He watched her back, and let his eyes run down the length of her hair. "I believe you could be snapping a charging rhino and not give an inch until you'd perfected the shot." There was a slight pause as she remained turned away from him. "I saw that photo you took of a burned-out tenement in New York. It was remarkable. Hard, clean and desperate."

Wary of the compliment, Autumn faced him. She knew Lucas wasn't generous with praise. Hard, clean and desperate, she thought. He had chosen the words perfectly. She didn't like discovering that his opinion still mattered. "Thank you." She turned back to focus on a grouping of trees. "Still having trouble with your book?"

"More than I'd anticipated," he muttered. Suddenly, he swooped her hair up into his hands. "I never could resist it, could I?" She continued to give her attention to the trees. Her answer was an absent shrug, but she squeezed her eyes tightly shut a moment. "I've never seen another woman with hair like yours. I've looked, God knows, but the shade is always wrong, or the texture or the length." There was a seductive quality in his voice. Autumn stiffened against it. "It's unique. A fiery waterfall in the sun, deep and vibrant spilling over a pillowcase."

"You always had a gift for description." She adjusted her lens without the vaguest idea of what she was doing. Her voice was detached, faintly bored, while she prayed for him to go. Instead, his grip tightened on her hair. In a swift move, he whirled her around and tore the camera from her hands.

"Damn it, don't use that tone with me. Don't turn your back on me. Don't ever turn your back on me."

She remembered the dark expression and uncertain temper well. There'd been a time when she would have dissolved when faced with them. But not anymore, she thought fleetingly. Not this time.

"I don't cringe at being sworn at these days, Lucas." She tossed her head, lifting her chin. "Why don't you save your attention for Julia? I don't want it."

"So." His smile was light and amused in a rapid-fire change.

"It was you. No need to be jealous, Cat. The lady made the move, not I."

"Yes, I noticed your mad struggle for release." Even as she spoke, she regretted the words. Annoyed, Autumn pushed away, but was only caught closer. His scent teased her senses and reminded her of things she'd rather forget. "Listen, Lucas," she ground out slowly as both anger and longing rose inside her. "It took me six months to realize what a bastard you are, and I've had three years to cement that realization. I'm a big girl now, and not susceptible to your abundant charms. Now, take your hands off me and get lost."

"Learned to sink your teeth in, have you, Cat?" To her mounting fury, his expression was more amused than insulted. His eyes lowered to her mouth for a moment, lingered then lifted. "Not malleable anymore, but just as fascinating."

Because his words hurt more than she had thought possible, she hurled a stream of abuse at him.

His laughter cut off her torrent like a slap. Abandoning verbal protest, Autumn began to struggle with a wild, furious rage. Abruptly, he molded her against him. Tasting of punishment and possession, his mouth found hers. The heat was blinding.

The old, churning need fought its way to the surface. For three years she had starved, and now all that hunger spilled out in response. There was no hesitation as her arms found their way around his neck. Eager for more, her lips parted. His mouth was urgent and bruising. The pain was like heaven, and she begged for more. Her blood was flowing again. Lucas let his mouth roam over her face, then come back to hers with new demands. Autumn met them and fretted for more. Time flew backward, then forward again before he lifted his face.

His eyes were incredibly dark, opaque with a passion she recognized. For the first time she felt the faint throbbing where his
hands gripped her and his hold eased to a caress. The taste of
him lingered on her lips.

"It's still there, Cat," Lucas murmured. With easy familiarity,
he combed his fingers through her hair. "Still there."

All at once, pain and humiliation coursed through her. She
pulled away fiercely and swung out a hand. He caught her wrist
and, frustrated, she drew back with her other hand. His re-
flexes were too sharp, and she was denied any satisfaction. With
both wrists captured, she could only stand struggling, her breath
ragged. Tears burned at her throat, but she refused to acknowl-
edge them. He won't make me cry, she vowed fiercely. He won't
see me cry again.

In silence, Lucas watched her battle for control. There was no
sound in the forest but Autumn's own jerking breaths. When
she could speak, her voice was hard and cold. "There's a difference between love and lust, Lucas. Even you should know one
from the other. What's there now may be the same for you, but
not for me. I loved you. I *loved* you." The words were an accusation in their repetition. His brows drew together as his gaze
grew intense. "You took it all once—my love, my innocence, my
pride—then you tossed them back in my face. You can't have
them back. The first is dead, the second's gone and the third
belongs to me."

For a moment, they both were still. Slowly, without taking
his eyes from hers, Lucas released her wrists. He didn't speak,
and his expression told her nothing. Refusing to run from him
a second time, Autumn turned and walked away. Only when
she was certain he wasn't following did she allow her tears their

freedom. Her statements about pride and innocence had been true. But her love was far from dead. It was alive, and it hurt.

As the red bricks of the inn came into view, Autumn dashed the drops away. There would be no wallowing in what was over. Loving Lucas changed nothing, any more than it had changed anything three years before. But she'd changed. He wouldn't find her weeping, helpless and—as he had said himself—malleable.

Disillusionment had given her strength. He could still hurt her. She'd learned that quickly. But he could no longer manipulate her as he had once. Still, the encounter with him had left her shaken, and she wasn't pleased when Helen approached from a path to the right.

It was impossible, without being pointedly rude, for Autumn to veer off and avoid her. Instead, she fixed a smile on her face. When Helen turned her head, the livid bruise under her eye became noticeable. Autumn's smile faded into quick concern.

"What happened?" The bruise looked painful and aroused Autumn's sympathy.

"I walked into a branch." Helen gave a careless shrug as she lifted her fingers to stroke the mark. "I'll have to be more careful in the future."

Perhaps it was her turmoil over Lucas that made Autumn detect some hidden shade of meaning in those words, but Helen seemed to mean more than she said. Certainly the eyes which met Autumn's were as hot and angry as the bruise. And the mark itself, Autumn mused, looked more like the result of contact with a violent hand than with any stray branch. She pushed the thought aside. Who would have struck Helen? she asked herself. And why would she cover up the abuse? Her own carelessness made more sense.

"It looks nasty," Autumn commented as they began to walk toward the inn. "You'll have to do something about it. Aunt Tabby should have something to ease the soreness."

"Oh, I intend to do something about it," Helen muttered, then gave Autumn her sharp-eyed smile. "I know just the thing. Out early taking pictures?" she asked while Autumn tried to ignore the unease her words brought. "I've always found people more interesting subjects than trees. I'm especially fond of candid shots." She began to laugh at some private joke. It was the first time Autumn had heard her laugh, and she thought how suited the sound was to Helen's smile. They were both unpleasant.

"Were you down at the lake earlier?" Autumn recalled the two figures she had spotted. To her surprise, Helen's laughter stopped abruptly. Her eyes grew sharper.

"Did you see someone?"

"No," she began, confused by the harshness of the question. "Not exactly. I saw two people by the lake, but I was too far away to see who they were. I was taking pictures from the ridge."

"Taking pictures," Helen repeated. Her mouth pursed as if she were considering something carefully. She began to laugh again with a harsh burst of sound.

"Well, well, such good humor for such early risers." Julia drifted down the porch steps. Her brow lifted as she studied Helen's cheek. Autumn wondered if the actress's shudder was real or affected. "Good heavens, what have you done to yourself?"

Helen's amusement seemed to have passed. She gave Julia a quick scowl, then fingered the bruise again. "Walked into a branch," she muttered before she stalked up the steps and disappeared inside.

"A fist more likely," Julia commented, and smiled. With a

shrug, she dismissed Helen and turned to Autumn. "The call of the wild beckoned to you, too? It seems everyone but me was tramping through forests and over mountains at the cold light of dawn. It's so difficult being sane when one is surrounded by insanity."

Autumn had to smile. Julia looked like a sunbeam. In direct contrast to her own rough jeans and jacket, Julia wore delicate pink slacks and a thin silk blouse flocked with roses. The white sandals she wore wouldn't last fifty yards in the woods. Whatever resentment Autumn had felt for the actress attracting Lucas vanished under her open warmth.

"There are some," Autumn remarked mildly, "who might accuse you of laziness."

"Absolutely," Julia agreed with a nod and a smile. "When I'm not working, I wallow in sloth. If I don't get going again soon, my blood will stop flowing." She gave Autumn a shrewd glance. "Looks like you walked into a rather large branch yourself."

Bewilderment crossed Autumn's face briefly. Julia's eyes, she discovered, were very discerning. The traces of tears hadn't evaporated as completely as Autumn would have liked. Helplessly she moved her shoulders. "I heal quickly."

"Brave child. Come, tell mama all about it." Julia's eyes were sympathetic, balancing the stinging lightness of the words. Linking her arm through Autumn's, she began to walk across the lawn.

"Julia..." Autumn shook her head. Inner feelings were private. She'd broken the rule for Lucas, and wasn't certain she could do so again.

"Autumn." The refusal was firmly interrupted. "You do need to talk. You might not think that you look stricken, but you do."

Julia sighed with perfect finesse. "I really don't know why I've become so fond of you; it's totally against my policy. Beautiful women tend to avoid or dislike other beautiful women, especially younger ones."

The statement completely robbed Autumn of speech. The idea of the exquisite, incomparable Julia Bond placing herself on a physical plane anywhere near Autumn's own seemed ludicrous to her. It was one matter to hear the actress speak casually of her own beauty, and quite another for her to speak of Autumn's. Julia's voice flowed over the gaping silence.

"Maybe it's the exposure to those two other females—one so dull and the other so nasty—but I've developed an affection for you." The breeze tugged at her hair, lifting it up so that the sunlight streamed through it. Absently, Julia tucked a strand behind her ear. On the lobe a diamond sparkled. Autumn thought it incongruous that they were walking arm in arm among her aunt's struggling daffodils.

"You're also a kind person," Julia went on. "I don't know a great many kind people." She turned to Autumn so that her exquisite profile became her exquisite full face. "Autumn, darling, I always pry, but I also know how to keep a confidence."

"I'm still in love with him," Autumn blurted out, then followed that rash statement with a deep sigh. Before she knew it, words were tumbling out. She left out nothing, from the beginning to the end, to the new beginning when he had come back into her life the day before. She told Julia everything. Once she'd begun, no effort was needed. She didn't have to think, only feel, and Julia listened. The quality of her listening was so perfect, Autumn all but forgot she was there.

"The monster," Julia said, but with no malice. "You'll find all men, those marvelous creatures, are basically monsters."

Who was Autumn to argue with an expert? As they walked on in silence, she realized that she did feel better. The rawness was gone.

"The main trouble is, of course, that you're still mad about him. Not that I blame you," Julia added when Autumn made a small sound of distress. "Lucas is quite a man. I had a tiny sample last night, and I was impressed." Julia spoke so casually of the passion Autumn had witnessed, it was impossible to be angry. "Lucas is a talented man," Julia went on. By her smile, Autumn knew that Julia was very much aware of the struggle that was going on within Autumn. "He's also arrogant, selfish and used to being obeyed. It's easy for me to see that, because I am, too. We're alike. I doubt very much if we could even enjoy a pleasant affair. We'd be clawing at each other before the bed was turned down."

Autumn found no response to make to the image this produced, and merely walked on.

"Jacques is more my type," Julia mused. "But his attentions are committed elsewhere." She frowned, and Autumn sensed that her thoughts had drifted to something quite different. "Anyway." Julia made an impatient gesture. "You just have to make up your mind what you want. Obviously, Lucas wants you back, at least for as long as it suits him."

Autumn tried to ignore the sting of honesty and just listened.

"Knowing that, you could enjoy a stimulating relationship with him, with your eyes open."

"I can't do that, Julia. The knowing won't stop the hurting. I'm not sure I can survive another...relationship with Lucas.

And he'd know I was still in love with him." A flash frame of their parting scene three years before jumped into her mind. "I won't be humiliated again. Pride's the only thing I have left that isn't his already."

"Love and pride don't belong together." Julia patted Autumn's hand. "Well then, you'll have to barricade yourself against the assault. I'll run interference for you."

"How will you do that?"

"Darling!" She lifted her brow as the slow, cat smile drifted to her lips.

Autumn had to laugh. It all seemed so absurd. She lifted her face to the sky. The black clouds were winning after all. For a moment, they blotted out the sun and warmth. "Looks like rain."

Her gaze shifted back to the inn. The windows were black and empty. The struggling light fell gloomily over the bricks and turned the white porch and shutters gray. Behind the building, the sky was like slate. The mountains were colorless and oppressive. She felt a tickle at the back of her neck. To her puzzlement, Autumn found she didn't want to go back inside.

Just as quickly, the clouds shifted, letting the sun pour out through the opening. The windows blinked with light. The shadows vanished. Chiding herself for another flight of fancy, Autumn walked back to the inn with Julia.

Only Jacques joined them for breakfast. Helen was nowhere in sight, and Steve and the Spicers were apparently still hiking. Autumn trained her thoughts away from Lucas. Her appetite, as usual, was unimpaired and outrageous. She put away a healthy portion of bacon, eggs, coffee and muffins while Julia nibbled on a single piece of thin toast and sent her envious scowls.

Jacques seemed preoccupied. His charm was costing him visible effort. Memory of the muffled argument in the lounge came to Autumn's mind. Idly, she began to speculate on who he had been annoyed with. Thinking it over, the entire matter struck her as odd. Jacques LeFarre didn't seem to be the sort of man who would argue with a veritable stranger, yet, as Autumn knew, both Lucas and Julia had been preoccupied elsewhere.

Appearing totally at ease, Julia rambled on about a mutual friend in the industry. But she's an actress, Autumn reminded herself. A good one. She could easily know the cause of last night's animosity and never show a sign. Jacques, however, wasn't an actor. The distress was there; anger lay just beneath the polished charm. Autumn wondered at it throughout the meal, then dismissed it from her mind as she left to find her aunt. After all, she reflected, it wasn't any of her business.

Aunt Tabby was, as Autumn had known she would be, fussing with Nancy the cook over the day's menu. Keeping silent, Autumn let the story unfold. It seemed that Nancy had planned on chicken while Aunt Tabby was certain they had decided on pork. While the argument raged, Autumn helped herself to another cup of coffee. Through the window, she could see the thick, roiling clouds continue their roll from the west.

"Oh, Autumn, did you have a nice walk?" When she turned, Autumn found her aunt smiling at her. "Such a nice morning, a shame it's going to rain. But that's good for the flowers, isn't it? Sweet little things. Did you sleep well?"

After a moment, Autumn decided to answer only the final question. There was no use confusing her aunt. "Wonderfully, Aunt Tabby. I always sleep well when I visit you."

"It's the air," the woman replied. Her round little face lit with pleasure. "I think I'll make my special chocolate cake for tonight. That should make up for the rain."

"Any hot coffee, Aunt Tabby?" Lucas swept into the kitchen as if he enjoyed the privilege daily. As always, when he came into a room, the air charged. This phenomenon Autumn could accept. The casual use of her aunt's nickname was more perplexing.

"Of course, dear, just help yourself." Aunt Tabby gestured vaguely toward the stove, her mind on chocolate cake. Autumn's confusion grew as Lucas strode directly to the proper cupboard, retrieved a cup and proceeded to fix himself a very homey cup of coffee.

He drank, leaning against the counter. The eyes that met Autumn's were very cool. All traces of anger and passion were gone, as if they had never existed. His rough black brows lifted as she continued to stare. The damnable devil smile tugged at his mouth.

"Oh, is that your camera, dear?" Aunt Tabby's voice broke into her thoughts. Autumn lowered her eyes.

The camera still hung around her neck, so much a part of her that she'd forgotten it was there.

"My, my, so many numbers. It looks complicated." Aunt Tabby peered at it through narrowed eyes, forgetting the glasses that dangled from her chain. "I have a very nice one, Autumn. You're welcome to use it whenever you like." After giving the Nikon another dubious glance, she beamed up with her misty smile. "You just push a little red button, and the picture pops right out. You can see if you've cut off someone's head or have your thumb in the corner right away, so you can take another picture. And you don't have to grope around in that darkroom either. I don't know how you see what you're doing in there." Her brows drew close, and she tapped a finger against her cheek. "I'm almost certain I can find it."

Autumn grinned. She was compelled to subject her aunt to yet another bear hug. Over the gray-streaked head, Autumn saw that Lucas was grinning as well. It was the warm, natural grin which came to his face so rarely. For a moment, she found she could smile back at him without pain.

Chapter Four

When the rain came, it didn't begin with the slow drip-drop of an April shower. As the sky grew hazy, the light in the lounge became dim. Everyone was back and the inn was again filled with its odd assortment of guests.

Steve, expanding on his role of bartender, had wandered to the kitchen to get coffee. Robert Spicer had trapped Jacques in what seemed to be a technical explanation of open-heart surgery. During the discussion, Julia sat beside him, hanging on every word—or seeming to. Autumn knew better. Occasionally, Julia sent messages across to her with her extraordinary eyes. She was enjoying herself immensely.

Jane sat sullen over a novel Autumn was certain was riddled with explicit sex. She wore dull brown again, slacks and a sweater. Helen, her bruise livid, smoked quietly in long, deep drags. She reminded Autumn eerily of Alice in Wonderland's caterpillar. Once or twice, Autumn found Helen's sharp eyes on her. The speculative smile left her confused and uncomfortable.

Lucas wasn't there. He was upstairs, Autumn knew, hammering away at his typewriter. She hoped it would keep him busy for hours. Perhaps he'd even take his meals in his room.

Abruptly, the dim light outdoors was snuffed out, and the room plunged into gloom. The warmth fled with it. Autumn shuddered with a sharp premonition of dread. The feeling surprised her, as storms had always held a primitive appeal for her. For a heartbeat, there was no sound, then the rain began with a gushing explosion. With instant force, instant fury, it battered against the windows, punctuated by wicked flashes of lightning.

"A spring shower in the mountains," Steve observed. He paused a moment in the doorway with a large tray balanced in his hands. The friendly scent of coffee entered with him.

"More like special effects," Julia returned. With a flutter of her lashes, she cuddled toward Robert. "Storms are so terrifying and moving. I find myself longing to be frightened."

It was straight out of *A Long Summer's Evening*, Autumn noted, amused. But the doctor seemed too overcome with Julia's ingenuous eyes to recognize the line. Autumn wanted to laugh badly. When Julia cuddled even closer and sent her a wink, Autumn's eyes retreated to the ceiling.

Jane wasn't amused. Autumn noticed she was no longer sullen but smoldering. Perhaps she had claws after all, Autumn thought, and felt she would like her better for it. It might be wise, she mused as Steve passed her a cup of coffee, if Julia concentrated on him rather than the doctor.

"Cream, no sugar, right?" Steve smiled down at her with his California blue eyes. Autumn's lips curved in response. He was a man with the rare ability to make a woman feel pampered without being patronizing. She admired him for it.

"Right. You've got a better memory than George." Her eyes

smiled at him over the rim of her cup. "You serve with such style, too. Have you been in this line of work long?"

"I'm only here on a trial basis," he told her with a grin. "Please pass your comments on to the management."

Lightning speared through the gloom again. Jacques shifted in his seat as thunder rumbled and echoed through the room. "With such a storm, is it not possible to lose power?" he addressed Autumn.

"We often lose power." Her answer, accompanied by an absent shrug, brought on varying reactions.

Julia found the idea marvelous—candlelight was so wonderfully romantic. At the moment, Robert couldn't have agreed more. Jacques appeared not to care one way or the other. He lifted his hands in a Gallic gesture, indicating his acceptance of fate.

Steve and Helen seemed inordinately put out, though his comments were milder than hers. He mumbled once about inconveniences, then stalked over to the window to stare out at the torrent of wind and rain. Helen was livid.

"I didn't pay good money to grope around in the dark and eat cold meals." Lighting another cigarette with a swift, furious gesture, she glared at Autumn. "It's intolerable that we should have to put up with such inefficiency. Your aunt will certainly have to make the proper adjustments. I for one won't pay these ridiculous prices, then live like a pioneer." She waved her cigarette, preparing to continue, but Autumn cut her off. She aimed the cold, hard stare she had recently developed.

"I'm sure my aunt will give your complaints all the consideration they warrant." Turning pointedly away, she allowed Helen's sharp little darts to bounce off her. "Actually," she told Jacques, noting his smile of approval, "we have a generator. My uncle was as practical as Aunt Tabby is…"

"Charming," Steve supplied, and instantly became her friend.

After she'd finished beaming at him, Autumn continued. "If we lose main power, we switch over to the generator. With that, we can maintain essential power with little inconvenience."

"I believe I'll have candles in my room anyway," Julia decided. She gave Robert an under-the-lashes smile as he lit her cigarette.

"Julia should have been French," Jacques commented. His moustache tilted at the corner. "She's an incurable romantic."

"Too much…romance," Helen murmured, "can be unwise." Her eyes swept the room, then focused on Julia.

Before Autumn's astonished gaze, Julia transformed from mischievous angel to tough lady. "I've always found that only idiots think they're wise." Statement made, she melted back into a celestial being so quickly, Autumn blinked.

Seeing her perform on the screen was nothing compared to a live show. It occurred to Autumn that she had no inkling which woman was the real Julia Bond—if indeed she was either. The notion germinated that she really didn't know any of the people in that room. They were all strangers.

The air was still vibrating with the uncomfortable silence when Lucas entered. He seemed impervious to the swirling tension. Helplessly, Autumn's eyes locked on his. He came to her, ignoring the others in his cavalier fashion. The devil smile was on his face.

She felt a tremor when she couldn't stop the room from receding, leaving only him in her vision. Something of that fear must have been reflected in her face.

"I'm not going to eat you, Cat," Lucas murmured. Against the violent sounds of the storm, his voice was low, only for her. "Do you still like to walk in the rain?" The question was offhand, and didn't require an answer as he searched her face. "I remember when you did." He paused when she said nothing. "Your aunt sent you this." Lucas held out his hand, and Autumn's gaze dropped to it. Tension dissolved into laughter. "I haven't heard that in a long time," Lucas said softly.

She lifted her eyes to his again. He was studying her with a complete, singleminded intensity. "No?" As she accepted Aunt Tabby's famous red-button camera, her shoulders moved in a careless shrug. "Laughing's quite a habit of mine."

"Aunt Tabby says for you to have a good time with it." Dismissively, he turned his back on her and walked to the coffeepot.

"What have you got there, Autumn?" Julia demanded, her eyes following Lucas's progress.

Flourishing the camera, Autumn used a sober, didactic tone. "This, ladies and gentlemen, is the latest technological achievement in photography. At the mere touch of a button, friends and loved ones are beamed inside and spewed out onto a picture which develops before your astonished eyes. No focusing, no need to consult your light meter. The button is faster than the brain. Why, a child of five can operate it while riding his tricycle."

"It should be known," Lucas inserted in a dry voice, "that Autumn is a photographic snob." He stood by the window, carelessly drinking coffee while he spoke to the others. His eyes were on Autumn. "If it doesn't have interchangeable lenses and filters, multispeed shutters and impossibly complicated operations, it isn't a camera, but a toy."

"I've noticed her obsession," Julia agreed. She sent him a delicious look before she turned to Autumn. "She wears that black box like other women wear diamonds. She was actually tramping through the forest at the break of dawn, snapping pictures of chipmunks and bunnies."

With a good-natured grin, Autumn lifted the camera and snapped Julia's lovely face.

"Really, darling," Julia said with a professional toss of the head. "You might have given me the chance to turn my best side."

"You haven't got a best side," Autumn countered.

Julia smiled, obviously torn between amusement and insult while Jacques exploded with laughter. "And I thought she was such a sweet child," she murmured.

"In my profession, Miss Bond," Autumn returned gravely, "I've had occasion to photograph a fair number of women. This one you shoot from the left profile, that one from the right, another straight on. Still another from an upward angle, and so on." Pausing a moment, she gave Julia's matchless face a quick, critical survey. "I could shoot you from any position, any angle, any light, and the result would be equally wonderful."

"Jacques." Julia placed a hand on his arm. "We really must adopt this girl. She's invaluable for my ego."

"Professional integrity," Autumn claimed before placing the quickly developing snapshot on the table. She aimed Aunt Tabby's prize at Steve.

"You should be warned that with a camera of any sort in her hands, Autumn becomes a dangerous weapon." Lucas moved closer. He lifted the snap of Julia and studied it.

Autumn frowned as she remembered the innumerable photographs she had taken of him. Under the pretext that they were art, she'd never disposed of them. She'd snapped and focused and crouched around him until, exasperated, he'd dislodged the camera from her hands and effectively driven photography from her mind.

Lucas saw the frown. With his eyes dark and unreadable, he reached down to tangle his fingers in her hair. "You never could teach me how to take a proper picture, could you, Cat?"

"No." The battle with the growing ache made her voice brittle. "I never taught you anything, Lucas. But I learned quite a bit."

"I've never been able to master anything but a one-button job myself." Steve ambled over. Autumn's camera sat on the table beside her. Picking it up, he examined it as if it were a strange contraption from the outer reaches of space. "How can you remember what all these numbers are for?"

When he perched on the arm of her chair, Autumn grasped at the diversion. She began a lesson in basic photography. Lucas wandered back to the coffeepot, obviously bored. From the corner of her eye, Autumn noticed Julia gliding to join him. Within moments, her hand was tucked into his arm, and he no longer appeared bored. Gritting her teeth, Autumn began to give Steve a more involved lesson.

Lucas and Julia left, arm in arm, ostensibly for Julia to nap and Lucas to work. Autumn's eyes betrayed her by following them.

When she dragged her attention back to Steve, she caught his sympathetic smile. That he understood her feelings was too obvious. Cursing herself, she resumed her explanations of f-stops, grateful that Steve picked up the conversation as if there had been no lull.

The afternoon wore on. It was a long, dreary day with rain beating against windows. Lightning and thunder came and went, but the wind built in force until it was one continuous moan.

Robert tended the fire until flames crackled and spit. The cheery note this might have brought to the room was negated by Jane's sullenness and Helen's pacing. The air was tight.

Evading Steve's suggestion of cards, Autumn sought the peace and activity of her darkroom. As she closed and locked the door behind her, the headache which had started to build behind her temples eased.

This room was without tensions. Her senses picked up no nagging, intangible disturbances here, but were clear and ready to work. Step by step, she took her film through the first stages of development, preparing chemicals, checking temperatures, setting timers. Growing absorbed, she forgot the battering storm.

While it was necessary, Autumn worked in a total absence of light. Her fingers were her eyes at this stage and she worked quickly. Over the muffled sound of the storm, she heard a faint rattle. She ignored it, busy setting the timer for the next stage of developing. When the sound came again, it annoyed her.

Was it the doorknob? she wondered. Had she remembered to lock the door? All she needed at that point was for some layman to blunder in and bring damaging light with him.

"Leave the door alone," she called out just as the radio she had switched on for company went dead. There went the power, she concluded. Standing in the absolute darkness, Autumn sighed as the rattle came again.

Was it someone at the door, or just someone in the kitchen? Curious and annoyed, she walked in the direction of the door to make sure it was locked. Her steps were confident. She knew every inch of the room now. Suddenly, to her astonishment, pain exploded inside her head. Lights flashed and fractured before the darkness again became complete.

* * *

"Autumn, Autumn, open your eyes." Though the sound was far off and muffled, she heard the command in the tone. She resisted it. The nearer she came to consciousness, the more hideous grew the throbbing in her head. Oblivion was painless.

"Open your eyes." The voice was clearer now and more insistent. Autumn moaned.

Reluctantly, she opened her eyes as hands brushed the hair from her face. For a moment, she felt them linger against her cheek. Lucas came into focus gradually, dimming and receding until she forced him back, clear and sharp.

"Lucas?" Disoriented, Autumn could not think beyond his name. It seemed to satisfy him.

"That's better," he said with approval. Before any protest could be made, he kissed her hard, with a briefness that spoke of past intimacy. "You had me worried there a minute. What the hell did you do to yourself?"

The accusation was typical of him. She barely noticed it. "Do?" Autumn lifted a hand to touch the spot on her head where the pain was concentrated. "What happened?"

"That's my question, Cat. No, don't touch the lump." He caught her hand in his and held it. "It'll only hurt more if you do. I'm curious as to how you came by it, and why you were lying in a heap on the floor."

It was difficult to keep clear of the mists in her brain. Autumn tried to center in on the last thing she remembered. "How did you get in?" she demanded, remembering the rattling knob. "Hadn't I locked the door?" It came to her slowly that he was cradling her in his arms, holding her close against his chest. She struggled to sit up. "Were you rattling at the door?"

"Take it easy," he ordered as she groaned with the movement.

Autumn squeezed her eyes shut against the pounding in her head. "I must have walked into the door," she murmured, wondering at the quality of her clumsiness.

"You walked into the door and knocked yourself unconscious?" She couldn't tell if Lucas was angry or amused. The ache in her head kept her from caring one way or the other. "Strange, I don't recall you possessing that degree of uncoordination."

"It was dark," she grumbled, coherent enough to feel embarrassed. "If you hadn't been rattling around at the door..."

"I wasn't rattling around at your door," he began, but she cut him off with a startled gasp.

"The lights!" For a second time, she tried to struggle away from him. "You turned on the lights!"

"It was a mad impulse when I saw you crumpled on the floor," he returned dryly. Without any visible effort, he held her still. "I wanted to see the extent of the damage."

"My film!" Her glare was as accusing as her voice, but he responded with laughter.

"The woman's a maniac."

"Let go of me, will you?" Her anger made her less than gracious. Pushing away, she scrambled to her feet. At her movement, the pain grew to a crashing roar. She staggered under it.

"For God's sake, Autumn." Lucas rose and gripped her shoulders, steadying her. "Stop behaving like an imbecile over a few silly pictures."

This statement, under normal conditions, would have been unwise. In her present state of mind, it was a declaration of war.

Pain was eclipsed by a pure silver streak of fury. She whirled on him.

"You never could see my work as anything but silly pictures, could you? You never saw me as anything but a silly child, diverting for a while, but eventually boring. You always hated being bored, didn't you, Lucas?" She made a violent swipe at the hair that fell over her eyes. "You sit with your novels and bask in the adulation you get and look down your nose at the rest of us. You're not the only person in the world with talent, Lucas. My abilities are just as creative as yours, and my pictures give me as much fulfillment as your silly little books."

For a moment, he stood in silence, studying her with a frown. When he did speak, his voice was oddly weary. "All right, Autumn, now that you've gotten that out, you'd better get yourself some aspirin."

"Just leave me alone!" She shook off the hand he put on her arm. Turning, she started to take her camera from the shelf she had placed it on before beginning her work. Glancing down at the table, she flared again. "What do you mean by messing around with my equipment? You've exposed an entire roll of film!" Seething with fury, she whirled on him. "It isn't enough to interrupt my work by fooling around at the door, then turn on the lights and ruin what I've started. You have to put your hands into something you know nothing about."

"I told you before, I wasn't fooling around at your door." His eyes were darkening dangerously. "I came back after the power went out and the generator switched on. The door was open, and you were lying in a heap in the middle of the floor. I never touched your damned film."

There was ice in his voice now to go with the heat in his eyes but Autumn was too infuriated to be touched by either. "Foolish as it may seem," he continued, "my concern and attention were on you." Moving toward her, he glanced down at the confusion on her work table. "I don't suppose it occurred to you that in the dark you disturbed the film yourself?"

"Don't be absurd." Her professional ability was again insulted, but he cut off her retort in a voice filled with strained patience. Autumn pondered on it. As she remembered, Lucas had no patience at all.

"Autumn, I don't know what happened to your film. I didn't get any farther into the room than the spot where you were lying. I won't apologize for switching on the lights; I'd do precisely the same thing again." He circled her neck with his fingers and his words took on the old caressing note she remembered. "I happen to think your welfare is more important than your pictures."

Suddenly, her interest in the film waned. She wanted only to escape from him, and the feelings he aroused in her so effortlessly. Programmed response, she told herself. The soft voice and gentle hands tripped the release, and she went under.

"You're pale," Lucas muttered, abruptly dropping his hands and stuffing them into his pockets. "Dr. Spicer can take a look at you."

"No, I don't need—" She got no farther. He grabbed her arms with quicksilver fury.

"Damn it, Cat, must you argue with everything I say? Is there no getting past the hate you've built up for me?" He gave a quick shake. The pain rolled and spun in her head. For an instant, his face went out of focus as dizziness blurred her vision. Swearing with short, precise expertise, he pulled her close against him until the faintness passed. In a swift move, he lifted her into his arms. "You're pale as a ghost," he muttered. "Like it or not, you're going to see the doctor. You can vent your venom on him for a while."

By the time Autumn realized he was carrying her to her room, her temper had ebbed. There was only a dull, wicked ache and the weariness. Flagging, she rested her head against his shoulder and surrendered. This wasn't the time to think about the darkroom door or how it had come to be opened. It wasn't the time to think of how she had managed to walk into it like a perfect fool. This wasn't the time to think at all.

Accepting the fact that she had no choice, Autumn closed her eyes and allowed Lucas to take over. She kept them closed when she felt him lower her to the bed, but she knew he stood looking down at her a moment. She knew too that he was frowning.

The sound of his footsteps told her that he had walked into the adjoining bathroom. The faint splash of water in the sink sounded like a waterfall to her throbbing head. In a moment, there was a cool cloth over the ache in her forehead. Opening her eyes, Autumn looked into his.

"Lie still," he ordered curtly. Lucas brooded down at her with an odd, enigmatic expression. "I'll get Spicer," he muttered abruptly. Turning on his heel, he strode to the door.

"Lucas." Autumn stopped him because the cool cloth had brought back memories of all the gentle things he had ever done. He'd had his gentle moments, though she'd tried hard to pretend he hadn't. It had seemed easier.

When he turned back, impatience was evident in the very air around him. What a man of contradictions he was, she mused. Intemperate, with barely any middle ground at all.

"Thank you," she said, ignoring his obvious desire to be gone. "I'm sorry I shouted at you. You're being very kind."

Lucas leaned against the door and stared back at her. "I've never been kind." His voice was weary again.

Autumn found it necessary to force back the urge to go to him, wipe away his lines of fatigue. He sensed her thoughts, and his eyes softened briefly. On his mouth moved one of his rare, disarming smiles.

"My God, Cat, you always were so incredibly sweet. So terrifyingly warm."

With that, he left her.

Chapter Five

Autumn was staring at the ceiling when Robert entered. Shifting her eyes, she looked at his black bag dubiously. She'd never cared for what doctors carried inside those innocent-looking satchels.

"A house call," she said and managed a smile. "The eighth wonder of the world. I didn't think you'd have your bag with you on vacation."

He was quick enough to note her uneasy glance. "Do you travel without your camera?"

"*Touché.*" She told herself to relax and not to be a baby.

"I don't think we'll need to operate." He sat on the bed and removed the cloth Lucas had placed there. "Mmm, that's going to be colorful. Is your vision blurred?"

"No."

His hands were surprisingly soft and gentle, reminding Autumn of her father's. She relaxed further and answered his questions on dizziness, nausea and so forth while watching his face. He was different, she noted. The competence was still there, but his dapper self-presentation had been replaced by a quiet compassion. His voice was kind, she thought, and so were his eyes. He was well suited to his profession.

"How'd you come by this, Autumn?" As he asked he reached in his bag and her attention switched to his hands. He removed cotton and a bottle, not the needle she'd worried about.

She wrinkled her nose ruefully. "I walked into a door."

He shook his head with a laugh, and began to bathe the bruise. "A likely story."

"And embarrassingly true. In the darkroom," she added. "I must have misjudged the distance."

His eyes shifted and studied hers a moment before they returned to her forehead. "You struck me as a woman who kept her eyes open," he said a bit grimly, Autumn thought, before he smiled again. "It's just a bump," he told her and held her hand. "Though my diagnosis won't make it hurt any less."

"It's only an agonizing ache now," Autumn returned, trying for lightness. "The cannons have stopped going off."

With a chuckle, he reached into his bag again. "We can do something about smaller artillery."

"Oh." She eyed the bottle of pills he held and frowned. "I was going to take some aspirin."

"You don't put a forest fire out with a water pistol." He smiled at her again and shook out two pills. "They're very mild, Autumn. Take these and rest for an hour or two. You can trust me," he added with exaggerated gravity as her brows stayed lowered. "Even though I am a surgeon."

"Okay." His eyes convinced her and she smiled back, accepting the glass of water and pills. "You're not going to take out my appendix or anything, are you?"

"Not on vacation." He waited until she had swallowed the medication, then pulled a light blanket over her. "Rest," he ordered and left her.

The next time Autumn opened her eyes, the room was in shadows. Rest? she thought and shifted under the blanket. I've been unconscious. How long? She listened. The storm was still raging, whipping against her windows with a fury she'd been oblivious to. Carefully, she pushed herself into a sitting position. Her head didn't pound, but a touch of her fingers assured her she hadn't dreamed up the entire incident. Her next thought was entirely physical—she discovered she was starving.

Rising, she took a quick glance in the mirror, decided she didn't like what she saw and went in search of food and company. She found them both in the dining room. Her timing was perfect.

"Autumn." It was Robert who spotted her first. "Feeling better?"

She hesitated a moment, embarrassed. Hunger was stronger, however, and the scent of Nancy's chicken was too tempting. "Much," she told him. She glanced at Lucas, but he said nothing, only watched her. The gentleness she had glimpsed so briefly before might have been an illusion. His eyes were dark and hard. "I'm starving," she confessed as she took her seat.

"Good sign. Any more pain?"

"Only in my pride." Forging ahead, she began to fill her plate. "Clumsiness isn't a talent I like to brag about, and walking into a door is such a tired cliché. I wish I'd come up with something more original."

"It's odd." Jacques twirled his fork by the stem as he studied her. "It doesn't seem to me that you would have the power enough to knock yourself unconscious."

"An amazon," Autumn explained and let the chicken rest for a delicious moment on her tongue.

"She eats like one," Julia commented. Autumn glanced over in time to catch the speculative look on her face before it vanished into a smile. "I gain weight watching her."

"Metabolism," Autumn claimed and took another forkful of chicken. "The real tragedy is that I lost the two rolls of film I shot on the trip from New York."

"Perhaps we're in for a series of accidents." Helen's voice was as hard as her eyes as they swept the table. "Things come in threes, don't they?" No one answered and she went on, fingering her own bruise. "It's hard to say what might happen next."

Autumn had come to detest the odd little silences that followed Helen's remarks, the fingers of tension that poked holes in the normalcy of the situation. On impulse, she broke her rule and started a conversation with Lucas.

"What would you do with this setting, Lucas?" She turned to him, but found no change in his expression. He's watching all of us, she thought. Just watching. Shaking off her unease, Autumn continued. "Nine people—ten really, counting the cook—isolated in a remote country inn, a storm raging. The main power's already snuffed out. The phone's likely to be next."

"The phone's already out," Steve told her. Autumn drew out a dramatic "Ah."

"And the ford, of course, is probably impassable." Robert winked at her, falling in with the theme.

"What more could you ask for?" Autumn demanded of Lucas. Lightning flashed, as if on cue.

"Murder." Lucas uttered the six-letter word casually, but it hung in the air as all eyes turned to him. Autumn shuddered involuntarily. It was the response she'd expected, yet she felt a chill on hearing it. "But, of course," he continued as the word still whispered in the air, "it's a rather overly obvious setting for my sort of work."

"Life is sometimes obvious, is it not?" Jacques stated. A small smile played on his mouth as he lifted his glass of golden-hued wine.

"I could be very effective," Julia mused. "Gliding down dark passageways in flowing white." She placed her elbows on the table, folded her hands and rested her chin on them. "The flame of my candle flickering into the shadows while the murderer waits with a silk scarf to cut off my life."

"You'd make a lovely corpse," Autumn told her.

"Thank you, darling." She turned to Lucas. "I'd much rather remain among the living, at least until the final scene."

"You die so well." Steve grinned across the table at her. "I was impressed by your Lisa in *Hope Springs*."

"What sort of murder do you see, Lucas?" Steve was eating little, Autumn noted; he preferred the wine. "A crime of passion or revenge? The impulsive act of a discarded lover or the evil workings of a cool, calculating mind?"

"Aunt Tabby could sprinkle an exotic poison over the food and eliminate us one by one," Autumn suggested as she dipped into the mashed potatoes.

"Once someone's dead, they're no more use." Helen brought the group's attention back to her. "Murder is a waste. You gain more by keeping someone alive. Alive and vulnerable." She shot Lucas a look. "Don't you agree, Mr. McLean?"

Autumn didn't like the way she smiled at him. *Cool and cal-culating.* Jacques's words repeated in her mind. Yes, she mused, this was a cool and calculating woman. In the silence, Autumn shifted her gaze to Lucas.

His face held the faintly bored go-to-hell look she knew so well. "I don't think murder is always a waste." Again, his voice was casual, but Autumn, in tune with him, saw the change in his eyes. They weren't bored, but cold as ice. "The world would gain much by the elimination of some." He smiled, and it was deadly.

They no longer seemed to be speaking hypothetically. Shift-ing her gaze to Helen, Autumn saw the quick fear. *But it's just a game,* she told herself frantically and looked at Julia. The actress was smiling, but there was none of her summer warmth in it. She was enjoying watching Helen flutter like a moth on a pin. Noting Autumn's expression of dismayed shock, Julia changed the subject without a ripple.

After dinner, the group loitered in the lounge, but the storm, which continued unabated, was wearing on the nerves. Only Julia and Lucas seemed unaffected. Autumn noted how they huddled together in a corner, apparently enthralled with each other's company. Julia's laughter was low and rich over the sound of rain. Once, she watched Lucas pinch a strand of the pale hair between his fingers. Autumn turned away. Julia ran interference expertly, and the knowledge depressed her.

The Spicers, without Julia as a distraction, sat together on the sofa nearest the fire. Though their voices were low, Autumn sensed the strain of a domestic quarrel. She moved farther out of earshot. A bad time, she decided, for Jane to confront Robert on his fascination with Julia when the actress was giving another

man the benefit of her attentions. When they left, Jane's face
was no longer sullen, but simply miserable. Julia never glanced
in their direction, but leaned closer to Lucas and murmured
something in his ear that made him laugh. Autumn found she,
too, wanted out of the room.

It has nothing to do with Lucas, she told herself as she moved
down the hall. I just want to say good-night to Aunt Tabby.
Julia's doing precisely what I want her to—keeping Lucas entertained. He never even looked at me once Julia stepped in between. Shaking off the hurt, Autumn opened the door to her
aunt's room.

"Autumn, dear! Lucas told me you bumped your head." Aunt
Tabby stopped clucking over her laundry list and rose to peer at
the bruise. "Oh, poor thing. Do you want some aspirin? I have
some somewhere."

Though she appreciated Lucas's consideration in giving her
aunt a watered-down version, Autumn wondered at the ease
of their relationship. It didn't seem quite in character for Lucas
McLean to bother overmuch with a vague old woman whose
claim to fame was a small inn and a way with chocolate cake.

"No, Aunt Tabby, I'm fine. I've already taken something."

"That's good." She patted Autumn's hand and frowned briefly
at the bruise. "You'll have to be more careful, dear."

"I will. Aunt Tabby…" Autumn poked idly at the papers on
her aunt's desk. "How well do you know Lucas? I don't recall you
ever calling a roomer by his first name." She knew there was
no use in beating around the bush with her aunt. It would produce the same results as reading *War and Peace* in dim light—a
headache and confusion.

"Oh, now that depends, Autumn. Yes, that really does depend." Aunt Tabby gently removed her papers from Autumn's reach before she focused on a spot in the ceiling. Autumn knew this meant she was thinking. "There's Mrs. Nollington. She has a corner room every September. I call her Frances and she calls me Tabitha. Such a nice woman. A widow from North Carolina."

"Lucas calls you Aunt Tabby," Autumn pointed out before her aunt could get going on Frances Nollington.

"Yes, dear, quite a number of people do. You do."

"Yes, but—"

"And Paul and Will," Aunt Tabby continued blithely. "And the little boy who brings the eggs. And…oh, several people. Yes, indeed, several people. Did you enjoy your dinner?"

"Yes, very much. Aunt Tabby," Autumn continued, determined that tenacity would prevail. "Lucas seems very much at home here."

"Oh, I am glad!" She beamed at her niece as she took Autumn's hand and patted it. "I do try so hard to make everyone feel at home. It always seems a shame to have to make them pay, but…" She glanced down at her laundry bills and began to mutter.

Give up, Autumn told herself. She kissed her aunt's cheek and left her to her towels and pillowcases.

It was growing late when Autumn finished putting her darkroom back in order. She left the door open this time and kept all the lights on. The echo of rain followed her inside as it beat on the kitchen windows. Other than its angry murmur, the house was silent.

No, Autumn thought, old houses are never silent. They creak and whisper, but the groaning boards and settling didn't disturb her. She liked the humming quality of the silence. Absorbed and content, she emptied trays and replaced bottles. She threw her ruined film into the wastecan with a sigh.

That hurts a bit, she thought, but there's nothing to be done about it. Tomorrow, she decided, she'd develop the film she'd taken that morning—the lake, the early sun, the mirrored trees. It would put her in a better frame of mind. Stretching her back, she lifted her hair from her neck, feeling pleasantly tired.

"I remember you doing that in the mornings."

Autumn whirled, her hair flying out from her shoulders as quick fear brought her heart to her throat. Pushing strands from her face, she stared at Lucas.

He leaned against the open doorway, a cup of coffee in his hand. His eyes locked on hers without effort.

"You'd pull up your hair, then let it fall, tumbling down your back until I ached to get my hands on it." His voice was deep and strangely raw. Autumn couldn't speak at all. "I often wondered if you did it on purpose, just to drive me mad." As he studied her face, he frowned, then lifted the coffee to his lips. "But, of course you didn't. I've never known anyone else who could arouse with such innocence."

"What are you doing here?" The trembling in her voice took some of the power out of the demand.

"Remembering."

Turning, she began to juggle bottles, jumbling them out of their carefully organized state. "You always were clever with words, Lucas." Cooler now that she wasn't facing him, she meticulously studied a bottle of stop bath. "I suppose you have to be in your profession."

"I'm not writing at the moment."

It was easier to deliberately misunderstand him. "Your book

still giving trouble?" Turning, Autumn again noticed the signs of strain and fatigue on his face. Sympathy and love flared up, and she struggled to bank them down. His eyes were much too keen. "You might have more success if you'd get a good night's sleep." She gestured toward the cup in his hands. "Coffee's not going to help."

"Perhaps not." He drained the cup. "But it's wiser than bourbon."

"Sleep's better than both." She shrugged her shoulders carelessly. Lucas's habits were no longer her concern. "I'm going up." Autumn walked toward him, but he stayed where he was, barring the door. She pulled up sharply. They were alone. The ground floor was empty but for them and the sound of rain.

"Lucas." She sighed sharply, wanting him to think her impatient rather than vulnerable. "I'm tired. Don't be troublesome."

His eyes smoldered at her tone. Though Autumn remained calm, she could feel her knees turning to water. The dull, throbbing ache was back in her head. When he moved aside, she switched off the lights, then brushed past him. Swiftly, he took her arm, preventing what she had thought was going to be an easy exit.

"There'll come a time, Cat," he murmured, "when you won't walk away so easily."

"Don't threaten me with your overactive masculinity." Her temper rose and she forgot caution. "I'm immune now."

She was jerked against him. All she could see was his fury. "I've had enough of this."

His mouth took hers roughly; she could taste the infuriated desire. When she struggled, he pinned her back against the wall, holding her arms to her sides and battering at her will with his mouth alone. She could feel herself going under and hating herself for it as much, she told herself, as she hated him. His lips didn't soften, even when her struggles ceased. He took and took as the anger vibrated between them.

Her heart was thudding wildly, and she could feel the mad pace of his as they pressed together. Passion was all-encompassing, and her back was to the wall. There's no escape, she thought dimly. There's never been any escape from him. No place to run. No place to hide. She began to tremble with fear and desire.

Abruptly he pulled away. His eyes were so dark, she saw nothing but her own reflection. I'm lost in him, she thought. I've always been lost in him. Then he was shaking her, shocking a gasp out of her.

"Watch how far you push," he told her roughly. "Damn it, you'd better remember I haven't any scruples. I know how to deal with people who pick fights with me." He stopped, but his fingers still dug into her skin. "I'll take you, Cat, take you kicking and screaming if you push me much further."

Too frightened by the rage she saw in his face to think of pride, she twisted away. She flew down the hall and up the stairs.

Chapter Six

Autumn reached her door, out of breath and fighting tears. He shouldn't be allowed to do this to her. She couldn't allow it. Why had he barged back into her life this way? Just when she was beginning to get over him. *Liar.* The voice was clear as crystal inside her head. You've never gotten over him. Never. But I will. She balled her hands into fists as she stood outside her door and caught her breath. I will get over him.

Hearing the sound of his footsteps on the stairs, she fumbled with the doorknob. She didn't want to deal with him again tonight. Tomorrow was soon enough.

Something was wrong. Autumn knew it the moment she opened her door and stumbled into the dark. The scent of perfume was so strong, her head whirled with it. She groped for the light and when it flashed on, she gave a small sound of despair.

The drawers and closet had been turned out and her clothes were tossed and scattered across the room. Some were ripped and torn, others merely lay in heaps. Her jewelry had been dumped from its box and tossed indiscriminately over the mounds of clothes. Bottles of cologne and powder had been emptied out and flung everywhere. Everything—every small object or personal possession—had been abused or destroyed.

She stood frozen in shock and disbelief. The wrong room, she told herself dumbly. This had to be the wrong room. But the lawn print blouse with its sleeve torn at the shoulder had been a Christmas gift from Will. The sandals, flung into a corner and slashed, she had bought herself in a small shop off Fifth Avenue the summer before.

"No." She shook her head as if that would make it all go away. "It's not possible."

"Good God!" Lucas's voice came from behind her. Autumn turned to see him staring into her room.

"I don't understand." The words were foolish, but they were all she had. Slowly, Lucas shifted his attention to her face. She made a helpless gesture. "Why?"

He came to her, and with his thumb brushed a tear from her cheek. "I don't know, Cat. First we have to find out who."

"But it's—it's so spiteful." She wandered through the rubble of her things, still thinking she must be dreaming. "No one here would have any reason to do this to me. You'd have to hate someone to do this, wouldn't you? No one here has any reason to hate me. No one even knew me before last night."

"Except me."

"This isn't your style." She pressed her fingers to her temple and struggled to understand. "You'd find a more direct way of hurting me."

"Thanks."

Autumn looked over at him and frowned, hardly aware of what was being said. His expression was brooding as he studied her face. She turned away. She wasn't up to discussing Lucas McLean. Then she saw it.

"Oh, *no!*"

Scrambling on all fours, Autumn worked her way over the mangled clothes and began pushing at the tangled sheets of her bed. Her hands shook as she reached for her camera. The lens was shattered, with spiderweb cracks spreading over the surface. The back was broken, hanging drunkenly on one hinge. The film streamed out like the tail of a kite. Exposed. Ruined. The mirror was crushed. With a moan, she cradled it in her hands and began to weep.

Her clothes and trinkets meant nothing, but the Nikon was more to her than a single-reflex camera. It was as much a part of her as her hands. With it, she had taken her first professional picture. Its mutilation was rape.

Her face was suddenly buried against a hard chest. She made no protest as Lucas's arms came around her, but wept bitterly. He said nothing, offered no comforting words, but his hands were unexpectedly gentle, his arms strong.

"Oh, Lucas." She drew away from him with a sigh. "It's so senseless."

"There's sense to it somewhere, Cat. There always is."

She looked back up at him. "Is there?" His eyes were keeping their secrets so she dropped her own back to her mangled camera. "Well, if someone wanted to hurt me, this was the right way."

Her fingers clenched on the camera. She was suddenly, fiercely angry; it pushed despair and tears out of her mind. Her body flooded with it. She wasn't going to sit and weep any longer. She was going to do something. Pushing her camera into Lucas's hands, Autumn scrambled to her feet.

"Wait a minute." He grabbed her hand before she could rush from the room. "Where are you going?"

"To drag everyone out of bed," she snapped at him, jerking her hand. "And then I'm going to break someone's neck."

He didn't have an easy time subduing her. Ultimately, he pinned her by wrapping his arms around her and holding her against him. "You probably could." There was a touch of surprised admiration in his tone, but it brought her no pleasure.

"Watch me," she challenged.

"Calm down first." He tightened his grip as she squirmed against him.

"I want—"

"I know what you want, Cat, and I don't blame you. But you have to think before you rush in."

"I don't have anything to think about," she tossed back. "Someone's going to pay for this."

"All right, fair enough. Who?"

His logic annoyed her, but succeeded in taking her temper from boil to simmer. "I don't know yet." With an effort, she managed to take a deep breath.

"That's better." He smiled and kissed her lightly. "Though your eyes are still lethal enough." He loosened his grip, but kept a hold on her arm. "Just keep your claws sheathed, Cat, until we find out what's going on. Let's go knock on a few doors."

Julia's room adjoined hers, so Autumn steered there first. Her rage was now packed in ice. Systematic, she told herself, aware of Lucas's grip. All right, we'll be systematic until we find out who did it. And then…

She knocked sharply on Julia's door. After the second knock, Julia answered with a soft, husky slur.

"Get up, Julia," Autumn demanded. "I want to talk to you."

"Autumn, darling." Her voice evoked a picture of Julia snuggling into her pillows. "Even I require beauty sleep. Go away like a good girl."

"Up, Julia," Autumn repeated, barely restraining herself from shouting. "Now."

"Goodness, aren't we grumpy. I'm the one who's being dragged from my bed."

She opened the door, a vision in a white lace negligee, her hair a tousled halo around her face, her eyes dark and heavy with sleep.

"Well, I'm up." Julia gave Lucas a slow, sensual smile and ran a hand through her hair. "Are we going to have a party?"

"Someone tore my room apart," Autumn stated bluntly. She watched Julia's attention switch from the silent flirtation with Lucas to her.

"What?" The catlike expression had melted into a frown of concentration. An actress, Autumn reminded herself. She's an actress and don't forget it.

"My clothes were pulled out and ripped, tossed around the room. My camera's broken." She swallowed on this. It was the most difficult to accept.

"That's crazy." Julia was no longer leaning provocatively against the door, but standing straight. "Let me see." She brushed past them and hurried down the hall. Stopping in the doorway of Autumn's room, she stared. Her eyes, when they turned back, were wide with shock. "Autumn, how awful!" She came back and slipped an arm around Autumn's waist. "How perfectly awful. I'm so sorry."

Sincerity, sympathy, shock. They were all there. Autumn wanted badly to believe them.

"Who would have done that?" she demanded of Lucas. Autumn saw that Julia's eyes were angry now. She was again the tough lady Autumn had glimpsed briefly that afternoon.

"We intend to find out. We're going to wake the others." Something passed between them. Autumn saw it flash briefly, then it was gone.

"All right," Julia said. "Then let's do it." She pushed her hair impatiently behind her ears. "I'll get the Spicers, you get Jacques and Steve. You," she continued to Autumn, "wake up Helen."

Her tone carried enough authority that Autumn found herself turning down the hall to Helen's room. She could hear the pounding, the answering stirs and murmurs from behind her. Reaching Helen's door, Autumn banged against it. This, at least, she thought, was progress. Lucas was right. We need a trial before we can hang someone.

Her knock went unanswered. Annoyed, Autumn rapped again. She wasn't in the mood to be ignored. Now there was more activity behind her as people came out of their rooms to stare at the disaster in hers.

"Helen!" She knocked again with fraying patience. "Come out here." She pushed the door open. It would give her some satisfaction to drag at least one person from bed. Ruthlessly, she switched on the light. "Helen, I—"

Helen wasn't in bed. Autumn stared at her, too shocked to feel horror. She was on the floor, but she wasn't sleeping. She was done with sleeping. Was that blood? Autumn thought in dumb fascination. She took a step forward before the reality struck her.

Horror gripped her throat, denying her the release of screaming. Slowly, she backed away. It was a nightmare. Starting with her room, it was all a nightmare. None of it was real. Lucas's careless voice played back in her head. *Murder*. Autumn shook her head as she backed into a wall. No, that was only a game. She heard a voice shouting in terror for Lucas, not even aware it was her own. Then blessedly, her hands came up to cover her eyes.

"Get her out of here." Lucas's rough command floated through Autumn's brain. She was trapped in a fog of dizziness. Arms came round her and led her from the room.

"Oh my God." Steve's voice was unsteady. When Autumn found the strength to look up at him, his face was ashen. She struggled against the faintness and buried her face in his chest. When was she going to wake up?

Confusion reigned around her. She heard disembodied voices as she drifted from horror to shock. There were Julia's smoky tones, Jane's gravelly voice and Jacques's rapid French-English mixture. Then Lucas's voice joined in—calm, cool, like a splash of cold water.

"She's dead. Stabbed. The phone's out so I'm going into the village to get the police."

"Murdered? She was murdered? Oh God!" Jane's voice rose, then became muffled. Raising her head, Autumn saw Jane being held tightly against her husband.

"I think, as a precaution, Lucas, no one should leave the inn alone." Robert took a deep breath as he cradled his wife. "We have to face the implications."

"I'll go with him." Steve's voice was strained and uneven. "I could use the fresh air."

With a curt nod, Lucas focused on Autumn. His eyes never

left hers as he spoke to Robert. "Have you got something to put her out? She can double up with Julia tonight."

"I'm fine." Autumn managed to speak as she drew back from Steve's chest. "I don't want anything." It wasn't a dream, but real, and she had to face it. "Don't worry about me, it's not me. I'm all right." Hysteria was bubbling, and she bit down on her lip to cut it off.

"Come on, darling." Julia's arm replaced Steve's. "We'll go downstairs and sit down for a while. She'll be all right."

"I want—"

"I said she'll be all right," Julia cut off Lucas's protest sharply. "I'll see to her. Do what you have to do." Before he could speak again, she led Autumn down the staircase.

"Sit down," she ordered, nudging Autumn onto the sofa. "You could use a drink."

Looking up, Autumn saw Julia's face hovering over hers. "You're pale," she said stupidly before the brandy burned her throat and brought the world into focus with a jolt.

"I'm not surprised," Julia murmured and sank down on the low table in front of Autumn. "Better?" she asked when Autumn lifted the snifter again.

"Yes, I think so." She took a deep breath and focused on Julia's eyes. "It's really happening, isn't it? She's really lying up there."

"It's happening." Julia drained her own brandy. Color seeped gradually into her cheeks. "The bitch finally pushed someone too far."

Stunned by the hardness of Julia's voice, Autumn could only stare. Calmly, Julia set down her glass.

"Listen." Her tone softened, but her eyes were still cold. "You're a strong lady, Autumn. You've had a shock, a bad one, but you won't fall apart."

"No." Autumn tried to believe it, then said with more strength, "No, I won't fall apart."

"This is a mess, and you have to face it." Julia paused, then leaned closer. "One of us killed her."

Part of her had known it, but the rest had fought against the knowledge, blocking it out. Now that it had been said in cool, simple terms, there was no escape from it. Autumn nodded again and swallowed the remaining brandy in one gulp.

"She got what she deserved."

"Julia!" Jacques strode into the room. His face was covered with horror and disapproval.

"Oh, Jacques, thank God. Give me one of those horrible French cigarettes. Give one to Autumn, too. She could use it."

"Julia." He obeyed her automatically. "You musn't speak so now."

"I'm not a hypocrite." Julia drew deeply on the cigarette, shuddered, then drew again. "I detested her. The police will find out soon enough why we all detested her."

"*Nom de Dieu!* How can you speak so calmly of it?" Jacques exploded in a quick, passionate rage Autumn hadn't thought him capable of. "The woman is dead, murdered. You didn't see the cruelty of it. I wish to God I had not."

Autumn drew hard on her cigarette, trying to block out the picture that flashed back into her mind. She gasped and choked on the power of the smoke.

"Autumn, forgive me." Jacques's anger vanished as he sat down beside her and draped an arm over her shoulders. "I shouldn't have reminded you."

"No." She shook her head, then crushed out the cigarette. It wasn't going to help. "Julia's right. It has to be faced."

Robert entered, but his normally swinging stride was slow and dragging. "I gave Jane a sedative." With a sigh, he too made for the brandy. "It's going to be a long night."

The room grew silent. The rain, so much a part of the night, was no longer noticeable. Jacques paced the room, smoking continually while Robert kindled a fresh fire. The blaze, bright and crackling, brought no warmth. Autumn's skin remained chilled. In defense, she poured herself another brandy but found she couldn't drink it.

Julia remained seated. She smoked in long, slow puffs. The only outward sign of her agitation was the continual tapping of a pink-tipped nail against the arm of her chair. The tapping, the crackling, the hiss of rain, did nothing to diminish the overwhelming power of the silence.

When the front door opened with a click and a thud, all eyes flew toward the sound. Strings of tension tightened and threatened to snap. Autumn waited to see Lucas's face. It would be all right, somehow, as long as she could see his face.

"Couldn't get through the ford," he stated shortly as he came into the room. He peeled off a sopping jacket, then made for the community brandy.

"How bad is it?" Robert looked from Lucas to Steve, then back to Lucas. Already, the line of command had been formed.

"Bad enough to keep us here for a day or two," Lucas informed him. He swallowed a good dose of the brandy, then stared out the window. There was nothing to see but the reflection of the room behind him. "That's if the rain lets up by morning." Turning, he locked onto Autumn, making a long, thorough study.

Again he had, in his way, pushed everyone from the room but the two of them.

"The phones," she blurted out, needing to say something, anything. "We could have phone service by tomorrow."

"Don't count on it." Lucas ran a hand through his dripping hair, showering the room with water. "According to the car radio, this little spring shower is the backlash of a tornado. The power's out all over this part of the state." He lit a cigarette with a shrug. "We'll just have to wait and see."

"Days." Steve flopped down beside Autumn, his face still gray. She gave him her unwanted brandy. "It could be days."

"Lovely." Rising, Julia went to Lucas. She plucked the cigarette from his fingers and drew on it. "Well." She stared at him. "What the hell do we do now?"

"First we lock and seal off Helen's room." Lucas lit another cigarette. His eyes stayed on Julia's. "Then we get some sleep."

Chapter Seven

Sometime during the first murky light of dawn, Autumn did sleep. She'd passed the night lying wide-eyed, listening to the sound of Julia's gentle breathing beside her. Though she'd envied her ability to sleep, Autumn had fought off the drowsiness. If she closed her eyes, she might see what she'd seen when she opened Helen's door. When her eyes did close, however, the sleep was dreamless——the total oblivion of exhaustion.

It might have been the silence that woke her. Suddenly, she found herself awake and sitting straight up in bed. Confused, she stared around her.

Julia's disorder greeted her. Silk scarves and gold chains were draped here and there. Elegant bottles cluttered the bureau. Small, incredibly high Italian heels littered the floor. Memory returned.

With a sigh, Autumn rose, feeling a bit ridiculous in Julia's black silk nightgown; it neither suited nor fit. After seeing herself in the mirror, Autumn was glad Julia had already awakened and gone. She didn't want to wear any of the clothes that might have survived the attack on her room, and prepared to change back into yesterday's shirt and jeans.

A note lay on them. The elegant, sloping print could only have been Julia's:

Darling, help yourself to some undies and a blouse or sweater. I'm afraid my slacks won't fit you. You're built like a pencil. You don't wear a bra, and in any case, the idea of you filling one of mine is ridiculous.
J.

Autumn laughed, as Julia had intended. It felt so good, so normal, that she laughed again. Julia had known exactly how I'd feel, Autumn realized, and a wave of gratitude swept through her for the simple gesture. She showered, letting the water beat hot against her.

Coming back to the bedroom, Autumn pulled out a pair of cobwebby panties. There was a stack of them in misted pastels that she estimated would cost as much as a wide-angle lens. She tugged on one of Julia's sweaters, then pushed it up to her elbows—it was almost there in any case. Leaving the room, she kept her eyes firmly away from Helen's door.

"Autumn, I was hoping you'd sleep longer."

She paused at the foot of the stairs and waited for Steve to reach her. His face was sleep shadowed and older than it had been the day before. A fragment of his boyish smile touched his lips for her, but his eyes didn't join in.

"You don't look as if you got much," he commented and lifted a finger to her cheek.

"I doubt any of us did."

He draped an arm over her shoulder. "At least the rain's slowed down."

"Oh." Realization slowly seeped in and Autumn gave a weak laugh. "I knew there was something different. The quiet woke me. Where is..." She hesitated as Lucas's name trembled on her tongue. "Everyone?" she amended.

"In the lounge," he told her, but steered her toward the dining room. "Breakfast first. I haven't eaten myself, and you can't afford to drop any weight."

"How charming of you to remind me." She managed a friendly grimace. If he could make the effort to be normal, so could she. "Let's eat in the kitchen, though."

Aunt Tabby was there, as usual, giving instructions to a much subdued Nancy. She turned as they entered, then enfolded Autumn in her soft, lavender-scented arms.

"Oh, Autumn, what a dreadful tragedy. I don't know what to make of it." Autumn squeezed her. Here was something solid to hold on to. "Lucas said someone killed the poor thing, but that doesn't seem possible, does it?" Drawing back, Aunt Tabby searched Autumn's face. "You didn't sleep well, dear. Only natural. Sit down and have your breakfast. It's the best thing to do."

Aunt Tabby could, Autumn mused, so surprisingly cut through to the quick when she needed to. She began to bustle around the room, murmuring to Nancy as Autumn and Steve sat at the small kitchen table.

There were simple, normal sounds and scents. Bacon, coffee, the quick sizzle of eggs. It was, Autumn had to agree, the best thing to do. The food, the routine, would bring some sense of order. And with the order, she'd be able to think clearly again.

Steve sat across from her, sipping coffee while she toyed with her eggs. She simply couldn't summon her usual appetite, and turned to conversation instead. The questions she asked Steve about himself were general and inane, but he picked up the effort and went with it. She realized, as she nibbled without interest on a piece of toast, that they were supporting each other.

Autumn discovered he was quite well traveled. He'd crisscrossed all over the country performing various tasks in his role as troubleshooter for his father's conglomerate. He treated wealth with the casual indifference of one who has always had it, but she sensed a knowledge and a dedication toward the company which had provided him with it. He spoke of his father with respect and admiration.

"He's sort of a symbol of success and ingenuity," Steve said, pushing his own half-eaten breakfast around his plate. "He worked his way up the proverbial ladder. He's tough." He grinned and shrugged. "He's earned it."

"How does he feel about you going into politics?"

"He's all for it." Steve glanced down at her plate and sent her a meaningful look. Autumn only smiled and shook her head. "Anyway, he's always encouraged me to 'go for what I want and I better be good at it.'" He grinned again. "He's tough, but since I am good at it and intend to keep it that way, we'll both be satisfied. I like paperwork." He gestured with both hands. "Organizing. Refining the system from within the system."

"That can't be as easy as it sounds," Autumn commented, encouraging his enthusiasm.

"No, but—" He shook his head. "Don't get me started. I'll make a speech." He finished off his second cup of coffee. "I'll be making enough of those when I get back to California and my campaign officially starts."

"It just occurs to me that you, Lucas, Julia and Jacques are all from California." Autumn pushed her hair behind her back and considered the oddity. "It's strange that so many people from the coast would be here at one time."

"The Spicers, too," Aunt Tabby added from across the room, deeply involved in positioning pies in the oven. "Yes, I'm almost sure Dr. Spicer told me they were from California. So warm and sunny there. Well—" she patted the range as if to give it the confidence it needed to handle her pies "—I must see to the rooms now. I moved you next door to Lucas, Autumn. Such a terrible thing about your clothes. I'll have them cleaned for you."

"I'll help you, Aunt Tabby." Pushing away her plate, Autumn rose.

"Oh no, dear, the cleaners will do it."

Smiling wasn't as difficult as Autumn had thought. "I meant with the rooms."

"Oh…" Aunt Tabby trailed off and clucked her tongue. "I do appreciate it, Autumn, I really do, but…" She looked up with a touch of distress in her eyes. "I have my own system, you see. You'd just confuse me. It's all done with numbers."

Leaving Autumn to digest this, she gave her an apologetic touch on the cheek and bustled out.

There seemed nothing to do but join the others in the lounge.

The rain, though it was little more than a mist now, seemed to Autumn like prison bars. Standing at the window in the lounge, she wished desperately for sun. Conversation did not sparkle. When anyone spoke, it was around or over or under Helen Easterman. Perhaps it would have been better if they'd closeted themselves in their rooms, but human nature had them bound together.

Julia and Lucas sat on the sofa, speaking occasionally in undertones. Autumn found his eyes on her too often. Her defenses were too low to deal with what one of his probing looks could do to her, so she kept her back to him and watched the rain.

"I really think it's time we talked about this," Julia announced suddenly.

"Julia." Jacques's voice was both strained and weary.

"We can't go on like this," Julia stated practically. "We'll all go crazy. Steve's wearing out the floor, Robert's running out of wood to fetch and if you smoke another cigarette, you'll keel over." Contrarily, she lit another herself. "Unless we want to pretend that Helen stabbed herself, we've got to deal with the fact that one of us killed her."

Into the penetrating silence, Lucas's voice flowed, calm and detached. "I think we can rule out suicide." He watched as Autumn pressed her forehead to the glass. "And conveniently, we all had the opportunity to do it. Ruling out Autumn and her aunt, that leaves the six of us."

Autumn turned from the window and found every eye in the room on her. "Why should I be ruled out?" She shuddered and lifted her arms to hug herself. "You said we all had the opportunity."

"Motive, Cat," he said simply. "You're the only one in the room without a motive."

"Motive?" It was becoming too much like one of his screenplays. She needed to cling to reality. "What possible motive could any of us have had?"

"Blackmail." Lucas lit a cigarette as she gaped at him. "Helen was a professional leech. She thought she had quite a little gold-mine in the six of us." He glanced up and caught Autumn with one of his looks. "She miscalculated."

"Blackmail." Autumn could only mumble the word as she stared at him. "You're—you're making this up. This is just one of your scenarios."

He waited a beat, his eyes locked on hers. "No."

"How do you know so much?" Steve demanded. Slowly, Lucas's eyes swerved from Autumn. "If she were blackmailing you, it doesn't necessarily follow that she was blackmailing all of us."

"How clever of you, Lucas," Julia interjected, running a hand down his arm, then letting it rest on his. "I had no idea she was sticking her fangs in anyone other than the three of us." Glancing at Jacques, she gave him a careless shrug. "It seems we're in good company."

Autumn made a small sound, and Julia's attention drifted over to her. Her expression was both sympathetic and amused. "Don't look so shocked, darling. Most of us have things we don't particularly want made public. I might have paid her off if she'd threatened me with something more interesting." Leaning back, she pouted effectively. "An affair with a married senator..." She sent a lightning smile to Autumn. "I believe I mentioned him before. That hardly had me quaking in my shoes at the thought of exposure. I'm not squeamish about my indiscretions. I told her to go to hell. Of course," she added, smiling slowly, "there's only my word for that, isn't there?"

"Julia, don't make jokes." Jacques lifted a hand to rub his eyes.

"I'm sorry." Julia rose to perch on the arm of his chair. Her hand slipped to his shoulder.

"This is crazy." Unable to comprehend what was happening, Autumn searched the faces that surrounded her. They were

strangers again, holding secrets. "What are you all doing here?
Why did you come?"

"It's very simple." Lucas rose and crossed over to her, but unlike Julia, he didn't touch to comfort. "I made plans to come
here for my own reasons. Helen found out. She was very good at
finding things out—too good. She learned that Julia and Jacques
were to join me." He turned, half blocking Autumn from the
rest with his body. Was it protection, she wondered, or defense?
"She must have contacted the rest of you, and made arrangements to have all her...clients here at once."

"You seem to know quite a bit," Robert muttered. He poked
unnecessarily at the fire.

"It isn't difficult to figure out," Lucas returned. "I knew she
was holding nasty little threats over three of us; we'd discussed
it. When I noticed her attention to Anderson, and you and your
wife, I knew she was sucking elsewhere, too."

Jane began to cry in dry, harsh sobs that racked her body. Instinctively, Autumn moved past Lucas to offer comfort. Before
she was halfway across the room, Jane stopped her with a look
that was like a fist to the jaw.

"You could have done it just as easily as anyone else. You've
been spying on us, taking that camera everywhere." Jane's voice
rose dramatically as Autumn froze. "You were working for her,
you could have done it. You can't prove you didn't. I was with
Robert." There was nothing bland or dull about her now. Her
eyes were wild. "I was with Robert. He'll tell you."

Robert's arm came around her. His voice was quiet and soothing as she sobbed against his chest. Autumn didn't move. There
seemed no place to go.

"She was going to tell you I was gambling again, tell you about all the money I'd lost." She clung to him, a sad sight in a dirt-brown dress. Robert continued to murmur and stroke her hair. "But I told you last night, I told you myself. I couldn't pay her anymore, and I told you. I didn't kill her, Robert. Tell them I didn't kill her."

"Of course you didn't, Jane. Everyone knows that. Come with me now, you're tired. We'll go upstairs."

He was leading her across the room as he spoke. His eyes met Autumn's half in apology, half in a plea for understanding. She saw, quite suddenly, that he loved his wife very much.

Autumn turned away, humiliated for Jane, sorry for Robert. The faint trembling in her hands indicated she'd been dealt one more shock. When Steve's arm came around her, she turned into it and drew the comfort offered.

"I think we could all use a drink," Julia announced. Moving to the bar, she poured a hefty glass of sherry, then took it to Autumn. "You first," she ordered, pressing the glass into her hand. "Autumn seems to be getting the worst of this. Hardly seems fair, does it, Lucas?" Her eyes lifted to his and held briefly before she turned back to the bar. He made no answer. "She's probably the only one of us here who's even remotely sorry that Helen's dead."

Autumn drank, wishing the liquor would soften the words.

"She was a vulture," Jacques murmured. Autumn saw the message pass between him and Julia. "But even a vulture doesn't deserve to be murdered." Leaning back, he accepted the glass Julia brought him. He clasped her hand as she once again sat on the arm of his chair.

"Perhaps my motive is the strongest," Jacques said and drank once, deeply. "When the police come, all will be opened and studied. Like something under a microscope." He looked at Autumn, as if to direct his explanation to her. "She threatened the happiness of the two things most important to me—the woman I love and my children." Autumn's eyes skipped quickly to Julia's. "The information she had on my relationship with this woman could have damaged my suit for custody. The beauty of that love meant nothing to Helen. She would turn it into something sordid and ugly."

Autumn cradled her drink in both hands. She wanted to tell Jacques to stop, that she didn't want to hear, didn't want to be involved. But it was too late. She was already involved.

"I was furious when she arrived here with her smug smile and evil eyes." He looked down into his glass. "There were times, many times, I wanted my hands around her throat, wanted to bruise her face as someone else had done."

"Yes, I wonder who." Julia caught her bottom lip between her teeth in thought. "Whoever did that was angry, perhaps angry enough to kill." Her eyes swept up, across Steve and Autumn and Lucas.

"You were at the inn that morning," Autumn stated. Her voice sounded odd, thready, and she swallowed.

"So I was." Julia smiled at her. "Or so I said. Being alone in bed is hardly an airtight alibi. No…" She leaned back on the wing of the chair. "I think the police will want to know who socked Helen. You came in with her, Autumn. Did you see anyone?"

"No." Her eyes flew instantly to Lucas. His were dark, already locked on her face. There were warning signals of anger and impatience she could read too easily. She dropped her gaze to her drink. "No, I…" How could she say it? How could she think it?

"Autumn's had enough for a while." Steve tightened his arm

protectively around her. "Our problems don't concern her. She doesn't deserve to be in the middle."

"Poor child." Jacques studied her pale, strained face. "You've walked into a viper's nest, *oui?* Go sleep, forget us for a while."

"Come on, Autumn, I'll take you up." Steve slipped the glass from her hand and set it on the table. With one final glance at Lucas, Autumn went with him.

Chapter Eight

They didn't speak as they mounted the steps. Autumn was too busy trying to force the numbness from her brain. She hadn't been able to fully absorb everything she'd been told. Steve hurried her by Helen's door before stopping at the one beside Lucas's.

"Is this the room your aunt meant?"

"Yes." She lifted both hands to her hair, pushing its weight away from her face. "Steve." She searched his face and found herself faltering. "Is all this true? Everything Lucas said? Was Helen really blackmailing all of you?" She noted the discomfort in his eyes and shook her head. "I don't mean to pry, but—"

"No," he cut her off, then let out a long breath. "No, it's hardly prying at this point. You're not involved, but you're caught, aren't you?"

The word was so apt, so close to her own thinking, that she nearly laughed. Caught. Yes, that was it exactly.

"It seems McLean is right on target. Helen had information concerning a deal I made for the company—perfectly within the circle of the law, but..." He gave a rueful smile and lifted his shoulders. "Maybe not quite as perfectly as it should have been. There was an ethical question, and it wouldn't look so good on paper. The technicalities are too complicated to explain, but the gist of it is I didn't want any shadows on my career. These days, when you're heading into politics, you have to cover all the angles."

"Angles," Autumn repeated and pressed her fingers to her temple. "Yes, I suppose you do."

"She threatened me, Autumn, and I didn't care for it—but it wasn't enough to provoke murder." He drew a quick breath and shook his head. "But that doesn't help much, does it? None of us are likely to admit it."

"I appreciate you telling me anyway," Autumn said. Steve's eyes were gentle on her face, but the lines and strain of tension still showed. "It can't be pleasant for you to have to explain."

"I'll have to explain to the police before long," he said grimly, then noted her expression. "I don't mind telling you, Autumn, if you feel better knowing. Julia's right." His fingers strayed absently to her hair. "It's much healthier to get it out in the open. But you've had enough for now." He smiled at her, then realized his hands were in her hair. "I suppose you're used to this. Your hair's not easy to resist. I've wanted to touch it since the first time I saw it. Do you mind?"

"No." She wasn't surprised to find herself in his arms, his mouth on hers. It was an easy kiss, one that comforted rather than stirred. Autumn relaxed with it, and gave back what she could.

"You'll get some rest?" Steve murmured, holding her to his chest a moment.

"Yes. Yes, I will. Thank you." She pulled back to look up at him, but her eyes were drawn past him. Lucas stood at the doorway of his room, watching them both. Without speaking, he disappeared inside.

When she was alone, Autumn lay down on the white heirloom bedspread, but sleep wouldn't come. Her mind ached with fatigue. Her body was numb from it, but sleep, like a spiteful lover, stayed away. Time drifted as her thoughts ran over each member of the group.

She could feel nothing but sympathy for Jacques and the Spicers. She remembered the Frenchman's eyes when he spoke of his children and could still see Robert protecting his wife as she sobbed. Julia, on the other hand, needed no sympathy. Autumn felt certain the actress could take care of herself; she'd need no supporting arm or soothing words. Steve had also seemed more annoyed than upset by Helen's threats. He, too, could handle himself, she felt. There was a streak of street sense under the California gloss; he didn't need Autumn to worry for him.

Lucas was a different matter. Though he had nudged admissions from the rest of them, whatever threat Helen had held over him was still his secret. He had seemed very cool, very composed when he'd spoken of blackmail—but Autumn knew him. He was fully capable of concealing his emotions when there was a purpose to it. He was a hard man. Who knew better than she?

Cruel? Yes, she mused. Lucas could be cruel. She still had the scars attesting to it. But murder? No. Autumn couldn't picture Lucas plunging something sharp into Helen Easterman. Scissors, she remembered, though she tried hard not to. The scissors that had lain on the floor beside Helen. No, she couldn't believe him capable of that. She wouldn't believe him capable of it.

Neither could she rationally believe it of any of the others.

Could they all conceal such hate, such ugliness behind their shocked faces and shadowed eyes?

But, of course, one of them was the killer.

Autumn blanked it from her mind. She couldn't think of it anymore. Not just then. Steve's prescription was valid—she needed to rest. Yet she rose and walked to the window to stare out at the slow, hateful rain.

The knock at her door vibrated like an explosion. Whirling, she wrapped her arms protectively around her body. Her heart pounded while her throat dried up with fear. Stop it! she ordered herself. No one has any cause to hurt you.

"Yes, come in." The calmness of her own voice brought her relief. She was hanging on.

Robert entered. He looked so horribly weary and stricken, Autumn automatically reached out to him. She thought no more of fear. He clasped her hands and squeezed once, hard.

"You need food," he stated as he searched her face. "It shows in the face first."

"Yes, I know. My delicate hollows become craters very quickly." She made her own search. "You could use some yourself."

He sighed. "I believe you're one of those rare creatures who is inherently kind. I apologize for my wife."

"No, don't." His sigh had been long and broken. "She didn't mean it. We're all upset. This is a nightmare."

"She's been under a lot of strain. Before…" He broke off and shook his head. "She's sleeping now. Your head—" he brushed the hair from her forehead to examine the colorful bruise "—is it giving you any trouble?"

"No, none. I'm fine." The mishap seemed like some ridiculous comic relief in the midst of a melodrama now. "Can I help you, Robert?"

His eyes met hers, once, desperately, then moved away. "That woman put Jane through hell. If I'd just known, I would have put a stop to it long ago." Anger overpowered his weariness and he turned to prowl the room. "She tormented her, drained every drop of money Jane could raise. She played on a sickness, encouraging Jane to gamble to meet the payments. I knew nothing about it! I should have. Yesterday, Jane told me herself and I was going to enjoy dealing with the Easterman woman this morning." Autumn saw the soft, gentle hands clench into fists. "God help me, that's the only reason I'm sorry she's dead."

"Robert…" She wasn't certain what to say, how to deal with this side of his character. "Anyone would feel the same way," she said carefully. "She was an evil woman. She hurt someone you love." Autumn watched the fingers in his left hand relax, one at a time. "It isn't kind, but none of us will mourn her. Perhaps no one will. I think that's very sad."

He turned back and focused on her again. After a moment, he seemed to pull himself back under control. "I'm sorry you're caught up in this." With the anger gone from his eyes, they were vulnerable. "I'm going to go check on Jane. Will you be all right?"

"Yes."

She watched him go, then sank down into a chair. Each different crisis drained her. If possible, she was wearier now than before. When did the madness start? Only a few days ago she'd been safe in her apartment in Manhattan. She'd never met any of these people who were tugging at her now. Except one.

Even as she thought of him, Lucas strode in through the door. He stalked over to her, stared down and frowned.

"You need to eat," he said abruptly. Autumn thought of how tired she was of hearing that diagnosis. "I've been watching the pounds drop off you all day. You're already too thin."

"I adore flattery." His arrogant entrance and words boosted her flagging energy. She didn't have to take abuse from Lucas McLean anymore. "Don't you know how to knock?"

"I've always appreciated the understatedness of your body, Cat. You remember." He pulled her to her feet, then molded her against him. Her eyes flashed with quick temper. "Anderson seems to have discovered the charm as well. Did it occur to you that you might have been kissing a murderer?"

He spoke softly while his hand caressed her back. His eyes were mocking her. Her temper snapped at the strain of fighting her need for him.

"One might be holding me now."

He tightened his fingers on her hair so that she cried out in surprise. The mockery was replaced by a burning, terrifying rage. "You'd like to believe that, wouldn't you? You'd like to see me languishing in prison or, better yet, dangling from the end of a rope." She would have shaken her head, but his grip on her hair made movement impossible. "Would that be suitable punishment for my rejecting you, Cat? How deep is the hate? Deep enough to pull the lever yourself?"

"No, Lucas. Please, I didn't mean—"

"The hell you didn't." He cut off her protest. "The thought of me with blood on my hands comes easily to you. You can cast me in the role of murderer, can't you? Standing over Helen with the scissors in my hand."

"No!" In defense, she closed her eyes. "Stop it! Please stop it." He was hurting her now, but not with his hands. The words cut deeper.

He lowered his voice in a swift change of mood. Ice ran down Autumn's back. "I could have used my hands and been more tidy." A strong, lean-fingered hand closed around her throat. Her eyes flew open.

"Lucas—"

"Very simple and no mess," he went on, watching her eyes widen. "Quick enough, too, if you know what to do. More my style. More—as you put it—direct. Isn't that right?"

"You're only doing this to frighten me." Her breath was trembling in and out of her lungs. It was as if he were forcing her to think the worst of him, wanting her to think him capable of something monstrous. She'd never seen him like this. His eyes were black with fury while his voice was cold, so cold. She shivered. "I want you to leave, Lucas. Leave right now."

"Leave?" He slid his hand from her throat to the back of her neck. "I don't think so, Cat." His face inched closer. "If I'm going to hang for murder, I'd best take what consolation I can while I have the chance."

His mouth closed fast over hers. She struggled against him, more frightened than she'd been when she'd turned on the light in Helen's room. She could only moan; movement was impossible when he held her this close. He slipped a hand under her sweater to claim her breast with the swift expertise of experience. Heart thudded madly against heart.

"How can anyone so skinny be so soft?" he murmured against her mouth. The words he'd spoken so often in the past brought more agony than she could bear. The hunger from him was thunderous; he was like a man who had finally broken free of his tether. "My God, how I want you." The words were torn from him as he ravaged her neck. "I'll be damned if I'll wait any longer."

They sank onto the bed. With all the strength that remained, she flailed out against him. Pinning her arms to her sides, Lucas stared down at her with a wild kind of fury. "Bite and scratch all you want, Cat. I've reached my limit."

"I'll scream, Lucas." The words shuddered out of her. "If you touch me again, I'll scream."

"No, you won't."

His mouth was on hers, proving him right and her wrong. His body molded to hers with bittersweet accuracy. She arched once in defense, in desperation, but his hands were roaming, finding all the secret places he'd discovered over three years before. There was no resisting him. The wild, reckless demand that had always flavored his lovemaking left her weak. He knew too much of her. Autumn knew, before his fingers reached the snap of her jeans, that she couldn't prevent her struggles from becoming demands. When his mouth left hers to roam her neck, she didn't scream, but moaned with the need he had always incited in her.

He was going to win again, and she would do nothing to stop him. Tears welled, then spilled from her eyes as she knew he'd soon discover her pitiful, abiding love. Even her pride, it seemed, again belonged to him.

Lucas stopped abruptly. All movement ceased when he drew back his head to stare down at her. She thought, through her blurred vision, that she saw some flash of pain cross his face before it became still and emotionless. Lifting a hand, he caught a teardrop on his fingertip. With a swift oath, he lifted his weight from her.

"No, I won't be responsible for this again." Turning, he stalked to the window and stared out.

Sitting up, Autumn lowered her face to her knees and fought against the tears. She'd promised herself he'd never see her cry again. Not over him. Never over him. The silence stretched on for what seemed an eternity.

"I won't touch you like this again," he said quietly. "You have my word, for what it's worth."

Autumn thought she heard him sigh, long and deep, before his footsteps crossed to her. She didn't look up, but only squeezed her eyes closed.

"Autumn, I…oh, sweet God." He touched her arm, but she only curled herself tighter into a ball in defense.

The room fell silent again. The dripping rain seemed to echo into it. When Lucas spoke again, his voice was harsh and strained. "When you've rested, get something to eat. I'll have your aunt send up a tray if you're not down for dinner. I'll see that no one disturbs you."

She heard him leave, heard the quiet click of her door. Alone, she kept curled in her ball as she lay down. Ultimately, the storm of tears induced sleep.

Chapter Nine

It was dark when Autumn awoke, but she was not refreshed. The sleep had been only a temporary relief. Nothing had changed while she had slept. But no, she thought as she glanced around the room. She was wrong. Something had changed. It was quiet. Really quiet. Rising, she walked to the window. She could see the moon and a light scattering of stars. The rain had stopped.

In the dim light, she moved to the bathroom and washed her face. She wasn't certain she had the courage to look in the mirror. She let the cold cloth rest against her eyes for a long time, hoping the swelling wasn't as bad as it felt. She felt something else as well. Hunger. It was a healthy sign, she decided. A normal sign. The rain had stopped and the nightmare was going to end. And now she was going to eat.

Her bare feet didn't disturb the silence that hung over the inn. She was glad of it. She wanted food now, not company. But when she passed the lounge, she heard the murmur of voices. She wasn't alone after all. Julia and Jacques were silhouetted by the window. Their conversation was low and urgent. Before she could melt back into the shadows, Julia turned and spotted her. The conversation ceased abruptly.

"Oh, Autumn, you've surfaced. We thought we'd seen the last of you until morning." She glided to her, then slipped a friendly arm around her waist. "Lucas wanted to send up a tray, but Robert outranked him. Doctor's orders were to let you sleep until you woke up. You must be famished. Let's see what your Aunt Tabby left for you."

Julia was doing all the talking, and quite purposefully leading Autumn away. A glance showed her that Jacques was still standing by the window, unmoving. Autumn let it go, too hungry to object.

"Sit down, darling," Julia ordered as she steered Autumn into the kitchen. "I'm going to fix you a feast."

"Julia, you don't have to fix me anything. I appreciate it, but—"

"Now let me play mother," Julia interrupted, pressing down on Autumn's shoulder until she sat. "You're past the sticky-finger stage, so I really quite enjoy it."

Sitting back, Autumn managed a smile. "You're not going to tell me you can cook."

Julia aimed an arched glance. "I don't suppose you should eat anything too heavy at this time of night," she said mildly. "There's some marvelous soup left from dinner, and I'll fix you my specialty. A cheese omelette."

Autumn decided that watching Julia Bond bustle around a kitchen was worth the market price of an ounce of gold. She seemed competent enough and kept up a bouncy conversation that took no brainpower to follow. With a flourish, she plopped a glass of milk in front of Autumn.

"I'm not really very fond of milk," Autumn began and glanced toward the coffeepot.

"Now, drink up," Julia instructed. "You need roses in your cheeks. You look terrible."

"Thanks."

Steaming chicken soup joined the milk, and Autumn attacked it with singleminded intensity. Some of the weakness drained from her limbs.

"Good girl," Julia approved as she dished up the omelette. "You look nearly human again."

Glancing over, Autumn smiled. "Julia, you're marvelous."

"Yes, I know. I was born that way." She sipped coffee and watched Autumn start on the eggs. "I'm glad you were able to rest. This day has been a century."

For the first time, Autumn noticed the mauve shadows under the blue eyes and felt a tug of guilt. "I'm sorry. You should be in bed, not waiting on me."

"Lord, but you're sweet." Julia pulled out a cigarette. "I haven't any desire to go up to my room until exhaustion takes over. I'm quite selfishly prepared to keep you with me until it does. Actually, Autumn," she added, watching through a mist of smoke, "I wonder if it's very wise for you to be wandering about on your own."

"What?" Autumn looked up again and frowned. "What do you mean?"

"It was your room that was broken into," Julia pointed out.

"Yes, but…" She was surprised to realize she'd almost overlooked the ransacking of her room with everything else that had happened. "It must have been Helen," she ventured.

"Oh, I doubt that," Julia returned and continued to sip contemplatively. "I very much doubt that. If Helen had broken into your room, it would have been to look for something she could use on you. She'd have been tidy. We've given this some thought."

"We?"

"Well, I've given it some thought," Julia amended smoothly. "I think whoever tore up your things was looking for something, then covered the search with overdone destruction."

"Looking for what?" Autumn demanded. "I don't have anything anyone here could be interested in."

"Don't you?" Julia ran the tip of her tongue over her teeth. "I've been thinking about what happened in your darkroom."

"You mean when the power went off?" Autumn shook her head and touched the bruise on her forehead. "I walked into the door."

"Did you?" Julia sat back and studied the harsh ceiling light. "I wonder. Lucas told me that you said you heard someone rattling at the knob and walked over. What if..." She brought her eyes back to Autumn's. "What if someone swung the door open and hit you with it?"

"It was locked," Autumn insisted, then remembered that it had been open when Lucas found her.

"There are keys, darling." She watched Autumn's face closely. "What are you thinking?"

"The door was open when Lucas—" She cut herself off and shook her head. "No, Julia, it's ridiculous. Why would anyone want to do that to me?"

Julia lifted a brow. "Interesting question. What about your ruined film?"

"The film?" Autumn felt herself being pulled in deeper. "It must have been an accident."

"You didn't spoil it, Autumn, you're too competent." She waited while Autumn spread her hands on the table and looked down at them. "I've watched you. Your movements are very fluid, very assured. And you're a professional. You wouldn't botch up a roll of film without being aware of it."

"No," Autumn agreed and looked back up. Her eyes were steady again. "What are you trying to tell me?"

"What if someone's worried that you took a picture they don't want developed? The film in your room was ruined, too."

"I can follow your logic that far, Julia." Autumn pushed aside the remaining omelette. "But then it's a dead end. I haven't taken any pictures anyone could worry about. I was shooting scenery. Trees, animals, the lake."

"Maybe someone isn't certain about that." She crushed out her cigarette in a quick motion and leaned forward. "Whoever is worried enough about a picture to risk destroying your room and knocking you unconscious is dangerous. Dangerous enough to murder. Dangerous enough to hurt you again if necessary."

Staring back, Autumn controlled a tremor. "Jane? Jane accused me of spying, but she couldn't—"

"Oh yes, she could." Julia's voice was hard again, and definite. "Face it, Autumn, anyone pushed hard enough is capable of murder. Anyone."

Autumn's thoughts flicked back to Lucas and the look on his face when he had slipped his hand around her throat.

"Jane was desperate," Julia continued. "She claims to have made a full confession to Robert, but what proof is there? Or

Robert, furious at what Helen had put his wife through, could have done it himself. He loves Jane quite a lot."

"Yes, I know." The sudden, sweeping anger in Robert's eyes flashed through her mind.

"Or there's Steve." Julia's finger began to tap on the table. "He tells me that Helen found out about some unwise deal he put through, something potentially damaging to his political career. He's very ambitious."

"But, Julia—"

"Then there's Lucas." Julia went on as if Autumn hadn't spoken. "There's a matter of a delicate divorce suit. Helen held information she claimed would interest a certain estranged husband." She lit another cigarette and let the smile float up and away. "Lucas is known for his temper. He's a very physical man."

Autumn met the look steadily. "Lucas is a lot of things, not all of them admirable, but he wouldn't kill."

Julia smiled and said nothing as she brought the cigarette to her lips. "Then there's me." The smile widened. "Of course, I claim I didn't care about Helen's threats, but I'm an actress. A good one. I've got an Oscar to prove it. Like Lucas, my temper is no secret. I could give you a list of directors who would tell you I'm capable of anything." Idly she tapped her cigarette in the ashtray. "But then, if I had killed her, I would have set the scene differently. I would have discovered the body myself, screamed, then fainted magnificently. As it was, you stole the show."

"That's not funny, Julia."

"No," she agreed and rubbed her temple. "It's not. But the fact remains that I could have killed Helen, and you're far too trusting."

"If you'd killed her," Autumn countered, "why would you warn me?"

"Bluff and double bluff," Julia answered with a new smile that made Autumn's skin crawl. "Don't trust anyone, not even me."

Autumn wasn't going to let Julia frighten her, though she seemed determined to do so. She kept her eyes level. "You haven't included Jacques."

To Autumn's surprise, Julia's eyes flickered, then dropped. The smooth, tapering fingers crushed out her cigarette with enough force to break the filter. "No, I haven't. I suppose he must be viewed through your eyes like the rest of us, but I know..." She looked up again, and Autumn saw the vulnerability. "I know he isn't capable of hurting anyone."

"You're in love with him."

Julia smiled, quite beautifully. "I love Jacques very much, but not the way you mean." She rose then and, getting another cup, poured them both coffee. "I've known Jacques for ten years. He's the only person in the world I care about more than myself. We're friends, real friends, probably because we've never been lovers."

Autumn drank the coffee black. She wanted the kick of it. *She'd protect him*, she thought. *She'd protect him any way she could.*

"I have a weakness for men," Julia continued, "and I indulge it. With Jacques, the time or place was never right. Ultimately, the friendship was too important to risk messing it up in the bedroom. He's a good, gentle man. The biggest mistake he ever made was in marrying Claudette."

Julia's voice hardened. Her nails began to tap on the table again, quicker than before. "She did her best to eat him alive.

For a long time, he tried to keep the marriage together for the children. It simply wasn't possible. I won't go into details; they'd shock you." Tilting her head, Julia gave Autumn a smile that put her squarely into adolescence. "And, in any case, it's Jacques's miserable secret. He didn't divorce her, on the numerous grounds he could have, but allowed her to file."

"And Claudette got the children."

"That's right. It nearly killed him when she was awarded custody. He adores them. And, I must admit, they are rather sweet little monsters." The nails stopped tapping as she reached for her coffee. "Anyway, skipping over this and that, Jacques filed a custody suit about a year ago. He met someone shortly after. I can't tell you her name—you'd recognize it, and I have Jacques's confidence. But I can tell you she's perfect for him. Then Helen crawled her slimy way in."

Autumn shook her head. "Why don't they just get married?"

Julia leaned back with an amused sigh. "If life were only so simple. Jacques is free, but his lady won't be for another few months. They want nothing more than to marry, bring Jacques's little monsters to America and raise as many more as possible. They're crazy about each other."

Julia sipped her cooling coffee. "They can't live together openly until the custody thing is resolved so they rented this little place in the country. Helen found out. You can figure out the rest. Jacques paid her, for his children and because his lady's divorce isn't as cut-and-dried as it might be, but when Helen turned up here, he'd reached his limit. They argued about it one night in the lounge. He told her she wouldn't get another cent. I'm sure, no matter how much Jacques had already paid her, Helen would still have turned her information over to Claudette—for a price."

Autumn stared at her, unable to speak. She had never seen Julia look so cold. She saw the ruthlessness cover the exquisite face. Julia looked over, then laughed with genuine amusement.

"Oh, Autumn, you're like an open book!" The hard mask had melted away, leaving her warm and lovely again. "Now you're thinking I could have murdered Helen after all. Not for myself, but for Jacques."

Autumn fell into a fitful sleep sometime after dawn. This was no deep, empty sleep brought on by medication or exhaustion, but was confused and dream riddled.

At first, there were only vague shadows and murmured voices floating through her mind, taunting her to try to see and hear more clearly. She fought to focus on them. Shadows moved, shapes began to sharpen, then became fuzzy and disordered again. She pitted all her determination against them, wanting more than hints and whispers. Abruptly, the shadows evaporated. The voices grew to a roar in her ears.

Wild-eyed, Jane crushed Autumn's camera underfoot. She screamed, pointing a pair of scissors to keep Autumn at bay. "Spy!" she shouted as the cracking of the camera's glass echoed like gunfire. "Spy!"

Wanting to escape the madness and accusations, Autumn turned. Colors whirled around her, then there was Robert.

"She tormented my wife." His arm held Autumn firmly, then slowly tightened, cutting off her breath. "You need some food," he said softly. "It shows in the face first." He was smiling, but the smile was a travesty. Breaking away, Autumn found herself in the corridor.

Jacques came toward her. There was blood on his hands. His eyes were sad and terrifying as he held them out to her. "My children." There was a tremor in his voice as he gestured to her. Turning, she fell into Steve.

"Politics," he said with a bright, boyish smile. "Nothing personal, just politics." Taking her hair, he wrapped it around her throat. "You got caught in the middle, Autumn." The smile turned into a leer as he tightened the noose. "Too bad."

Pushing away, she fell through a door. Julia's back was to her. She wore the lovely, white lace negligee. "Julia!" In the dream, the urgency in Autumn's voice came at a snail's pace. "Julia, help me."

When Julia turned, the slow, cat smile was on her face and the lace was splattered with scarlet. "Bluff and double bluff, darling." Throwing back her head, she laughed her smoky laugh. With the sound still spinning in her head, Autumn pressed her hands to her ears and ran.

"Come back to mother!" Julia called, still laughing as Autumn stumbled into the corridor.

There was a door blocking her path. Throwing it open, Autumn dashed inside. She knew only a desperate need for escape. But it was Helen's room. Terrified, Autumn turned, only to find the door closed behind her. She battered on it, but the sound was dull and flat. Fear was raw now, a primitive fear of the dead. She couldn't stay there. Wouldn't stay. She turned, thinking to escape through the window.

It wasn't Helen's room, but her own. There were bars at the windows, gray liquid bars of rain, but when she ran to them, they solidified, holding her in. She pulled and tugged, but they were cold and unyielding in her hands. Suddenly, Lucas was behind her, drawing her away. He laughed as he turned her into his arms.

"Bite and scratch all you want, Cat."

"Lucas, please!" There was hysteria in her voice that even the dream couldn't muffle. "I love you. I love you. Help me get out. Help me get away!"

"Too late, Cat." His eyes were dark and fierce and amused. "I warned you not to push me too far."

"No, Lucas, not you." She clung to him. He was kissing her hard, passionately. "I love you. I've always loved you." She surrendered to his arms, to his mouth. Here was her escape, her safety.

Then she saw the scissors in his hand.

Chapter Ten

Autumn sat straight up in bed. The film of cold sweat had her
shivering. During the nightmare, she had kicked off the sheets
and blankets and lay now with only a damp nightgown for cover.
Needing the warmth, she pulled the tangled blanket around her
and huddled into it.

Only a dream, she told herself, waiting for the clarity of it to
fade. It was only a dream. It was natural enough after the late-
night conversation with Julia. Dreams couldn't hurt you. Autumn wanted to hang on to that.

It was morning. She trembled still as she watched the sunlight
pour into her window. No bars. That was over now, just as the
night was over. The phones would soon be repaired. The water
in the ford would go down. The police would come. Autumn sat,
cocooned by the blanket, and waited for her breathing to even.

By the end of the day, or tomorrow at the latest, everything
would be organized and official. Questions would be answered,
notes would be taken, the wheels of investigation would start
to turn, settling everything into facts and reality. Slowly her

muscles began to relax and she loosened her desperate grip on the blanket.

Julia's imagination had gotten out of hand, Autumn decided. She was so used to the drama of her profession that she had built up the scenario. Helen's death was a hard, cold fact. None of them could avoid that. But Autumn was certain her two misfortunes had been unconnected. *If I'm going to stay sane until the police come,* she amended, *I have to believe it.*

Calmer now, she allowed herself to think. Yes, there had been a murder. There was no glossing over that. Murder was a violent act, and in this case, it had been a personal one. She had no involvement in it. There wasn't any correlation. What had happened in the darkroom had been simple clumsiness. That was the cleanest and the most reasonable explanation. As for the invasion of her room... Autumn shrugged. It had been Helen. She'd been a vicious, evil woman. The destruction of Autumn's clothes and personal belongings had been a vicious, evil act. For some reason of her own, Helen had taken a dislike to her. There was no one else at the inn who would have any reason to feel hostility toward her.

Except Lucas. Autumn shook her head firmly, but the thought remained. Except Lucas. She huddled the blanket closer, cold again.

No, even that made no sense. Lucas had rejected her, not the other way around. She had loved him. And he, very simply, hadn't loved her. *Would that matter to him?* The voice in her brain argued with the voice from her heart. Ignoring the queaziness in her stomach, Autumn forced herself to consider, dispassionately, Lucas in the role of murderer.

It had been obvious from the beginning that he was under

strain. He hadn't been sleeping well and he'd been tense. Autumn had known him to struggle over a stage of a book for a week on little sleep and coffee, but he'd never shown the effects. All that stored energy he had was just waiting to take over whenever he needed it. No, in all her memory, she had never seen Lucas McLean tired. Until now.

Helen's blackmail must have disturbed him deeply. Autumn couldn't imagine Lucas concerning himself over publicity, adverse or otherwise. The woman involved in divorce must mean a great deal to him. She shut her eyes on a flash of pain and forced herself to continue.

Why had he come to the Pine View Inn? Why would he choose a remote place nearly a continent away from his home? To work? Autumn shook her head. It just didn't follow. She knew Lucas never traveled when he was writing. He'd do his research first, extensively if necessary, before he began. Once he had a plot between his teeth, he'd dig into his beachside home for the duration. Come to Virginia to write in peace? No. Lucas McLean could write on the 5:15 subway if he chose to. She knew no one else with a greater ability to block people out.

So, his reason for coming to the inn was quite different. Autumn began to wonder if Helen had been a pawn as well as a manipulator. Had Lucas lured her to this remote spot and surrounded her with people with reasons to hate her? He was clever enough to have done it, and calculating enough. How difficult was it going to be to prove which one of the six had killed her? Motive and opportunity he'd said—six people had both. Why should one be examined any closer than the others?

The setting would appeal to him, she thought as she looked out at mountains and pines. Obvious, Lucas had called it. An obvious setting for murder. But then, as Jacques had pointed out, life was often obvious.

She wouldn't dwell on it. It brought the nightmare too close again. Pushing herself from the bed, Autumn began to dress in her very tired jeans and a sweater Julia had given her the night before. She wasn't going to spend another day picking at her doubts and fears. It would be better to hang on to the knowledge that the police would be there soon. It wasn't up to her to decide who had killed Helen.

When she started down the stairs, she felt better. She'd take a long, solitary walk after breakfast and clear the cobwebs from her mind. The thought of getting out of the inn lifted her spirits.

But her confidence dropped away when she saw Lucas at the foot of the stairs. He was watching her closely, silently. Their eyes met for one brief, devastating moment before he turned to walk away.

"Lucas." She heard herself call out before she could stop herself. Stopping, he turned to face her again. Autumn gathered all her courage and hurried down the rest of the stairs. She had questions, and she had to ask them. He still mattered much too much to her. She stood on the bottom step so that their eyes would be level. His told her nothing. They seemed to look through her, bored and impatient.

"Why did you come here?" Autumn asked him quickly. "Here, to the Pine View Inn?" She wanted him to give her any reason. She wanted to accept it.

Lucas focused on her intensely for a moment. There was something in his face for her to read, but it was gone before she could decipher it. "Let's just say I came to write, Autumn. Any other reason has been eliminated."

There was no expression in his voice, but the words chilled her. *Eliminated.* Would he choose such a clean word for murder? Something of her horror showed in her face. She watched his brows draw together in a frown.

"Cat—"

"No." Before he could speak again, she darted away from him. He'd given her an answer, but it wasn't one she wanted to accept.

The others were already at the table. The sun had superficially lightened the mood, and by unspoken agreement, the conversation was general, with no mention of Helen. They all needed an island of normalcy before the police came.

Julia, looking fresh and lovely, chattered away. Her attitude was so easy, even cheerful, that Autumn wondered if their conversation in the kitchen was as insubstantial as her nightmare. She was flirting again, with every man at the table. Two days of horror hadn't dulled her style.

"Your aunt," Jacques told Autumn, "has an amazing cuisine." He speared a fluffy, light pancake. "It surprises me at times because she has such a charming, drifting way about her. Yet, she remembers small details. This morning, she tells me she has saved me a piece of her apple pie to enjoy with my lunch. She doesn't forget I have a fondness for it. Then when I kiss her hand because I find her so enchanting, she smiled and wandered away, and I heard her say something about towels and chocolate pudding."

The laughter that followed was so normal, Autumn wanted to hug it to her. "She has a better memory about the guests' appetites than her family's," Autumn countered, smiling at him. "She's decided that pot roast is my favorite and has promised to provide it weekly, but it's actually my brother Paul's favorite. I haven't figured out how to move her toward spaghetti."

She gripped her fork tightly at a sudden flash of pain. Very clearly, Autumn could see herself stirring spaghetti sauce in Lucas's kitchen while he did his best to distract her. Would she never pry herself loose from the memories? Quickly, she plunged into conversation again.

"Aunt Tabby sort of floats around the rest of the world," she continued. "I remember once, when we were kids, Paul smuggled some formaldehyde frog legs out of his biology class. He brought them with him when we came on vacation and gave them to Aunt Tabby, hoping for a few screams. She took them, smiled and told him she'd eat them later."

"Oh, God." Julia lifted her hand to her throat. "She didn't actually eat them, did she?"

"No." Autumn grinned. "I distracted her, which of course is the easiest thing in the world to do, and Paul disposed of his biology project. She never missed them."

"I must remember to thank my parents for making me an only child," Julia murmured.

"I can't imagine growing up without Paul and Will." Autumn shook her head as old memories ran through her mind. "The three of us were always very close, even when we tormented each other."

Jacques chuckled, obviously thinking of his own children. "Does your family spend much time here?"

"Not as much as we used to." Autumn lifted her shoulders. "When I was a girl, we'd all come for a month during the summer."

"To tramp through the woods?" Julia asked with a wicked gleam in her eyes.

"That," Autumn returned mildly, and imitated the actress's arched-brow look, "and some camping." She went on, amused by Julia's rolling eyes. "Boating and swimming in the lake."

"Boating," Robert spoke up, cutting off a small, nagging memory. Autumn looked over at him, unable to hang on to it. "That's my one true vice. Nothing I like better than sailing. Right, Jane?" He patted her hand. "Jane's quite a sailor herself. Best first mate I've ever had." He glanced over at Steve. "I suppose you've done your share of sailing."

Steve answered with a rueful shake of his head. "I'm afraid I'm a miserable sailor. I can't even swim."

"You're joking!" This came from Julia. She stared at him in disbelief. Her eyes skimmed approvingly over his shoulders. "You look like you could handle the English Channel."

"I can't even handle a wading pool," he confessed, more amused than embarrassed. He grinned and gestured with his fork. "I make up for it in land sports. If we had a tennis court here, I'd redeem myself."

"Ah well." Jacques gave his French shrug. "You'll have to content yourself with hiking. The mountains here are beautiful. I hope to bring my children one day." He frowned, then stared into his coffee.

"Nature lovers!" Julia's smiling taunt kept the room from sliding into gloom. "Give me smog-filled L.A. anytime. I'll look at your mountains and squirrels in Autumn's photographs."

"You'll have to wait until I add to my supply." She kept her voice light, trying not to be depressed over the loss of her film. She couldn't yet bring herself to think of the loss of her camera.

"Losing that film is like losing a limb, but I'm trying to be brave about it." Taking a bite of pancake, she shrugged. "And I could have lost all four rolls instead of three. The shots I took of the lake were the best, so I can comfort myself with that. The light was perfect that morning, and the shadows…"

She trailed off as the memory seeped through. She could see herself, standing on the ridge looking down at the glistening water, the mirrored trees. And the two figures that walked the far side. That was the morning she had met Lucas in the woods, then Helen. Helen with an angry bruise under her eye.

"Autumn?"

Hearing Jacques's voice, she snapped herself back. "I'm sorry, what?"

"Is something wrong?"

"No, I…" She met his curious eyes. "No."

"I would think light and shadow are the very essence of photography," Julia commented, flowing over the awkward silence. "But I've always concerned myself with looking into the lens rather than through. Remember that horrible little man, Jacques, who used to pop up at the most extraordinary times and stick a camera in my face. What was his name? I really became quite fond of him."

Julia had centered the attention on herself so smoothly that Autumn doubted anyone had noticed her own confusion. She stared down at the pancakes and syrup on her plate as if the solution to the mysteries of the universe were written there. But she could feel Lucas's eyes boring into her averted head. She could feel them, but she couldn't look at him.

She wanted to be alone, to think, to reason out what was

whirling in her head. She forced down the rest of her breakfast and let the conversation buzz around her.

"I have to see Aunt Tabby," Autumn murmured, at last thinking she could leave without causing curiosity. "Excuse me." She had reached the kitchen door before Julia waylaid her.

"Autumn, I want to talk to you." The grip of the slender fingers was quite firm. "Come up to my room."

From the expression on the enviable face, Autumn could see arguing was useless. "All right, right after I see Aunt Tabby. She'll be worried because I didn't say good-night to her yesterday. I'll be up in a few minutes." She kept her voice reasonable and friendly, and managed a smile. Autumn decided she was becoming quite an actress herself.

For a small stretch of silence, Julia studied Autumn's face, then loosened her grip. "All right, come up as soon as you've finished."

"Yes, I will." Autumn slipped into the kitchen with the promise still on her lips. It wasn't difficult to go through the kitchen to the mud room without being noticed. Aunt Tabby and Nancy were deep in their morning argument. Taking down her jacket from the hook where she had placed it the morning of the storm, Autumn checked the pocket. Her fingers closed over the roll of film. For a moment, she simply held it in the palm of her hand.

Moving quickly, she changed from shoes to boots, transferred the film to the pocket of Julia's sweater, grabbed her jacket and went out the back door.

Chapter Eleven

The air was sharp. The rain had washed it clean. Budded leaves Autumn had photographed only days before were fuller, thicker, but still tenderly green. Her mind was no longer on the freedom she had longed for all the previous day. Now, Autumn was only intent on reaching the cover of the forest without being seen. She ran for the trees, not stopping until she was surrounded. Silence was deep and it cradled her.

The ground sucked and skidded under her feet, spongy with rain. There was some wind damage here and there that she noticed when she forced herself to move more carefully. Broken limbs littered the ground. The sun was warm, and she shed her jacket, tossing it over a branch. She made herself concentrate on the sights and sounds of the forest until her thoughts could calm.

The mountain laurel hinted at blooms. A bird circled overhead, then darted deeper into the trees with a sharp cry. A squirrel scurried up a tree trunk and peered down at her. Autumn reached in her pocket and closed her hand over the roll of film. The conversation in the kitchen with Julia now made horrible sense.

Helen must have been at the lake that morning. From the evidence of the bruise, she had argued violently with someone. And that someone had seen Autumn on the ridge. That someone wanted the pictures destroyed badly enough to risk breaking into both her darkroom and her bedroom. The film had to be potentially damaging for anyone to risk knocking her unconscious and ransacking her room. Who else but the killer would care enough to take such dangerous actions? Who else? At every turn, logic pointed its finger toward Lucas.

It had been his plans that brought the group together in the first place. Lucas was the person Autumn had met just before coming across Helen. Lucas had bent over her as she lay on the darkroom floor. Lucas had been up, fully dressed, the night of Helen's murder. Autumn shook her head, wanting to shatter the logic. But the film was solid in her hand.

He must have seen her as she stood on the ridge. She would have been in clear view. When he intercepted her, he had tried to rekindle their relationship. He would have known better than to have attempted to remove the film from her camera. She would have caused a commotion that would have been heard in two counties. Yes, he knew her well enough to use subtler means. But he wouldn't have known she had already switched to a fresh roll.

He had played on her old weakness for him. If she had submitted, he would have found ample time and opportunity to destroy the film. Autumn admitted, painfully, that she would have been too involved with him to have noticed the loss. But she hadn't submitted. This time, she had rejected him. He would have been forced to employ more extreme measures.

He only pretended to want me, she realized. That, more than anything else, hurt. He had held her, kissed her, while his mind had been busy calculating how best to protect himself. Autumn forced herself to face facts. Lucas had stopped wanting her a long time ago, and his needs had never been the same as hers. Two facts were very clear. She had never stopped loving him, and he had never begun to love her.

Still, she balked at the idea of Lucas as a cold-blooded killer. She could remember his sudden spurts of gentleness, his humor, the careless bouts of generosity. That was part of him, too—part of the reason she had been able to love him so easily. Part of the reason she had never stopped.

A hand gripped her shoulder. With a quick cry of alarm, she whirled and found herself face-to-face with Lucas. When she shrank from him, he dropped his hands and stuffed them into his pockets. His eyes were dark and his voice was icy.

"Where's the film, Autumn?"

Whatever color was left in her face drained. She hadn't wanted to believe it. Part of her had refused to believe it. Now, her heart shattered. He was leaving her no choice.

"Film?" She shook her head as she took another step back. "What film?"

"You know very well what film." Impatience pulled at the words. He narrowed his eyes, watching her retreat. "I want the fourth roll. Don't back away from me!"

Autumn stopped at the curt command. "Why?"

"Don't play stupid." His impatience was quickly becoming

fury. She recognized all the signs. "I want the film. What I do with it is my business."

She ran, thinking only to escape from his words. It had been easier to live with the doubt than the certainty. He caught her arm before she had dashed three yards. Spinning her around, he studied her face.

"You're terrified." He looked stunned, then angry. "You're terrified of me." With his hands gripping hard on her arms he brought her closer. "We've run the gamut, haven't we, Cat? Yesterday's gone." There was a finality in his voice that brought more pain than his hands or his temper.

"Lucas." Autumn was trembling, emotionally spent. "Please don't hurt me anymore." The pain she spoke of had nothing to do with the physical, but he released her with a violent jerk. The struggle for control was visible on his face.

"I won't lay a hand on you now, or ever again. Just tell me where that film is. I'll get out of your life as quickly as possible."

She had to reach him. She had to try one last time. "Lucas, please, it's senseless. You must see that. Can't you—"

"Don't push me!" The words exploded at her, rocking her back on her heels. "You stupid fool, do you have any idea how dangerous that film is? Do you think for one minute I'm going to let you keep it?" He took a step toward her. "Tell me where it is. Tell me now, or by God, I'll throttle it out of you."

"In the darkroom." The lie came quickly and without calculation. Perhaps that was why he accepted it so readily.

"All right. Where?" She watched his features relax slightly. His voice was calmer.

"On the bottom shelf. On the wet side."

"That's hardly illuminating to a layman, Cat." There was a

touch of his old mockery as he reached for her arm. "Let's go get it."

"No!" She jerked away wildly. "I won't go with you. There's only one roll; you'll find it. You found the others. Leave me alone, Lucas. For God's sake, leave me alone!"

She ran again, skidding on the mud. This time he didn't stop her.

Autumn had no idea how far she ran or even the direction she took. Ultimately, her feet slowed to a walk. She stopped to stare up at a sky that had no clouds. What was she going to do?

She could go back. She could go back and try to get to the darkroom first, lock herself in. She could develop the film, blow up the two figures beside the lake and see the truth for herself. Her hand reached for the hated film again. She didn't want to see the truth. With absolute certainty, she knew she could never hand the film over to the police. No matter what Lucas had done or would do, she couldn't betray him. He'd been wrong, she thought. She could never pull the lever.

Withdrawing the film from her pocket, she stared down at it. It looked so innocent. She had felt so innocent that day, up on the ridge with the sun coming up. But when she had done what she had to do, she would never feel innocent again. She would expose the film herself.

Lucas, she thought and nearly laughed. Lucas McLean was the only man on earth who could make her turn her back on her own conscience. And when it was done, only the two of them would know. She would be as guilty as he.

Do it quickly, she told herself. Do it fast and think about it later. Her palm was damp where the film was cradled in it. You're going to have a whole lifetime to think about it. Taking a deep breath, Autumn started to uncap the plastic capsule she used to protect her undeveloped film. A movement on the path behind her had her stuffing the roll back into her pocket and whirling around.

Could Lucas have searched the darkroom so quickly? What would he do now that he knew she had lied to him? Foolishly, Autumn wanted to run again. Instead, she straightened and waited. The final encounter would have to come sooner or later.

Autumn's relief when she saw Steve approaching quickly became irritation. She wanted to be alone, not to make small talk and useless conversation while the film burned in her pocket.

"Hi!" Steve's lightning smile did nothing to decrease her annoyance, but Autumn pasted on one of her own. If she were going to be playing a game for the rest of her life, she might as well start now.

"Hello. Taking Jacques up on the hiking?" God, how normal and shallow her voice sounded! Was she going to be able to live like this?

"Yeah. I see you needed to get away from the inn, too." Taking a deep breath of the freshened air, he flexed his shoulders. "Lord, it feels good to be outside again."

"I know what you mean." Autumn eased the tension from her own shoulders. This was a reprieve, she told herself. Accept it. When it's over, nothing's ever going to be the same again.

"And Jacques is right," Steve went on, staring out through the thin leaves. "The mountains are beautiful. It reminds you that life goes on."

"I suppose we all need to remember that now." Unconsciously, Autumn dipped her hand in her pocket.

"Your hair glows in the sunlight." Steve caught at the ends

and moved them between his fingertips. Autumn saw, with some alarm, that warmth had crept into his eyes. A romantic interlude was more than she could handle.

"People often seem to think more about my hair than me." She smiled and kept her voice light. "Sometimes I'm tempted to hack it off."

"Oh no." He took a more generous handful. "It's very special, very unique." His eyes lifted to hers. "And I've been thinking quite a lot about you the last few days. You're very special, too."

"Steve…" Autumn turned and would have walked on, but his hand was still in her hair.

"I want you, Autumn."

The words, so gentle, almost humble, nearly broke her heart. She turned back with apology in her eyes. "I'm sorry, Steve. I really am."

"Don't be sorry." He lowered his head to brush her lips. "If you let me, I could make you happy."

"Steve, please." Autumn lifted her hands to his chest. If only he were Lucas, she thought as she stared up at him. If only it were Lucas looking at me like this. "I can't."

He let out a long breath, but didn't release her. "McLean? Autumn, he only makes you unhappy. Why won't you let go?"

"I can't tell you how many times I've asked myself the same question." She sighed, and he watched the sun shoot into her eyes. "I don't have the answer—except that I love him."

"Yes, it shows." Frowning, he brushed a strand of hair from her cheek. "I'd hoped you'd be able to get over him, but I don't suppose you will."

"No, I don't suppose I will. I've given up trying."

"Now I'm sorry, Autumn. It makes things difficult."

Autumn dropped her eyes to stare at the ground. She didn't want pity. "Steve, I appreciate it, but I really need to be alone."

"I want the film, Autumn."

Astonished, she jerked her head up. Without consciously making the step, she aligned herself with Lucas. "Film? I don't know what you mean."

"Oh yes, I'm afraid you do." He was still speaking gently, one hand stroking her hair. "The pictures you took of the lake the morning Helen and I were down there. I have to have them."

"You?" For a moment, the implication eluded her. "You and Helen?" Confusion turned into shock. She could only stare at him.

"We were having quite a row that morning. You see, she had decided she wanted a lump-sum payment from me. Her other sources were drying up fast. Julia wouldn't give her a penny, just laughed at her. Helen was furious about that." His face changed with a grim smile. "Jacques had finished with her, too. She never had anything worthwhile on Lucas in the first place. She counted on intimidating him. Instead, he told her to go to hell and threatened to press charges. That threw her off balance for a while. She must have realized Jane was on the edge. So...she concentrated on me."

He had been staring off into the distance as he spoke. Now, his attention came back to Autumn. The first hint of anger swept into his eyes. "She wanted two hundred and fifty thousand dollars in two weeks. A quarter of a million, or she'd hand over the information she had on me to my father."

"But you said what she knew wasn't important." Autumn let her eyes dart past his for a moment. The path behind them was empty. She was alone.

"She knew a bit more than I told you." Steve gave her an apologetic smile. "I could hardly tell you everything then. I've covered my tracks well enough now so that I don't think the police will ever know. It was actually a matter of extortion."

"Extortion?" The hand on her hair was becoming more terrifying with each passing moment. Keep him talking, she told herself frantically. Keep him talking and someone will come.

"Borrowing, really. The money will be mine sooner or later." He shrugged it off. "I just took some a little early. Unfortunately, my father wouldn't see it that way. I told you, remember? He's a tough man. He wouldn't think twice about booting me out the door and cutting off my income. I can't have that, Autumn." He flashed her a smile. "I have very expensive tastes."

"So you killed her." Autumn said it flatly. She was finished with horror.

"I didn't have a choice. I couldn't possibly get my hands on that much cash in two weeks." He said it so calmly, Autumn could almost see the rationale behind it. "I nearly killed her that morning down by the lake. She just wouldn't listen to me. I lost my temper and hit her. Knocked her cold. When I saw her lying there on the ground, I realized how much I wanted her dead."

Autumn didn't interrupt. She could see he was far from finished. Let him talk it out, she ordered herself, controlling the urge to break from him and run. Someone's going to come.

"I bent over her," he continued. "My hands were almost around her throat when I saw you standing up on the ridge. I knew it was you because the sun was shining on your hair. I didn't think you could recognize me from that distance, but I had to be sure. Of course, I found out later that you weren't paying attention to us at all."

"No, I barely noticed." Her knees were starting to shake. He was telling her too much. Far too much.

"I left Helen and circled around, thinking to intercept you. Lucas got to you first. Quite a touching little scene."

"You watched us?" She felt a stir of anger edge through the fear.

"You were too involved in each other to notice." He smiled again. "In any case, that's when I learned you'd been taking pictures. I had to get rid of that film; it was too chancy. I hated to hurt you, Autumn. I found you very attractive right from the first."

A rabbit darted down the path, veering off and bounding into the woods. She heard the call of a quail, faint with distance. The simple, natural texture of her surroundings gave his words a sense of unreality. "The darkroom."

"Yes. I was glad the blow with the door knocked you out. I didn't want to have to hit you with the flashlight. I didn't see your camera, but found a roll of film. I was so certain I had things taken care of. You can imagine how I felt when you said you'd lost two rolls, and that they were shots of your trip down from New York. I didn't know how the other roll had been ruined."

"Lucas. Lucas turned on the lights when he found me." Suddenly, through the horror came a bright flash of realization. *It hadn't been Lucas.* He'd done nothing but simply be who he was. She felt overwhelming relief at his innocence, then guilt at ever having believed what she had of him. "Lucas," she said again, almost giddy with the onslaught of sensations.

"Well, it hardly matters now," Steve said practically. Autumn snapped back. She had to keep alert, had to keep a step ahead of him. "I knew if I just took the film from your camera, you'd begin to wonder. You might start thinking too closely about the pictures you'd taken. I hated doing that to your things, breaking your camera. I know it was important to you."

"I have another at home." It was a weak attempt to sound unconcerned. Steve only smiled.

"I went to Helen's room right after I'd finished with yours. I knew I was going to have to kill her. She stood there pointing to the bruise and telling me it was going to cost me another hundred thousand. I didn't know what I was going to do…I thought I was going to strangle her. Then I saw the scissors. That was better—anyone could have used scissors. Even little Jane. I stopped thinking when I picked them up until it was over."

He shuddered, and Autumn thought, *Run! Run now!* But his hand tightened on her hair. "I've never been through anything like that. It was terrible. I almost folded. I knew I had to think, had to be careful, or I'd lose everything. Staying in that room was the hardest thing I've ever done. I wiped the handles of the scissors clean and tore up my shirt. Her blood was on it. I flushed the pieces down the toilet. When I got back to my room, I showered and went to bed. I remember being surprised that the whole thing took less than twenty minutes. It seemed like years."

"It must have been dreadful for you," Autumn murmured, but he was oblivious to the edge in her voice.

"Yes, but it was all working out. No one could prove where they were when Helen was killed. The storm—the phones, the power—that was all a bonus. Every one of us had a reason to want Helen out of the way. I really think Julia and I will be the least likely suspects when the time comes. The police should look to Jacques because he had more cause, and Lucas because he has the temper."

"Lucas couldn't kill anyone," Autumn said evenly. "The police will know that."

"I wouldn't bank on it." He gave her a crooked smile. "You haven't been so sure of that yourself."

She could say nothing when struck with the truth. *Why wasn't someone coming?*

"This morning, you started talking about four rolls of film, and the pictures you took of the lake. I could tell the moment when you remembered."

So much for my talent at acting, she thought grimly. "I only remembered there'd been people down by the lake that morning."

"You were putting it all together quickly." He traced a finger down her cheek and Autumn forced herself not to jerk away. "I had hoped to distract you, gain your affection. It was obvious you were hurting over McLean. If I could have moved in, I might have gotten my hands on that film without having to hurt you."

Autumn kept her eyes and voice steady. He'd finished talking now; she could sense it. "What are you going to do?"

"Damn it, Autumn. I'm going to have to kill you."

He said it in much the same way her father had said, *"Damn it, Autumn, I'm going to have to spank you."* She nearly broke into hysterical giggles.

"They'll know this time, Steve." Her body was beginning to shake, but she spoke calmly. If she could reason with him...

"No, I don't think so." He spoke practically, as if he considered she might have a viable point. "I was careful to get out without being seen. Everyone's spread out again. I doubt anyone even knows you went outside. I wouldn't have known myself if I hadn't found your jacket and boots missing. Then again, if I hadn't found the jacket hanging on a branch and been able to follow your tracks from there, I wouldn't have found you so easily."

He shrugged, as if showing her why his reasoning was better than hers. "When you're found missing, I'll make certain I come this way when we look for you. I can do a lot of damage to the tracks and no one will know any better. Now, Autumn, I need the film. Tell me where you've put it."

"I'm not going to tell you." She tossed back her head. As long as she had the film, he had to keep her alive. "They'll find it. When they do, they'll know it was you."

He made a quick sound of impatience. "You'll tell me Autumn, eventually. It would be easier for you if you told me now. I don't want to hurt you any more than I have to. I can make it quick, or I can make it painful."

His hand shot out so swiftly, Autumn had no time to dodge the blow. The force of it knocked her back into a tree. The pain welled inside her head and rolled through, leaving dizziness. She clutched at the rough bark to keep her balance as she saw him coming toward her.

Oh no, she wasn't going to stand and be hit again. He'd gotten away with it twice, and twice was enough. With as much force as she could muster, she kicked, aiming well below the waist. He went down on his knees like a shot. Autumn turned and fled.

Chapter Twelve

She ran blindly. *Escape!* It was the only coherent thought in her brain. It wasn't until the first wave of panic had ebbed that Autumn realized she had run not only away from Steve, but away from the inn. It was too late to double back. She could only concentrate as much effort as possible into putting distance between them. She veered off the path and into thicker undergrowth.

When she heard him coming after her, Autumn didn't look back, but increased her pace. His breathing was labored, but close. Too close. She swerved again and plunged on. The ground sucked and pulled at her boots, but she told herself she wouldn't slip. If she slipped, he would be on top of her in a moment. His hands would be at her throat. *She would not slip.*

Her heart was pounding and her lungs were screaming in agony for more air. A branch whipped back, stinging her cheek. But she told herself she wouldn't stop. She would run and run and run until she no longer heard him coming after her.

A tree had fallen and lay drunkenly in her path. Without

breaking stride, Autumn vaulted it, sliding for a moment when her boots hit the mud, then pounding on. He slipped. She heard the slick sound of his boots as they lost traction, then his muffled curse. She kept up her wild pace, nearly giddy at the few seconds his fall had given her.

Time and direction ceased to exist. For her, the pursuit had no beginning, no end. It was only the race. Her thoughts were no longer rational. She knew only that she had to keep running though she'd almost forgotten why. Her breath was coming in harsh gasps, her legs were like rubber. She knew only the mindless flight of the hunted—the naked fear of the hunter.

Suddenly, she saw the lake. It glistened as the sun hit its surface. With some last vestige of lucidity, Autumn remembered Steve's admission that morning. He couldn't swim. The race had a goal now, and she dashed for it.

Her crazed approach through the woods had taken her away from the ridge where the incline graduated for easy descent. Instead, she came to the edge of a cliff that fell forty feet in a sheer drop. Without hesitation, Autumn plunged down at full speed. She scrambled and slid, her fingers clawing to keep herself from overbalancing. Like a lizard, she clung to the mountain. Her body scraped on jagged rocks and slid on mud. Julia's designer sweater shredded. Autumn realized, as the pain grew hot, that her skin suffered equally. Fear pushed her beyond the pain. The lake beckoned below. Safety. Victory.

Still, he came after her. She could hear his boots clatter on the rocks above her head, jarring pebbles that rained down on her. Autumn leaped the last ten feet. The force of the fall shot up her legs, folding them under her until she rolled into a heap. Then she was scrambling and streaking for the lake.

She heard him cry out for her. With a final mad impetus, she flung herself into the water, slicing through its surface. Its sharp frigidity shocked her system and gave her strength. Clawing through it, she headed for depth. She was going to win.

Like a light switched off, the momentum which had driven her so wildly, sapped. The weight of her boots pulled her down. The water closed over her head. Thrashing and choking, Autumn fought for the surface. Her lungs burned as she tried to pull in air. Her arms were heavy, and her feeble strokes had her bobbing up and down. Mists gathered in front of her eyes. Still, she resisted, fighting as the water sucked at her. It was now as deadly an enemy as the one she had sought to escape.

She heard someone sobbing, and realized dimly it was her own voice calling for help. But she knew there would be none. The fight was gone out of her. Was it music she heard? She thought it came from below her, deep, beckoning. Slowly, surrendering, she let the water take her like a lover.

Someone was hurting her. Autumn didn't protest. Darkness blanketed her mind and numbed the pain. The pushing and prodding were no more irritating to her than a faint itch. Air forced its way into her lungs, and she moaned gently in annoyance.

Lucas's voice touched the edges of her mind. He was calling her back in a strange, unnatural voice. Panic? Yes, even through the darkness she could detect a note of panic. What an odd thing to hear in Lucas's voice. Her eyelids were heavy, and the darkness was so tempting. The need to tell him was stronger. Autumn forced her eyes open. Blackness receded to a verge of mist.

His face loomed over her, water streaming from it and his hair. It splattered cold on her cheeks. Yet her mouth felt warm, as if his had just left it. Autumn stared at him, groping for the power of speech.

"Oh God, Autumn." Lucas brushed the water from her cheeks even as it fell on them again from his own hair. "Oh God. Listen to me. It's all right, you're going to be all right, do you hear? You're going to be all right. I'm going to take you back to the inn. Can you understand me?"

His voice was desperate, as were his eyes. She'd never heard that tone or seen that expression. Not from Lucas. Autumn wanted to say something that would comfort him, but lacked the strength. The mists were closing in again, and she welcomed them. For a moment, she held them off and dug deep for her voice.

"I thought you killed her, Lucas. I'm sorry."

"Oh, Cat." His voice was intolerably weary. She felt his mouth touch hers. Then she felt nothing.

Voices, vague and without texture, floated down a long tunnel. Autumn didn't welcome them. She wanted her peace. She tried to plunge deeper into the darkness again, but Lucas had no respect for what anyone else wanted. His voice broke into her solitude, suddenly clear and, as always, demanding.

"I'm staying with her until she wakes up. I'm not leaving her."

"Lucas, you're dead on your feet." Robert's voice was low and soothing, in direct contrast to Lucas's. "I'll stay with Autumn. It's part of my job. She's probably going to be floating in and out all night. You wouldn't know what to do for her."

"Then you'll tell me what to do. I'm staying with her."

"Of course you are, dear." Aunt Tabby's voice surprised Autumn even in the dim, drifting darkness. It was so firm and strong. "Lucas will stay, Dr. Spicer. You've already said it's mainly a matter of rest, and waiting until she wakes naturally. Lucas can take care of her."

"I'll sit with you, Lucas, if you'd like...all right, but you've only to call me." Julia's voice rolled over Autumn, as smoky as the mists.

Suddenly, she wanted to ask them what was happening. What they were doing in her own private world. She struggled for words and formed a moan. A cool hand fell on her brow.

"Is she in pain?" Was that Lucas's voice? Autumn thought. Trembling? "Damn it, give her something for the pain!"

The darkness was whirling again, jumbling the sounds. Autumn let it swallow her.

She dreamed. The deep black curtain took on a velvet, moonlight texture. Lucas stared down at her. His face seemed oddly vivid for a dream. His hand felt real and cool on her cheek. "Cat, can you hear me?"

Autumn stared at him, then drew together all her scraps and rags of concentration. "Yes." She closed her eyes and let the darkness swirl.

When her eyes reopened, he was still there. Autumn swallowed. Her throat was burning dry. "Am I dead?"

"No. No, Cat, you're not dead." Lucas poured something cool down her throat. Her eyes drooped again as she tried to patch together her memory. It was too hard, and she let it go.

Pain shot through her. Unexpected and sharp, it rocketed down her arms and legs. Autumn heard someone moan pitifully. Lucas loomed over her again, his face pale in a shaft of moonlight. "It hurts," she complained.

"I know." He sat beside her and brought a cup to her lips. "Try to drink."

Floating, like a bright red balloon, Autumn felt herself drift through space. The pain had eased as she stumbled back into consciousness. "Julia's sweater," she murmured as she opened her eyes again. "It's torn. I think I tore it. I'll have to buy her another."

"Don't worry about it, Cat. Rest." Lucas's hand was on her hair and she turned her face to it, seeking reassurance. She floated again.

"I'm sure it was valuable," she murmured, nearly an hour later. "But I don't really need that new tripod. Julia lent me that sweater. I should have been more careful."

"Julia has dozens of sweaters, Cat. Don't worry."

Autumn closed her eyes, comforted. But she knew her tripod would have to wait.

"Lucas." She pulled herself back, but now the moonlight was the gray light of dawn.

"Yes, I'm here."

"Why?"

"Why what, Cat?"

"Why are you here?"

But he moved out of focus again. She never heard his answer.

Chapter Thirteen

The sunlight was strong. Used to darkness, Autumn blinked in protest.

"Ah, are you with us to stay this time, Autumn, or is this another quick visit?" Julia bent over her and patted her cheek. "There's a bit of color coming back, and you're cool. How do you feel?"

Autumn lay still for a moment and tried to find out. "Hollow," she decided, and Julia laughed.

"Trust you to think of your stomach."

"Hollow all over," Autumn countered. "Especially my head." She glanced confusedly around the room. "Have I been sick?"

"You gave us quite a scare." Julia eased down on the bed and studied her. "Don't you remember?"

"I was…dreaming?" Autumn's search for her memory found only bits and pieces. "Lucas was here. I was talking to him."

"Yes, he said you were drifting in and out through the night. Managed to say a word or two now and again. Did you really think I'd let you sacrifice your new tripod?" She kissed Autumn's cheek, then held her a moment. "God, when Lucas carried you in, we thought…" Shaking her head briskly, she sat up. Autumn saw that her eyes were damp.

"Julia." Autumn squeezed her eyes a moment, but nothing came clear. "I was supposed to come to your room, but I didn't."

"No, you didn't. I should have dragged you with me then and there. None of this would have happened." She stood up again. "It appears Lucas and I were both taken in by those big green eyes. I don't know how much time we wasted searching for that damn film before he went back to find you."

"I don't understand. Why…" As she reached up to brush at her hair, Autumn noticed the bandages on her hands. "What are these for? Did I hurt myself?"

"It's all right now." Julia brushed away the question. "I'd better let Lucas explain. He'll be furious that I chased him downstairs for some coffee, and you woke up."

"Julia—"

"No more questions now." She cut Autumn off as she plucked a robe from a chair. "Why don't you slip this on. You'll feel better." She eased the silk over Autumn's arms and covered more bandages. The sight of them brought added confusion, more juggled memories. "Just lie still and relax," Julia ordered. "Aunt Tabby already has some soup simmering, just waiting for you. I'll tell her to pour it into an enormous bowl."

She kissed Autumn again, then glided to the door. "Listen, Autumn." Julia turned back with a slow, cat smile. "He's been through hell these past twenty-four hours, but don't make it too easy for him."

Autumn frowned at the door when Julia had gone and wondered what the devil she was talking about.

Deciding she wouldn't find any answers lying in bed, Autumn dragged herself out. Every joint, every muscle revolted. She nearly succumbed to the desire to crawl back in, but curiosity was stronger. Her legs wobbled as she went to the mirror.

"Good God!" She looked, Autumn decided, even worse than she felt. The bruise on her temple had company. There was a light discoloration along her cheekbone and a few odd scratches. There was a sudden, clear memory of rough bark scraping against her hands. Lifting them, Autumn stared at the bandages. "What have I done to myself?" she asked aloud, then belted the robe to disguise the worst of the damage.

The door opened, and in the reflection she watched Lucas enter the room. He looked as though he hadn't slept in days. The lines of strain were deeper now and his chin was shadowed and unshaven. Only his eyes were the same. Dark and intense.

"You look like hell," she told him without turning. "You need some sleep."

He laughed. In a gesture of weariness she had never seen in him, he lifted his hands to run them down his face. "I might have expected it," he murmured. He sighed, then gave her a smile from the past. "You shouldn't be out of bed, Cat. You're liable to topple over any minute."

"I'm all right. At least I was before I looked in the mirror." Turning, she faced him directly. "I nearly fainted from shock."

"You are," he began in quiet, serious tones, "the most beautiful thing I've ever seen."

"Kindness to the invalid," she said, looking away. That had hurt, and she wasn't certain she could deal with any more pain. "I could use some explanations. My mind's a little fuddled."

"Robert said that was to be expected after..." He trailed off and jammed clenched fists into his pockets. "After everything that's happened."

Autumn looked again at her bandaged hands. "What did happen? I can't quite remember. I was running..." She lifted her eyes to his and searched. "In the woods, down the cliff. I..." She shook her head. There were only bits and pieces. "I tore Julia's sweater."

"God! You would latch on to a damn sweater!" His explosion had Autumn's eyes widening. "You almost drowned, and all you think about is Julia's sweater."

Her mouth trembled open. "The lake." Memory flooded back in a tidal wave. She leaned back against the dresser. "Steve. It was Steve. He killed Helen. He was chasing me. The film, I wouldn't give it to him." She swallowed, trying to keep calm. "I lied to you. I had it in my pocket. I kept running, but he was right behind me."

"Cat." She backed away, but he wrapped his arms around her. "Don't. Don't think about it. Damn it, I shouldn't have told you that way." He pressed his cheek against her hair. "I can't seem to do anything properly with you."

"No. No, let me think it through." Autumn pushed away. She wanted the details. Once she had them all, the fear would ease. "He found me in the woods after you'd gone in. He'd been with Helen down by the lake the morning I was taking pictures. He told me he had killed her. He told me everything."

"We know all of it," Lucas cut her off sharply. "He let out with everything once we got him back here. We got through to the police this morning." He whipped out a cigarette and lit it swiftly. "He's already in custody. They've got your film, too, for whatever it's worth. Jacques found it on the path."

"It must have fallen out of my pocket. Lucas, it was so strange." Her brow knitted as she remembered the timeless incident with Steve. "He apologized for having to kill me. Then when I told him I wouldn't give him the film, he slugged me so hard I saw stars."

Face thunderous, Lucas spun around and stalked to the window. He stared out without speaking.

"When he came at me again, I kicked him, hard, where I knew it would do the most damage."

She heard Lucas mutter something so uncharacteristically vulgar she thought she misunderstood. For a time she rambled about her flight through the woods, talking more to herself than to him.

"I saw you when you started your suicidal plunge down the cliff." His back was still to her, his voice still rough. "How in God's name you managed to get to the bottom without cracking your skull…" Lucas turned when Autumn remained silent. "I'd been tracking you through the woods. When I saw you were making for the lake, I veered off and started for the ridge. I hoped to cut Anderson off." He pulled on his cigarette, then took a long, shuddering breath. "I saw you flying down those rocks. You never should have made it down alive. I called you, but you just kept tearing for the lake. I was on him before you hit the water."

"I heard someone call. I thought it was Steve." She pushed a bandaged hand against her temple. "All I could think about was getting into the water before he caught me. I remembered he couldn't swim. Then when I had trouble keeping myself up, I panicked and forgot all those nifty rules you learn in lifeguard class."

Very slowly, very deliberately, Lucas crushed out his cigarette. "By the time I finished kicking his head in, you were already floundering. How you got out so far after the run you'd had, and with boots that must weigh twenty pounds, I'll never know. I was a good ten yards from you when you went under the last time. You sank like a stone."

He turned away again to stare out the window. "I thought…" He shook his head a moment, then continued. "I thought you were dead when I dragged you out. You were dead white and you weren't breathing. At least not enough that I could tell." He took out another cigarette and this time had to fight with his lighter to get flame. He cursed and drew deeply.

"I remember you dripping on me," Autumn murmured into the silence. "Then I thought I died."

"You damn near did." The smoke came out of his lungs in a violent stream. "I must have pumped two gallons of water out of you. You came around just long enough to apologize for thinking I killed Helen."

"I'm sorry, Lucas."

"Don't!" His tone was curt as he swung around again.

"But I should never have—"

"No?" He cut her off with one angry word. "Why? It's easy enough to see how you reached your conclusions, culminating with my last attack about the film."

After a moment, Autumn trusted herself to speak. "There were so many things you said that made me think…and you were so angry. When you asked me for the film, I wanted you to tell me anything."

"But instead of explanations, I bullied you. Typical of me, though, isn't it?" He drew a breath, but his body remained tense.

"That's another apology I owe you. I seem to have chalked up quite a few. Would you like them in a group, Cat, or one at a time?"

Autumn turned away from that. It wasn't an apology she wanted, but an explanation. "Why did you want it, Lucas? How did you know?"

"It might be difficult for you to believe at this point, but I'm not completely inhuman. I wanted the film because I hoped, if I had it and made it known that I did, that you'd be safe. And…" She turned back as a shadow crossed his face. "I thought you knew, or had remembered what was on the film, and that you were protecting Anderson."

"Protecting him?" Astonishment reflected in her voice. "Why would I do that?"

He moved his shoulders in a shrug. "You seemed fond of him."

"I thought he was nice," Autumn said slowly. "I imagine we all did. But I hardly knew him. As it turns out, I didn't know him at all."

"I misinterpreted your natural friendliness for something else. Then compounded the mistake by overreacting. I was furious that you gave him what you wouldn't give me. Trust, companionship. Affection."

"Dog in the manger, Lucas?" The words shot out icily.

A muscle twitched at the corner of his mouth in contrast to another negligent shrug. "If you like."

"I'm sorry." With a sigh, Autumn pushed wearily at her hair. "That was uncalled for."

"Was it?" he countered and crushed out his cigarette. "I doubt that. You're entitled to launch a few shafts, Cat. You've taken enough of them from me."

"We're getting off the point." She moved away. Julia's silk robe whispered around her. "You thought I was protecting Steve. I'll accept that. But how did you know he needed protecting?"

"Julia and I had already pieced together a number of things. We were almost certain he was the one who had killed Helen."

"You and Julia." Now she turned to him, curious. Autumn gestured with her hands, then stopped as the pain throbbed in them. "You're going to have to clear things up, Lucas. I might still be a little dim."

"Julia and I had discussed Helen's blackmail thoroughly. Until her murder, we centered on Jacques's problem. Neither Julia nor I were concerned with the petty threats Helen held over us. After she was killed and your room broken into, we tossed around the idea that they were connected. Autumn, why don't you get back in bed. You're so pale."

"No." She shook her head, warding off the creeping warmth the concern in his voice brought her. "I'm fine. Please, don't stop now."

He seemed about to argue, then changed his mind. "I'd never believed you'd ruin your own film, or knock yourself senseless. So, Julia and I began a process of elimination. I hadn't killed Helen, and I knew that Julia hadn't. I'd been in her room that night receiving a heated lecture on my technique with women until I came down to see you. And I'd passed Helen in the hall right before I'd gone into Julia's room, so even if Julia'd had the inclination to kill Helen, it's doubtful that she would have had two identical white negligees. There'd have been blood." He shrugged again. "In any case, if Julia had killed her, she probably would have admitted it."

"Yes." Autumn gave a murmured agreement and wondered what Julia's lace-clad lecture had included.

"I've known Jacques for years," Lucas continued. "He's simply not capable of killing. Julia and I all but eliminated the Spicers. Robert is entirely too dedicated to life to take one, and Jane would dissolve into tears."

Lucas began to pace. "Anderson fit the bill. And, for reasons of my own, I wanted it to be him. Our intrepid Julia copped the spare key from Aunt Tabby and searched his room for the shirt he had worn the night of the murder. I nearly strangled her when she told me she'd done it. She's quite a woman."

"Yes." Jealousy warred with affection. Affection won. "She's wonderful."

"The shirt wasn't there. Julia claims to have an unerring eye for wardrobe, and I wanted to believe her. We decided you should be put on guard without going into specifics. I thought it best if you were wary of everyone. We decided that Julia would talk to you because you'd trust her more quickly than you'd trust me. I hadn't done anything to warrant your trust."

"She frightened me pretty successfully," Autumn recalled. "I had nightmares."

"I'm sorry. It seemed the best way at the time. We thought the film had been destroyed, but we didn't want to take any chances."

"She was telling Jacques that night, wasn't she?"

"Yeah." Lucas noted the faint annoyance in her tone. "That way there would have been three of us to look out for you."

"I might have looked out for myself if I'd been told."

"No, I don't think so. Your face is a dead giveaway. That morning at breakfast when you started rambling about a fourth roll and remembered, everything showed in your eyes."

"If I'd been prepared—"

"If you hadn't been a damn fool and had gone with Julia, we could have kept you safe."

"I wanted to think," she began, angry at being kept in the dark.

"It was my fault." Lucas held up a hand to stop her. "The whole thing's been my doing. I should have handled things differently. You'd never have been hurt if I had."

"No, Lucas." Guilt swamped her when she remembered the look on his face after he had dragged her from the lake. "I'd be dead if it weren't for you."

"Good God, Cat, don't look at me like that. I can't cope with it." He turned away. "I'm doing my best to keep my word. I'll get Robert; he'll want to examine you."

"Lucas." She wasn't going to let him walk out that door until he told her everything. "Why did you come here? And don't tell me you came to Virginia to write. I know—I remember your habits."

Lucas turned, but kept his hand on the knob. "I told you before, the other reason no longer exists. Leave it."

He had retreated behind the cool, detached manner he used so well, but Autumn wasn't going to be shoved aside. "This is my aunt's inn, Lucas. Your coming here, however indirectly, started this chain of events. I have a right to know why you came."

For several seconds, he stared at her, then his hands sought his pockets again. "All right," he agreed. "I don't suppose I have any right to pride after this, and you deserve to get in a few licks after the way I've treated you." He came no closer, but his eyes locked hard on hers. "I came here because of you. Because I had to get you back or go crazy."

"Me?" The pain was so sharp, Autumn laughed. She would not cry again. "Oh Lucas, please, do better." She saw him flinch before he walked again to the window. "You tossed me out, remember? You didn't want me then. You don't want me now."

"Didn't want you!" He whirled, knocking over a vase and sending it crashing. The anger surrounding him was fierce and vivid. "You can't even comprehend how much I wanted you, have wanted you all these years. I thought I'd lose my mind from wanting you."

"No, I won't listen to this." Autumn turned away to lean against the bedpost. "I won't listen."

"You asked for it. Now you'll listen."

"You told me you didn't want me," she flung at him. "I never meant anything to you. You told me it was finished and shrugged your shoulders like it had been nothing all along. Nothing, *nothing's* ever hurt me like the way you brushed me aside."

"I know what I did." The anger was gone from his voice to be replaced by strain. "I know the things I said to you while you stood there staring at me. I hated myself. I wanted you to scream, to rage, to make it easy for me to push you out. But you just stood there with tears falling down your face. I've never forgotten how you looked."

Autumn pulled herself together and faced him again. "You said you didn't want me. Why would you have said it if it weren't true?"

"Because you terrified me."

He said it so simply, she slumped down on the bed to stare at him. "Terrified you? *I* terrified *you?"*

"You don't know what you did to me—all that sweetness, all that generosity. You never asked anything of me, and yet you asked everything." He began to pace again. Autumn watched him in bewilderment. "You were an obsession, that's what I told myself. If I sent you away, hurt you badly enough to make you go, I'd be cured. The more I had of you, the more I needed. I'd wake up in the middle of the night and curse you for not being there. Then I'd curse myself for needing you there. I had to get away from you. I couldn't admit, not even to myself, that I loved you."

"Loved me?" Autumn repeated the words dumbly. "You loved me?"

"Loved then, love now and for the rest of my life." Lucas drew in a deep breath as if the words had left him shaken. "I wasn't able to tell you. I wasn't able to believe it." He stopped pacing and looked at her. "I've kept close tabs on you these past three years. I found all sorts of excuses to do so. When I found out about the inn, and your connection with it, I began to fly out here off and on. Finally, I admitted to myself that I wasn't going to make it without you. I mapped out a plan. I had it all worked out." He gave her an ironic smile.

"Plan?" Autumn repeated. Her mind was still whirling.

"It was easy to plant the idea in Aunt Tabby's head to write you and ask you to visit. Knowing you, I was sure you'd come without question. That was all I needed. I was so sure of myself. I thought all I'd have to do would be to issue the invitation, and you'd fall right back into my arms. Just like old times. I'd have you back, marry you before you sorted things out and pat myself on the back for being so damn clever."

"Marry me?" Autumn's brows flew up in astonishment.

"Once we were married," Lucas went on as if she hadn't interrupted, "I'd never have to worry about losing you again. I'd simply never give you a divorce no matter how you struggled. I deserved a good kick in the teeth, Cat, and you gave it to me. Instead of falling into my arms, you turned up your nose and told me to get lost. But that didn't throw me off for long. No, you'd loved me once, and I'd make you love me again. I could deal with the anger, but the ice…

"I didn't know I could be hurt that way. It was quite a shock. Seeing you again…" He paused and seemed to struggle for words. "It was torture, pure and simple, to be so close and not be able to have you. I wanted to tell you what you meant to me, then every time I got near you I'd behave like a maniac. The way you cringed from me yesterday, telling me not to hurt you again, I can't tell you what that did to me."

"Lucas—"

"You'd better let me finish," he told her. "I'll never be able to manage this again." He reached for a cigarette, changed his mind, then continued. "Julia roasted me, but I couldn't seem to stop myself. The more you resisted, the worse I treated you. Every time I approached you, I ended up doing the wrong thing. That day, up in your room…" He stopped and Autumn watched the struggle on his face. "I nearly raped you. I was crazy with jealousy after seeing you and Anderson. When I saw you cry—I swore I'd never be responsible for putting that look on your face again.

"I'd come up that day, ready to beg, crawl, plead, whatever it took. When I saw you kissing him, something snapped. I started thinking about the men you'd been with these past three years. The men who'd have you again when I couldn't."

"I've never been with any man but you," Autumn interrupted quietly.

Lucas's expression changed from barely suppressed fury to confusion before he studied her face with his familiar intensity. "Why?"

"Because every time I started to, I remembered he wasn't you."

As if in pain, Lucas shut his eyes, then turned from her. "Cat, I've never done anything in my life to deserve you."

"No, you probably haven't." She rose from the bed to stand behind him. "Lucas, if you want me, tell me so, and tell me why. Ask me, Lucas. I want it spelled out."

"All right." He moved his shoulders as he turned back, but his eyes weren't casual. "Cat…" He reached up to touch her cheek, then thrust the hand in his pocket. "I want you, desperately, because life isn't even tolerable without you. I need you because you are, and always were, the best part of my life. I love you for reasons it would take hours to tell you. Take me back, please. Marry me."

She wanted to throw herself into his arms, but held back. *Don't make it too easy on him.* Julia's words played back in her head. No, Lucas had had too much come too easily to him. Autumn smiled at him, but didn't reach out.

"All right," she said simply.

"All right?" He frowned, uncertain. "All right what?"

"I'll marry you. That's what you want, isn't it?"

"Yes, damn it, but—"

"The least you could do is kiss me, Lucas. It's traditional."

Lightly, he rested his hands on her shoulders. "Cat, I want you to be sure, because I'll never be able to let go. If it's gratitude, I'm desperate enough to take it. But I want you to think about what you're doing."

She tilted her head. "You did know I thought it was you with Helen on that film?"

"Cat, for God's sake—"

"I went into the woods," she continued mildly. "I was just about to expose that film when Steve found me. Lucas." She inched closer. "Do you know how I feel about the sanctity of film?"

His breath came out in a small huff of relief as he lifted a hand to either side of her face. He grinned. "Yes. Yes, I do. Something about the eleventh commandment."

"Thou shalt not expose unprocessed film. Now—" she slid her arms up his back "—are you going to kiss me, or do I have to make you?"

* * * * *